PORTAL TRAVELER

REBEKAH OLSON

PORTAL TRAVELER

ISBN 978-1-7349262-0-0

Formatting by:

Heather Dowell, Unicorn Nightporium, LLC
http://unicornnightporium.com/

Cover by:

BetiBup33, The Book Cover Designer
http://thebookcoverdesigner.com/designers/betibup33/

Chapter 1

ADAM'S LEG THROBBED. He probably shouldn't have punched the doctor the day before. Even if the jerk had deserved a good solid sock in the nose. He had no cause to complain about having to do his job. It wasn't like Adam had shot himself, or asked for it.

The base Oberst had called Adam into his office, then let him stand there for a few minutes. He tried to maintain proper posture while keeping as much of his weight on his good leg as possible. Even so it felt like it was bleeding again, unless that was his imagination dripping down his thigh and soaking into his uniform's pant leg.

Finally, the Oberst pulled a thick file out of his desk and slapped it open. "You have a penchant for trouble. Three fights within the first week of your arrival. You should know, I almost asked for you to be transferred out then. Glad I didn't. You're a damn good interpreter."

Adam clenched his teeth to keep them from chattering. He wasn't cold. He was shaking. And it got worse with every throbbing pulse through his leg.

"You're in a fight at least once a month, if not two or three times a month." The Oberst flipped through page after page in the file. Incident reports, Adam had to assume. "Now granted, most of them you didn't start. In fact, in a lot of them I'd have done the same as you. But still... How do you get yourself in so much trouble so often?"

Was that rhetorical? Adam hoped so since the only answer he could think of would most likely be taken as sass. He remained quiet. The Oberst didn't demand a response. So, rhetorical.

The next question needed a response. "Why did you break the doctor's nose yesterday?"

Adam answered with no hesitation. "He punched my leg where the POW shot me."

"He says he didn't," the Oberst said. "He just grabbed you a bit hard to try to get you to sit still so he could stitch it up, which he only did because you tend to cause more trouble in the infirmary than the average patient. And he was in a hurry with you, what with a bus load of wounded coming in fresh from the lines."

So, it was one man's word against another. No resolving that. Not even by pointing out that doubling your fist and smacking someone with it wasn't grabbing them, not by any stretch of the imagination.

"As valuable as you are to the war effort here, you've become more of a problem than I have the time to deal with." The Oberst shut the file without reaching the end. He leaned back in his chair, interlacing his fingers over his stomach. "You've been recalled. I've fought it for the past two weeks. But this last incident yesterday…" He shook his head.

"Explain this to me again," the Oberst said. "Give me something, anything, that will make this easier for me and I'll do what I can to keep you here behind the lines."

Where Adam would continue interpreting for POW's as they had information beaten out of them? He had volunteered for the war effort under the delusion that if he could just talk to the enemy, he could explain to them why they were wrong. He'd swallowed the Fuhrer's talk that obviously God must favor the Fatherland in this war or the supplies to fuel the war machine wouldn't be miraculously appearing out of thin air.

Except none of the POW's believed that, and no amount of talking could convince them. This most recent one was just another in a batch who had been trying to figure out where the mystery supplies were coming from. The Allies had a harder time sabotaging supply lines if they couldn't find the source and cut it off.

So Obersoldat Adam Weiss watched them beaten, one after another after another, asking the questions he was given to ask, interpreting their answers, or defiant refusals to answer, to the officer overseeing the interrogations.

Which was maybe why he didn't interfere much when one picked the locks on his cuffs and grabbed a walther. Adam had been shot. But at least he was alive, unlike the others that had been in the room, including the POW.

"Well?" the base Oberst asked.

After watching so many men beaten, some killed that way, Adam deserved worse than being stationed behind the lines. He certainly deserved worse than a bullet passing through the meat in his thigh. Though he should probably phrase it with more acceptable verbiage. He said, "Sir, I'll go wherever the Fatherland needs me."

The base Oberst grimaced before his face drooped with resignation. After that, he said nothing. He handed Adam some paperwork and gestured for him to leave. Not even a proper dismissal. The Oberst's aide was the one who directed Adam to pack his belongings and leave with the daily courier. Which gave him less than an hour.

That gave him neither the time nor the opportunity to ditch the contraband book buried in the bottom of his sack. Probably for the better. He would have been caught with indecision, likely unable to force himself to get rid of it. Disguised as it was among his other language dictionaries, he hadn't even yet had a chance to thumb through it.

He threw what little he owned into his sack and hobbled out to the courier truck. When he showed his papers, the man glanced through them, checked the date was current, 15 May 1948, checked Adam's identification and description against the name on the transfer papers signed by some general named Wattenberger: dark blonde hair, hazel eyes, 5'10", 170 lbs, age 19, etc. Then he glanced down at Adam's injured leg.

"You want to get that seen to in the infirmary real quick?" he asked.

"I'm fine." Adam passed him and tossed his sack in the truck.

"Have it your way." The courier said with a shrug. "Long as you don't slow me down."

The courier drove and Adam watched the base recede in the distance from the back of the truck, tucked in among all the other parcels. They wended their way along the roads, the driver stopping several times, or driving off the road to avoids spots he suspected might conceal a buried mine. They detoured around field littered with debris and shrapnel where he said there might still be live fire ready to go off if looked at wrong.

The towns and burgs they passed through showed little sign of civilian life. The shutters were closed, the traffic on the public streets furtive and sparse. Until they met a supply convoy in one.

Everyone was out in the streets. You'd have thought it was a party except for all the uniforms and weapons and military vehicles. The young girls of the village flirted with the soldiers and were rewarded with extra rations. The old sang praises of worship to God for the miraculous influx of supplies. Boys were allowed to handle the weapons and pretend they were shooting down enemy troops from the vehicles.

Adam bit his tongue. He'd been one of those boys a couple of years ago, before the supplies started flooding into the war machine from seemingly nowhere. Despite everything his dad had told him, despite his mother crying and begging him not to, he'd gone and volunteered. And now, less than a year later, the illusion was shattered. Now, he'd believe in magic before he believed this was some miracle from God.

Six years of war since the Fuhrer had invaded Poland in 1942, and Adam could see the devastation on the land now as he rode through it with the courier. Not like the newscasters reported in the cinemas and on the public radio broadcasts. The POW's they captured acted nothing like he'd been told they acted. The wounded were hurting, not proud they had martyred their bodies and their limbs in service of the Fatherland. So what else had the government lied about? The miraculous nature of supplies appearing out of thin air by the grace of God? As some Americans had told him, if it sounded too good to be true it probably was.

After a couple of days criss-crossing the countryside and passing through small populations, the courier entered the city of Neuberg. Where Adam's papers said his destination lay. Where Adam had grown up. Where his parents and younger brother still lived.

Knowing the layout of the city, Adam figured they'd go to the industrial section the military had cordoned off and restricted for the past couple of years.

On the other side of town from his family's house. Which made it easier to pretend he had no interest in asking for leave to visit them. If he did that, he'd have to admit to them that his father had been right about the evils of war.

His mother would have a fit over his leg anyway. It still throbbed. It wasn't bleeding anymore. But it was seeping some kind of clearish liquid. And it looked swollen. Or maybe that was just his imagination because it felt that way. And it felt on fire.

Once dropped off, Adam followed an unteroffizier to an office with the nameplate Wattenberger on a desk. At least he tried to. He could hardly walk. Every step, when he put weight on his leg, a pulse of dizziness flashed through his head making him nauseous. The unteroffizier harumphed with impatience and took Adam's sack, urging him to hurry up.

Thankfully, the Wattenberger guy, Generaloberst Wattenberger according to his insignias, allowed Adam to sit. Then he steepled his fingers and smiled. Or was that more of a leer?

"You're a lucky man," Wattenberger said. "If your previous base Oberst had fought your transfer any longer, it would have been too late for you to embark on the opportunity of a lifetime."

The Generaloberst paused. Adam hoped he wasn't expected to say anything. The office was cold and he was trying to keep from shivering. As it was, he managed to keep his teeth from chattering by clenching them.

"What do you know about magic?" Wattenberger asked. Adam frowned. Wattenberger held up one finger. "Let me rephrase that. What would you think about working with a people so primitive they think a scientifically measured phenomenon is magic?"

Adam managed to unclench his teeth long enough to respond. "If they're primitive, they can think of it however they want."

"Good answer." Wattenberger's leer broadened. "Because there's been a bit of a problem, and I needed precisely that answer in order to have you help smooth things over."

"Problem, sir?"

"Oh, yes. You see, the wrong information was found in the wrong hands. As a result the government wants to send you, your brother, and mother to a labor camp after your father's trial finds him guilty next week and shoots him for treason."

The previous nausea punched Adam in the face, nearly doubling him over. Wattenberger's tone turned patronizing. "Now, now. There's no need to turn green like that. I already told you this is the opportunity of a lifetime. And here's the opportunity part. I run an operation that's short on interpreters. You agree to work for me, and I'll pull some strings that makes sure your father is sent home on house arrest instead."

The nausea didn't ease. Adam's breath hitched as his stomach rose. He dry swallowed, trying to keep it down.

"You must be having some trouble understanding all this," Wattenberger said.

"This is a choice?" Adam choked out. "Not a recall?"

"Let me give you some details to help you out." Wattenberger leaned forward. "While I run a military operation and could simply issue you an order, I need your total cooperation in this. And some of the orders and stipulations will sound odd to you. First of all, there will be no contact with anyone here in the Fatherland from the moment you walk out of my office. Second, you'll receive an automatic promotion, a little incentive for you. Third, you'll be required to remove all symbols and patches and medals from our current Reich."

"Something covert?" Adam asked.

"Sort of, but not really," Wattenberger said. "The natives will know you're there. Some of them. They have some odd ideas, like their belief in magic. But that's something you'll have to deal with them on, not disillusion them. That's the fourth point. And fifth, considering how important this is and the circumstances your family is in, you can't screw this up. Not in any way. Not even once. If you get in trouble over there at all we'll strand you there. Because there won't be anyone for you to come home to. Understood?"

No longer trusting his voice, Adam nodded. That also proved a mistake as it set the room to spinning.

"So are you fully cooperative?" Wattenberger asked.

What choice did Adam have? Cooperate or kill his family? Not a choice. He said, "Yes."

"Good," Wattenberger said slapping open palms on his desk. He stood. "My adjutant will assist you from here. You're dismissed."

Adam barely managed to get to his feet and through the proper salute and protocols. He stumbled to the door. Outside the office he put his back to the wall and slid to sit on the floor.

Someone found him there and helped him up. He managed to mumble, "I'm sorry."

"Don't worry about it," the man said, whoever he was. He helped Adam move into and up some kind of corridor. "You'd be surprised how many people come out of his office as dejected as this when they're told the stipulations of going over. You're limping though. That's a bit unusual. And you feel kind of feverish. You need to go to the infirmary?"

So they could decide he was unfit for service? If he was unfit, would that mean they would withdraw the chance to save his family? Adam said, "I'm fine."

"If you say so." They entered some kind of room set up with bunks like a barracks. "Did Wattenberger give you the orientation manual?"

"Manual?"

Adam lost track of things a bit after that. Someone added papers and a booklet to his sack. He was given a bunk. Then he slept until someone woke him and told him he had to fall in for formation. It was time to go.

His leg was on fire. Others around supported his weight, helping him limp to where they were supposed to go. Someone commented on his condition. Wattenberger's voice said, "Their problem now. Don't really care how they take care of it. So long as he goes and we have leverage. And it'll get them to quit nagging me for another interpreter."

After that, Adam found himself in a group of men with issued traveling sacks the same as his. People talked. Wattenberger gave some sort of pep speech.

Then they moved into a warehouse where Adam started hallucinating. At least he thought he was hallucinating. He couldn't think of any other explanation. In the center of the huge open space sat a glowing circle about twice as tall as the average man. It swirled and spiraled, like fire in a vortex. Only flat. And vertical. And pallets of supplies flowed into it and disappeared.

A Hauptmann stood near, checking off every pallet on a clipboard. At least Adam assumed he was a Hauptmann. That's how others addressed him. With the hallucinations, Adam couldn't see any ranks or symbols on the man's uniform. When the pallets stopped flowing, the Hauptmann called out names. One by one, the group Adam stood among stepped up and disappeared through that glowing, opaque circle.

When it was Adam's turn the Hauptmann used the wrong rank to call him. Despite that, whoever was helping Adam stepped him over to the glowing circle and let go. He stumbled through that hallucination like everyone else had.

Putting weight on his leg spread the fire through his entire body. Dizziness flipped the floor sideways, hitting him with nausea so hard he doubled over and retched.

Falling prone got the weight off his leg. That helped some. And the stone floor felt nice and cool on his cheek. Now if only it would hold still and stop rocking. Then he could sleep peacefully in the darkness overtaking everything.

Chapter 2

A DEEP VOICE RUMBLED somewhere in the fog where Adam floated. "Why wouldn't he get something like that treated?"

"It was treated." Another voice. This one much smoother, almost oily, like a politician. "It just wasn't treated well. And if anyone had done any follow up, it would have been caught sooner."

Adam slitted his eyes open. He lay in a bed, stripped down to his undershorts, covered with a blanket up to his chin. Two uniformed men stood over by the door of the room, one as thick and solid looking as a tree, the other wearing a white doctor coat and a stethoscope looped over the back of his neck.

"Papers say he was transferred to us in a rush." The rumble came from the solid man. "Arrived from his last base with just a few hours to spare."

"That would explain the lack of follow up. No time," the doctor slicked. He saw Adam awake. "Or did you just tell everyone you were fine?"

"I'm fine enough to go wherever I'm needed." Adam rolled to one side and sat up. "Can I still go?"

"You've already done gone and gotten here," the solid man said. "You didn't have a chance to read that orientation book, did you."

"His fever was pretty high," the doctor said. "He may not have understood it even if he did have time."

"I'm not sick," Adam said.

The doctor scowled. "No, you're injured. And that got infected. And don't tell me again that you're fine, or I'll shoot you in the other leg."

"Calm down." One side of the solid man's mouth twitched, almost a half grin. He said to Adam, "I'm Oberst Gerhardt. I run the field of operation on this mission. This is Oberstarzt Lieber. Most of us just call him Doc Lieber. He's in charge of my medical personnel."

"Irritate me," Lieber said. "Please. So I can make you miserable in return."

"You're an interpreter." Gerhardt held up some papers in his hand and flipped through them. "How many languages do you speak?"

Adam started tallying them up on his fingers. Lieber raised an eyebrow. Gerhardt said, "Okay, if you have to count, that's good enough for me. What's the fastest you've learned a language you've never heard?"

"Well enough to translate some?" Adam averaged in his head the ones he'd learned the quickest. "A couple of months."

"See if you can half that time. We're desperate. What do you need?"

"To hear it. To practice it."

"I'll try and get you a native then."

The doctor grumbled, "That might be problematic."

"Fritz will manage it." Gerhardt turned and stepped out of the little room. "Meantime, I'll send Jorgan in here to give orientation."

"Give it a day or so for more recovery." Lieber followed. Then he smirked over his shoulder at Adam. "For now, he's fine."

Alone, Adam leaned back on his hands and released tension in a long sigh. His family was safe for the moment. Now he just had to keep them that way.

He was in a room with wooden walls, no plaster finish. The furnishings were stark, just the bed, a three-legged stool, a small cabinet style table by the bed with a drawer. The outside wall with the window was made of stone mason work. From his angle he couldn't see outside. While his leg didn't pain him nearly as much as it had, getting up just to look out would be too much effort.

Gerhardt rumbled softly from somewhere, perhaps the next room over by the sound of it. Lieber's political tones slicked a reply. Something about someone else getting sick coming through... a portal? Why didn't they just say transport? Or door? They weren't on a ship. Weren't doors on ships called portals? Or was that ports?

Adam shook his head. Jargon made no sense. He was so good at picking up languages everyone assumed he could learn lingo, slang, and jargon just as easy. Then they got mad at him when he didn't understand what they babbled about.

Footsteps receded, Gerhardt and Lieber's voices receding with them. Adam looked over at his sack propped up against the wall by the door. He couldn't tell if anyone had opened and gone through it. The only way to tell was to check. And until he had somewhere completely private, with no risk of anyone popping in unexpectedly, he didn't dare check to see if his contraband book was still hidden in there.

The open window let in the scent of pines, thick with the pungent fragrance of layers of dropped needles. He breathed in deep. This wasn't Neuberg. He didn't remember leaving the city but there was nowhere within its boundaries that smelled so deeply of old forest.

A couple of people walked past the door, talking quietly to each other. Adam's eyes dropped out of focus, his attention solely on the sounds coming out of their mouths. They spoke in a language he had never heard before. It had some of the soft slurring the French used, but with inflections more like Russian.

Adam pushed away the blanket and stood. Immediately he fell to the floor with a crash, his leg refusing to support his weight. The talking ceased. He crawled across the floor the short space to his bag. He ripped open the top and dug in.

His writing tools were on top, just where he'd put them. He snatched them out and scribbled away, recording the sounds he heard before they faded from his brain. He dug further into his bag, pulling out his notes. He compared the new sounds, searching for anything similar. When he couldn't find anything, he dug back in for his dictionaries. He took out only a few, making sure to leave the forbidden one with some camouflage. Then he flipped through page after page after page, looking for any words with similar structure to what he'd heard.

Lieber stepped into the room with a clipboard and a leather case. "What are you doing over here on the floor?"

"I'm—"

11

"Don't say you're fine!"

"—studying," Adam quickly amended what he'd been about to say.

Lieber set his stuff down on the little cabinet table. He reached for Adam. "Back to bed. I'm not examining you on the floor."

"I can do it." Adam grabbed at his tools and resources, trying to fend off Lieber from picking him up. "I walked around like normal before I got here."

"You mean before you took a bullet in the leg?" Lieber hooked his arms under Adam's and hauled him up. "Or do you just not remember all the people who helped you? Unless you think limping around is normal."

Lieber dragged Adam back to the bed, away from about half his dictionaries. Before he could protest, the doctor used a foot to gently push the stack of books over beside the bed and set the sack next to them. He opened his leather case and took out a glass thermometer.

Adam tried waving it off. "I'm not sick."

"Prove it." Lieber pushed Adam's hand aside and stuck the thermometer in his mouth. "Your fever's down but I don't think it's gone. Let me get the rest of your vitals and check on your leg."

Adam endured the doctor's prodding. It was the quickest way to get him to leave. He wore a pressure cuff and let Lieber count his pulse. He took deep breaths for the stethoscope. He nearly lost his temper when Lieber studied his ears and looked up his nose. That was just getting ridiculous. Who in their right mind would look up someone else's nose?

Lieber backed off and took the thermometer. He twisted it in his fingers examining the mercury through the glass. Then he shook it down with his left hand while writing a bunch of figures on the clipboard with his right.

He took a few vials out of the case and set them on the table with some gauze pads. Then he took the dressing off of Adam's leg. The flesh around the bullet hole was red and puffy, pretty angry looking. The bandage had pussy looking goop soaked into it.

"This is looking better," Lieber said.

If that was better Adam didn't want to know what it had looked like before. He sat still, not protesting in the slightest when Lieber dabbed some liquid from one of the vials onto one of the pads and laid it over the wound.

At first contact about a thousand bees swarmed into his leg all at once. Then, just as suddenly, the sting subsided and the flesh went numb.

"I tell you…" Lieber hadn't even glanced up when Adam had flinched and gasped. "The natives here, they don't have much in the way of pharmaceuticals. But what they do have makes up for it."

"You're using native medicines?" Adam asked.

"Don't get paranoid on me," Lieber said. "I've studied them well and they work, no matter how primitive you might think they are."

"I'm not paranoid." Adam lifted his pencil over his new notes. "I want the names. Do you know them?"

"No." Lieber doused the wound with a liquid from a different vial. "I've named them for categorization purposes. I don't know what the natives call them."

Adam let the pencil drop onto his paper. His shoulders drooped. Lieber asked, "Are you really that eager to get to work? Or are you putting on a show to try and impress us?"

"Words fascinate me," Adam said. "You can follow trails of them through several different languages, with small changes from pronunciation, accent, and transliteration. That's why so many of them are so similar, like the romantic languages."

"Fascinating." Lieber sounded drolly sarcastic, not interested in the least.

He finished up whatever he was doing and re-wrapped the dressing on Adam's leg. He packed up his tools, made more markings on the clipboard, picked everything up and left with the parting words, "Stay put. Off your leg."

That suited Adam. For now. He dove back into his notes and various language dictionaries.

Eventually, someone brought him something to eat. The doctor came in a few times more to bother him with claims of taking vitals. Aside from those annoyances, he was able to keep at his favorite hobby until it started getting dark. There was no light fixture in the room. No wires or switches on the walls. So he assumed there was no electricity. He put his study tools back into his sack, rolled over, and went to sleep.

Chapter 3

N THE MORNING, Lieber declared Adam's fever gone, and let him up. He got to stand by himself. He crossed the room a couple of times unaided. He walked slow, and limped. But he walked.

"All right," the doctor begrudged, scrutinizing his every move. "You can leave my infirmary if you promise not to overdo it."

"Course not." Adam smiled at the idea of leaving a doctor's care. He sat down, just to prove he wouldn't overwork his leg.

"Hmph," Lieber grunted skeptically. He turned to leave. "Wait here 'til Jorgan comes."

Adam dug out his only change of uniform. Once he had it on, he went to the window. From a second story vantage, he looked across a large dirt yard to a tall stone wall, thick enough it would make a good perimeter defense for a medieval town or castle. The trees of a pine forest stood tall on the other side, far enough away that a large space must separate them from the wall. The ends of their branches wore the light green tufts of spring, giving the forest a multi-toned shade of light and dark as the trees spread farther and farther back. Beyond that, a hill rose up into sight a few miles away. Its top lay bare of trees, crowned in the green of grasses instead.

A skinny man, maybe a year or two older than Adam, came to the doorway holding a clipboard. He looked like the same guy with the clipboard Adam had seen standing next to the hallucination of the big, round, glowing disc in the warehouse. He said, "Hi. I'm Gruber. Jorgan Gruber."

"Hauptmann?" Adam asked. That was how everyone had addressed him, though he still wore no insignias, patches, or symbols.

"That's right," he said with a nod. "You're Leutnant Weiss? Yes?"

"Obersoldat Adam Weiss," Adam corrected.

"Nah." Gruber smiled, making his eyes sparkle with warmth. "You got promoted by coming here, Leutnant."

"I didn't go through any kind of officer training."

Jorgan shrugged. "Neither did I. Just accept it. That kind of training doesn't matter so much here, and the rank gets you extra privileges. Like a private room to yourself." He nodded to the window. "Enjoying the view? Not much to see from here."

Adam looked outside. "Where are we?"

"In a castle," Gruber said. "We call it Far Base. I have no idea what the locals call it. They won't tell us."

"A castle where?" Adam asked. Too many castles from the past centuries dotted the European landscapes for that to be relevant in regard to location.

"Close to the border between Brend and Shontarra," Jorgan said. "The native language you'll be learning is called Brendish. Not sure if it's because Brend is larger, or for some other reason. That's another thing the locals won't tell us."

Adam turned to look at Jorgan. Either the man had a poker face, or he wasn't trying to pull a fast one. Adam said, "Wait, back up. Between where? Brend and Shontarra? Are those code names or something?"

"Don't try and place them on a map from any of your geography lessons," Jorgan said. "They're countries on no map you've ever seen."

"I've never heard of them."

"No one has. Except the few of us sent here, and the chain of command we answer to back in the Fatherland. We trade with one of the leaders in Shontarra. From what we can figure, it's about a third the size of Brend to the north. To the west is the ocean. To the east are mountains. We're not sure what's south of Shontarra, but we think it's a city state's territory, and then a large body of water."

"You're right." Adam held up his hands. "This isn't fitting any geography lesson. Can't you tell me something more general, like maybe what continent we're on?"

"Sorry," Jorgan said. "We're not on any continent you'd recognize. We're not on Earth."

Everything out the window had looked normal. Nothing strange. It still looked like mid-March, just like at home. "Where else would we be?"

"I don't know. Some other world. And I don't just mean another planet like Mars or Venus. From what we can tell this place is in an entirely different universe, or something."

"What are you talking about?" Was Adam still hallucinating audibly? Maybe the doctor had released him too early after all.

"I'll try to explain on the way to your room." Jorgan reached for Adam's sack.

"I can get that." Adam also reached for it.

Jorgan hefted it anyway. "Of course you can. I'm being courteous. Follow me."

He walked backwards up the corridor, slowly, so Adam could gimp after him without much effort. "We're on the second floor. Your room isn't far."

He stepped around a wooden bench by an open door still moving backwards. Adam tried going around the bench while using the wall for support. The wooden seat wasn't quite narrow enough. He let go and attempted an unaided step.

"Please be careful." Jorgan frowned. "If you mess up your leg you'll never hear the end of it from Lieber."

Lieber came into the doorway from the room. "No, you won't. And I'll come up with the most miserably boring jobs I can possibly think of for Gerhardt to assign you as punishment."

"I'm walking carefully." Adam took another step to prove it. "Were you waiting around close by just to monitor or something?"

"That's his office where he does a lot of his work," Gruber told him. Then he said to Lieber, "He was using the wall for support before the bench got in the way. Too bad we don't have any crutches."

"Don't get me started on all the things we don't have," Lieber grumbled. He watched Adam take another couple of steps past the bench and the doorway to put his hand back on the wall. "I think he'll be okay for now without them."

Adam pushed on. Lieber's office was the last room in the corridor before it ended at a landing. To the right a wide set of stairs led down to an open foyer. To the left another set of narrower stairs led up and out of sight.

"Don't you dare." Lieber shook his finger from the hall. "You stay off of stairs. If your room wasn't on this floor, I'd keep you here."

"I'm not using stairs." Adam rolled his eyes at the doctor's paranoia. "I was just curious where they went."

"They go up to the third and fourth floors where most of the men share their quarters." Jorgan headed backward across the balcony overlooking the foyer. He pointed downstairs. "That's the main entry of the castle. If you need to go outside you either go out that door, or you fight through the kitchen or laundry. The natives we have working for us get mean if you do that too many times."

There was a noisy crowd around somewhere. And smells of food that set Adam's mouth to watering. He turned his back on it and gimped into the far corridor after Jorgan. The Hauptmann stopped in front of another open door and patiently addressed whoever was in there. "Helmut, what have I told you about getting dressed with your door open?"

"Everybody is downstairs," a thick voice responded. "No one will see me."

"That doesn't matter," Jorgan said. "What have I told you about getting dressed with your door open?"

"To not to." The door shut.

Jorgan moved on to another door, saying to Adam, "This one's yours."

"I really get this all to myself?" The room was about the same small size as the one he'd just left. Smaller than the one he'd had at his parents' house. He hadn't thought anything of it back then. Now that he'd spent the better part of the past year sharing quarters with strangers, he had a new appreciation for privacy.

"All yours." Jorgan set the sack on the narrow, wood framed bed. "We passed mine two doors up on this side. You heard me talk to Helmut next to you. Across from me is Fritz. Next to him is Strom, on the rare occasions he's here. And be glad your room isn't on that side of the corridor. Their windows open into the mess hall, not outside."

"I like this room already." Adam looked out the window. They were on the same side of the castle as the infirmary. The hill still towered over the landscape making a nice view.

"Fritz and Strom are the other two interpreters," Jorgan said. Adam opened his sack and took out the top few items while Jorgan continued. "Eventually, you'll meet them both. For now, Strom is at the palace, as usual. And Kiefer Fritz is in trouble. Again."

"Does that happen often?" Adam asked.

"Quite often. Always when the portal opens every third month," Jorgan said. Adam frowned. There was that word again. Jorgan went on, "Usually he's only in trouble and isolated before the portal opening. This time, he really did do quite bad, so he's still in trouble afterward."

"Portal?" Adam asked.

"Yes. Portal. You know. That glowing spiral you stepped through to get here."
Adam's jaw dropped open. "That was *real*?"

Jorgan laughed. "Yes. What did you think that was?"

"I thought I was hallucinating."

"Nope." Jorgan opened the booklet he carried and slowly flipped through the pages. "I suppose you also thought you were hallucinating when you were told magic is real. Or did Wattenberger even get that far? He tends to try and avoid the subject."

"Magic is for fairytales." Adam set down what he'd taken out of his sack and reached in for more.

"And for here." Jorgan stopped on a page toward the back. He handed the booklet over and pointed. "Read this paragraph right here."

WITH THE SCIENTIFIC MEASUREMENTS TAKEN OF THE ENERGIES PRODUCED BY THE HUMAN BODY, A METHOD OF HARNESSING AND CONTROLLING IT WAS SOUGHT AND ACHIEVED BY ZIEGFRIED KLEIN, CIVILIAN AND EXPERT IN OCCULT KNOWLEDGE AND LORE. ALTHOUGH HE HAS PUT THE ARCHAIC LABEL

OF 'MAGIC' ON THIS PHENOMENON, IT IS AS REAL AND WORKABLE AS ELECTRICITY.

Adam stared at the page. He read the passage again. He read the paragraph before it. He read the paragraph after it. He had to have missed something somewhere.

He studied the cover of the booklet. All the official signs and symbols were in their proper places. It looked like a real document, not a forgery or a hoax. He turned back to the paragraph and reread it.

"Honestly," Jorgan said. "I think if we could get here any other way than magic, Wattenberger wouldn't have written anything about it at all."

Adam put his finger on the words. "It says it's energy."

Jorgan nodded. "He doesn't like the word 'magic'. Even though that's the best description of it."

"Magic?"

"Yes."

"Magic."

"That's right."

"It says energy."

"We can go round as many times as you want." Jorgan spread his hands helplessly. "It won't change anything. And you better get used to the idea. You're going to be working with the natives. They think of this energy as magic. So does Ziegfried. And he controls the only way back home."

"This is crazy." Adam slapped the booklet shut. "Maybe a hundred years ago I might believe this. Science has progressed a little since then."

"And a hundred years ago, people would have thought electricity was magic." Jorgan chuckled and started ticking a list off on his fingers. "Not to mention radio, films, and cars. Let's not even start on aircraft. Science has measured this. It just has an archaic label because it's so diverse we don't know what else to call it."

"I suppose I'll have to get used to it then?" Adam tossed a couple more items from his sack onto the bed.

"Yup," Jorgan said. His eyes focused on the few items Adam had unpacked. His face went blank of emotion. "Is that a photo of your family?"

"Yeah." Adam picked it up and stared at it fondly. "This was taken the only time we ever went to visit my uncle in the Alps. We had to show him how to work the camera so he could take the picture."

"Hide it." Jorgan's face turned wistful. He looked like many other soldiers when they got nostalgic over peaceful times. "Not everyone has a tangible reminder of loved ones. And a photo, any photo, is a little piece of home. Pieces of home are barter items here and prone to theft. Hide that somewhere while I go get you some breakfast."

He left the room and Adam slipped the photo into one of his pockets. He picked up a couple of items. There had to be somewhere in the room for them to belong. He glanced around at the sparse furnishings: a narrow bed, a three-legged stool, a cabinet style square table with a drawer, and a skinny, freestanding closet. All his. For now. For how long? He hadn't stayed at any base for more than a few months. Maybe he shouldn't unpack after all.

He sat down on the bed with a sigh. Tired already and the sun hadn't even climbed halfway up the morning sky. His leg throbbed. He slouched and dropped the items he'd picked up back onto the bed. He took the photo back out of his pocket. One thing he remembered clearly. He couldn't mess this up. Not even once.

"Jorgan?" The thick voice Jorgan had named Helmut called out. A large man passed Adam's door. His uniform was perfect except for his untied shoes. He went several paces up the corridor, then started back. "Jorgan?"

He passed by the door and called out again. Then his footsteps returned. His large frame filled Adam's door. "Do you know where Jorgan is? He was here earlier."

"Jorgan?" Adam stopped to think and place the name. "Oh, you mean Gruber?"

"Yes. Jorgan Gruber. I need some help. Is that a photograph?" The big man pointed at the back of the photo. "You should hide that. Jorgan says we should hide our photograph pictures. He lost one. I don't like hiding pictures. So I draw them. I drew him a picture of the one he lost. Do you know where he is?"

"He went to get me some breakfast." Adam slipped the photo back into his pocket.

"Oh." Helmut stuck his lower lip out in a childlike pout. He looked mournfully down at his untied shoes. "Can you help me? I made rabbit ears and they keep getting twisted up every time I try to make one of them go around a post and look for a hole to go through. I don't think bunnies really do this."

Adam shook his head in confusion. "What are you talking about?"

"I don't think bunnies tie shoes." Helmut sat down and fiddled with his laces. "I wish I had boots. I got my shoes before the supplies came by magic, and no one will give me boots now, because I have shoes. I wish they had buckles. My shoes at home had buckles. I can remember buckles easier."

"You need help tying your shoes?" Who didn't know how to tie shoes? And how did such a person get into the military? Adam had been told that all people of slow mental faculties were put into institutions to be cared for.

"I can make rabbit ears easy." Helmut demonstrated as he spoke. "But I can't remember where the post is for them to go around and find the hole to go through and they keep getting twisted up."

He wrapped one loop around the other a couple of times and then stuck it through the loop at the top. He tried to pull it tight. As soon as he let go, it loosened and came undone. He sighed with frustration and let his hands drop to the floor. He gave Adam a pleading look. "Can you help me?"

"For one thing…" Taking pity on the big man, Adam sat next to him and took the laces to try and help. "You can't make both the rabbit ears at the beginning. You only make one loop, like this. The other lace is like a rabbit getting chased by a fox. It goes around the post that the loop has made. Then it ducks into this hole. Now you have two loops that you can pull tight, and those are the rabbit ears."

"You made that look easy!" Helmut gasped. He pulled the bow undone and clapped his hands. "Do it again!"

Jorgan came back. "Helmut, what are you doing? You can't sit in doorways like this. You'll trip anyone trying to get in or out of the room."

"Sorry, Jorgan." Helmut looked up at him. "I'll move. He was just helping me with my shoes. He's nice. I wish I had boots."

"Or buckles, I know," Jorgan said. "I'll help you with your shoes. Let me through."

Helmut squeezed to one side. Jorgan turned sideways to step through. He handed Adam a bowl of some sort of gruelish porridge. "The food here's not the greatest. It's pretty bland. But it fills. Now, Helmut, let's get your shoes tied."

"I tried to make rabbit ears," Helmut said. "And they were chased by a fox around each other and they jumped into holes. I still couldn't do it right."

"Someone else tried to help you again, didn't they?"

"Doctor Koen showed me yesterday since you weren't here. He's nice."

"He doesn't know how to explain things to you properly. That's why you're confused." Jorgan squatted in front of the big man. "Make a loop that's approximately five centimeters tall. Now take the other lace and circle it around the back of the loop. Don't make it a complete circle. Stop a few degrees short."

"So go around only 340 degrees instead of 360?" Helmut's fingers worked the laces following the directions.

"Uh, sure, that sounds about right," Jorgan said. "Now, see where there's a space under the lace that you used to wrap?"

"Yes."

"Poke a midsection of the same lace through that space so that it's overlapping itself."

"Hey! That made another loop!"

"Now, using the sides of the loops where the laces are twined together, pull them both tight."

Helmut cheered. "I did it!"

"Good job!" Gruber praised. "Now do the other one."

Helmut laboriously went through the process again whispering the instructions to himself as he worked. When he finished, he cheered again.

"Very good." Gruber patted one of his beefy arms. "Now, have you eaten breakfast?"

Helmut shook his head. "I was getting dressed. My buttons kept getting crooked when I put my shirt on."

"Did you count both the buttons and the holes before you started?"

"Most people don't have to do that. I want to be like other people."

"Most other people are stupid." Jorgan put his hands on Helmut's wide shoulders and looked him square in the face. "Not like you. You're too smart to be as stupid as them. Now, how many steps does it take to get from this room to the mess hall?"

"I haven't counted from this room," Helmut said. He looked up at the ceiling and put his tongue in the corner of his mouth. His fingers twitched at his sides and he mumbled, "This room is five away from my door, so if I add that to the number of steps from there, then it comes up to—"

"Verify it," Jorgan interrupted. He stood up, "Go count it out and make sure you're right."

"Okay." Helmut jumped to his feet and walked down the corridor counting every step he took.

"That was interesting," Adam said.

"He's a genius with math and geometry," Jorgan said. "He has perfect recall of everything he's ever seen. He can draw really well too. He's just not so good with everyday things, like tying his shoes, so most people think he's a simpleton. He made a really good intelligence operator back home, believe it or not. There was just a few too many people who didn't know how to deal with him properly."

"Him working as an intelligence operator is a lot easier to believe than magic being real," Adam said.

"It sure is!" Jorgan agreed with an easy laugh.

Chapter 4

ADAM SAT HALFWAY DOWN THE STAIRS. He scribbled on his paper so rapidly he could barely read his own writing. Stacks of more notes were spread out on the steps around him. Kiefer Fritz, the other interpreter, sat in the kitchen at the bottom holding conversation in the Brendish language with one of the natives that worked there.

For some reason, people kept offering Adam condolences when they found out he worked closely with Kiefer. He couldn't figure out why. There had been a few hazing incidences. But that couldn't be why. That was expected. All the new guys got hazed. So what? Aside from that, there wasn't really any reason for people to hate Kiefer as much as they did.

He was a little grumpy sometimes. So was Adam. And if people spoke to Adam the way they spoke to Kiefer, he'd be more than just grumpy. His short temper would explode. Not Kiefer. He just ignored whatever insult people threw at him, like water off a duck's back. Then if he got really mad, he got cleverly nasty about his revenge.

Helmut had given the entire story about why Kiefer had been in so much trouble when Adam had arrived. He had sneaked a powerful laxative out of the infirmary and laced someone's mouth with it.

Helmut's heavy tread clomped down the stairs from above. He got as far as where Adam sat. Looking down at all the papers spread out, he shuffled to one side and lifted a foot. Then he shuffled to the other side and lifted a foot. He touched the toe of one shoe in between two of the papers.

"Here." Adam gathered them up and stacked them.

"Thank you." Helmut continued down. After a couple of steps, he stopped and looked back up at Adam. "Can I sit with you?"

"What are you supposed to be doing?" Adam asked.

"Drawing." Helmut grinned, holding up the stack of blank paper in his hand. "I'm going to draw the basements of the castle. I was going to do it in the kitchen because it smells nice. But I like you. And it smells just as nice here. Can I sit with you?"

Adam shrugged. "Sure."

"Thank you!" Helmut plopped down on one of the steps with another grin.

His pencil scratched away and Adam re-tuned his ears to the Brendish conversation below. After a week of convalescing, Doctor Lieber had allowed him to use stairs. A week more of sitting, listening, and taking notes, he was getting a grasp on the flow and cadence of the language. He had picked up some of the linking words right away: is, and, too, but, with, etc. Now he was picking out specific nouns and verbs with their conjugal forms. He tried a few of them on his tongue.

Helmut lifted his pencil from the paper. "You sound like Kiefer. I didn't know you could do that."

"It's my job to do that," Adam said.

"Jorgan used to try and make sounds like that." Helmut went back to his drawing while he talked. "Kiefer laughed at him. So did the natives. I don't think it was very nice. Kiefer is nice to me, and he's usually nice to Jorgan, but sometimes he's not nice. I don't think he means to. He was just treated bad. So he doesn't always know how to be nice to other people. He's always nice to Ernest, though."

"Ernest?"

"Oberst Ernest Gerhardt." Helmut briefly looked up from his drawing without stopping his pencil. "He got sent here because he asked permission to leave his post to go home to talk to his wife when she cheated on him. I don't know how she cheated. He wasn't home to play games with her."

"Uh…" Adam stared at his paper. Maybe if he stared down hard enough, avoiding eye contact, Helmut wouldn't tell him anything else he shouldn't know. That sometimes worked with his brother.

"That's not as sad as Conrad." Helmut shook his head. Adam squinted at his paper. Helmut carried on. "Oberstleutnant Conrad Grippe. He has a tattoo with the name of the girl he loved when he was a teenager. She was killed by a bomb in an air raid. I don't like it when people die. It makes me sad. Does it make you sad?"

"Yes," Adam said. Even when the person who died was a POW who shot him in the leg. It still made him sad. He just tried not to think about it.

"I had a friend once that died." Helmut sniffed and wiped his nose on the upper arm of his sleeve. Then he smiled. "But now I have Jorgan. He's my friend. And Kiefer's my friend. And Velig's my friend, too."

Adam looked up again. Had Helmut not used Major Velig's first name because he didn't know it? Or out of respect because Velig was the discipline enforcer on this base?

Helmut leaned toward Adam, whispering with a hand to the side of his mouth. "His first name is Ulfric. He doesn't like it, so he asked me not to call him that."

"If he asked you not to call him that, you probably shouldn't go around telling other people."

"Oh." Helmut's eyes widened and he nearly dropped his pencil, making a smudge on his drawing. "I never thought of that. You're probably right. No one ever told me that. Thank you. You're nice. You'll be my friend too?"

"Sure." Adam leaned forward for a better look at Helmut's paper. The markings looked more like an architect's schematic than an artist's rendering. "You're drawing all these rooms and corridors just from memory?"

"It's just counting." Helmut bobbed his head from side to side, his version of shrugging something off. "I don't know why more people don't do it. It's really simple. So simple, I can do it."

"If it really was simple, more people really would do it." Adam leaned back again. "Jorgan was right. You must be some kind of genius or something."

"You're just being nice." Helmut tipped his chin down and his cheeks flushed. He caught sight of the writing on the papers Adam had stacked. "Those don't look like normal letters."

"They're not." Adam added a few more to the paper currently on his lap. "They're phonetic symbols."

"What's that?"

"Phonetics is the study of sounds," Adam said. "I made up a different letter for every sound I could think of in our language. Then, when I hear other languages, I can write down the sounds. And every time I hear a new sound, I make a new letter for it."

Helmut's eyes glazed over. He nodded anyway. Adam smiled and said, "Think of them as sound pictures, instead of letters."

"Oh." Helmut's mouth made a perfect circle. "Pictures of sounds! Even I can't draw sounds!"

"You can write, can't you?"

"Yes."

"Then you're drawing pictures of sounds."

"Oh!" Helmut repeated, even more enthusiastic this time. "Show me more!"

Adam wrote out a quick key for him of all basic letters of the alphabet according to the sounds they made, then went back to taking notes from the conversation going on in the kitchen below. After a few minutes, Helmut handed him a paper full of words spelled phonetically. He asked, "Like this?"

"Wow, Helmut," Adam looked over the words. "This is perfect. You picked this up really fast."

Every native in the kitchen down below stopped talking. Which meant someone else must have come in. Whoever it was, they spoke in German. "Excuse me, I'm looking for Kiefer Fritz."

"Who's asking?" Kiefer demanded. "And why?"

"I was told to register a food complaint and a meal request through him," the man said.

"You're complaining about the food? What do you think this is? Your mother's confectionery? Do you want us to come wait on you hand and foot, too?"

"Not my complaint," the man said a bit too hasty. "Not mine. I have no complaints. None whatsoever. But my Unteroffizier, he sent me."

"Uh-huh."

"He said to ask you for a pork roll."

"Then he sent you on a snipe hunt." Kiefer's tone was flat. "There isn't any pork here. Doesn't even come through the portal from home."

"No, no, he said you have some and hide it. Because you're a... uh..."

Kiefer's tone dropped in pitch and he spoke very slow. "A what?"

"Oh, what was the word he used. Something French. Oh yes. I have it!" The man slowly enunciated, and still mangled, the French word for cannibal. "That's what it was. So he said you have pork to eat. And he wants some."

That was basically accusing Kiefer of being less than an animal. Adam found himself at the bottom of the stairs and moving with no memory of getting there. He barreled into the kitchen and grabbed the soldier by the shirt with his fists. "Who told you to call him that? Why would you call *anyone* that!"

"Whoa!" The soldier cringed, leaning backward away from Adam. "I don't even know what it means!"

"Hey!" Kiefer laid a hand on Adam's upper arm. "Calm down. It's not a big deal. This guy's obviously being hazed. You're picking on the victim, stupid."

No getting in trouble. No fighting. Adam repeated the reminders to himself a few times in his head. He let go with one hand, then the soldier jerked himself out of the other hand.

Kiefer brushed off the soldier's shirt and said, "See? No harm done. Go tell your Unteroffizier I hide the pork rolls with the fallopian tubes. It's a good hiding place, since all the fallopian tubes think he's repulsive and do whatever it takes to hide from him."

"What's a fallopian tube?" the soldier asked.

"Ask your Unteroffizier," Kiefer said. "If he has no deficiencies in his education, he'll know what it is. If not, well, then he doesn't deserve to be around them anyway."

Helmut giggled from where he'd come to the bottom of the stairs. The soldier wrinkled his nose at the big man and snarled. "It's not funny!"

"Leave him alone," Adam put some growl into his voice.

The soldier turned and stomped out of the kitchen. Helmut still giggled. He said, "Kiefer, you're naughty. Karl is going to be mad at you. He doesn't like it when you play this joke."

"Karl?" Adam asked.

"Doc Lieber," Kiefer told him.

Even knowing he would be teased for asking, Adam had to know what the unfamiliar word was. "What's a fallopian tube? Some kind of medicine in the infirmary?"

"I guess your education is deficient too." Kiefer snorted and chortled. He said. "If you want to think of one that way though, it might be better classified as a drug that makes men lose their mind. And when they get addicted to one, if it's the right one, they'll go to the ends of the earth through every trial and misery imaginable while claiming they're the happiest man alive."

"Sounds dangerous," Adam said. "So what exactly is it?"

Helmut bellowed in gales of laughter and as he said, "It's a woman part! There's no fallopian tubes here on base, because there's no women!"

Heat crept up Adam's face. This embarrassment was a little worse than anticipated. He deserved to be laughed at for it. Educational deficiency indeed. He ground his teeth.

"Hey, cheer up." Kiefer slapped Adam on the back. "At least I gave someone else a bad time. How many hazings have I given you now?"

"Five," Adam said. "Six if you count when you tried to push me out the window."

"I don't count that one," Kiefer said. "I wasn't really going to. And it wasn't funny after you punched me."

"It served you right," Helmut said. "You shouldn't push people out of windows. They could get hurt."

"I wasn't really going to," Kiefer repeated.

"Good," Helmut said. "He's my friend. He makes sound pictures."

Keifer raised his eyebrows in confusion. "Sound pictures?"

"I'll show you!" Helmut ran back to the stairs where Adam had left all his notes.

The native in charge of the kitchen workers stood at Kiefer's shoulder, staring holes into Adam. As soon as the two made eye contact, the native pointedly looked over to the stairwell, then back at Adam.

"I think he wants me to leave," Adam said.

"Probably because you're stinky," Kiefer said with a snicker. "He doesn't want anyone coming in, smelling you, and thinking they're poisoning the food."

Adam rolled his eyes. "That's your weakest attempt yet."

They both headed for the stairs. Helmut met them at the bottom, all Adam's notes in hand perfectly aligned into one neat stack. He held them up, about an inch from Kiefer's face. "See? Sound pictures."

Kiefer leaned back, putting a few more inches between the papers and his face. He took them and held them down where he'd be able to see them better. "What kind of writing is this?"

"It's sound picture writing," Helmut said.

"Phonetics," Adam said.

"Phonetics," Kiefer repeated. "As in… the study of sounds?"

"That's right," Adam said. "There's a finite number of sounds the human mouth is capable of forming. So I made a letter for each one, with variations indicating which part of the mouth and tongue is used."

"Huh," Kiefer grunted. He flipped through a few pages, glancing them over. "Would this help with something like pronunciation of regional accents?"

"That's what originally got me started," Adam said. "I was tired of sounding different. I figure if I talk to a foreigner and he can't pinpoint that I'm not from the same country as him, or even the same part of the same country as him, then I'm speaking properly."

"Interesting." Kiefer flipped through a few more pages then handed them back. "Maybe you're not as stupid as I thought."

"He's not stupid," Helmut said. "He's smart enough he said I'm a genius."

"He's smart enough to recognize that?" Kiefer smirked. "Yeah, I guess he's okay then."

Chapter 5

ADAM WENDED HIS WAY through the lines of tables with his lunch. He stopped near a group conversing all with different accents and sat at the table next to them. There, he could easily eavesdrop, drinking in the different pronunciations.

"No, no, you've got them mixed up." the man with the northern accent hawked. "Andreno is that native lord that we trade with."

"So Ziegfried is the sorcerer that opened that doorway portal thing." The man next to him slurred with a softer, more southern accent.

"Did anyone else feel a little dizzy after stepping through that?" The man across the table had a more middle accent, but also had a nasal twang, pushing too much air through his nose.

"Everyone feels dizzy after going through the portal." Hawk talked with food in his mouth. "Some people claim that Gruber doesn't. I think he's just been back and forth so many times that he's gotten used to it."

"Back to the subject." Twang jabbed his fork at Hawk. "Who else should we know that isn't here at base?"

"Lord Andreno answers to Prince Sanbralio, his uncle." Hawk swallowed this time. As always, the presence or absence of food in the mouth slightly changed the pronunciation of words. "It's not likely you'll ever meet the prince. You'll probably meet the dozen or so bodyguards Ziegfried has."

"A dozen!" Slur and Twang exclaimed together.

"Or so. Give or take. I think they're at about nineteen or twenty right now. They rotate in and out of shifts." Hawk shoveled in more food. "It's so he had protection 24/7. Then there's the radio operators and the interpreter we sent to the palace. Ziegfried put a spell on himself, so he can communicate just fine, so the interpreter is for the com guys and Lord Andreno. He has to make a good impression on the natives and the nobility, so we sent the real guy instead of the monkey."

"The monkey?" Twang asked.

"Kiefer Fritz." Hawk swallowed and took another bite. "The real guy's name is Strom. Not sure if you'll get to meet him or not."

Adam clenched his fork so tight in nearly broke through the skin of his palm. He stabbed at his food. Detached it. Stabbed again. He couldn't get in trouble. He couldn't get in trouble.

"Are Strom and Ziegfried always at the palace with Andreno?" Twang asked.

"Not always," Hawk said. "Ziegfried comes here at least every third month to open the portal. Then the monkey gets himself in trouble and has to stay in his room. Personally, I think he should always stay in his room so he doesn't sully the rest of us. But at least he's kept away from the important people. You know, one would think he'd learn how to behave better for superiors, with how much time he spends with Helmut. Even that dunce knows how to behave properly."

Adam wrapped his fist around his tin drinking cup and flipped it around, using the momentum to hurl the vessel at Hawk's head. It beaned him right above the ear, splashing water all over him, his plate, and the table.

Hawk surged to his feet, holding his ear, looking around for where the cup had come from. Several fingers from other tables pointed at Adam. Jorgan bee-lined through the rows of tables. He stopped in front of Hawk. "What did you do that got him so upset?"

"Me!" Hawk rubbed his ear. "He attacked and you come after *me*? Are you going to defend him too, like you defended Fritz when he used laxatives on me?"

Several snickers broke out among surrounding tables. Jorgan sniffed disdainfully. "You're so full of crap, it didn't hurt you to let some out."

The snickers pitched to gales of laughter. Jorgan looked around. Everywhere his gaze fell, heads ducked and the laughter died. He leaned over, both palms flat on the table. "Were you talking about Fritz and Helmut again? Calling them a monkey and a moron?"

Hawk stuck out his chin. "They are."

Gruber looked at the water stain. "Your uniform's a mess. Go change."

"I'm not finished eating."

Gruber took Hawk's water cup and poured it out over his lunch. "Oh, look. You just made a bigger mess. You really should learn to be more careful. The only people I've seen this messy are babies. Clean this up. Then go get a diaper change and a fresh uniform. Before Velig hears you were talking that way again."

Red faced, grumbling, casting evil glances at Jorgan, Hawk collected his soggy tray. Jorgan leaned over Twang and Slur. "You should know, verbal slander about Fritz or Helmut is the fastest way to earn you crap duty. You haven't been here long, so you may not know exactly what that is. Ask your friend. He's been on it lots."

Gruber turned and picked up Adam's tray. Adam followed him across the mess hall to where Helmut sat. The big man lit up with a grin. "Adam! Are you going to sit and eat with me?"

"Yes, he is." Jorgan set Adam's tray down and said to him. "I was coming to tell you that after lunch, we're expecting visitors. Our monthly shipment of goods."

Helmut bounced in his seat. "That's today?"

"Yes," Jorgan said, then turned back to Adam. "These are the goods that Andreno trades us for."

"These are the goods that the orientation booklet said are fueling the war machine?" Adam asked.

"That's what it says." Jorgan's voice was monotone, as if it was a phrase he often repeated, but didn't believe. "I have to go. Oh, and Weiss, be more careful who you sit by with that temper of yours. No more lobbing dishes at people."

Adam hung his head. He shouldn't have done it in the first place. Helmut watched Jorgan walk away. Then he looked at his food and sighed. "I need paper."

Adam sat next to him. "To eat?"

"No," Helmut said. "To draw, silly."

"Draw what? You've already drawn everything in the entire castle, haven't you?"

"I can draw you pictures of the people who are coming so you'll recognize them when they get here. I can't do it after. That won't help you. And I'll be busy counting everything. They always have packages and boxes and crates that get sent home. Once, somebody tried sneaking into one of the big boxes so he could go home. It was full of leather, and he got caught throwing some of it out to make room for himself. He got crap duty. That's not what everybody else calls it. I'm not supposed to use the word everybody else uses. Jorgan said so. I say it the way he says it."

"What's crap duty?"

"We're not supposed to talk about it while we're eating." Helmut took another bite. "We have to take all of our poop out to a pit, mix it with kerosene and straw, and burn it. I had to do that once when I got in trouble. Kiefer has to do it lots."

"Jorgan's right." Adam pushed away his half-eaten food. "You shouldn't talk about that while we're eating. Anyway, I'd give you some of my paper, but I'm out."

"I'll go to the Stabsgefreiter in the acquisitions basement and get some." Helmut polished off his lunch. "You want to come with me?"

"Will the Stabsgefreiter give it to you?" Adam followed him out of the Mess and toward the nearest stairs to the first basement. "He yelled at me when I tried to get some."

"He's grumpy, because too many people ask for silly things," Helmut said. "You have to ask Velig to tell him to give you paper. That's what I did. Now he gives me as much as I want!"

The Stabsgefreiter glared at Adam. He scowled at Helmut. He grumbled while he got the paper. Then he handed it over along with a fistful of pencils Helmut hadn't even asked for.

On the way up the stairs, Helmut handed Adam several sheets and a few pencils. "I'll share with you until you can get him to give you your own. I like sharing. Sharing is nice. And you're my friend. I like friends. I share with my friends."

Somewhere outside, a bugle sounded a short blast, followed by two longer ones. After about five seconds, the bugle repeated. Helmut grabbed Adam's new writing tools. "I'll put these in your room. Run outside! Hurry!"

Now that Adam had the new supplies, he didn't want to let them go. Except Helmut obviously knew more about what was going on than Adam did. Adam had just gotten out of one spot of trouble, he didn't need to risk another. And who knew? Maybe he could redeem his behavior in the mess hall if he proved himself both useful and obedient. He relinquished the paper and pencils. Helmut dashed toward their rooms with them.

Adam headed for the entrance. All around him, uniformed men came out of the woodwork like cockroaches when the lights go out. Strange as it was seeing the uniforms with no symbols or patches, no insignias to indicate rank, they acted with so much precision it was a testament to their military training. All scurried through the front entrance. Outside, they lined up in formation.

"Adam," Kiefer called, waving him to come over by Jorgan and the brass near the corner of the castle that went around to the stables.

One of the men at the top of the gate called. Winches creaked. The gate opened. Five large, enclosed wagons sat unmoving at the line of trees outside the wall. Men on horses surrounded them. Only one man came through the gate. He dismounted and strolled toward the brass with the smile of a door-to-door salesman.

"This isn't the right group," Gerhardt growled.

"Keniv," Velig snarled, teeth clenched, hand hovering over his luger.

"Fritz!" The native smiled, waved, and kept talking. Adam didn't understand all the words spoken, but he got the general gist of the greeting. "So nice to see you again."

"Keniv, what are you doing here," Kiefer demanded.

"I've been..." he used a phrase Adam thought was akin to pulling strings to get something. "I like you (he used the plural form, so he had to mean all the Germans as a group)."

"You like what you think you can get from us," Kiefer said with a sneer.

"Who is this?" Keniv tipped his chin to Adam. "And why is he staring at me like an idiot?"

"That idiot can understand you," Kiefer said.

"Is that Strom?" Keniv turned his fake smile on Adam. "I thought he was at the palace."

Adam gave his surname. "I am Weiss."

Keniv looked around at the formations. "How many of you are here now?"

"None of your business." Kiefer poked the man, prodding him back toward his horse. "You get out of here. Where's the real caravan driver? And where are the rest of the wagons?"

"The other drivers are gone." Keniv only backed up half a step for every third or fourth poke from Kiefer. "I paid them for the goods. And the other wagons are someplace else. If you want them, you deal with me."

Adam translated to the brass. Gerhardt turned away. Walking to the castle, he said, "Gruber. Staff meeting. Now. Set it up."

Following Gerhardt, Oberstleutnant Grippe pointed at the native and said, "Get that filth off my base before I have him shot."

"Why are they walking away?" Keniv put his hands on his hips, watching the Brass turn away from him. "Where are they going?"

"None of your business," Kiefer repeated.

Keniv tensed along his shoulders and bared his teeth. "It is if you want your goods."

Goose pimples rose up on Adam's arms. He had a short enough temper, he recognized the symptoms when he saw them in another man. If they couldn't get him to leave before he lost control, they really would receive orders to kill him.

Kiefer also turned his back to the native. "We don't deal with thieves."

"I never stole anything!" Keniv's hands left his hips, balling into fists. That might actually be a good thing. It put his hands further from the knives he wore in sheathes on each hip.

"Everything pointed to you," Kiefer said.

Keniv's face turned red. "It was all fake!"

"Calm down," Adam said.

Keniv shot him an angry glance. Then he looked around again at the men in formation. He took a deep breath, his normal color returning to his face. His hands opened and dropped to his sides. "I brought you gifts. Some might replace things you've had trouble getting from your home. I can get you more. I have more to gain from trading with you than from stealing from you. Please. Give me a chance."

"We did." Kiefer crossed his arms. "Then you stole from us. We don't deal with thieves."

Keniv took in a small breath and stopped. The skin around his eyes tightened. His fingers stretched out, something most people took as a sign of control. When Adam did that, it was fear of losing control.

"You need to leave." Adam nodded over to Velig, whose hand was still near his gun. "Before someone kills you."

"You haven't been here long enough. You don't know everything happening here." The tension in Keniv's voice gave away his anger. He said to Kiefer, "I can tell you who stole. It was blanketed (Covered? Disguised?). You think you got the items back. You didn't. I know where they are."

"Get rid of him before I do." Velig drew his gun. "He has about five more seconds."

Keniv backed away, even without a translation, his gaze fixed on the luger. He mounted his horse. Walking the animal slowly toward the gate, he called over his shoulder, "If you want your goods, I'll be in the village."

The gate shuddered to a close behind him. Velig stuffed his luger back into its holster. Kiefer nudged Adam toward the castle. "Let's go."

Chapter 6

ADAM OBEDIENTLY FOLLOWED KIEFER hoping for some kind of elaboration on what had just taken place. Kiefer said nothing. When he turned down the corridor where the brass did most of their work, Adam hesitated.

"Where exactly are we going?" he asked.

"You heard Gerhardt call a staff meeting." Kiefer took his upper arm and steered him down the corridor. "If we hold everything up, he'll make us pay. Oh, and what you said to Keniv was grammatically incorrect."

"Which part?"

"You said, 'You would be best advised to leave before a person deads you'."

"I knew I wasn't getting everything right."

"You did really good for the short time you've been learning. Way better than Strom could have hoped for in the same amount of time."

"Better than you?" Adam jibed.

Kiefer's face darkened. "Different circumstances." He rolled his shoulders in a half shrug. "Anyway, Keniv got the point. You did well enough."

"What's the right way to say it?"

Kiefer walked him through the vocabulary, the grammar, and the proper syntax while leading him to a room he had never entered. A German flag draped over one wall, the only one Adam had seen since arriving at this base. Another had a board with scads of notices tacked to it. A large table ringed with wooden chairs dominated the floor. Jorgan was busy laying maps out on it. Men stood around that Adam identified more with their jobs than their names.

The Stabsgefreiter burst into the room with Velig calmly following. The Stabsgefreiter slapped his hands on the table, leaning close to Gerhardt, demanding, "Did I hear right! Did the wagons turn around and leave?"

"You heard right," Gerhardt said.

"Keniv tried to get back in our good graces," Grippe added.

Stabsgefreiter got look very near panic. "You didn't let him, did you?"

Velig narrowed his eyes. "Did you bet anything on it?"

"Of course not," Stabsgefreiter said just a tad too quickly. "Did you kill him?"

"Anyone come to you asking for shovels?" Velig asked.

"No."

"Then I guess I didn't get to kill him. Yet."

"What about the goods?" Stabsgefreiter turned to Gerhardt. "Without them we won't make even close to quota. Andreno's gold will be cut short. We'll have him out here breathing down our necks."

"Or Ziegfried," one of the other officers chimed.

"Or both," another muttered.

"Prep for both," Gerhardt told Grippe. "Expect Ziegfried."

Kiefer let out a colored stream of swearing right in front of all the officers. None of them looked the least bit surprised at the brazenness. Velig just glanced at him and said, "Can it."

"It's not his normal time to be here," Kiefer complained. "What if he stays until the portal opening. That's over a month away! I don't want to pretend to be in trouble for over a month!"

"Keep it up!" Velig snarled. "You won't have to pretend!"

"I'll figure something out to keep you separated from him," Gerhardt told Kiefer, then turned to Adam. "Weiss, that means I may have to send him away for a bit. I don't want this base to be without an interpreter, if it can be avoided. And whichever of them comes, Andreno or Ziegfried, they'll take interest in you. Practice up."

Adam snatched at the opportunity to ask what Helmut had advised. "May I have paper?"

Stabsgefreiter snapped at him. "You don't need paper to practice speaking a language."

"How would you know?" Kiefer sassed. "How many foreign languages have you ever learned? You think we can just cast a spell that interprets everything for us?"

"I said can it!" Velig warned.

"You really need paper?" Grippe asked Adam.

"I write out the words and their translations for practice and as part of my memorization process," Adam said. "Helmut loaned me some, but I'd rather not borrow."

Grippe ordered Stabsgefreiter, "Give him all the paper and pencils he asks for."

"But..." Stabsgefreiter stammered. "But..."

Grippe shook a finger at him. "Don't make me remind you again of your place in this hierarchy."

"Fine!" Stabsgefreiter spat the word. "It's not like paper is expensive here. I already have to waste it on one complete moron. What's one more?"

Grippe growled. "Watch it."

"I'm watching our numbers in the stockrooms." Stabsgefreiter crossed his arms. "Paper included. Very closely since Wattenberger cut our provisions in half for not meeting quota the last several openings. What do you think he'll do this next time?"

Gerhardt didn't look or sound concerned. "We'll have enough to meet the minimum requirements with the next caravan."

"Unless Keniv gets hold of that one too," Stabsgefreiter said.

"Andreno will prevent that," Gerhardt said.

Stabsgefreiter rolled his eyes. "Oh, sure. Because he's stepped in and taken care of so many things like that in the past."

"Because if Keniv gets hold of any more caravans, Andreno doesn't get his gold," Gerhardt said. He turned to the Hauptmann in charge of communications. "Get a message to the palace. I want Andreno told I'm incensed that Keniv is making the delivery and I demand compensation."

"He'll just go find the original caravan drivers and make them do the delivery." The Hauptmann shrugged. "He'll claim that's more compensation than we deserve and find some way to blame us."

"As long as I get to find out whether or not he knew about this," Gerhardt said. "I'll settle for whatever he offers."

"You're not going to demand the goods Keniv got hold of?" Stabsgefreiter's eyes bulged. "How many more times do you think we can send minimal amounts home before we start getting notices of family detentions and executions?"

"We have enough leeway," Gerhardt said. "Take Weiss down to the storeroom and get him all the paper he wants."

Stabsgefreiter's eyes bulged. "You're dismissing me?"

"You're talking too much," Gerhardt said.

Stabsgefreiter stomped out of the room. Adam quickly followed. He was cussed at the entire way down to the first basement. There, Stabsgefreiter took a ream of paper and shoved it into his arms. Then he dug in a box and threw pencils at him.

Adam offered a gesture of peace. "Can I help you with anything in return?"

Stabsgefreiter threw more pencils. "Get out!"

Adam picked up a handful of them and made his escape. He ran up to his room. The paper that Helmut had given to him sat squarely in the exact center of the little table by the bed. Adam made a mental note to return it now that he had access to his own.

He sat down and wrote out notes of everything that had occurred with Keniv, marking anything he had questions about, outlining what Kiefer had already corrected him on.

After a while, Kiefer joined him and they went over some of the material. As his notes grew, he got so involved that he had no idea how much time had passed when Helmut's heavy trod went up and down the hall.

"Jorgan?" Helmut passed Adam's open door, heading in the wrong direction, away from Gruber's room. "Jorgan? Jorgan?"

"Uh oh," Kiefer said.

"Jorgan?" Helmut came back the other way and passed the door again.

"Helmut," Kiefer called. "What do you need?"

Helmut came to the door, his large frame filling the entire space. His ham-hands were full of several sheets of drawings. "Do you know where Jorgan is?"

"Jorgan is always busy this time of day," Kiefer said. "What do you need?"

Helmut held up the papers. "I ran out of space on my walls."

"That's because you can't tack up every drawing you make," Kiefer said. "You're going to have to take some down."

"But I like them."

"Do you like your new drawings?"

"Yes."

"Then you're going to have to make room for them by taking down some others," Kiefer repeated.

"Which ones?"

"Which ones are oldest?" Adam asked. That was what his mother always asked when he or his brother needed to cull a collection of odds and ends.

Helmut's eyes teared up. "I like the oldest ones."

"I'm going to have to go help him sort through things," Kiefer said. Helmut backed out into the hall. Kiefer whispered to Adam, "Wish me luck."

"Can I put some in Strom's room?" Helmut asked.

Kiefer stepped out into the hall with him. "You'd have to ask him."

Helmut led the few steps to his room. "He's not here."

"That makes it difficult to ask," Kiefer said.

Adam poked his head out into the hallway. How many pictures did Helmut have? Kiefer was already stepping into Helmut's room. Adam peeked in. He couldn't see much, until Helmut moved from the doorway and sat on the bed.

Every wall was covered. Paper lined up with paper, ruler straight, edge to edge, little presents tacked up for the eyes to feast on like snicker doodle cookies that melted on the tongue. Bowls of Fruit. Furniture. Rooms. Doors. Kitties. Puppies. Other various animals. Faces. Parts of faces. People. Groups of people. Helmut could have put all those pictures together into a mansion, furnished it, stocked its icebox and pantry, and populated it with a family and a menagerie of pets all at once.

Kiefer pointed to a wall with filigreed wood drawn as a decorative top. "What about this one?"

"I like that one," Helmut said. "It was the border in my first friend's favorite room."

Kiefer pointed to a set of stairs. "This one?"

"They curve perfect," Helmut said. "I like it."

Kiefer pointed to an apple. "How about this one?"

"Apples are good for you," Helmut said. "They're yummy. I like them."

Adam figured he probably should just walk away. Kiefer seemed to have this well in hand, and displayed the patience that Helmut needed. And yet, he somehow couldn't bring himself to walk away without at least trying to help one more time. He asked, "Have you ever thought of binding them into a book?"

"I haven't drawn any books," Helmut said. He opened the drawer in the little table identical to the one in Adam's room, took out paper and pencil.

"Not now." Kiefer put his hand on the paper, stopping Helmut from drawing on it. He asked Adam, "Do you know how to bind books?"

"I have a basic idea," Adam said. "Matthias, my brother, does it all the time. Takes his own photographs for them, writes little articles about the pictures. The first ones were terrible. The more he did it, the better he got. And all these drawings, they could be bound into a book and then they'd be safe. And take up less space on the wall, leaving room for more."

Helmut jumped up from the bed. "You must be some kind of genius or something!"

"You'd probably be better off with a professional than someone with just a basic idea," Kiefer said. "I'll ask around. See if we can find someone for you."

"That would be great!" Helmut threw his hands up in the air. Then he wrapped his arms around Kiefer, a bear hugging a rabbit, lifting him off the floor in ferocious cuddles. "Thank you! Thank you!"

"Ach!" Kiefer wriggled. "Leggo! Can't breathe! Put me down!"

Helmut let go. Kiefer rubbed his arms where they had been grabbed. "Good grief, Helmut. You have the strength of an ox, you big galoot."

Helmut giggled. Then he badgered Adam until he described the few basics he knew about book binding. Helmut immediately started gathering up drawings he wanted to try it on.

"Hold it." Kiefer gently took the papers. "Set these aside for a book for later. You don't want to try this the first time on your drawings. Why don't you try it with blank paper? Then if you mess it up that's okay, because you won't mess up your drawings."

"And if you don't mess it up—" Adam said— "you can go back through and draw on all the pages."

They spent the rest of the evening folding paper, hunting up needle and thread, making stacks, and miserably failing at getting any of the leafs sewn together. How had Matthias always made this look so easy? They hadn't even approached attaching a cover to it.

Chapter 7

I N THE MORNING, the discussion on book binding continued between the three of them over breakfast. About halfway through the meal, a bugle at the wall sounded three short blasts followed by a long one. Kiefer threw his fork down on the table and cussed.

"What?" Adam asked. "What is that?"

"Are they mad at us again?" Helmut asked.

Kiefer rose from his seat. "When are they not?"

"What's going on?" Adam asked.

"Morse code, letter U." Kiefer beckoned Adam to leave his meal and follow him. "First letter of the word *Ureinwohner.* We've got a native knocking on our door. The only natives that do that, are the villagers."

They exited through the front door as the bugle repeated the pattern a second time. The gate was already closing. They could see the tail end of a horse disappearing around the castle toward the stable. Kiefer swore again.

Adam stared after the horse. "They already let the visitor in?"

"Means they know who it is." Kiefer headed that way. "It's either the glutton of a mayor, or his dullard of a son. They're the only ones the gate isn't supposed to keep waiting."

In the stable, holding onto the horse and glaring at the workers, was a man who could have stepped right out of an English Robin Hood legend.

From his boots, up his belted tunic, all the way to the pointy feathered hat on his head, he made the perfect picture.

Kiefer spoke to him in Brendish with a bored monotone. "Welcome. We're glad to have you. Hope we can be friends. Blah, blah, blah, blah, you know everything else I'm supposed to say."

The native slapped leather gloves against his thigh. "Where is the regular man to take my horse?"

"Eating breakfast." Kiefer waved at the other workers. "They're fine. Give them your horse. Or you can stay out here where no one will come talk to you."

"You'd like that." The native held out the reins to one of the workers. He swished his gloves in Adam's direction. "Who is that?"

"That's Adam. He's learning your language." Kiefer turned and headed out of the stable without watching to see if the native followed.

The native kept up just fine. "Is he as stupid as that other one? The one that went to the Shontese Palace?"

"Strom? Oh, no," Kiefer said. "He's much smarter than Strom. Nicer than me, too. You might like him. But then again, you don't have much brains so you may not like someone as smart as him."

The native said a phrase with vocabulary Adam hadn't heard yet. From the sneer on the man's face, it couldn't have been anything polite. When they reached the second floor of the castle the native passed Kiefer and automatically headed down the command corridor.

"What was that phrase he used?" Adam repeated it.

"It was an idiom," Kiefer said. "Loosely translated, I'd have better luck chasing a will-o-wisp than finding an intelligent thought in my head."

They passed the room where they'd held the meeting the day before. They passed the locked room with the radio setup. At the end of the corridor, the native strode into the large, comfortable sitting room with the big picture windows along the outside wall. Tapestries of battles hung on the walls, interspersed with antlers that had been modified as candelabras. A worn bearskin rug covered the floor between two facing couches that had seen better days.

Oberstleutnant Grippe leaned casually against the wall between two of the windows. Four helmeted soldiers, walthers at their hips, mausers held cross body, lined up against one of the tapestries. The native took them all in with a glance. He put his hands on his hips. "Where is your leader?"

"Grippe leads this location," Kiefer told him. Adam filed away the exact word used for location, unsure if he had the translation accurate. The way Kiefer had used it, it could mean something closer to facility, or base of operation.

The native crossed his arms. "I came here to speak with Gerhardt."

"Tell him Gerhardt sends his apologies," Grippe responded to the familiar name before an interpretation was given. "He's in the middle of a com with our men at the palace."

Adam listened carefully. Kiefer used different words and conjunctions than when he conversed with the workers in the castle. While he interpreted into Brendish, Grippe continued, "If he's here about anything that concerns this base, our men, or relations between us and his village, he speaks to me. Not Gerhardt."

The native glowered as he listened to the interpretation. The grip on his gloves tightened, along with his lips and the skin around his eyes. "My father wants to know why you sent the caravan to our village."

Adam relayed that in German. Kiefer snickered and said, "Demand. The word is demand, not want. And he said Mayor, not father. Although this Mayor really is this guy's father. And you left out accursed. His Mayor wants to know why we sent the accursed caravan—"

"Enough." Grippe held up his hand. "Tell him we merely sent them away. We don't deal with thieves. We certainly wouldn't point them toward the village. Tell the Mayor to do as he pleases with the caravan and its leader."

After Kiefer interpreted, the native still didn't look mollified. He said, "They did bad things (crime?). We want (no, demand) payment."

"They want recompense for wrongdoings," Adam told Grippe. This time, Kiefer didn't snicker.

"For what?" Grippe glared at the native, then snorted. "For keeping Andreno from breathing down their necks like he did when we first got here? For running off that poacher? For clearing out the wolves that kept stealing their livestock and killed those two kids? What more recompense do they want?"

"No," was all the answer Kiefer gave to the native.

"We demand—"

"No," Kiefer interrupted. "We've more that paid you in the past. Tell your leader father that."

"How dare you!" The native bared his teeth. He swiped his gloves two inches from Kiefer's face, mimicking a slap. "My father is not a leader! He is the Mayor!"

Adam frowned. Something didn't add up. He had a word wrong somewhere. Grippe took a couple of steps toward them, wearing the same look Velig did when he bore down on men that needed discipline. "What exactly did you say to him?"

"He took offense to Fritz referring to his father with a word I thought meant leader," Adam said. "What does it really mean?"

"Fathead," Kiefer said. "Indirectly translated. Same connotation."

"Goddamn it!" Grippe barked.

Kiefer shrugged. "Well, he is."

Adam swallowed a lump in his throat. If the brass got mad while he was on the job, would they take into account that a different person had caused the problem? Or would the situation endanger his family regardless? He wasn't familiar enough with them to know. Nor was he familiar enough to know if they would be angered if he overstepped his authority. Regardless, he had to do something or he would forever wonder. He began trying to diffuse the tension just in case.

"Please accept our apologies," he said to the native as best he could. "My comrade was wrong to use that word of your father."

The native stared at him with wide eyed shock. His mouth opened. His body froze all other movement. Then he shook himself. "That was a quick apology. What of our payment? The caravan men did bad things last night."

"Is that word crimes?" Adam asked Kiefer. He nodded. Adam switched back to his garbled version of Brendish. "Take payment from the men who did the crimes."

"All they have is leather, cloth, grains…" he listed a couple of other items Adam didn't know the translation to. "We have enough. What would we do with more?"

"Sell them to us?" Adam suggested.

The native gaped again. Kiefer laughed. Grippe asked, "What? What is he saying?"

"He just suggested the village do exactly what we wanted them to do at the start." Kiefer chortled. "He said they should trade with us."

The native frowned at the laughter. "We don't trade with the accursed."

"That's us, this time," Kiefer quickly said to Adam before he could respond. "Not the caravan. They think this castle is cursed, and so is anyone living in it."

Adam amended what he had been about to say to the native. "Then don't trade. Keep what you think you can trade to others. Could we please have the rest, to help us out of our curse? That would serve the caravan men right since they are in the village to avoid giving us the goods."

The native stared at Adam with utter confusion on his face. Kiefer laughed so hard he bent over and had to hold his sides. "That was so mangled, I barely understood it."

He rephrased everything, wiping away the native's look of confusion. Then the man nodded at Adam. "You try hard. You seem good. Just working for the wrong people. I'll speak with my father about trading this one time, just to get rid of the caravan men."

After Adam interpreted back to German, Grippe said, "Kiefer, escort him back to the stable for his horse. Then meet us in the conference room."

Chapter 8

ONCE THE TWO OF THEM LEFT THE ROOM, Grippe dismissed the armed soldiers. He watched out the large picture windows where Kiefer could be seen leading the native toward the stable. Then he waited until the man rode out.

He strode from the room motioning for Adam to follow. He passed the conference room, pointing to it and saying, "Go in and wait for us."

Adam obeyed. Maps still hung on the walls and lay on the table. Some of them looked like Helmut had drawn them. He studied, trying to make heads or tails of the local geography.

Kiefer entered. Jorgan followed saying, "Seriously, if you can't stop calling people childish names—"

"Go on with you." Kiefer snorted with derision. "He is a fathead. You know it. The brass know it. The villagers know it. His son knows it."

"That doesn't mean you should blurt it out and insult the very people—"

"I didn't insult the people." Kiefer leaned against a wall map with one shoulder. "Just their fathead leader. Our people know a lot about what life is like under the dictatorship of a fathead leader."

Grippe stepped into the room with a file folder. With a searing look at Kiefer he said, "I can hear you all the way out in the hall. Can it."

Kiefer snapped to attention, over-exaggerating a salute he shouted, "Yes, sir!"

Ignoring the sarcasm Grippe plopped the folder onto the table, opened it, sat, and perused. With barely a glance at Adam he said, "Weiss, let's square away some things here in the few minutes we have to spare. What put the thought in your head that you could take charge of a situation?"

"I apologize, sir," Adam said. "I overstepped my place."

"No, you didn't." Grippe lowered the paper and looked at him square in the eye. "You maybe got us exactly what we needed. But most people would indeed think you overstepped. They would never even consider taking charge of a situation like that. That's more of an American trait than European."

Adam cocked his head to the side. "Sir?"

Grippe leaned back. "In battle the leaders are targeted because if you can take them out the men will throw up a defensive position and hold out as long as they can until they either receive new orders or a new leader. Unless they're American. Those damned devils. You may as well fight a hydra. If you kill their leader, two more rise up and take his place. Then they counterattack instead of falling back. Where did you get this trait? Did you spend time in their country? Or did someone who had a strong influence on you?"

"My father was a POW in an American camp during the Great War," Adam said.

"He teach you to take charge if something goes wrong?"

"Yes, sir."

"That's it then." Grippe leaned over the open file. "Keep doing it. We're desperate for leaders here. Now, as for your language skills. Gerhardt doesn't care so much about every little detail. I find them useful. Exactly how many languages do you speak, and which ones are they?"

"Fluently?" Adam asked. "Or conversationally? Or just a smattering of vocabulary words and phrases?"

Grippe frowned. "Does it matter?"

"Yes, sir," Adam said.

Kiefer nodded. "It really does. There's a difference."

"Fine," Grippe said. "Count them all together."

Adam tallied them on his fingers. He began with German, his first language. He could also fluently speak Spanish, French, Italian, Russian, and English. Should he lump the three romantic languages together as one?

Probably not, if Grippe was looking for exact numbers. There were more differences between them than just vocabulary pronunciations. So that made six.

Add to that, he could hold limited basic conversations in Polish, Portuguese, Danish, and Greek. That summed it up for Europe and the Western Hemisphere for ten. He should probably include Latin in that lineup, even though that language technically was dead. So eleven.

He could hold crippled conversations in Farsi, Japanese, and Mandarin Chinese. Fourteen. Add to that a smattering of vocabulary words in Swahili, Arabic, Korean, and… should he mention that last one? If his contraband book had caused his transfer to this place, the brass had to already know about it, even if he hadn't been able to go through it yet. If he didn't mention it, how much trouble would he get into? His family couldn't afford him to get in any trouble.

"You stopped counting." Grippe stared at Adam's fingers. "You stopped at seventeen? Eighteen? Which ones are they and put them in the classifications you mentioned."

Adam went back through them, aloud this time. He still hesitated with the last one. Grippe stared at him, his eyes boring holes through Adam's skull, screaming silently for him to admit his guilt. The Oberstleutnant asked, "Is that all?"

"Sir, it's purely for academic purposes," Adam confessed. "I know I should have turned it in. But running across it was a once in a lifetime opportunity. I doubt I'll ever get another chance to learn anything about that language. It's purely academic."

Grippe blinked at him. "What are you talking about?"

"The book that got me transferred here," Adam said.

"What book?"

"Generaloberst Wattenberger said a contraband item was found on the wrong person." Adam's gut tightened up. Grippe wasn't acting like he already knew. Nothing for it now. If he tried to backpedal, he would only make things worse. "I can only assume he referred to a book in my possession that I should have surrendered to be burned."

"Generaloberst Wattenberger referred to classified information your father dug up," Grippe said. "You got sent here partly to keep him toeing the line, since the government would like to have the organizations he keeps putting together to distribute the products his business partner procures. You have a banned book in your possession?"

Adam swallowed and nodded. Grippe pursed his lips. Then said, "Go get it. Bring it here. Now."

Numbness hit Adam on the way to his room. What had he just done? How much would this cost his parents and his brother? Their freedom? Their lives? He pulled his still partially filled bag out from under his bed. With wooden fingers he dug into it down to the bottom and extracted the contraband book. He took it back and laid it on the table by Grippe's hand.

Grippe picked it up and thumbed through it. "What is this? I can't read it."

"It's a language dictionary," Adam said. He pointed to some of the words. "This side of the page is in American English."

Gripped drew his finger down the column on the other side of the page. "What are these symbols?"

"Letters."

Grippe peered at them so close his nose nearly brushed the page. "No letters I recognize."

"They're called Chaldean flame letters."

"Hebrew?" Kiefer stood bolt straight. "You have a Hebrew dictionary?"

"It's purely academic," Adam repeated.

"Relax." Grippe tossed the book on the edge of the table. "You're safe. Just make sure none of the men see it or find out about it."

"Yes, sir." Adam's breath released with a whoosh.

Kiefer leaped forward and snatched the book. Adam flinched, fighting the instinct to hit him and take it back. Did Kiefer count as one of the men Grippe had referred to? Couldn't be. He already knew now. And Grippe didn't appear to have a problem with Kiefer taking the book. Perhaps if Adam shared it that would further please the brass? His muscles slowly unclenched as Kiefer handled it, tenderly turning pages, skimming up and down the words, holding it as reverently as if it was the Holy Bible.

Adam asked Grippe, "Are you all right with me sharing it with Kiefer?"

"Sure," Grippe said with a shrug.

Kiefer beamed. Gerhardt and Velig walked in. Velig frowned at him and asked, "What's got you so worked up?"

Kiefer lifted the book above his head like a trophy. "Look! Look at this! A Hebrew Dictionary!"

Velig barked at him. "Then stop waving it around for everyone to see."

Gerhardt dropped a stack of folders on the table. "Go hide that."

Kiefer stuffed the book down his shirt and ran from the room. Grippe said, "Jorgan, go with him. Make sure he comes right back instead of holing up and reading it."

"Where'd he get that?" Gerhardt asked as Jorgan stepped out.

"Weiss." Grippe nodded his head at Adam. "He thought that was the contraband item that got him sent here."

Gerhardt asked Adam. "Where did you get it?"

"Off a wounded British POW," Adam said. "I don't think the others cataloging his possessions knew what it was, or they'd have made sure it burned."

"Likely," Gerhardt said. "Don't tell anyone else you have it. That's the type of thing that could turn into a sword of Damocles over your head."

"Yes, sir," Adam agreed. He didn't dare ask why the brass had no problem with him possessing it.

Jorgan pushed a very reluctant looking Kiefer back into the room. Gerhardt handed Grippe and Velig each a folder off his stack. "Down to business. First thing's first. Kiefer, insult the locals again and the next time Ziegfried is here I won't take pains to keep you two separated."

Kiefer pouted. He actually stuck out his lower lip like a toddler denied candy. The brass ignored it. Grippe asked Gerhardt, "What did you get from the com?"

"Andreno and Ziegfried left the palace a few days ago," Gerhardt said.

"To go where?" Velig studied the folder he had opened. "You only wrote the destination is unverified."

"Strom claimed he couldn't verify," Gerhardt said. "He thinks they're going to visit the home of some important noble somewhere near the Brendish border."

Velig frowned. "He claimed? Or did he just not bother to find out?"

"He claimed," Gerhardt repeated. "After I threatened to come out there and roll a few heads. He said he'll send out a fast riding messenger to catch them. He wrote down what happened, so only Ziegfried will be able to read it."

"That doesn't mean Ziegfried won't share it with Andreno." Grippe flipped over to the second page. "You still think Andreno might come here?"

"Depends on how important this noble is that he's visiting," Gerhardt said. "He likes impressing nobles. But if he thinks his gold supply might get cut short, he might forgo that particular pleasure. Weiss, you suggested to the Mayor's son that they trade with us?"

"Only as a method for them to get rid of the caravan," Adam said.

Gerhardt nodded approval. "It's a step in the right direction. If they'll trade with us once, it'll make it that much easier to do it a second time. Maybe eventually you could convince them to let me meet their District Premiere, or send a letter of greeting to their King in Brend."

Adam froze. He couldn't promise something he had no idea how to deliver. At the same time, he'd just escaped a fire unscathed with that book. He didn't want to disappoint.

"Don't worry about it for now," Gerhardt said. "Best not to ask too much of them all at once. Just keep it in mind for future reference."

Chapter 9

ADAM STARED AT THE PAGES OF NOTES spread out on his bed and the little square table next to it. He told himself once more not to get irritated. It solved nothing.

He wanted to glean practice. The natives still wouldn't converse with him. He couldn't sit and listen to conversations because Kiefer was sitting in his room sulking. He couldn't even hide and listen to them work because they had gone practically silent. Too many of the soldiers ran pell mell around the castle. Velig and Grippe had nearly everyone cleaning, scrubbing, primping, and preening every last nook, cranny, crack, and hole, including the few places the natives worked.

"Count yourself lucky," he scolded himself.

Adam hadn't been assigned any cleaning jobs except his room. They wanted him to focus more on the language, to be as ready as possible to show off for Ziegfried Klein. The problem, if he stared at his notes much longer without using the words on them, his eyes would start leaking tears of blood.

He turned away from them. Outside the window, the hill stood steadfast. The lightest green colors of mid-spring had darkened. Some of the beiges and darker greens, the first signs of the coming summer, sprinkled their way up the wooded slope.

Closing his eyes, he let his newest favorite imagining run like a film behind his eyelids. One thing he'd learned at his uncle's place in the Alps, sound carried upward quite well. He could stand on a slope and hear much of what went on in the valley below. He pictured himself on top of that hill, the conversations of the village at its base carrying up to him, washing him in their language.

Helmut's heavy tread interrupted the reverie. Instead of walking up and down the hall calling for Jorgan, he stopped at Adam's open door. "Can you help me?"

"What do you need?" Adam asked.

"I need somewhere to hang my drawings." Helmut held stacks of them in his hands.

Jorgan came up behind him. "Helmut, I already told you. Lay them neatly in a drawer."

Helmut's eyes started watering. "They're not in a book yet for people to read. They need to hang up where people can see them."

"You can re-hang them after your room passes inspection." Jorgan put a skinny hand on the big man's shoulder and tried to lead him away. He didn't budge.

"Can you help me, please?" Helmut held his drawings out to Adam. He looked around the room. "You could put them... Wait, where are all the ones I hung up for you in here?"

"I told him to take them down," Jorgan said. Adam winced, knowing what the reaction would be. Sure enough, Helmut started crying.

"Why?" His word was more akin to a moan of despair than a question.

"For the same reason I told you to." Jorgan gently pried the drawings away from Helmut one by one. "We have to pass inspection. Your drawings will be fine if you put them safe in your drawer. Put them right beside that book you're working on making. The drawer keeps that safe. Right? They'll be fine. Just like last time. And the time before that. And you know you can get them back out and hang them up right away once you pass."

Helmut sniffled. "I don't like inspections."

Jorgan led him away. "Nobody likes inspections."

Another pair of feet clacked in the hall, the sharp tack of shoes rather than the dull thud of boots. Whoever approached had been issued their footwear before the supplies had started 'miraculously' replenishing themselves and leather became more available.

"Hi!" Helmut enthusiastically greeted whoever it was, as if he hadn't been on the verge of tears mere moments before.

"Hi," Velig's voice responded. "Is your room ready yet?"

Helmut gasped. His heavy footfalls ran the couple of steps to his room. The door slammed shut while he shouted, "Not yet! Not yet!"

"I'll give you until I inspect everyone else's room in this corridor. No longer," Velig called. Adam went around his room, frantically looking for anything wrong that he could fix in a jiffy. He lucked out. Velig banged on a different door. "Fritz! Open up!"

"Ah man!" Kiefer opened his door complaining. "Why can't you inspect someone else's room first?"

"Because," Velig said.

Adam continued going around his own room. He smoothed out a wrinkle where he'd sat on the bed. No dust balls had rolled in underneath the frame since the last time he'd checked. He gathered up all his notes to put into a tidy stack.

In the other room, Velig said, "You actually put some effort into this."

"I told you I would," Kiefer groused.

"Hmph," Velig grunted. "Pack. You're going out."

"Out?" Kiefer now sounded excited. "Really? Where to? How long?"

"As long as the written contingency is satisfied," Velig said. Some papers crinkled and rustled. "Read up."

His shoes clacked back into the hall. Adam picked up his stack of papers. He should put them somewhere. His drawer was full. He had no shelf. Anywhere else would look like clutter. Maybe he could get someone else to hold them for him, just for a few minutes, until the inspection was done. He whipped around to leave the room, too quickly, spilling some of the papers onto the floor. He bent and retrieved them. Then straightened again to Velig standing in the doorway. It startled him enough he nearly dropped the papers again.

"What are those?" Velig asked.

"My notes on the Brendish language," Adam said.

"Very well," Velig said.

He stepped into the room and looked around. Adam stood to the side out of the way. Velig went through everything. He opened the closet and checked for loose threads on the seams of the uniforms. He looked under the bed, brushed his hand on the floor, brought it out and checked his fingers for dirt. He pulled out the sack Adam still had stashed under there and opened it up.

He dumped it onto the bed. "You still haven't put all of this away?"

"Those are mostly just my language dictionaries." Adam curled his toes in his boots to keep from shuffling his feet. "I don't have a bookshelf, sir. So I keep them neatly out of the way."

Velig held up the cigarette case that had also been stashed with the books. "This is a language dictionary?"

"I thought it prudent to keep that hidden, sir," Adam said. "No one else here is much interested in dictionaries. I figured no one would look in there."

Velig opened the case. "You still have quite a few. More than most."

"I don't smoke much, sir." Adam didn't bother adding that he felt guilty every time he did. His mother had always scorned smoking as a dirty, filthy habit.

Velig held up Adam's deck of playing cards. "Gamble much?"

"No, sir. Not at all. I use those for solitaire tableaus."

"You sure?" Velig looked at him out of the corner of his eye. "A single cigarette is a high stake. One of the other men had this many that he got all from his winnings."

"Sir, If I gambled, I wouldn't have any cigarettes at all. I'm told I have a terrible poker face."

The corner of Velig's mouth twitched upward. He slapped the case shut and dropped it back on the bed with the dictionaries. He picked up the hat, mittens, and scarf Adam's mother had knitted for him and brandished them. "You don't think these go in the closet?"

"Not if someone is going to steal them," Adam answered. He'd already lost one set his mother had made him, and a bowie knife that had been taken from a POW. He was more sore over losing the knife than the winter wear. "I don't know what the rate of theft is here. So I keep them hidden."

"If they turn up missing next winter, let me know," Velig said. He opened the table drawer. "This is where you keep your writing materials? You have several of Helmut's drawings."

"He ran out of space on his walls."

"He does that. Before you hang anything up in here, you need to let someone in charge approve it."

"Jorgan Gruber picked these."

"Good enough." Velig stopped rifling through the drawer and closed it. "I see room for improvement. I'll give you some leeway. Judging by the notes in your hands, you were focused on doing your primary job."

Velig left the room. Adam sagged with relief. In the hall, Velig said something quiet that Kiefer responded to. Then he rapped on another door. "Gruber! Open up!"

"I'm ready!" Helmut shouted. "You can inspect my room. I'm ready now."

"Very good," Velig said. "Let's do that. Then you need to pack to go out for a few days."

"Where?" Helmut sounded almost as excited as Kiefer had.

"Talk to Fritz when we're done here," Velig said. "Gruber, you go talk to Fritz now. I'm doing your room next, and then you're packing to go too."

Adam looked out into the corridor. Jorgan came out of Helmut's room and went to Kiefer's. Velig took only a couple of minutes for the inspection. Then he came out, calling for Jorgan to come to his room. Helmut danced his way into the hall, knocking against his door frame and bumping the walls.

"I cleaned my room good!" He trilled in a singsong rhythm. "I get to go out now! I cleaned my room good!"

Adam clapped for him. "Good job!"

"Do you get to go too?" Helmut asked.

Kiefer called from his room. "We don't want Adam to go."

Helmut stopped dancing. "We don't?"

Kiefer stuck his head out the door, wearing the same grin he got whenever he pulled a joke on someone. "He's a party pooper."

"He is not!" Helmut shook a finger at Kiefer. "You be nice!"

"Have you ever been to a party with him?"

"No."

"Then how do you know he's not a party pooper?" Kiefer asked. Helmut looked back and forth between the two of them with consternation. Kiefer laughed. "I'm just joshing you. They need him here at the base without me. Maybe he can go somewhere next time. Go finish packing."

Helmut dove back into his room. Kiefer checked up and down the hallway. Then he came out of his room with the Hebrew dictionary and handed it to Adam. "Velig said I have to give it back."

The bugle at the wall sounded. Two longs, followed by two shorts. Then a few seconds later, long short long. Kiefer blanched. Adam stuck the book behind his back when Helmut popped back out of his room, slack jawed and wide eyed saying, "That's not enough days. I counted. This is too soon."

Velig came out into the hall with Jorgan behind. Jorgan said, "He's not coming from the palace. The number of days won't be the same."

Kiefer's nearly whispered, "I'm leaving. It's all right. I'm leaving. I won't be around him."

"Contingent on if he—" Velig jabbed a finger at Adam— "is ready to work as a fully functioning interpreter. Or did you conveniently forget that part."

Adam wasn't ready. Not to function without assistance from someone who knew the language better. He could probably manage all right. But since he hadn't been able to practice with anyone except Kiefer he couldn't know for sure.

"He's ready," Kiefer said, his voice pitched slightly high as if he were on the edge of panic. "Aren't you, Adam? Tell him you're ready."

The desperation was plain on his face, his eyes pleading. For someone who could manage people insulting him as often as they did, what was it about this Ziegfried that had him so on edge? No one else acted this way about it.

Velig held up a hand, cutting Kiefer off. He turned to Adam. "Are you ready?"

"I'll manage," Adam said. He tried shrugging off his misgivings. "I got the message across with the mayor's son, didn't I?"

"All right, then you have about thirty seconds to slap on your dress uniform and get outside," Velig told him. He said to the others, "The rest of you, pack fast. Let's get you out before he knows you're here."

Adam ducked into his room and snagged his dress uniform while shedding his everyday one. In the hall, Jorgan said, "If we use the gate, he'll know. We'll need to use the underground exit."

There was another exit? Adam looked out into the hall. Velig put a hand on his face, pushed him back into his room, and shut the door saying, "Get ready!"

By the time he got his dress uniform on and went back out into the hall, it was empty. He straightened and buttoned and buckled it all as best he could on his way down the stairs to the front yard while dodging men scurrying around like ants when you stomp on their hill.

Most of them were busy putting on the last touches of whatever cleaning they'd been doing, and hiding their tools and supplies. Others had also donned their dress uniforms and ran the same way as Adam, also straightening buckles and straps with every footfall.

Grippe already stood out there between the main door to the castle and the gate. He scrutinized the uniformed men lining up, then called Adam over.

The men Adam stepped away from stood in two short rows. Some of the faces were those who claimed to have been stationed there the longest. Most of them represented different functions inside the operation.

The gate opened. Men wearing German military uniforms and riding horses entered first. Adam lost count after thirteen or fourteen. They couldn't have numbered more than twenty. All of them had the typical blond hair and blue eyes favored by the administration. None of them had any darker features, like a sprinkling of men at the base did. None of them had any faces he had seen before.

Behind them rolled a horse drawn, enclosed carriage. After that came two times the number of men than those in German uniforms. They also rode horses. Their double-breasted shirts were dyed such a deep scarlet they may as well have dripped blood. Everything else was gray: their pants, belt sashes, the braids on their shoulders, even the buttons up either side of their shirts.

The carriage stopped a few feet away from Grippe. The door opened and a little man stepped out. If he hadn't borne wrinkles on his face, and gray in his thinning hair, anyone could have mistaken him for a boy just out of adolescence, a little bit pudgy, giving the impression that the baby fat hadn't quite left him yet. At about five feet, his short height didn't help. He planted his stubby hands on his narrow hips, looked over the men in the two rows, and scowled just enough that it almost made him look cute.

"Welcome back to Far Base, Ziegfried," Grippe said.

"I don't see Ernest." Ziegfried's voice was the high pitch of an adolescent that hadn't yet dropped a couple of octaves.

"*Oberst Gerhardt* is occupied at the moment." Grippe put emphasis on the honorific and proper name.

"Occupied? I abandoned Andreno and traveled all the way here instead of his destination, and Ernest can't even make the time to greet me?" Apparently Ziegfried felt comfortable enough using Gerhardt's first name, whether appropriate for the setting or not.

"Why don't we go inside where you can get more comfortable until he's available?" Grippe turned to the side and swept one arm toward the castle.

Ziegfried sighed a little and said, "Fine."

He took mincing steps in that direction. Grippe nudged Adam to follow, then came right behind him. Inside, no one scurried about any longer. Ziegfried climbed the stairs to the second floor and turned down the command corridor. He went right to Gerhardt's office and burst inside.

Ziegfried glowered at the empty office. "Where is he?"

"I told you," Grippe said. "He's occupied."

"Is he in the com room?" Ziegfried looked up the hall to the door where the radio wires ran from under the door, tacked down where the wall met the floor, snaking their way to the tower where the antenna was located.

"I don't keep track of his every movement," Grippe said. "I keep track of the events on this base. And right now, the biggest event is you."

"The biggest event is the supplies he turned away." Ziegfried headed toward the room at the back of the castle where the villager had spoken with them.

"It was." Grippe followed him. "Now it's you."

Ziegfried threw wide the door to the room and strode inside. He plopped his chubby butt onto one of the couches and sprawled. Adam could just about see his mother bearing down, wooden spoon in hand in case she needed to beat someone, pointing at Ziegfried's shoes on the furniture. "*Füße auf die Boden!*"

Ziegfried wiggled his feet, grinding the heels of his shoes on the furniture. Not the kind of person Adam's mother would shower with an embarrassing number of hugs and kisses, then over-stuff with pork pie. He heaved out an elongated sigh, closed his eyes, rolled his head around, and rubbed the back of his chubby neck.

"Traveling on these roads is such a pain." Ziegfried opened his eyes and stared up at the ceiling. "Where's Kiefer?"

"Fritz is off base on assignment," Grippe said.

"Kiefer doesn't go off base on assignments." Ziegfried sounded skeptical.

"He does sometimes, when we have a need for him to," Grippe said. "And with the caravan in the village instead of here dropping off the materials for trade, we have a need for him to."

"How long before he gets back?" Ziegfried asked.

"Since it's been a while since he's done any field training exercises, we're taking advantage of the situation and making him do one," Grippe said. "No getting out of it this time. He's already out there. And we're not letting him back in until he does this."

Ziegfried frowned. "He'd do it just if Gerhardt ordered it. You're just trying to keep us separate."

"Think what you wish," Grippe said.

"Well, since I'm going to be here for a longer time—"

"Oh yes, on that topic," Grippe interrupted him. "Last time you came, you complained about the food. So we had some shipped in from the palace."

"I already knew that. Why are you bringing it up?"

"Since you're here so much earlier than anticipated, we're going to run out before you leave. You're going to have to eat the same as the rest of us."

"I hate this place," Ziegfried muttered.

"On a happier note," Grippe continued. "The new interpreter is ready to work."

"He only came through with the last portal opening," Ziegfried said. "Two months isn't long enough to learn a language."

"Apparently it is if you're gifted and smart enough," Grippe said. He gestured to Adam. "Meet Weiss."

"Two months isn't long enough," Ziegfried insisted.

"Fritz says's he's usable for the bare minimum," Grippe said. "We've already tried him out."

Ziegfried wriggled his foot on the couch again. "We should have him get on the radio and let Strom verify."

"No need." Grippe shook his head. "Fritz is a good judge."

"But Strom—"

"—didn't learn the Brendish language the same way Fritz did and, therefore, doesn't have the same finesse and comprehension of the nuances of the language."

Zigfried swung his feet down to the floor with a little bit of a growl. The sudden animosity hit Grippe with about as much affect as throwing water at a duck. He didn't even twitch his hands, still loosely clasped in front of him.

"Don't bother," he said. "My ears are deaf to your many excuses. And it's a change of subject. You asked us to present the new translator as soon as he was usable. Here he is. If you're satisfied, I'll dismiss him."

"No, don't do that," Ziegfried said a little too quickly. He stood, drawing himself up to his full, less than impressive height. He eyed Adam up and down, a look in his eye that was a little bit more predator than evaluator. He held out his hand like an American seeking a friendly handshake. "I'm Ziegfried Klein. Pleasure to meet you. What was your name again?"

"I already told you his name." Grippe stuck his arm in between the two of them, forestalling the handshake. "Weiss, since Gruber is gone with Fritz, Commander Gerhardt is without his normal aide. Go find him and see if he needs anything you can help him with."

"Yes, sir," Adam said.

Ziegfried reached out. "Wait."

Grippe moved, standing between them. Adam didn't stick around.

Chapter 10

ADAM WENT STRAIGHT TO GERHARDT'S OFFICE. The Oberst now sat behind his desk, writing reports or something. Adam didn't know what, and he had no desire to try and take a peek to find out.

Gerhardt didn't look up from his papers. "You meet Ziegfried?"

"Yes, sir," Adam said.

"Grippe send you?"

"Yes, sir. He said to ask if you need anything."

Gerhardt pointed with his pen to a seat close to the window that looked out on the mess hall. "I need you to make sure that chair doesn't fly away."

"Sir?"

Gerhardt pointed again. "Sit."

Adam sat. Gerhardt's pen scratched away. He flipped the paper to the side and started another. Adam looked out the window. He would never have thought of windows as looking inward to another room in the building. But every room on this side of the corridor did that.

He could see across the vaulted mess hall to the second story windows on the other side. Those would be the personal quarters of those in the hallway where Adam's room was located. He knew Kiefer was one of those windows. So were Gerhardt, Grippe, and Velig. He rested his chin on his hand with his elbow on the sill. The outside view was much better, even the side of the castle that couldn't see the hill.

At least here he could entertain himself watching all the comings and goings in the large room below. In his head, he went through name and titles of activities and items in other languages, listing things he could see one by one, language after language. Stringing the words together into sentences. Now he had yet more words he could add, since he understood more Brendish. Eventually he was going to find some private space where he could hole up with that forbidden dictionary and learn those words too.

"Weiss, that's really distracting." Gerhardt was giving him the evil eye. Maybe he hadn't kept all the words in his head. Sometimes when he got too absorbed, some of them slipped out of his mouth.

"Sorry, sir," Adam said.

"Here." Gerhardt held out some of the many papers he had written and set to the side. "Take these to Webmuller. Tell him to relay this info to Gruber when he checks in."

"Webmuller, sir?" Adam had heard the name before, and wasn't connecting it to the many faces he had been introduced to.

"The Hauptmann in charge of communications," Gerhardt said. "First, grab that special dictionary of yours. Show it to Webmuller. Tell him I want you to hide someplace to study it. I don't care if he goes with you and works on his pet project. Just don't let anyone see you until supper."

Adam grinned. He went to his room and dug out his book. He brought along a stack of notes, and blank paper to write more. Then he went to the locked com room and banged on the door. One of the com guys opened and accepted the messages. Then Webmuller came out with a set of keys and beckoned Adam to follow.

They went to the small, inconspicuous door that Jorgan claimed led up the tower that held the antennae and most of the communication equipment. Adam hadn't actually been in there. Webmuller selected a key and fit it into the lock. When they both had entered, he relocked it.

"Entire tower is private." He headed up the stairs. "Best view is the room at the top."

Adam didn't need a view to study a dictionary. But it might make a nice change after watching the mess hall. He headed up.

In most of the towers of castles that he'd toured back at home, the stairs ran up the circular, outside wall. This tower was square. Each floor had a room with a few pieces of radio equipment. The top one had a door with a keyhole that was swung ajar. The only other choice was the ladder that went up to a trapdoor in the ceiling. Adam entered the door.

A cot with a blanket was against one wall. A wobbly stool sat under the only window. Outside, the hill rose in all its grandeur. No radio equipment in here. Barely anything at all in here.

"I come up here to read or catch some naps from time to time. It's nice and quiet." Webmuller was already digging through a satchel leaning against the wall. He pulled paper and pencils out, and then smirked at Adam. "I hear you have an evil book. Are you writing it, or did you come across it?"

"Came across it." Adam sat in the corner opposite him, spreading out his notes and writing materials.

"Rats," Webmuller said with a smirk. "I was hoping you'd say you were writing it. I'd have offered to read it for you. I was only able to bring a couple of books, so I've read them several times. Something new might be nice. I don't suppose you'd let me read it even if you're not writing it?"

"It's just a language dictionary," Adam said, holding it up. Webmuller's face fell with disappointment. Then he sighed and bent over his own papers.

Adam opened his dictionary and stared at the words. This was the first time he'd actually been able to sit down and go through it at leisure. He didn't memorize any words. For now, he simply studied the letters, trying to let them unravel themselves in his head into a semblance of order and pattern.

He got about halfway through the book when he realized he was looking at the Chaldean flame letters backwards. Like many eastern languages, it read from right to left, not left to right like the English words on the other half of the page. He laughed.

"Must be a hilarious dictionary." Webmuller didn't look up from his writing. "I hope my book's as funny."

"You're writing your own book?" Adam lowered his.

"Trying to," Webmuller said. "It's a very sarcastic piece with fools for leaders. My last Oberst didn't find it very amusing. He burned my manuscript and got me sent here."

"You're re-writing it?"

"Not exactly the same. I put one leader in it this time that isn't a fool. Gerhardt prove that they do exist. They're just rare as hen's teeth."

"Does everybody have a reason they were sent here?" Adam asked. "I've heard others talking about it."

"Every one of us," Webmuller said. "We're all too dangerous to have around at home, and too useful to shoot. In some cases, our use is just to keep family obedient at home. Hostage, I guess you could say. Others, they want something from us, and this place keeps us contained until they want to pressure us more to cooperate. Not all of us know the exact reason we're here. It's not like command back at home is real forthcoming with information when they send us, and the brass here doesn't talk about it at all. But some of us, the reason is so obvious that we'd have to be stupid to not know."

The bugle call for supper blared. Adam gathered up his notes and papers that he had ended up not using. Webmuller walked him down the stairs and said, "I'll let you out."

"You're not going to eat?" Adam asked.

"Gerhardt usually has one of the radio operators bring me something when he gives me leave to work on my writing." Webmuller unlocked the door.

Ziegfried, coming up the corridor, spotted Adam the moment he stepped through the door. He looked like he was trying to stride with powerful steps, but his short little legs just looked silly. A goose trying to march. "There you are! What were you doing up in the tower?"

"I delivered a message to the com Hauptmann," Adam told half the truth.

"Webmuller?" Ziegfried eyed the door askance. "I swear, he's up to something in that tower. Nobody needs to spend that much time on stored radio equipment."

"I didn't see anything I considered wrong," Adam said.

"Anyway..." Ziegfried shrugged it away. "I was just about to make Ernest have someone go search for you. Come have supper with me."

"I don't want to bother you." Adam held up the stack of papers and notes that made camouflage for his book. "And I need to put this away."

He walked away. Unfortunately, either Ziegfried didn't get the clue that Adam didn't want to eat with him, or he didn't care. He tagged along. He didn't try to enter Adam's room, so that left enough opportunity to properly hide the book. But he was still there when Adam came back out.

Ziegfried smiled. "Ready now?"

Did Adam have the right to refuse? The brass had gone out of their way to keep the two of them separate. And yet they still acted respectfully to him. Jorgan had said Ziegfried controlled the only way back home. Did that mean that if he was displeased, he could also send messages back home that endangered people's families? It was probably best to keep him happy until Adam knew more.

He followed Ziegfried to the large room at the end of the command corridor. A small table by one wall had been set with food, better than the usual slop in the mess hall. Grippe and a few others were there too.

Ziegfried frowned a little. "What are you doing here?"

"You complained earlier about the lack of company," Grippe said. "I got you some company to eat with."

Ziegfried pointed to Adam. "I already found some company."

"And now you have more," Grippe said.

Ziegfried waved at the other men with a little swish of his hand. "This really isn't necessary. One guest for a meal is enough."

"I wouldn't want to miss the opportunity to bask in your presence." Grippe made the statement sound insulting.

"Fine." Ziegfried sighed a little petulantly. He plopped down in a chair and dished up a plate. He held it out to Adam. "Here. Sit down, and we can talk."

Grippe took the offered plate and set it on the table. "Don't touch him."

Ziegfried dished up another plate. "Paranoia will raise your blood pressure."

Every other man in the room had a carefully blank face. None of them gave Adam any clue what to make of this interaction. Grippe sat. One of the men served him. He pointed Adam to the first plate, so he sat too.

"Tell me about yourself," Ziegfried said to Adam. Then before anything could be said, he kept right on talking. "Myself, I come from a pretty normal family. We weren't rich. We weren't poor. I got picked on in school. Everyone hated me. I think they knew, deep down inside, that I was superior to them all, and it made them jealous."

He shoveled forkfuls into his mouth between words. The others ate, some of the salivating heavily over the quality of the food. Grippe maintained dignity, eating sparingly, keeping an eye on everyone at the table.

Ziegfried kept talking. He was a great person. It made everyone jealous. Everyone picked on him. Over and over, he related case after case. Most of them were just him being ignored, not actually picked on the way he claimed. Adam tuned him out and just enjoyed the food. It still wasn't as good as his mother's cooking. It was certainly better than what he'd been eating since leaving home to join the army.

Ziegfried leaned in close to Adam, whispering, "Then I gave him a taste of my real power."

Grippe paused, frozen in mid-bite, glaring, tense. Ziegfried sat straight and went back to talking normal. "He never picked on me again. Everyone avoided me even more after that. I think they were all afraid I'd also prove to them how superior I was."

He nudged Adam's arm with his elbow, grinning conspiratorially, like he'd just shared some kind of private joke. Grippe tapped the handle of his fork on the table and loudly cleared his throat. Ziegfried didn't even look. He took another bite. Too bad it didn't garble his talking.

"I think that was the incident that got me noticed by the military," Ziegfried continued. "Of course, they were very discreet at first. I hardly ever even saw them, and then only as they passed by me on the streets. They didn't contact me until I forced my way into a politician's office to let them know that I was ready for them to exploit my talents."

Adam finished his plate faster than he wanted to. Then again, maybe it wasn't such a bad thing. As good as the food tasted, the company was almost enough to spoil the appetite. Others started cleaning up. He stood to gather his own plate and utensils.

"Wait." Ziegfried put his stubby-fingered hand on Adam's arm. Grippe stood, bumping the table and making everything on it clatter. Ziegfried finally turned to him. "I'm not doing anything."

Adam slid his arm out from under the contact. Someone else took his plate, and all the other men disappeared with the dishes. That left him with just Ziegfried and Grippe.

"Don't even think about it," Grippe said to Ziegfried.

"I just want a little taste," Ziegfried said. "I was going to ask permission first."

"Permission from someone who doesn't understand what you're asking? Your answer is no."

"I'm not asking you."

"I'm answering you anyway."

Ziegfried stood. "You say he's ready to interpret, after only two months. That's outlandish. Unless I get a taste for his skills, and they're able to do what you claim, I don't believe you."

Adam bridled at the slight on his abilities. "I can interpret. You want me to talk to you in Brendish? Would that prove it?"

"Anything spoken in Brendish, I hear in German," Ziegfried said. "I use a translation spell. I won't know which of the two languages you're using."

"Then how were you planning on getting a taste for my skill?" Adam asked.

"Like this." Ziegfried leered, and touched Adam's hand.

A cold tingle shivered up Adam's spine. A wave of sleepiness mixed with nausea clubbed him over the head. He staggered and caught the back of the nearest chair to keep himself upright.

Grippe slapped Ziegfried's hand away. Adam gasped, all the air in his lungs doing no good. He might as well have taken a plunge into icy waters and swam under the surface for twelve miles.

"Damn it, Ziegfried!" Grippe shouted. "If you've made him unusable…"

"No, no." Ziegfried looked smug. He licked his lips. "I'm satisfied. His talent matches what you describe. I believe you."

"Get out," Grippe growled. He kept himself between them as Ziegfried moved past Adam and left the room with a gloat. Grippe pulled out the chair Adam clung to and maneuvered him into it. "Sit. Catch your breath."

"I'm fine," Adam wheezed.

"Stay here," Grippe said.

He left the room. Adam dropped his head into his hands. What had just happened? He was dizzy. That didn't help with the nausea. Maybe he was hyperventilating? Except he had felt dizzy before gasping for air. He let his head sink lower until it was between his knees.

He tried to straighten up when the door opened, admitting Grippe and Lieber. The sudden movement made him dizzy all over again.

Lieber steadied him. "Take it easy."

"I'm fine."

"Yeah, you look it." Sarcasm dripped from Lieber's voice. He felt for a pulse on Adam's wrist.

Adam didn't resist the medical attention. "I don't know what happened."

"Don't let Ziegfried touch you." Grippe explained while Lieber continued his checking. "He can suck the energy right out of you. It's what he uses to cast spells. If you have a skill that he wants to utilize, stay away from him entirely. Or if he's drained himself, stay away from him then too. This time, we got lucky. He just wanted to get a feel for your talents and skills. I don't think he'll do it to you again."

"Better not." Lieber examined Adam's eyes with a flashlight. "Or he might wake up some morning with a terribly itchy rash."

"He could retaliate against some of the men," Grippe said. "Don't do it."

Chapter 11

THE LAST CARAVAN WAGON rolled out through the gate. One by one, all ten of them had come in, emptied their contents, turned around, and left. None of the drivers had spoken with Adam, no matter how hard he had tried.

While the men who offloaded the wagons complained that there were twice as many as normal, Helmut bounced around between the crates. "Can I count now? Can I count now? Can I count now?"

"Wait," Jorgan told him, flipping through pages on his clipboard, examining the markings on each crate, checking them off from his lists.

They had gone through this round with all ten wagons now. And in between Helmut's nagging, Jorgan was beset with a line of people asking questions. He dealt with them one by one, first come first serve, despite others coming up from behind with claims of needing his immediate attention. With about every other person, he had to stop and tell Helmut, once more, to wait.

Adam couldn't help with the line of questioners. He didn't even understand half of them, they were so full of jargon. But there was one person he could distract to give Jorgan some room.

"Hey, Helmut!" Adam called the big man over. "I still don't understand why I'm needed here. Can you explain it to me again, please?"

Helmut leaned down to whisper in Adam's ear, loud enough to startle a cow. "I think it's for pretends." Then, thankfully, he stood straight and talked normal. "We used to keep Kiefer away from Ziegfried this way. We would pretend he needed to come out and interpret for the people bringing in the crates, even though they never ever talked to him much. And then he would pretend to try and mess me up when I counted everything. And then we would all pretend he was in trouble for trying to mess me up, even though nothing ever messed up my counts. And then Zigfried would have to leave him alone while he was in pretend trouble! Isn't that clever? I would never have thought of that!"

"He's not here right now." Adam scuffed his toe in the dirt. "And I thought you and Jorgan came to base only long enough to take in these wagon loads."

"Right," Helmut said, nodding. "Then me and Jorgan get to go back out and do a training exercise with Kiefer. He's supposed to be setting it up now that he got the caravan to leave the village and come here. Did I tell you he did that?"

"Yes, you did." Adam went on the assumption that he had to be there to continue the charade, so Kiefer could continue playing it the next time. He didn't bother asking. Helmut's answer would likely be confusing and meander through many different subjects. Jorgan still needed more time, though. Adam continued the conversation. "This caravan of wagons comes every month? I don't remember it last month."

"It didn't come." Helmut scuffed his toe the same as Adam had. He stared at Adam's posture then mimicked him exactly. "We didn't know why. Jorgan says that's probably when Keniv first was trying to take over. We didn't worry too much. Some months it doesn't come. It's happened before. And this time I get to go out because of it."

"You like going outside the castle walls?"

"Oh, yes." Helmut smiled wide. "Going out is exciting. It gets boring just drawing and counting everything here."

Adam pointed to his favorite piece of landscape. "Have you ever climbed that hill?"

"Yes."

"What's it look like from the top?"

"There's grass on top where the trees end," Helmut said. "And there's one tree there all by itself. I wonder sometimes if it gets lonely. And I found a cave once. But Jorgan wouldn't let me explore it."

"Can you see the village from there?"

"Only the tall building," Helmut said. "Kiefer said you can't see the others because they're short and hide behind the trees."

"Can you see this castle?"

"Yes," Helmut said. "And the other castle too."

"Other castle?"

"There's another castle farther away that way." Helmut pointed directly at the hill. "Way, way, way, over, a long ways away. And if the sky isn't clear enough, you can't see it."

Indistinct shouting floated across the yard. Several heads turned. Most of the men saw that it was just Ziegfried, screaming at Velig, stamping his feet, and waving his arms. They quickly went back to work, carefully keeping their faces turned away from the confrontation.

Helmut stared. "You don't act like that."

"Why would I act like that?" Adam asked. Gerhardt came out and talked to Ziegfried. He stopped throwing such a tantrum, but his face was red and he still gesticulated rather wildly.

"He drew from you," Helmut said. "He usually acts a little like the people he draws from. Unless he draws from lots of people at once. Then he's just weird. But he drew from you. And you don't act like that."

"I have a short temper." Adam's face flushed a bit. "But you're right. I try not to act like a little kid having a fit."

"Sometimes I don't like Ziegfried very much," Helmut whispered loudly. Speaking normal, "Don't tell anyone. Most people say I like everybody. Sometimes, I don't know about Ziegfried. There was this one other person I thought I liked. Then he killed my friend with a gun. So I didn't like him anymore."

"Didn't?" Adam asked. "Or don't?"

"Um… Well…" Helmut opened his hands in front of him. Staring at them, he started crying. "I'm so sorry. I didn't know my hands would kill him. I'm sorry. I didn't mean to."

"Whoa, whoa, hey." Adam patted his arm. "It's okay. Don't cry. Please. I'm sorry I brought it up."

"Jorgan says it's okay to not like everybody." Helmut sniffled, wiped his nose, and brushed away some of the tears. It took several brushes before they stopped flowing.

"Jorgan's right, you don't have to like everybody," Adam said. He nodded his head toward Gerhardt herding Ziegfried back inside. "Some people make themselves difficult to like."

"Yeah." Helmut giggled, still wiping away the last of the tears. "They do. I bet Jorgan's wife doesn't make it hard. She's probably really nice. I know she's pretty."

"Wife?"

"Yeah. He has a wife. Her name is Gretel. And she's really pretty. He lost her picture. It was in his Bible. And somebody stole his Bible. I drew him a new picture of her. It's one of the ones hanging in his room."

"Helmut." Jorgan walked over to them. "That's enough. You can go count what's in the crates now."

"Yay!" Helmut skipped away, waving his hands in the air. Some of the men pried open one of the crates and he dove in head first.

Adam took a deep breath. "He just dumped a few bombshells of information on me."

"I know. I heard," Jorgan said. "Sorry. Partly my fault. I should have warned you he might cry if he talks too much about his friend."

"Not just that." Adam looked away. "Are you really? Married?"

"I sure hope so," Jorgan mumbled, sifting through some of the papers on his clipboard.

"You don't know?"

Jorgan sighed. He flipped a couple more pages. He looked around. No one was within hearing. Still, he spoke softly. "Five days after the wedding, two SS officers drove up in a black car, stuffed me in the back, told me I was enlisted, and drove me to basic training. I wasn't allowed to write her a letter, or telephone her, or anything. I'm lucky I had... Well, that's gone now too, so it doesn't matter."

"You didn't even get to phone her when you finished basic?"

"I didn't finish basic," Jorgan said. "Before I finished, I was transferred here."

Helmut popped up from inside the crate. "Done!"

Jorgan strode over to him, flipping pages on the clipboard. "Very good!"

"Hey!" One of Ziegfried's bodyguards trotted toward Adam. "Are you Leutnant Weiss? The new interpreter?"

"Yes," Adam said.

"Soon as you're done here, Ziegfried wants you."

"I have to report to Velig soon as I'm done here," Adam told him.

"Ziegfried first," the bodyguard said. "Then Velig."

"I follow orders from chain of command before a civilian." Adam put a hand behind his back and dug his nails into his palm. "Command gets testy if I do it the other way around."

"Look, I'm going to level with you." The man drew close, speaking quietly. "We need some help. He drew from you, and now he's flying off the handle with no control, mad at everything. You seem pretty calm and collected. Give him some tips how you do it."

"I'm the wrong person to ask." Adam dug his nails deeper. "I'm fighting the urge to punch you in the face just for asking me to risk getting in trouble. Because you know I would if I ignore orders from Velig."

"Fine," the man hissed.

He said nothing more. He didn't leave, either. He tapped his foot. He crossed and uncrossed his arms. He glared at anyone and everyone. Finally, Jorgan got fed up and told Adam, "Get out of here, and take that guy with you."

Adam went straight to Velig, Zigfried's man tagging along as a shadow. Velig was conferencing or something with Grippe. Grippe told him, "Go shut yourself in your room and study. If I see your face again before dinner, I'll have someone lock you in the radio tower with nothing but your dictionaries, paper, and pencils."

"Ziegfried needs him," the bodyguard said.

"Ziegfried can grow up and stop throwing tantrums like a two-year-old before I let him expose anyone else to his current behavior," Grippe told him.

Adam couldn't keep the smile off his face as he went to his room. There, he enjoyed the time to himself as he went through his forbidden dictionary,

78

along with a few others. When supper rolled around someone brought him food, so he didn't even have to come out then.

He stayed in his room studying over the next couple of days while Jorgan and Helmut finished the fresh inventory count. Then they were sent back out to join Kiefer and the others on their training exercise. Once they were gone, Adam turned into the rope in a tug-of-war between the brass and Ziegfried.

He enjoyed the few times Grippe ordered him into seclusion to study, or into hiding spots to listen to the natives converse. It was far better than any time he got stuck with Ziegfried. Every time he left that little man, he felt tired and physically drained. Then he had to seclude himself anyway, just to keep hold on his temper, instead of flying off the handle at any and every perceived provocation.

Not all of the orders the Brass gave him were so enjoyable. They sent him to the acquisitions officer to haggle for something that he didn't want to issue, and they didn't need. Another time, he had to sort dirty socks on the claim that someone had to do it. Then he had to assist with the crap burning, because he hadn't done it yet. Never mind the fact that there were plenty of others who also hadn't done it yet. He almost would have preferred getting tired in Ziegfried's company. Almost.

After two weeks, Kiefer, Helmut, Jorgan, and the few with them returned from the training exercise. They all looked exhausted, and from the way they talked, they really had been training, not goofing around to avoid Ziegfried.

Chapter 12

ONE MONTH AFTER Keniv's attempt to enter the base, another caravan arrived with five wagons full of goods. Everything went smoothly this time, so the regular drivers and leader must have returned. The wagon drivers were disinclined to converse. It wasn't just Adam this time, like with the natives staffing the castle. They wouldn't talk much to Kiefer either. Just the leader spoke, conveying pertinent information for the brass. And he talked to both the interpreters. That was rather satisfying. Until he finished. Then he clammed up. Adam shifted back into being useless while Jorgan organized everyone and took stock of the goods.

"Can I count the next one now?" Helmut tapped Jorgan on the shoulder hard enough to jostle the clipboard.

"Wait." Jorgan dipped his shoulder down away from the tapping. He steadied the clipboard and continued writing. He erased something, checked off something else, sent away the person who had just spoken with him, turned to the next one, then had to hold up his hand for the next few to wait when they called for their turn.

One of Ziegfried's bodyguards approached. "Leutnant Weiss, you finished here yet? Ziegfried wants you again."

"I haven't been dismissed," Adam told him.

The bodyguard stuck his hand over Jorgan's clipboard, getting his attention. "You don't really need two interpreters for this, do you? You probably don't even really need one."

"Can I count the next one now?" Helmut tapped again.

"Hey, Helmut!" Kiefer grinned impishly. "One tabulator, one counter, one bodyguard, and two interpreters. How many people is that?"

Helmut stopped tapping Jorgan to roll his eyes at Kiefer. "Duh, silly. That's five."

"And how many of them are stupid enough to think that interpreters aren't needed to read the writing on the crates?"

The bodyguard bridled. "Hey!"

Helmut giggled. "That's not nice."

The bodyguard took his hand off the clipboard, repeatedly stabbed a pointing finger in the direction of the crates. "By now, everyone knows which markings are for which goods. Interpreters aren't needed for the counts."

Kiefer rocked back on his heels enough that his toes lifted slightly. "And you know this because you've done... how much translation work?"

The bodyguard just growled in answer. Jorgan ignored them, answered a question and sent two more people away. He stepped over to the next questioner and flipped through papers on his clipboard looking for a specific number. One of the Soldats who worked for the Stabsgefreiter came running up. "Hauptmann Gruber? Sir?"

"For pity's sake!" Jorgan ground his teeth and moved farther away.

"Weiss," the bodyguard said. "You should come now."

No way was Adam going to risk getting in trouble for leaving his post until he was dismissed. "Tell Ziegfried he'll have to wait."

"Can I count the next one?" Helmut sounded like a broken record.

Kiefer caught his arm before he could follow Jorgan. He turned the big man away, asking about the numbers of various different things: stones in the walls, boards nailed to the floor of his room, how many animals were on base if they included the men who liked Ziegfried.

Kiefer was definitely doing his part to keep Jorgan's distractions down to a minimum. Adam could help too. He stepped in front of the Stabsgefreiter's Soldat, holding out his hand to stop the man. "What do you need?"

"I'm supposed to tell him to wait to stage everything in the corridor," the man said. "My boss has a better method of organizing it."

"Tell your boss his answer is no," Kiefer interjected while Helmut was busy counting the stones in the wall's mason work.

The Soldat sneered without even looking at Kiefer. "I'm not asking a monkey."

Adam moved before thinking. He plowed his right fist into the Soldat's left eye. His head snapped to the side, his left shoulder coming around as he crumpled in on himself with buckling knees. That gave perfect momentum. All Adam had to do was hold up his left fist and the idiot rammed his own chest into it. With one little push after that, he fell to the ground.

Adam coiled to spring on top to pound him further. Someone snaked their arms under his from behind, yanking him off balance. Kiefer jumped in front of him, also pushing him back and shouting. "Hey! Hey! No! Back off!"

"What is going on?" Jorgan shouted from the line of questioners. Everyone stared at Adam, some of them with jaws slack.

Helmut's mouth made a perfect circle of astonishment. Then he said, "That was naughty."

It was Ziegfried's bodyguard who had grabbed Adam from behind. He let go but stayed close. Kiefer had one hand on Adam's chest, like a nonverbal message to stay back.

Jorgan strode over demanding, "Someone explain! Now!"

"What does it look like?" The Soldat put a hand over his reddening eye and pointed at Adam. "He attacked me for no good reason."

The bodyguard cocked his head with a smug look. "He didn't attack you. You tripped and fell and punched yourself in the face."

Helmut pointed at the idiot. "He called Kiefer a monkey again."

Jorgan narrowed his eyes and turned his head to glare down his nose at the Soldat. "Then he deserved to get hit."

The idiot got to his feet. It looked like he tried to jump to his feet, but he staggered some. That ruined it. Still holding his eye, he bared his teeth at Adam. "Just you wait until Velig hears about this."

Kiefer held up his other hand, the one not signaling Adam to stay back. "There's no need to report about you tripping and falling."

"He should get that eye looked at though," the bodyguard said. "Maybe have Doc Lieber check on his sudden dizzy spell. He might need to take precautions to make sure he doesn't trip hard enough to sock himself in the face in the future."

"I didn't trip!" the idiot snarled.

"I saw it," the bodyguard said. "Good thing for you Leutnant Weiss was right there to catch you or you might have hurt yourself more than you did."

"I'm reporting this attack to Velig," the idiot said. He tipped his chin down at Adam. "You're finished."

"Yeah, he'll get a slap on the wrist," Jorgan said. "But only if you really want to suffer what Velig will do to you for calling Kiefer a monkey. You sure you want to report it?"

The idiot blanched. His hand dropped away from covering his swelling eye. He shifted his weight. The bodyguard smirked, grabbed his collar, and marched him back to the castle saying, "Come on, let's get you to Doc Lieber and make sure your dizzy spell won't come back."

Jorgan went back to the crates and the line of questioners. Helmut stood stock still, eyes a little too wide. Kiefer shook his head and looked Adam right in the eye, "You need to keep a lid on that temper."

"Sorry," Adam mumbled. It was stupid. But there really was nothing more to say.

"You will be," Kiefer said. He hiked a thumb over his shoulder to point at the bodyguard taking the idiot inside. "He's going to claim that you owe him now, since he covered for you. So now you're not going to be able to get out of spending more time with Ziegfried."

Adam ground his teeth at the prospect. Not that he didn't deserve it. He could all but hear his father's voice telling him, "Boy, if you don't like punishment then learn to stop earning it."

At supper, just as Kiefer predicted, Adam got stuck spending time with Ziegfried. The little man stuffed his face while he spouted his normal geyser of braggadocio. Tonight's speech was interlaced with how unavailable he would be the next day because it was time to open the portal again.

"I know a lot of the men will be disappointed that they can't spend more time with me." Ziegfried sopped some bread on his plate and crammed it in his mouth. "I hate to do that to them. I know how it feels to be denied time with someone. I certainly wanted to spend more time with Ernest. Or even Kiefer. I still think that he would do better with the proper influence. But, it is what it is. I have a duty to perform. And it takes a lot of time, effort, and concentration. Which I'm sure is why Ernest didn't get to spend as much time with me either."

"Probably." Adam made sure to put in a word every now and then, making it appear he listened politely. "Jorgan says Oberst Gerhardt is pretty busy."

"Good man, that Jorgan Gruber, despite his whacko religion." Ziegfried swirled the water in his cup as if it were a fine wine.

"He said he came over with you right at the first."

"Jorgan? Yes. Don't think even he knows the reason behind it. Ernest does. He knows the reason behind every man being here. He just won't talk about it. Not even to me." Ziegfried set his water back down and picked up his fork again. "Anyway, as I was saying, I'm going to be too busy to talk to you very soon, and after the portal closes I sleep, and then leave to go back to the palace the next day. I usually sleep the entire way. It's the reason I have my own bodyguards, that vulnerability."

He looked up from his plate, just enough of a pause to give Adam time to grunt acknowledgment. Oh, the lecture Ziegfried would have received from Adam's parents, decrying the sins of pride, extolling the virtues of paying more attention to others than to yourself. He hadn't said anything about the bruises Adam hand given himself on the knuckles of his right hand when he'd punched that idiot Soldat. Adam had sat at this meal for the better part of an hour and he couldn't tell if Ziegfried had even noticed.

Their plates were almost empty. Not soon enough. Adam had his left hand under the table hiding that he was digging his nails into his palm, struggling to keep his calm. Soon it would hurt more than the bruises on his right knuckles if he kept this up.

He couldn't mouth off. He couldn't mess up. He had already skated too close to the line today. He couldn't let loose his temper and give this little man the tongue lashing he repeatedly deserved. His family's lives depended on him. Whether they knew it or not. He would bite his tongue, in some cases literally, hard enough to draw blood. And he would stay out of trouble.

"So what I'm getting around to…" Ziegfried continued his ramblings. "I've kind of been putting off talking to you about it. Well, at first I wasn't. I hadn't even thought of it because I didn't know you yet. It didn't take long. I'm a very good judge of character. I can always tell if someone's got good genes. And I could tell before that first day was over that you have very good genes. Like me."

Ziegfried continued verbal circles, a buzzard too lazy to make its own kill. Adam nodded. He interjected a response or two. Never once did the little man say anything he hadn't said in other meals. Until Adam polished off his plate and pushed away from the table to leave.

"I still haven't exactly said what I needed to, and we're already out of time." Ziegfried sighed. He dabbed at his mouth a little bit with the corner of his napkin. "I'll just have to come right out in the open and say it directly. I put in a request on your behalf this afternoon for a transfer to the palace. There. I said it."

"You did what?" Adam half turned back to the table. "You requested I be transferred?"

"I put it in under your name." Ziegfried dropped his napkin next to his plate and stood. "We need someone else there who speaks the language. Strom can't be in two places at once. Andreno needs him. And I'm too busy to always play interpreter for my bodyguards, so I really need a second one with them. And I doubt I need to tell you much more about the palace. I'm sure you already know how great an opportunity this is for you. So I forged your handwriting, and submitted the request, to save you time and effort."

"Excuse me." Adam strode from the room, gnawing on the inside of his cheek. His tongue was too sore from biting it too often in the past several days. He went directly to the Oberst's office.

"Weiss, come in," Gerhardt said. He tapped a piece of paper on his desk. "I was going to call you in after supper anyway to talk to you about this."

"Is that the transfer request?" Adam bared his teeth at the paper. "I didn't write it. In fact, I just now found out about it."

Gerhardt nodded. "Thought so. Is there any reason I should or should not grant the request?"

"Besides the fact that it's forged?"

"That's a reason not to," Gerhardt said. "Any reason I should?"

Adam shook his head. "Not that I can think of."

"You had to have given some sort of indication that you might like the transfer, or he wouldn't have thought you'd go along with it. He drew from you. He can pick up on your subtlest cues that you might not even be aware of."

Adam clenched and unclenched his fists at his sides. "Whatever he thinks may have caught my interest wouldn't be worth having to spend so much time with him."

"Maybe so." Gerhardt leaned back from his desk and interlaced his fingers. "We should still figure this out. You must have had your interest piqued by something. I assume he talked to you frequently about life in the palace. Think. What did he say?"

"He said there are women," Adam said the first thing that came to mind.

"Every man here would be interested in that," Gerhardt said. "Some of us haven't seen anything female for months straight. There had to have been something else. What did he ramble about?"

Adam ticked off on his fingers, trying to recall as many things as possible. "He said the food is better. The beds are softer. There are women. Strom is there instead of Kiefer. I'd be used a lot more since Andreno keeps Strom close by and Ziegfried's bodyguards need their own interpreter. There are always foreign guests that speak other languages."

"That one." Gerhardt sat forward. "There was a flicker in your eyes when you said it. Did he mention it by itself? Or while he talked about another subject?"

"He was talking about Strom trying to pick up some of the slang and other dialects of the Brendish language."

"And yet you spoke like the other languages were the main point, not Strom." He picked up the paper and looked it up and down. "You're really that interested in other languages? Knowing more than a dozen isn't enough for you?"

"I love words."

"I suppose he's right on one thing. We really could use a second interpreter at the palace more than here. I'm just not sure I want any more of my men that close to Ziegfried. He can drain a person so fast it almost makes me believe some of the old vampire legends. I could put in the stipulation that you're to be assigned to Andreno, and Strom to Ziegfried and his bodyguards. Are you willing to do this?"

"If it's beneficial to this operation—" and if compliance kept his family safe— "I'll do whatever is needed."

"Very well." Gerhardt signed the paper at the bottom. "Get packed."

Adam left the office. What had he just gotten himself into? And how had it happened so abruptly? Or did it really even matter at this point? It wasn't like he could go back in and say he'd changed his mind. And if he could, would he? Probably not. Not with the opportunity to use the Brendish language more, and possibly learn others besides.

He went to his room and pulled out his sack. Packing didn't take long. He had most of it done before Helmut caught him.

The big man stood aghast in the door, spreading his hands out in a pleading way. "What are you doing?"

"I'm packing," Adam said. "I got orders to go to the palace."

"No, no, no, no, no." Helmut grabbed Adam's bag from him and pulled things back out of it. "You can't go. You can't. You're my friend! I want you here. You have to stay."

"Helmut?" Kiefer called from the hall, then leaned into the room. "What's wrong? Why are you crying?"

"I just got transfer papers to the palace." Adam tried to gently pry his sack out of Helmut's cling. He may as well have tried to wrench a pipe out of a vise clamp.

"Oh. I see." Kiefer came all the way into the room. He squatted by Helmut and wiped at his tears with a slow hand. "Now Helmut, you know he doesn't have a choice. If he got papers, he has to go."

Helmut wailed. "He's my friend!"

"He'll be back," Kiefer said. "Strom has come back from time to time. You always get excited to see him, don't you? Adam will come back too."

"I guess so." Helmut sniffled. He wiped at his nose, letting go of the bag. Then he jumped to his feet and ran out saying, "I'm going to ask Ernest to make him not go!"

Kiefer asked Adam. "You didn't request this, did you?"

"Ziegfried did." Adam slowly replaced some of what Helmut had taken out.

"I can just imagine what form of request he put in." Kiefer snorted and rolled his eyes. He got to his feet. "Good luck. And be sure and keep a tight grip on your temper there."

"You think Helmut will adjust okay?"

"He'll be all right," Kiefer said. "Me and Jorgan will cheer him up. Don't worry about it."

"Thanks for helping me with him," Adam said. "I think I'm going to have to reorganize everything. He dug all the way down to the bottom and pulled stuff out from there."

Adam picked up his Hebrew dictionary from the pile of things Helmut had extracted. Kiefer eyed it hungrily. A pang of guilt stabbed Adam. Here he was, going someplace where he could practice other languages, where he might not have time to even open the cover. Here was Fritz, stuck in a place where people hated him for some unknown reason, with plenty of time and privacy on his hands to make good use of the book.

It was better for it to get used. He held it up. "You want to keep this somewhere safe for me?"

Kiefer caught his breath. "Are you sure?"

He reached with both hands, stopping just shy of touching. Adam nodded reluctantly and put the book in his hands. Kiefer cradled it with as much reverence as he had the first time. He backed out of the room and disappeared from Adam's sight.

He didn't see anyone else for the rest of the evening. He could hear plenty through the thin walls, though. Helmut cried in his room later. Jorgan tried consoling him. Adam stayed out of it. He probably would have felt better if he stole Easter chocolate from a room full of Kindergartners.

Chapter 13

AFTER BREAKFAST, EVERYONE immediately stacked all the tables and benches against one wall of the mess hall. Then they all scrambled to their various assignments. Velig sent Adam to help keep people away from Jorgan.

Only one person approached while Jorgan was in his room donning his dress uniform. Helmut and Kiefer jumped the guy and dragged him out of the hall. Adam didn't have to do a thing. Jorgan must have heard the altercation, though. He grumbled.

"Idiots." He stood in front of a full-length mirror attached to the inside of his closet door. "For some reason they all think that since I step through the portal that I can somehow sneak a message through to someone."

"You do have a reputation for solving puzzles," Adam said.

"If I could get any message through, I'd send one to my wife." Jorgan yanked and tugged at the cut of the cloth, jerking everything straight.

"How many of them even know you're married?" Adam asked.

Jorgan sighed and dropped his hands to his sides. He glanced over at the Helmut-drawn picture of the pretty woman tacked to his wall by his bed. He picked up his hat and worried it in his hands. "None of them know. So I guess it's not really fair to hold that against them. If I could get a message through, any kind of message, maybe she wouldn't think I'm dead, or just plain give up and go get an annulment or something. She deserves a husband

90

who's there to protect and provide for her. Not someone who's absent and leaves her to take care of everything and make her own way."

Helmut and Kiefer returned. Jorgan tapped his hat atop his head and shut his door saying, "Give me a moment."

"Poor Jorgan," Helmut said. "He misses his Gretel most when the portal opens. He showed me a picture once, before someone stole it with his Bible. She's really pretty. I drew him a picture. But I don't have any colors to put on it for him. He said she has yellow hair and green eyes. Like yours. Your eyes are green."

"My eyes are hazel," Adam said.

"Hazel?" Helmut frowned. "Like hazelnuts? Hazelnuts are brown. Your eyes are green. Not hazelnut."

"They're hazel," Adam repeated. "So sometimes they look green."

"Nuh-uh." Helmut shook his head. "They're green."

"Adam has freaky eyes." Kiefer smirked. "They change colors. Sometimes they're blue, sometimes gray, and sometimes they're green."

Helmut squinted at Adam's face. "Nobody's eyes change color."

"They do if they're a freak like him," Kiefer said. He put a hand to the side of his mouth and leaned sideways to Helmut. "When he's really mad, they definitely turn green, and get gold flecks, so it looks like he's trying to shoot electric sparks out at you."

Adam took a half-hearted swing at Kiefer, aimed right at his shoulder where it wouldn't hurt much if it connected. Kiefer sidestepped as if he was used to having punches thrown at him. He laughed and said to Helmut, "See? What did I tell you? Really mad."

"That's really naughty," Helmut said.

"Yeah." Kiefer laughed some more and shook a finger at Adam. "Naughty, naughty, naughty. You apologize. And then maybe I'll think about forgiving you."

Adam threw up his hands. "You're impossible!"

Jorgan came out of his room. Without a word, he headed for the stairs. Adam, Kiefer, and Helmut followed him down, meeting up with the brass and several others outside the doors to the mess hall. It sounded like a bonfire raged inside, a dragon swallowing everything in the room.

Someone yawned. Another leaned casually against the wall. A couple of others held a conversation swallowed up by the noise. Adam shifted his feet, glancing between the door and all the people not reacting.

"Relax," Gerhardt told him. "It always sounds like this. Ziegfried will get it under control."

Adam tried leaning against the wall. That didn't calm him. He tapped his fingers on his thighs to let out nervous energy. That didn't help. He was going to have to resort to the one thing that worked every time.

He took the word for fire and translated it into every language he knew how to. Then he took synonyms and did the same. He went through descriptions. Antonyms. Then moved on to homonyms and rhyming words. That was always amusing. The words no longer rhymed when translated to other tongues.

"Stop it," Kiefer said, elbowing him. Several others were staring. He still hadn't figured out how to do it entirely in his head. The words had slipped out of his mouth again.

Someone grumbled off to the side about how only idiots show off. Adam looked over. It was the same guy he'd thrown his water cup at, the one that had called Helmut a moron and Kiefer an animal. When he saw Adam looking, he narrowed his eyes, crossed his arms, and tilted his nose up.

Kiefer used English to say, "Don't react. It's what he wants."

"It's hard," Adam responded, also in English.

"It's strategic," Kiefer said. "People like him, if they don't get what they want they usually do one of two things. They either stop, or they get worse. Both are good."

"How is getting worse good?"

"Because the worse they get—" Kiefer grinned impishly— "the more likely they'll get themselves in trouble."

The grumbling turned into snide comments about how there was no need to learn other languages. Because once the Fuhrer won the war all other nations would have to learn German. Whoever he was grumbling to snickered. Someone else said, "Yeah, unless they're part of a sub-human species and are too stupid to learn the language of their superiors."

Velig spun on his heel. He grabbed the original grumbler and the person who made the sub-human comment and dragged them around a corner. Some smacks and yelps followed that. Velig came back. The other two didn't.

Kiefer smirked again and said, "See?"

Just then, one of Ziegfried's bodyguards came and told them, "The portal is stable. It's safe now."

Gerhardt swung open the double door. Everyone flowed inside. Adam froze in the doorway. A couple of people bumped him when they moved around. He blinked, mesmerized by the spiraling ring in the center of the room.

It stood twice as high as a man and just as wide. Flat as a piece of paper, it still took up a good chunk of the large room. It reminded Adam of the flaming hoop a circus trainer made a lion jump through. Except this hoop was opaque. And a lot bigger. And it was flat on the bottom where it met with the floor.

The flames spiraled instead of rising, with every color of the rainbow. The outer rim was hard red. That faded in to orange. Inward from that, the orange muted to yellow. Then it turned green and spiraled in to blue and royal purple, with a pinpoint of indigo at the very center.

"We shouldn't stand in the doorway," Helmut said from behind Adam. "Jorgan will get upset if we don't move out of the way. He says we can't stand in doorways because people might trip over us."

Helmut herded Adam to the side where the brass and the doctors stood. Kiefer laughed at him and said, "What's wrong with you? It's not like you haven't seen it before."

"I don't remember all this detail," Adam said.

"It's pretty." Helmut stared at it, openly displaying his awe. "I like looking at the portal. I can't draw it, though. I don't have any colors. It wouldn't look right without the colors."

After several minutes another of Ziegfried's bodyguards came and told Gerhardt, "It's usable."

Gerhardt nodded to Jorgan. "Go."

Jorgan set his jaw and walked through the flames in the center of the spiral. Several minutes passed. Then the front edge of a pallet emerged from the flames. Helmut bounced over to the half dozen men that rushed forward. A couple of them caught it, pulling to bring it the rest of the way through.

They trundled it along on a flat hand-truck, Helmut dancing along beside it. Another pallet emerged. More men grabbed it. Then another.

Adam stopped counting after a while. The men who had taken the first pallet came back for more. All the men cycled back, like a carousel that trundled the goods along as if on a conveyor system in a manufacturing plant. And all the while, Helmut skipped and jumped and danced around, telling everyone he was going to count it all.

One came through with a paper list tacked to it. No other pallets came through after that. Gerhardt frowned. One of the men said, "That's it? This is all they're supplying us with? This isn't even as much as last time."

"And we thought that was only a little," another grumbled.

Grippe called out, "Cut the complaints. We'll make do. Reverse the flow."

Kiefer said to Adam, "Here's where we earn our pay."

The men now trundled in the goods that had come in on the native caravans. Each crate had a manifest tacked to it with the identification code assigned to it. Adam and Kiefer doubled checked each identification code, ensuring that the manifest matched the native markings scrawled on the crate.

Adam triple and quadruple checked them. Keifer said, "You're going a little bit slow. You're good enough with the verbal I didn't think you'd have trouble with the writing."

"I can't mess up," Adam said. "Not when they have to know on the other side that I'm helping with this. Not when it could affect my family."

After another couple of crates, Kiefer said in English, "They really don't care over there. This stuff, it doesn't make any difference. It's mostly for appearance. The men on this mission are told these are the 'miracle' supplies that are fueling the war machine. So we send them."

Adam responded in English. "And you're willing to risk your family's lives if you mess it up?"

Kiefer went silent. He worked a muscle in his cheek and didn't look at Adam for the rest of the time the crates of native goods flowed into the portal. When they stopped flowing, he stiffly walked out of the large room without a leave or dismissal, and without a backward glance.

Adam glanced at the brass, half tempted to ask leave to go check on him, make sure he was okay. But if he did, that would draw attention to the fact that he'd left. And Adam might have to explain why and how he'd been upset. Which might lead to explaining that Kiefer had a very lackadaisical attitude over the quality of the translations on the crates.

No. Adam wouldn't do that to him. He let it be. With this many people in the room moving and shuffling about, maybe the brass wouldn't notice Kiefer's absence.

Pallets reversed direction once again, coming out of the portal from Germany. This time, they stopped them in the room and opened each one. All of them held gold bars. Helmut dove in and counted them all right there. The Stabsgefreiter recorded the counts in every crate before they were closed up again and finally carted off.

There was another pause. Not only did the pallets stop, but so did the men in the large room. Adam glanced at the brass hoping they still wouldn't notice Kiefer's absence. They weren't looking around. Their attention was on the portal.

Men stepped through the portal from home, one at a time, totaling about a dozen. They wore everyday uniforms and carried their sacks on their shoulders. At least half of them stumbled when they stepped out of the portal. One of them keeled over and fell flat on his face. Lieber and the other doctors immediately went and pulled him away.

"Every time," Velig muttered. "Damn Ziegfried. Every time, there's someone who can't handle it. I thought you were going to talk to him about not drawing from new men coming through to us."

"Pick your battles," Gerhardt said. "This is minor. We have other more important concerns."

Jorgan came back through at last. He turned to Ziegfried's bodyguard by the door, and gave a cut-off signal, drawing his hand flat across his throat. The bodyguard ran off.

Jorgan handed his clipboard to Gerhardt. "That's all."

"Can I go count now?" Helmut asked.

"Wait," Gerhardt told him, glancing through the pages on the clipboard. He got to the last page, handed it back to Jorgan and said, "Go count the fresh inventory."

"What little bit they sent us," Velig groused.

Gerhardt addressed the new men with a standard orientation speech. The brass were introduced by their names. The new arrivals were told to toe the line and threatened with disciplinary measures if they caused trouble. They were handed off to people who would process them, get them quarters, and trooped out of the room.

Grippe clapped his hands together, getting the attention of everyone left in the room, "The rest of you, get the mess hall put back together. We're done here."

And Kiefer hadn't gotten in trouble. And it seemed Adam's family was safe for at least a little while longer. He let out his breath in relief.

Chapter 14

ZIEGFRIED SNORED. FOR MOST OF THE TRIP, Adam had avoided him, riding on one of the wagons. Every time they had passed through any kind of population center like a town or village, even a few buildings huddled on the side of the road, the bodyguards stuffed him in the carriage with the insufferable little man.

He had seen this population center from a distance before they made him sit inside, the largest one yet, surrounding the towers of a castle. Even though Ziegfried kept the windows of the carriage closed, all the smells and sounds penetrated. Adam pressed his ear to the shutters, ignoring the odors as best he could, drinking in the buzz of life all around.

Merchants called out their wares. Women made propositions to the soldiers passing with the carriage and wagons. Scuffles broke out. The soldiers cussed at some thieves.

After a while the carriage came to a stop. Someone shouted for a gate to open. Metal creaked. The carriage rolled forward again. The sounds and smells of the populace faded into more tranquil ones and the gate clanked shut behind them.

The carriage stopped again. Someone knocked on it. Ziegfried snorted and slurped at the string of drool leaking from the corner of his mouth. He fumbled around a bit. His face stretched and contorted with efforts to open his eyes.

Adam opened the carriage. A blond haired, blue eyed man in native clothes stood outside. He spoke in German. "You must be Adam. Heard you were coming in with Ziegfried. You don't mind me calling you by your first name, do you? I don't really care for military formalities."

"Mmpf," Ziegfried mumbled a little, grinding fists in his eyes. "Mrrgh aahm zzrg sshlggh."

"Did he sleep the whole way?" the blonde asked.

"Yes." Adam jumped out, away from Ziegfried.

"That's weird," the blonde said. "He's usually in a little better shape by the time he gets all the way here."

"And you are?" Adam asked.

"Oh, sorry. I'm Strom." He smiled. For one who didn't like military formalities, why was he giving his last name? Superiority complex? Before Adam could ask, Strom turned and opened his arms to their surroundings. "Welcome to the Shontese palace."

The place could have passed for a walled in, private park. There were lines of trees with flowers planted at their bases. Fountains tinkled. Birds warbled inside large cages. Gravel paths meandered between everything, dotted here and there with stone statues and manicured bushes.

"Pretty, isn't it," Strom said. "First time I saw this place, it took my breath away. Kind of odd, how someplace so primitive that they don't even have a working toilet can be so pleasant and lovely."

Ziegfried fell out of the carriage. A couple of the bodyguards picked him up. Strom said, "Find him a refill. Andreno's back, and he'll want to talk."

"Back already?" Schneider, the man in charge of the bodyguards, didn't assist his ward. He left all that work to the other bodyguards.

"He got in yesterday," Strom said. "And he's been asking every few hours if Ziegfried has arrived yet. Take Adam in. We'll meet you outside Andreno's room."

A quarter of the bodyguards went with Strom and Ziegfried around the side of the castle. Adam followed Schneider inside. He navigated through the high-ceilinged rooms and corridors with the confidence of someone familiar with the layout.

Adam half expected people to eye their uniforms and the walthers on their hips. No one did. But then, no one eyed all the daggers and swords people wore either. Did they not know the guns were weapons? Or did they just not care because everyone was armed?

Some people didn't look at them at all. They swept along, shoulders back, head held high, passing everyone else as if they were the only person in existence. Others stared at Adam and Schneider openly. Still others, the ones with unhealthy pallors, limps, and visible injuries, cast their eyes down and bowed their head every time anyone passed them.

They stopped outside a door trimmed with gold and carved with oak leaves around the edges. A couple of bored looking guards stood to either side. Several natives of the staring variety loitered in the corridor. Adam stared right back, just to see what they would do. They didn't react at all, just continued silently staring. After only a couple of minutes, Ziegfried came strolling up with his bodyguards and Strom in his wake.

"Inform Lord Andreno that Ziegfried has arrived and answered his summons," Strom said to the bored guards. One of them entered the room.

"Stay out here," Ziegfried told his bodyguards. Then he turned to Adam. "When we go in, don't say anything unless you're asked a direct question."

The guard re-emerged, held the door open and said to Ziegfried, "Enter."

Strom and Adam both followed Ziegfried in. Adam caught his breath at the opulence of the room. Heavily brocaded curtains with sequins and pearls framed the windows. The spread over the bed and its fringed canopy matched. Rugs covered almost every inch of the floor. The corners of the walls were leafed in silver and gold swirls where tapestries didn't soften the space. A fireplace dominated one wall with patterns chiseled on every brick. Surrounding this, was a sitting area with two chairs and a sofa.

On the sofa lounged a skinny man with a pinched face. His pointy nose stuck out too far, like a rat's snout. His shoes were off. A few unhealthy looking people were scrambling toward the door. He yelled at them as they went. "That's right. When I say to get out, I mean right at that moment. That doesn't mean you finish what you're doing first. I can't believe what I have to put up with. Stremion!"

One of the bored guards at the door entered the room. "Yes, Lord Andreno."

"Beat them." Andreno waved a negligent hand at the poor looking people running away from him. "Maybe they'll figure out that I shouldn't have to tell them something more than once. And make sure every other servant in the palace knows about it. If I'm lucky, that'll get the message across to all of them at the same time."

Adam hoped he had the translations wrong in his head. What was the matter with this person? Did he have no gratitude for servants? Did he honestly think that beating someone over nothing would make everyone want to serve him better, rather than sabotaging him out of hatred?

Andreno stood up from the sofa, spread his arms wide in a welcoming gesture, gave a political smile that greatly improved the shape of his face, and said to Ziegfried, "Welcome back, my friend. Did everything go all right without me?"

"Please don't get me started." Ziegfried shuddered, a little bit over dramatic. "It was a nightmare without you. Everything that could go wrong, did go wrong. And every time I turned around, someone was asking me where you were to help us straighten it all out."

Even though Andreno spoke in the native tongue and Ziegfried used German they both seemed to understand each other perfectly fine. It had to be that translation spell that Ziegfried had mentioned. Strom certainly didn't look surprised by it.

"What did you tell them?" Andreno asked.

"Nothing," Ziegfried said. "They have no right to ask after the affairs of their superiors. You complain about incompetent servants here. At least they know that you're their superior."

Andreno's smile didn't waver. "True enough."

"Did you find what you were looking for in Brend?"

"More!" Andreno's smile broadened into something more genuine. He motioned for Ziegfried to sit. Adam looked to Strom for an indication on what he should do. Strom didn't move. So neither did Adam.

"First..." Andreno plopped back down to his lounging position on the sofa. "I got a good amount of attention from the princess, so I had the opportunity to lay some good groundwork there for the future when I figure out how to get them to give her to me in marriage. She's prettier than I thought she would be, which is pleasant."

Ziegfried leaned forward in his chair, propping his elbows on his knees. "What did they say about the water?"

"They told the populace that some sick animal up in the mountains drowned in the river and contaminated the water with some sort of illness." Andreno chuckled. "Commoners are so stupid. They'll believe anything."

"Do you think their King believed that?"

"I think he and his core staff know more. How much more, I don't know."

"Care to take a guess?"

"I know they had visitors from the mountains, some shaman woman and her son. I know the Brendish court magician came up with some way of being able to tell if the water was pure or tainted. I brought you back a sample of what he used."

"Really?" Ziegfried broke out in a smile almost as wide as Andreno's.

"Before I give that to you, ask me how my other search went."

"Did you find him? Was he there?"

"Yes, I found him. And yes, he was there. *Was.*" Andreno paused to cackle like a naughty child getting away with mischief. "I escorted his body back, which is why I've returned home so much sooner than planned."

"You killed him already?" Ziegfried sat back, wiggling his butt and settling a little more into his seat. "I thought you were going to wait a bit."

Adam glanced over at Strom again. He leaned his back against the wall and picked at his fingernails, completely nonchalant. Was he not listening? Or was talk of murder an everyday occurrence in this place?

Andreno wore a gloat. "I didn't have to do a thing. He went and got himself killed."

Ziegfried laughed. "That proves what you've said about him all along!"

Andreno joined in the laughter. "He was crazy and stupid."

"You okay?" Strom whispered to Adam. He nodded numbly, unwilling to admit that the conversation made him ill. Strom pushed, "You sure? You're looking a little green."

"I'm fine," Adam whispered back. He added an excuse. "I think I may have some of the interpretations wrong, that's all."

"You want me to tell you what he's saying?" Strom asked.

Did he? That might reflect poorly on his claim that he could work as a fully functioning interpreter. Then again it was usually better to double check and be sure rather than realizing too late that you were in over your head. That usually ended up with fakery. Adam nodded. After that, Strom whispered a repeat in German of everything Andreno said.

Ziegfried grinned. "You really didn't have to do a thing to get rid of him."

"I think the Brendish General suspects I had something to do with it anyway," Andreno said. "He's the one who suggested I leave and take the body with me. He's probably investigating the whole affair."

Strom whispered the interpretation to Adam. The words were correct. He didn't have them wrong in his head. He bit his tongue, preventing himself from shouting at Ziegfried and Andreno. It wouldn't do any good. And it might get himself into trouble.

Apparently oblivious to Adam's discomfort, Ziegfried carried on the conversation. "And if he does drum up some way to twist blame so that it falls on you?"

"Even if I had ordered him executed, it's not like there's anything he could do to me." Andreno stretched his arms across the back of the sofa. "And the best part is, I've been able to use this to gain status here at home. Even though he was just a bastard and not worthy of any honor, a lot of people still claim he was Uncle's only grandson. Everyone is singing my praises for being generous to those undeserving out of sheer respect for Uncle. It's wonderful!"

Adam put a fist behind his back, hiding it, digging his nails into his palm, keeping from punching either of these two idiots. Or from punching Strom for not stopping them. It wasn't like Adam was any better. He wasn't stopping them either.

Ziegfried nodded approval to Andreno and said, "People will start treating you with proper recognition."

"It's a start," Andreno said with a shrug. "How about you? Any changes this time?"

Ziegfried's face brightened with a grin. "You remember I told you last time they sent through someone who was supposed to train as an interpreter?"

"Yes."

"Here he is!" Ziegfried waved at Adam. Andreno turned and looked at him for the first time. Ziegfried stood. "Turns out, they sent someone competent. Not like we feared."

"Really?" Andreno eyed Adam skeptically. "Why is Strom translating everything for him then?"

Ziegfried looked at him and Strom. "Yes, why is that?"

"The speech is formal," Adam answered in the native tongue. Even though it was true, it was still an excuse. He had understood the formal conjugations just fine. He just didn't like them. And since he'd committed to just listening rather than interfering, he now had to follow through. They were staring at him. So he finished it out. "The words are a little different than what I learned from Kiefer."

"Of course someone like Kiefer used only casual forms. He's not good enough to know better, and he was speaking only with lowly commoners for you to listen to," Ziegfried said. He turned back to Andreno. "Other than the proper formalities he's fluent, even after such a short period of time."

"Yes, I heard that. He said it in my language." Andreno smiled. "You still can't tell, can you?"

Ziegfried grinned sheepishly. "No."

"They finally gave you something you demanded." Andreno jiggled his propped feet from side to side, just like Ziegfried did from time to time. "Will they start listening to you on other matters now?"

"I think we got lucky with this." Ziegfried sobered. "If we could fill their list of desired and needed items every time, that would help."

"We need the mountains for that." Andreno stilled his feet. "You know what I need to manipulate that into taking place."

"I need a better method of refill to help you with that," Ziegfried said.

"I have an idea there," Andreno said. "Dismiss the interpreters."

"Does it have to do with whatever the Brendish magician used on the water?"

"Oh, that!" Andreno jumped to his feet. He went to a small chest on a shelf, took a box from inside it, and handed that to Ziegfried. "He said it's just sugar that he put a spell on. Whatever it dissolves in will glow and show the colors of any magic associated with it."

"Very clever." Ziegfried opened the little box and peered inside. "From what I've seen here, I wouldn't have thought a traditionally minded magician would come up with something like this."

"Uncle's court magician certainly wouldn't." Andreno snorted with derision. "You didn't see how much he did when we tested it here, running around in circles, calling in colleagues for advice, trying to figure it out."

Ziegfried ran his finger through the contents of the box. "You said the Brendish had visitors from the mountains. Did you get any indications of how they were regarded? Any hostilities there at all?"

"None. We'll have to try the other method."

"I still think you may want to get a higher political position first."

"I have an idea for that too. But again, you need better refills."

"Strom," Ziegfried said. "You got Adam those special quarters I asked you to?"

"Yes, sir," Strom said.

"Go get him settled in." Ziegfried turned away from them. Adam, ashamed that he'd chosen wrong by staying silent to maintain a false sense of integrity, followed Strom out.

Chapter 15

THE NUMBER OF LOITERERS in the corridor had decreased some. The people who stared were the most numerous, and the majority of those wore guard uniforms. Strom walked by them like they didn't exist.

"You're going to love it here." Strom spoke German while they traversed the rooms and corridors. Adam tried to keep track of which direction they headed, sure that he would never be able to find the entrance again. Strom continued talking. "Your job should be simple enough. You're assigned to Andreno. If he treats you the way he treats me, you'll just sit in the background and be generally ignored. You're kind of a status decoration. But you'll get to listen in on everything and soak up all the juicy gossip that makes women so giddy."

"Great." Adam didn't even try to force enthusiasm into that word. The corridors narrowed with every turn. The confident people disappeared. The staring people were fewer. Most everyone they passed were of the head bowing variety now, except one of the guards that followed them a ways behind.

"This place is so much better than Far Base." Strom turned at yet another intersecting hallway. "This is where they house the men who have the ears of important people. We have so many more advantages here than even some of the places at home!"

"Like electricity, and running water, and working showers, and toilets?"

"Ha, ha, very funny," Strom said. He headed up the corridor. He tapped on one of the doors as he passed. "This one's mine."

He opened the next door and entered. "This one's yours."

The room didn't look much different than the one Adam had used at base. The dimensions were slightly larger. The floor had a rug. So a little better. Not a lot different on the whole.

"The best part of this room is the view." Strom leered and pointed at the unshuttered, uncurtained window.

There was nothing special. There wasn't even a pretty hill to decorate the horizon. Adam shrugged. "It's just a wall on the far side of a kitchen garden. Big deal."

"That's the outer wall of the palace grounds," Strom said. "That's not what I'm talking about. Get closer to the window and look down."

Adam stepped over to the window and looked down. His hands flew up to cover his eyes and he stumbled backward. "Whoa! Oh! Whoa, whoa, whoa! That's not right."

He didn't stumble back fast enough. And his hands wouldn't keep his eyes covered. His eyes revolted against the morals his parents had taught him and peeked, despite all his efforts to tear away his gaze.

"I do believe you're blushing." Strom laughed. "Haven't you ever seen a naked woman before?"

He had not. But a battalion of American Teufelhunden couldn't have dragged an admission out of Adam. Not after some of the hazing he'd seen happen to other soldiers making that mistake. Since leaving home for the military, he'd been to pubs with dancers wearing costumes that left little to the imagination. He'd seen bits and pieces of naked female flesh here and there. This was his first time seeing it all in one showing.

And there was so much showing! There had to be a dozen women down there of varying size, shape, shade, and voluptuousness. Lounging around tubs of water, or lathering themselves up, or scrubbing each other off, all of them were appealing in their own way. His eyes darted back and forth, his brain trying to take it all in and yet trying to focus on each one individually. It was too much.

He pointed. "Do they know we're up here and can see them?"

"Don't point." Strom quickly pushed Adam's finger down. He wiped his smile from his face and looked out the window down at the bathing women below. "Of course they know we're up here. They're watching for someone on this floor to point, or wave, or smile, or give any other indication. Then they come up to that room expecting to exchange favors."

Two of the women giggled, setting different parts of them to jiggling and wiggling. They waved up at Adam and Strom in the window. A woman with thick, black, wavy hair came up behind them. She arched her back, stretching her arms above her head, peeling her torso bare.

The two women turned to see what had drawn Adam's attention. One of them got up and tackled the half-undressed woman. They fell over the side of the bath and into the water. A flurry of scratching, hair pulling, and clawing splashed water everywhere. The partially dressed woman got the upper hand and held the other's head under the water. Then suddenly she let go with a hopeful expression, her line of sight fixed on the window two rooms down from Adam's.

"That's Marietta," Strom said. "She's feisty. A lot of fun. I could give her *some* favors but not the one she's really after. So she stopped coming to my room."

Adam backed away from the window, the only way to force his eyes off the bathing women. "Does Gerhardt know about this?"

"Of course not." Strom still ogled shamelessly. "That's one of the advantages of the palace over Far Base. We don't have the Brass breathing down our necks so we have more leeway."

Adam looked around the room again, at everything, studying anything, except the window and the scene outside it. The bed had a smooth mattress and pillow. No apparent lumps. The frame looked like pine. His sack sat on the floor beside it. There was a narrow bureau five drawers high. Another cabinet style table beside the bed. That must be a favored piece of furniture in this land. There was no room for a chair, but the bed was close enough he could use it as a seat for the little table.

"I don't suppose there are any larger rooms available," Adam said. "I need a closet to hang my uniforms. And a shelf for my dictionaries. And maybe a file for all my notes."

"No." Strom turned from the window, laughing. He clapped Adam on the shoulder. "You must be one of those guys that does better with privacy."

"Yeah, that," Adam said, voice squeaking as he choked on the lie. Privacy wasn't the issue. Morals and respect were the issue.

If he was stuck with this room he was going to have to spend as much time as possible away from it. The temptation outside was too great. He didn't have *that* much willpower. And in order to spend time away from the room he would need to know how to navigate the building. He said, "Before privacy, could you show me around?"

"Sure," Strom said. "I was going to suggest it anyway. And Gerhardt's left orders for you to check in. I thought maybe you might want to wait until after you relaxed and enjoyed yourself. But we can get it over with now if you prefer."

"I prefer," Adam said.

"Then follow me," Strom said, and led the way back out of the room.

The guard who had followed them earlier stuck at it during the tour. The basic layout of the palace was only a little more complex than the castle of Far Base. Its dimensions were more eye appealing, closer ceilings, rooms that were more squarish than overlong rectangles. There were also a few corridors that displayed quite a bit of luxury and wealth. Like the one with Andreno's room. Wide. Cushioned benches. Well lit with chandeliers. Decorative trim. Paintings. Strom claimed that was for the private chambers that belonged to the royal family. Prince Sanbralio was at one end. Andreno was at the other, as far away as he could be put and still remain in the corridor.

Another corridor was just a step down from that kind of fancy. Ziegfried's room was here. The only seats were in windows at either end. Lots of people passed by them, heads high, eyes straight ahead. According to Strom, these were high or low nobles, residing in the palace, or there as guests for business or pleasure. He had no idea, nor seemed to care, what the difference was between the high and the low, just that the variation existed. There was plenty of talk in this corridor, between the nobles, between their people, between the guards, including the one that shadowed them. Adam would happily have stayed there, maybe sit in one of the window seats taking notes. But Strom moved on.

Adam was shown the laundry, the privy, the baths, the best place to find page boys in case he needed to send a message to anyone, and where he would take his meals. That was a room about the size of the mess hall at Far Base, and set up about the same with rows of tables and benches.

Lastly, Strom took him up a tower where two of their men manned a com station. They raised Far Base and had Adam report in that Ziegfried and everyone with him had arrived at the palace. Then they put Kiefer Fritz on the line.

"Howdy!" Kiefer spoke in English. "Command here has a question that the other interpreter guy there doesn't need to know."

Adam responded in kind. "He doesn't know English?"

"Nope. And he doesn't know where your host there at the palace was taking off to when we had our little incident here with the supply wagons and the thief."

"He went to the nation north of this one," Adam said. "I forget the name."

"That's okay. He'd recognize the name anyway." There was a pause in the communique. Then Kiefer came back. "Well, damn, now command here is in a foul mood. Something about missing an opportunity to broaden our contacts since we had to pull our magician back to base. How did you find out so quickly, anyway?"

"They were just talking about it," Adam said. "Why didn't they just ask the magician while he was at base."

"They did," Kiefer said. "They're smart enough not to trust him. Good thing. What you said is completely different from what he claimed."

With that, they ended the communique and signed off. Strom leaned against the wall by the door examining his fingernails. His clenched jaw and narrowed eyes gave away that he was more than irritated.

"You speak English," he said, not looking up at Adam. He left the tower room and headed down the stairs.

Adam followed him. "Among others. What do you speak?"

"French, Spanish, and Italian. You?"

"I speak those." Adam didn't give more. With the way Strom was acting he wasn't sure what kind of a response he would get.

"And English?" Strom led them out of the tower and back into the winding rooms and corridors. "Anything else?"

"Yes," Adam said. "Why are you upset that I speak English?"

"I'm not," Strom claimed, though he said it through gritted teeth. "Do you speak any other languages that Fritz knows that I don't?"

"I speak all the languages he does," Adam admitted.

"He could have used any one of those. He didn't have to use the one language I tried to learn and couldn't pick up. Damn Americans. The language was probably fairly straight forward a couple hundred years ago, before they got hold of it. They pollute and confuse everything."

"Seriously?" Adam couldn't believe what he was hearing. "Even school kids learn English. It's hard, but I don't think Americans made it impossible."

"It is if your arrogant father tries to insist that the foreign languages you already know aren't good enough, that you have to keep adding just one more, just one more, just one more..."

That was probably closer to the real reason Strom hadn't learned the language. The Americans were just a convenient excuse. And knowing Kiefer, he was probably laughing his head off right now knowing full well he had irritated Strom from a distance.

Adam sighed. Being the neutral man between these two wasn't going to be any fun. He mentally repeated his motivation to himself, over and over and over. Stay out of trouble. Keep the family safe. Stay out of trouble. Keep the family safe. His parents and brother were depending on him, whether they knew it or not.

Chapter 16

O VER THE NEXT SEVERAL DAYS, Adam quickly became familiar with his schedule and duties. They sounded deceptively simple. He sat in the background just as Strom had predicted. No one cared if he took notes. No one cared if he read one of his dictionaries. At one point he even broke out his deck of cards and played solitaire just to see if anyone would react. No one even noticed as far as he could tell.

In the mornings Andreno spent some of his time in Prince Sanbralio's throne room while court was held. Adam wasn't allowed in there, which was fine with him. With all the snobbery that oozed out the doors when they finally opened, he doubted he missed much. Then he was sent to eat lunch. After that, he had to sit through the afternoon while Andreno spent his time doing... whatever. Adam didn't always know. Like the throne room sometimes Adam was purposely shut out of the proceedings, even if they were with Ziegfried.

The evenings were his to do with as he pleased. He usually ate supper with Strom, some of Ziegfried's bodyguards, and perhaps one of the radio guys if they felt like showing their face. Then he retreated to a window seat at the end of the noble guest corridor to play solitaire while he listened to the conversations of the passing people.

Simple. Not easy. Not given the social structure of this place. Those with higher social status treated those with lower status like animals to be smacked around. Unless they had the ear of someone even higher in status. It was stupid and confusing.

Home was better. Respect. Respect elders. Respect officers. Respect women. Respect clergy. Respect teachers. Respect parents. Simple. Easy.

He should probably count himself fortunate. Everyone associated him with Andreno and Ziegfried. No one tried to abuse him the way they did others.

The hardest part was that he had to remain silent while people did atrocious things to each other. And Andreno was one of the worst offenders. Every time he smacked one of the servants over nothing Adam fought the urge to step in and smack him back.

About a week after arriving at the palace Adam had to get up and leave the room lest he lose control. Some traders had come and told Andreno he'd have to pay higher prices for their goods. He reacted by going on a prolonged rampage, summoning servants just so he could beat them the moment they were in reach. Adam sat in the corridor reminding himself over and over in several different languages not to get himself in trouble by interfering.

Since none of Ziegfried's bodyguards showed up for supper that evening, Adam complained to Strom about it then said, "I don't suppose there's anyone else we can deal with besides Andreno."

"Not really," Strom said.

"What about the next nation over?" Adam asked. "What's it called? Brend? They're bigger, aren't they? Wouldn't they have more access to resources anyway? Andreno's already complaining about the difficulty of obtaining what our leaders back home are trying to get from him. That's what the fiasco was over today. Someone charging higher prices for the goods he trades to us."

"He's complained about that for a while now." Strom propped his elbow on the table and yawned. "And no, we can't go to Brend. Zigfried says the fact that they're bigger is part of the reason why. They wouldn't need us the way Andreno does. Ziegfried and his bodyguards do projects for him on the side sometimes to keep him happy."

"What kind of projects?" Adam pushed his bland food around on his plate. Some spices on it might be nice. Or some vinegar. Or maybe some pork. He hadn't eaten a single dish with pork since stepping through the portal.

"I don't know much." Strom wasn't eating much either. "I don't ask. I know every once in a while Ziegfried makes something with magic. Even though that always causes trouble with Masorno."

"Who?"

"The local magician here at the palace. I think he's some kind of minor noble or something."

"Maybe I should talk to him." Adam gave up on the food and set down his fork. "We should probably learn more about magic. Ziegfried said he discovered it by accident. These people here have been dealing with it through the history of their society. They're bound to know quite a bit."

"Don't bother." Strom managed another bite then talked with his mouth full. "Masorno hates us. He says Ziegfried has no right to use magic, he's doing it wrong, he's a hazard to human life in general, and all of us associated with him should be executed or banished from the country."

Across the room a hand smacked against flesh followed by a loud taunt and a chortle. Adam didn't have to look to know who it was. He growled a low complaint. "Can't we get through one evening without him hitting someone?"

Strom abandoned his effort to eat, pushing away his plate. "Not likely."

Adam clenched his fists. "Why doesn't that guard stop this?"

"What guard?" Strom asked.

"One of the guards keeps following me around everywhere."

"Why would he stop it?" Strom shrugged. "This is normal here."

The smacking continued. Adam halfway turned. Strom reached over and took his shoulder. "Hey, we're not supposed to rock the boat. Remember? Put your mind elsewhere. Like on that new girl in the baths. What do you think of her? Cute, yeah?"

"I haven't been watching," Adam admitted.

Strom's face went slack with shock. "*What?*"

"I have better things to do with my time than play voyeur."

"Like what?"

"Like my job. I still have a lot to learn about this language. The speech is more formal here, less conversationally casual. I spend the evenings watching people and trying to listen in on their conversations. Or I go over my notes. Or I try to find someone willing to let me talk with them so I can practice."

Strom shook his head. "You're taking this far too seriously."

"I can't screw up here," Adam said.

Strom snorted with derision. "That's what they tell everyone who comes here. 'Don't screw up or your family is dead.' Personally, I say screw my family. They're the reason I'm stuck here in the first place. I figure, if something bad happens it's their own fault."

A woman yelped and pleaded in time with the slaps on the other side of the room. Strom looked over. "Oh, man. It's Marietta from the baths. She's still getting over the broken wrist he gave her the night you got here. He also cheated her, didn't give her the favor she traded for. He just took from her without giving anything back."

Adam stood so fast he knocked into the table, rattling the dishes. Strom flinched. "Hey! Watch it. Where are you going?"

Adam's feet took on a will of their own carrying him across the room. Marietta knelt before the man, leaning away from his onslaught. She took blow after blow crying, "I just want what you promised."

Adam grabbed the man's arm before he could hit her again. He shoved against Adam then tossed a kick at Marietta. Adam stepped between them taking the foot to his shins. Then he shoved back. The man toppled backward. He jumped back to his feet with a growl.

The guard that had been shadowing Adam stepped in, grabbing the man's collar and shoving him back down. "You attack one of Lord Andreno's personal guests?"

"He attacked me," the man snarled. The guard looked at Adam.

"In my country we protect women," Adam said. "We do not allow men to hit them."

"She's not a woman." The man regained his feet more slowly this time, non-threatening. "She's just a (unfamiliar word). I can do whatever I like to her."

"Not really," the guard said. He asked the woman, "Marietta, did he pay you?"

She shook her head. The guard turned back to the man. "So not only do you offend one of Lord Andreno's guests, you're a thief. That's grounds for expulsion from the palace."

"I'm here as the servant of the Heir to the Sanquilla District!" The man tilted his nose up.

"Yes, we've been hinting that it's time for him to leave," the guard said. His mouth smiled. His eyes did not. "Now that we learn he has a thief associated with him we have the perfect excuse to turn him out. His father will be most displeased with him. And you."

He raised his hand above his head and snapped his fingers. A couple more palace guards melted out of the corners of the room. They took hold of the man and dragged him off with smug expressions.

Adam offered a hand to Marietta. "Are you all right?"

She stared at his hand. Strom came up behind him. The guard asked him, "Is that true? You're not supposed to let anyone hit women in your country?"

Strom averted his eyes and nodded guiltily. He mumbled, "It happens anyway. And we're not supposed to make trouble here."

"Is that so?" The guard's tone was droll. He looked back to Adam with his creepy blank eyes. He nodded his head toward the nearest corridor leading out. "You and I should have a talk."

He headed away. Adam picked up a foot to follow. Marietta snagged the cuff of his pants with her fingers. She whispered to him, "Don't go."

Strom gave her his best smile. "It's all right. I'll take care of you."

"Don't trust him," Marietta said to Adam, glancing at the guard, ignoring Strom. "Come with me instead. I'll pay you my thanks."

Adam could only imagine the kind of thanks she would pay. He swallowed hard, tamping down his urges. He'd best stay away from this woman.

The guard put a hand on his shoulder, "Please. Come."

Adam snagged the opportunity for escape and followed the guard out of the room. They went up a couple of flights of stairs to an open landing the size of a sitting room. Adam asked, "What do you need to speak to me about?"

"Some of your people." The guard didn't stop in the sitting room. He headed for one of the corridors that led off from it. "You're getting better and better at this language in the short time you've been here."

"I study." Adam followed. If he had his bearings correct, this corridor ran parallel to, and one level higher than the guest rooms where Adam favored the window seat.

"Yes, I know." The guard paused at the entrance to the corridor, letting Adam pass him. "Keep it up and eventually you'll probably even get rid of your accent."

"I would like that." Adam looked around, chills going up his spine.

The corridor might once have been as fancy as its twin on the floor below. Now it was choked with dust. The doors swung ajar where they hung crooked in their frames. The carpet running up the center had holes and frayed edges. The wall plaster was spider-webbed with cracks. The chandeliers held no candles. The grimed window at the end cast gloom everywhere instead of light. Nothing was right with this corridor.

Adam took a step backward then turned to leave. The guard socked him with a left fist to the right cheek and grabbed his right arm. He stepped around Adam, twisting the arm behind his back, pushing him to the floor. The weight held him down, his left arm pinned under his body. A dagger flashed just at the edge of his sight by his face.

Adam writhed, kicking his feet. "What are you *doing*?"

"I can't accuse Andreno directly." The guard yanked Adam's right arm. The bones jolted at the wrong angle, wrenching a gasp out of him. "So I'll get information from his newest person. Where are Ziegfried's bodyguards? Tell me what they're doing."

"I do not know."

"Wrong answer." The guard flicked the dagger. It stung just in front of Adam's right ear. "Try again. Where are they?"

"I only know they did not come to eat supper." If Adam could twist just enough, or get a leg up under himself, it might give him leverage.

"How does Andreno plan to take the throne? How is he planning on getting Yaquerro out of the way?"

"Who is Yaquerro?"

"I'm not playing games with you!"

He sliced through the seam of Adam's shirt, biting into his shoulder. He flinched, which gave him just enough room to get his left leg curled up underneath. That gave his left arm some room. He scrabbled for the walther on his right hip.

"Tell me what you know," the guard said.

Adam's fingertips brushed his gun. Another dagger flick deepened the cut on his shoulder. He flinched again, sucking in his breath at the burning sting. His fingers wrapped around the gun. He pulled. The gun didn't clear the holster. Not enough room against the floor.

Adam pushed with his leg, hoping to gain a few inches. The guard lifted off his back, letting go of his arm. Overcompensating, Adam went flying through a sitting position and hit the wall behind him. His left arm swung wildly to counterbalance. Still gripping the gun, it released from the holster. Unfortunately he now held it upside down. The guard slapped it away. It skittered a foot across the floor.

The guard whapped Adam's forehead with a palm. His head snapped back, hitting the wall again. Spots flared in his vision. He kicked out. One of his steel-toed boots connected. The guard grunted, then pressed his forearm against Adam's throat. The dagger sliced through the front of his shirt and across the top of the left side of his chest.

The guard hissed, "Kick me again, and I'll cut out an eye."

Adam stretched as far as he could, reaching for his walther. The guard plunged the dagger into his hand. the blade slipped between the bones. The tip came out the underside and nailed his hand to the wood floor. He heard himself shriek more than he felt himself make the noise.

The guard thrust his face in Adam's. "You think I don't know that thing is a weapon?"

Strom called from out in the sitting room landing. "Weiss!"

The guard leaned in, pressing his arm against Adam's throat, cutting off all air. Adam swiped his right fist at the guard's left temple. He missed wide and hit the man in the side of the neck instead, just below the ear. He flinched. Adam brought his right knee up into the man's ribs. The jostling tore at the knife in his hand and released some of the weight from his throat. He gasped and yelped at the same time.

Strom ran up the corridor with his own walther in his hand. "Get off him!"

Adam yelled for Strom to pull the trigger. "*Ershiess ihn!*"

Strom shifted to a two-handed grip on his weapon. He took aim. Ground his teeth. Exhaled properly, steadying the shot. And never pulled the trigger.

Adam drew up his right leg, planted his boot on the guard's chest, and pushed. It pulled at his hand again. He reached over and yanked out the dagger. It hurt almost more than when it had been stabbed in. He rose to his feet brandishing the blade.

Ziegfried approached behind Strom. "Put it down."

Andreno stood at the mouth, not entering the corridor. Ziegfried wheezed for breath, pale as a bleached sheet. He clutched his chest with his right hand like a heart attack victim. With his left, he leaned against the wall with every step. He looked almost as bad as he had immediately after opening the portal to home.

"I've had my eye on you." Andreno shook his finger at the guard. "You spend far too much time with Charlass. She's almost as bad as her brother was."

Ziegfried got within arm's reach of the guard. He raised his chin, defiant yet resolute. Ziegfried grabbed hold. The man spasmed like he'd received a jolt of electricity. His eyes glassed over. An ashy, gray color curled across his skin. It crept out from under his clothes away from the spot where Ziegfried gripped him. His back arched. His hands curled. His head threw backward, his mouth open in silent agony. He shriveled up that way, no longer filling out his clothes. His hair fell out. His skin pulled taut, stretching his mouth into a rictus grin. Within moments of Ziegfried's touch, he fell to the floor as a desiccated corpse.

Chapter 17

ADAM PRESSED HIMSELF AGAINST THE WALL. His left hand dripped blood down the cracking plaster. His right hand still gripped the dagger. Not that he could use it to stave off the horror in front of him now.

The temperature plummeted. Everyone's breath frosted. The gloomy light from the window at the end of the corridor dimmed. Sorrowful moans and wails emanated from some of the rooms. A frigid wind whipped up the hall toward Andreno. He gasped, his eyes showing white all around.

"Leave me alone!" he screamed as he fled, disappearing out into the sitting room.

The wind stopped just short of leaving the corridor. There it died. Cobwebs stopped fluttering. The temperature went back up. Whatever cloud had obscured the window passed. Dirty crystals on the chandeliers still wobbled back and forth, little pendulum testimonies of the disturbance.

"That was a rather nasty draft." Ziegfried chuckled, standing straight, his skin glowing with health and vitality.

Strom still held his walther with a two-handed grip, the muzzle of the gun now pointed at the floor. It shook and trembled in his hands, the shivers going all the way up his arms. Adam stumbled past him.

"I'm sorry." Strom caught his arm. He holstered the gun. "Here, lean on me."

Adam pulled away. "I'm fine."

Careening and reeling, he managed to avoid smashing into anything and emerged into the sitting room. Andreno was still out there. He hadn't retreated far. His bodyguards cowered on the side of the room farthest from him, eyeing him warily.

"I sent for a doctor," Andreno said.

Adam looked back up the corridor. Ziegfried stood over the corpse, blocking it from view. Adam said, "Why? No doctor can help him. He is dead."

"Not for him, for you." Andreno said. With that he swept out of the sitting room, his bodyguards following.

Adam grumbled in German. "I don't need a doctor."

"Your blood says otherwise." Strom put a hand on his elbow, offering support again. Adam jerked his arm away and nearly swiped him with the dagger. Strom jumped back.

"Sorry." Adam set the dagger on the arm of one of the chairs. His congealed blood on the blade smeared the upholstery.

"No. I'm sorry." Strom hung his head. "I couldn't make my finger pull the trigger. He could have killed you. And I froze up."

"I'm just glad you came." Adam dropped into the chair, his knees giving out. The shakes set in. He folded his arms, tucking in his hands to keep it from showing until it stopped.

"Marietta was frantic," Strom said. "I've never seen her that way before. She said Dalrien was mad at his son, and desperate, and acting irrational."

"Who's Dalrien?"

"That guard that just attacked you. I didn't know his name. But she did."

Ziegfried marched out of the corridor. He thrust a leather dagger sheath at Adam. "Here. You'll need this to keep that dagger."

Adam looked away. "I'm not keeping it."

"It's the custom here." Ziegfried still pushed the sheath at him. "If you're attacked with a blade and the attacker dies in the fight, you keep the blade."

Adam recoiled, keeping Ziegfried from touching him. "I didn't kill him."

"Doesn't matter," Ziegfried said, frowning at the dagger. He took out a handkerchief, picked up the weapon, and wiped it down. "You're supposed to clean it after being used. Otherwise it rusts and dulls."

A man stepped up the stairs into the sitting room carrying a leather satchel similar to ones doctors in Germany carried when making house calls. He set down the satchel and gave a cursory look at each of Adam's injuries. He took out some cloths and cleaned up some of the blood, just enough to examine the cuts more closely. Adam sat still and endured. At this point letting a doctor touch him was preferable to Ziegfried.

"Learn to take proper care of this." Ziegfried snapped the dagger into the sheath and slapped it back down onto the arm of the chair. "If you don't, you'll hurt yourself."

A couple of guards showed up. One of them said, "Andreno told us to come dispose of a body."

"This way." Ziegfried reentered the creepy corridor. The guards followed.

"He isn't going to be any fun for the next week or two," Strom muttered. "He'll be marching around and giving orders like we're all soldiers."

"We *are* soldiers," Adam reminded him.

"You know what I mean," Strom said, as if that explained anything at all.

Ziegfried marched back out of the corridor. He grunted approval at the doctor. Then he left in the same direction Andreno had gone.

Adam mumbled in one of the languages Strom didn't know. "*Good riddance.*"

"There's a lot of blood down the side of his neck," Strom said to the doctor. "Are you sure he's not badly hurt there?"

The doctor glanced at the slice by Adam's ear. "It's just a small cut. Head (unfamiliar word) bleed a lot."

"Did he just say head wounds?" Adam asked in German.

"Yes," Strom said. Adam whispered the word to himself a few times. Strom frowned at him. "Don't do that just now. Save it for later."

"Do what?"

"You have a tendency to mutter new words over and over in several different languages. So far I've counted eight of them I don't know. It's embarrassing."

"Why?"

"Because I don't think I could learn that many if I tried. Is that really how many you know? Or is it more?"

Adam cleared his throat and looked away. The doctor dabbed something from a dark colored bottle onto the stab wound through Adam's hand. Instant burn hit and spread through his hand, passed his wrist, and writhed up his arm.

"Ow!" Adam jerked his hand away. The doctor grabbed hold and kept dabbing, making the burn worse. "That hurts! What are you *doing*?"

"This will prevent sickness." The doctor kept a firm grip despite Adam's attempts to keep pulling away.

"Sickness?" Adam asked Strom in German. "That word doesn't quite fit."

"Unbelievable." Strom shook his head and looked rather disgusted. "You can switch between languages without even a moment's pause to reorient your thinking and you stumble over a little word like that?"

Adam ground his teeth. "Just tell me."

"Infection. He said it will prevent infection."

"Infection, infection." Adam repeated the new word.

"Stop that!"

A page boy entered the room. When studying history Adam had always thought that pages would be pre-pubescent. He had yet to see any here that were younger than about fifteen. The kid handed a slip of paper to Strom. That was another strange thing. They never said anything. They never spoke to the person they delivered messages to unless directly questioned.

Strom read the note. "Andreno's summoning us both. As soon as you're available. Not sure why he didn't just say so before he hightailed it out of here. I didn't think he was squeamish at the sight of blood."

Adam stood, saying to the doctor. "I am done. Get away from me."

"I'm not finished." The doctor wouldn't let go of his arm. He pulled Adam back into the seat. "You still need bandages. You still need medicine. And some of these need sewing on."

Adam shuddered. "You are not sewing anything on me."

"Stitches." Strom laughed as he interpreted the word. "Not sewing. Stitches."

"I have an excuse to get away from him," Adam said in German. "Don't spoil it."

The doctor let go. "It's all right. I understand."

"You do?" Adam screwed up his face in confusion. He and Strom had used German. The doctor couldn't possibly have understood.

"You want to get away from that corridor." The doctor pointed. "People only come this close when they want to tell themselves scary stories, or do something they're not supposed to."

"Why?" Adam asked.

"Many people have died in there." The doctor wrapped a bandage around Adam's hand. "No one uses those rooms anymore, unless they're doing something they want to hide. Even before that people heard wind and moans on still nights. Screams in empty rooms. Knocks on doors when no one is there."

"You make it sound like there are (unfamiliar word) in there," Strom said. Before Adam could ask after the word, Strom glanced at him and said in German, "Ghosts."

"There are," the doctor said.

"There's no such things as ghosts," Strom said.

"You sure?" Adam asked in German. "Magic is real. Why not ghosts?"

"Everyone knows ghosts aren't real."

"Everyone knows magic isn't real."

Strom clucked his tongue and said, "That's different."

"Why?"

"Because in the case of ghosts, everyone is correct."

"They're wrong about magic."

The doctor interrupted the argument. "No one used this corridor after Lord Andreno's parents were murdered in one of these rooms. They insisted on staying here for a week to prove to him that ghosts aren't real. One morning they didn't wake up. Suffocated in their sleep. What a terrible morning that was. Poor Andreno hasn't set foot in there ever since."

Strom cocked his head and looked at the doctor out of the corner of his eye. "I thought people here weren't supposed to talk about the affairs of the nobility?"

"True," the doctor said. "I talk about it only when it serves a good purpose."

"What purpose?" Adam asked.

"Getting you to be still long enough for me to keep working." The doctor grinned. He'd been dabbing at cuts the entire time. "Put on a clean shirt. You have blood all over this one. It's unhealthy."

Adam looked down at himself. "I have no clean shirt. My other one is in the laundry."

"I'll go borrow one for you. Stay here." Strom ran off.

Adam slumped back into the chair. The doctor pulled out needle and thread. Adam said, "I need no stitches."

"No, not if you want scars." The doctor threaded the needle. "If you don't want scars, then you need stitches. And some further medicines from me over the next week."

"Medicines, medicines." Adam whispered the word to himself. It wasn't quite the same word he knew for it. The last syllable was slightly different. He made a mental note to ask about it. The way it was used it could mean doses, or treatments.

He went back through the words that Strom had stopped him from practicing. He repeated them to himself over and over in different languages, always coming back to what he was memorizing. The doctor corrected his pronunciation a couple of times, so he went through and asked after the pronunciations and accents of several other words too. By the time the doctor was packing up his medical torture devices, Strom returned.

He held up a shirt. "What do you think?"

Adam grabbed for it. "Thanks."

Strom held it just beyond reach. "I asked what you think. You didn't even look at it."

"I think it's a shirt," Adam said.

"Unrefined ingrate," Strom muttered, handing it over.

He waited just long enough for Adam to peel off the bloodied uniform shirt and pull on the new one. Then he turned in the same direction Andreno and Ziegfried had gone. Adam had to hurry to keep up.

The guards outside Andreno's door didn't even make an attempt to hinder them. They entered without asking permission or stating they were sent for. Ziegfried stood nearby in a stance similar to a proud soldier in formation. Andreno lounged on his favorite couch as if nothing had just happened. Disgusted with the display from both of them, Adam couldn't keep the sneer off his face.

"Which doctor did the treatment?" Andreno asked.

"Shullian," Strom said.

"Good," Andreno said. "He can make it so there's no scars. Scars are good on bodyguards. Makes them look tough. On servants like interpreters it's not necessary."

"Servants," Adam muttered. Clenching his teeth, he glared at Ziegfried. Even knowing he should just let it alone he couldn't help ask. "Speaking of bodyguards, where are yours?"

"I'm not sure what's got you so riled." Andreno sat up. "You could at least show enough respect to speak my language."

Adam repeated the question in Brendish. "Where are your bodyguards, Ziegfried?"

"None of your business," Ziegfried snapped.

Adam didn't bother keeping his voice down. "It is when I get attacked by someone demanding to know where they are."

"So that's what he was after." Andreno lay back. He laced his fingers behind his head and propped one foot on the arm at the other end of the couch. "They're resting. I sent them on an assignment."

Adam jabbed a finger in Andreno's direction. "You do not have that right."

"I gave him permission," Ziegfried said.

Adam turned his finger on Ziegfried. "Which you do not have the right to do."

Ziegfried bared his teeth. "They're mine to do with as I please."

"They're assigned to protect you." Adam swiped his hand through the air, nearly hitting Strom beside him. "Not to obey you. Not to act as servants. Not to run errands. Does Gerhardt know you do this?"

"You are way out of line!" Ziegfried tipped his chin down, glowering, probably trying to look a little bit dangerous. Given his diminutive stature it only looked a little bit ridiculous.

"You are obviously (unfamiliar word)," Andreno said.

"Distraught," Strom whispered to Adam before he could ask.

"Go back to your room." Andreno continued. "Enjoy one of the women from the baths. Relax. When you're more yourself again, tell me what favor she wants and I'll pay it."

Strom went slack jawed. He asked, "For both of us?"

Andreno tossed him a disdainful sneer. "Were you attacked by someone trying to slander my reputation? I think not. You didn't even really help him out expect to notify us. I'll pay for Adam, just so everyone in the palace sees how generous I am to someone standing for my good name."

"I did not stand for you," Adam said.

"Don't spoil this," Strom whispered at him, pushing him out of the room. "Go. Take advantage. Before he changes his mind and tosses you in chains for being ungrateful for his generosity."

Adam let Strom push him down the corridor. "Would he really? Toss me in chains?"

"Yes!" Strom let go. He took a deep breath, held it for a moment, then slowly let it out. "I'll go tell him that you're hurting, which makes for a short temper. You go do what you were told. Or at least make it seem like you did."

Before Adam could ask what that last statement was supposed to mean, Strom stepped back into the room. Was it well known that he didn't partake of those women? At least well enough that Strom had heard? Andreno obviously hadn't. Either that, or he just didn't care. Probably the latter.

Adam went to his room, taking care to stay away from the window as always. There was far too much temptation out there. If he gave in to his desire to watch, he'd also eventually give in to the desire to call one of those women up to his room. Best to stay away from that entirely.

Instead of going through his dictionaries and notes, he smoked one of his precious cigarettes and broke out his deck of cards. Laying out a solitaire tableau on his bed, one game turned into two. Then three. On and on, wiping everything else from his mind. He spoke aloud the names of the cards and the moves he made. Each game he used a different language. That relaxed him more than the cards and the cigarette combined.

He continued until the sun set and took the light with it.

He never lit his lamp. That would draw attention. He peeled off his clothes, starting with the stupid shirt Strom had made such a deal of. Every cut had stiffened, especially his hand. He climbed between the sheets of his bed hoping he wasn't so sore that it would keep him from sleeping.

Chapter 18

SLEEP WAS JUST TAKING HOLD when Adam's door opened. Groggy, he forced his eyes open. The light from the baths outside spilled across his ceiling, casting shadow on the female figure just inside the room.

"You have the wrong room," Adam mumbled. He lay his head back down on the flat pillow, letting his eyes droop shut again.

"I have the right room," the woman said.

"I do not want a woman in here," Adam forced himself to say. Now he was going to go to hell for lying.

"I know," she said. "I have some friends who might interest you. I just came to ask if you would like to meet them."

She brought with her the scent of some kind of flower, just like his mother fresh out of the shower. Just like some of the girls at the school he'd graduated from. Lavender? Roses? He wasn't so good at figuring out which scent went with which flower.

Hold it. What had she said? "What do you mean you know? You know what?"

"You like men, don't you?"

"Wh-what?" Adam stammered.

"I know you don't want a woman," she said. "But I owe you a favor."

Adam sat up. "No, no, no, no."

"Yes I do." She took a couple of mincing steps, bringing her halfway across the room. "You stopped that man from hitting me where everyone was eating. You embarrassed him for embarrassing me."

"Marietta?" Adam guessed.

"That's me." A smile played through her voice. Then her shoulders shrugged in the dim light and her voice turned bland again. "Unless you want my name to be something else. Whatever. I only sent your friend after you. That doesn't pay for the favor you did me. I owe you."

"You do not owe me for that."

"I wouldn't if I were the guest and you were the whore. Then you would have just been doing your duty. But I'm the whore. I pay my debts. All of them. Now, I can convince a few of my man friends to come. You can pick whichever of them you want."

"No, no, no, no, no, no." Adam vigorously shook his head. This wasn't really happening. It couldn't really be happening. Could it?

"It's okay. They don't mind. They want to come. You're pretty good looking, even though you have light coloring."

"Why would you think I like men that way?" Adam asked.

"Because you never come to your window."

"I could be killed if people think I like men that way," Adam said. "And not just me, my entire family!"

Marietta almost gasped, just a slight intake of breath. She hugged her arms around herself. "You're from a nation where men liking men is bad?"

"Very bad."

"Oh dear. I've insulted you. Now I owe you twice." She paused. Then she half shrugged again, dropped her arms, and finished crossing the room to sit on the bed. "Oh, well. If you like women, then I can repay you once now, and again later whenever you want."

"No, no, no, no." Adam drew up his feet, his knees shielding his chest, not caring that he sounded like a scratched record. She wouldn't know what that was anyway.

"Are you angry?" She sat back towards the foot of the bed, away from him. "I'm sorry. We didn't think. It's not a bad thing here."

"It is bad where I come from."

"It used to be bad here," she said. "Then Prince Yaquerro presented his lover in court. Now it's fashionable. A lot of men have tried it, just to try it."

"Prince Yaquerro?" There was that name again.

"Andreno's cousin. Prince Sanbralio's son. Heir to the throne. He'll be our next ruler when Prince Sanbralio dies."

Adam flipped through faces in his mind. None of them matched the name Yaquerro. "I do not know which person he is."

"He's in the mountains on his annual hunting trip with his lover. They left just before you arrived."

Adam leaned over the side of his bed and pulled out his bag. He dug through in the dark until he found his cigarette case. He got out the matches and lit the candle he'd never used on the little bedside table.

"That's a first." Marietta stared at the candle with raised eyebrows. She looked at the spent match curiously. "Your friend in the next room doesn't use those little fire sticks to light candles anymore."

"He probably ran out." Adam got out paper and pencil. "How many people know you are here?"

"Several of my friends."

"Then will they stop thinking I like men?" Adam asked.

"I guess. If I stay and don't ask for them to come."

Adam wrote down everything she had told him about Prince Yaquerro. It wasn't much. He likely wouldn't forget. Better to be safe than sorry. Besides, word would need to get back to base that he'd been attacked. And he was damn sure going to tell them everything. Especially the parts that Ziegfried might like left out.

Marrietta remained quiet until he put down his pencil. Then asked, "What are you writing?"

"What happened today..." he said. "...what you told me about Yaquerro... I need to tell Gerhardt."

"Gayerhart?" She said the name slowly, and still mangled it.

"Gerhardt," he re-said it correctly. "My leader while I am in this country."

"Ziegfried isn't your leader?"

Adam shook his head.

"That's interesting. Strum never said anything about that."

"Strum? Oh. Strom."

"Yes, him." She tucked her feet up under herself. "You people have strange names. I can't even pronounce his first name he gave us. No one could. So he just told us to call him Strum, er, Strom. And that's another thing. Before him, I never met anyone with more than one name. Do you have more than one name? I've heard him call you both Adam and Vise."

"Weiss," he corrected her pronunciation again. She said the first consonant sound a little too soft, not quite enough snap. "The second name is the name of our entire family we come from. Everyone in my family is named Weiss. Everyone in Strom's family is named Strom."

"Oh, I see," she said. "That makes more sense. I guess."

She rocked a bit, hugging her knees and wriggling her toes. Her black hair curled full, framing her olive tanned face and dark eyes. Thick lashes stretched up, almost touching her eyebrows. She noticed him looking at her, and she stretched out, arching her back, extending long legs off the edge of the bed. What she wore looked like some sort of shapeless nightgown. It clung to her body, showing off every curve, every bump.

He averted his eyes, clearing his throat, trying to catch his breath. He leaned away from her, folding the paper and tucking it into his bag for morning.

"I can't leave until I pay you," she said.

"You owe me nothing," Adam told her.

"If I leave without paying you, I'll get kicked out of the palace."

"And stop having to be a whore? Would that be so bad?"

"Don't talk like you understand." She curled up again, drawing into herself. "What do you think I'd be doing outside the palace walls. I have nothing else. At least here, there's a chance that…"

She stopped talking and looked away. She hugged her knees again, resting her chin on them. "Are you one of those people who thinks you're too good for a whore?"

"My parents taught me it is wrong to treat women this way." Adam pushed his bag back under the bed. "My mother said if I ever got a woman pregnant before I married her, she would take that woman as a daughter and tell me I am not her son until I make her my wife. My father, well, I do not want to think of what my father would do. And I have to set the example for my younger brother."

"As if any of them would know," she said. "They're not here."

"If I get used to doing something wrong just because I think I will not get caught, then I will end up doing it where I will get caught. Best to just not do it."

"You really think being a whore is wrong?"

"I think treating a woman like a whore is wrong."

"Even if she really is one?"

"Yes."

"So if you were to make me your wife, you would let me do whatever I want?"

"Whatever you want? Or whatever I want?"

Marietta smiled, her white teeth gleaming in the dim light. "Do you even know what you want? Have you ever done this before?"

Adam looked away again, the heat of a blush creeping up his face. Her smile penetrated her voice making her sound intrigued. "You haven't, have you. That's all right. If you want to wait for marriage, I wish you luck. But I'll have to find some other way to pay you."

"You can make sure Strom doesn't think I like men," Adam said. "That would be a very big favor to me."

"I can do that easily enough," she said. "Unless you don't want anyone even thinking that you've slept with a woman."

"Most of my comrades assume all of us have," Adam said. "Me included. If you do not want to lie, I will not ask it of you."

"Not a problem," she said. "I'll make everyone believe it. That's one. I need something else to pay you for insulting you by offering men."

Adam thought for a moment. Then asked, "If Andreno told me to bring what you want to him, will I get in trouble if I do not?"

"Likely."

"Then what favor do you want?" Adam asked. "You can help me by letting me take that to him."

"Then I'll owe you a third time."

"No," Adam said. "This will make us even. I cannot get in trouble here. At all. My family will pay the price with their lives."

"If you do me a favor that saves your family? How does that even make sense?"

"Please?" He wasn't about to go on about how dangerous things were at home, what with the war, and insurgents, and malcontents, and spies, and air raids, and rumored conditions of prisoner camps, and who knew what all else.

"I'd have to be crazy to trust you like this." She turned and put her feet on the floor. Leaning forward, she rested her elbows on her knees and hung her head, her thick hair draping and hiding her profile. "I want a better life for my sister."

"You want a favor for your sister?"

"She'll be fifteen soon. An adult. If she could have some training as a seamstress, or a laundress, or a maid, or kitchen help, or something, then she won't have to... be like me."

"I will tell Andreno," he said. "Thank you."

She peeked at him between locks of her hair. "For insulting you?"

"For not laughing at me for not having done this before. Many people would."

"I would never laugh at someone who actually respects me." She reached over and patted his cheek. Then she silently stood and left the room.

Chapter 19

ADAM'S CLOTHES WERE MISSING. The extra shirt hadn't come back from laundry like it was supposed to. Both pairs of pants were gone. All his socks. His coat. Even his boots. Gone. All of it. The only things that remained were his belt, his walther, and the winter hat, gloves, and scarf from his mother that he'd hidden away.

There was some sort of outfit and shoes on the little bedside table. He unfolded them. They looked about the right size for him. He could either put them on and go look for his uniforms, or strip the bed and wrap the blanket around himself toga-style.

He opted for the clothes. Then he went and banged on Strom's door. Strom yanked it open, rubbing sleep from his eyes. "What do you need?"

"I need my uniforms," Adam said.

"Why?"

"They're missing. Who do I talk to about finding them?"

"What you're wearing is fine." Strom opened the door wider, stepping away to pick up a robe to toss over his shoulders.

A brunette woman raised her head from the pillow, blinking groggily. She saw Adam, smiled, and said, "You look nice."

"There, see?" Strom continued in German. "You look nice."

Adam used better manners, speaking in Brendish for the benefit of the woman. "These clothes are not mine."

"Andreno wants you to dress better," Strom said. "So you have better clothes. Live with it."

"Marietta said you were very sweet." The woman was still smiling. "She liked it."

Adam blushed. Strom laughed at him. "It's nothing to be ashamed of. It's a perfectly natural human function."

His line of sight shifted from Adam, to just behind him. Adam turned. A page boy stood behind him, holding out a note. Adam took it. Strom asked, "Who wants you?"

Adam showed him the note, written in German. "The radio guys."

"Probably Gerhardt," Strom said. "I had to report yesterday's incident. He wanted you. I told him you were with the doctor and then ordered to rest."

"Rest is not what I was ordered."

"Gerhardt doesn't need to know that. Not if you want to stay out of trouble." Strom ogled the woman in his bed. "Now get out of here. I want to owe this beauty another favor before breakfast."

That left Adam to make his way alone up to the tower where the radio had been set up. He'd only been there once. By the time he found the entrance to the bottom level of it, one of the two radio operators was there watching for him.

"About time," the man said. "Gerhardt's hot to trot about getting you on the box."

They climbed all the way to the top where Gerhardt's voice scratched through the radio demanding to know if Adam had arrived yet. The other radio operator manning the equipment saw them, pushed the button to talk, and spoke into the microphone. "He just walked in."

Adam had to go through the rounds. He grit his teeth reliving the details. Lieber got on too and asked about what treatments were used, as if Adam knew all the medical lingo. Gerhardt asked more detail about where Ziegfried's bodyguards were for the same reason Adam had. Once he was satisfied, he gave Adam leave to go and told the radio operators to get Ziegfried on.

One of the operators said to Adam, "I don't suppose we could get you to give him the message?"

"I just missed breakfast," Adam complained. "I'm sure Andreno's getting ready for court by now and he'll probably be mad that I haven't showed up yet."

"If you're already late, what's a couple more minutes?" the operator said. "Besides, it's a lot easier for you, since you don't have to write it all out and then hope the message gets to the right person. You can just tell them."

"Fine," Adam said.

He trudged back down into the corridors of the palace. He detoured to Ziegfried's room. It was empty. Strom wasn't even there. He went looking for a page boy to ask Ziegfried's location. The first one he found said he was in Andreno's room. Adam went there.

Andreno's bodyguards stood just outside the closed door, not allowing anyone to approach. People lined the corridor, most of them arguing and jockeying for a better position. All of them claimed they should be first to have access to Andreno the moment he unlocked his door.

"He locked the door?" Adam asked one of the bodyguards.

"Yes," the man said. "Back off."

"I thought he'd be in court by now."

"His presence in court is a privilege for others around him, not a requirement on his part." The guard said the words so quickly and with so little inflection, it had to be rehearsed rather than something he believed.

"Is Ziegfried in there with him?"

"None of your business," the guard said.

"Ziegfried's leader wants him. Commands him to report."

"He'll have to wait until Andreno is finished and unlocks the door," the guard said.

Yet another man came striding up the corridor to stand face to face with the bodyguards, brushing Adam aside. "I'm here to speak with Andreno, sent by Prince Sanbralio. Open the door."

"All these people were sent by Prince Sanbralio." The bodyguard swept his hands out, indicating everyone in the corridor. "Step away. When Andreno makes himself available, you'll wait your turn."

Adam went back to the page boys. He wrote down a message for them to take to the radio tower. Ziegfried was currently inaccessible.

He returned to the corridor. There, he waited. And waited. The more time went by, the more agitated people got. Eventually, Strom wandered up and asked, "Are Ziegfried's bodyguards in with him and Andreno? I can't find any of them. Not even the off-duty ones."

"How should I know?" Adam hitched his shoulders with irritation. "I haven't been allowed in."

More people kept trickling in. When court let out for the day a flock of people sifted through, gossiping. Usually, they stayed just outside the throne room for their socializing. Why were they all squeezing through the crowded corridor, speculating on which noble lady Andreno would visit with first?

A guard with gold piping on the seams of his red and gray uniform marched up the corridor. The sea of people parted, as if Moses himself approached. Andreno's bodyguards snapped to attention. The newcomer demanded, "Why are the people Sanbralio sent all loitering out here in the hall? How many of them has Andreno seen?"

"None, sir," said one of the bodyguards, the same one who had refused everyone else.

"Who's in there with him now?"

"His foreign friend Ziegfried, sir."

"Open the door."

"I can't, sir." The bodyguard paled. "Lord Andreno took my key and locked it from the inside."

The newcomer's face darkened. He pressed his lips together. The skin around his eyes went taut. A muscle in his jaw twitched. The bodyguard cast his eyes to the floor and swallowed hard.

"Prince Sanbralio sent me to fetch him." The newcomer spoke through clenched teeth. "And you're telling me you don't even have access to your charge?"

He reached past the bodyguard and pounded on the door with a fist. When there was no response, he thumped it with his foot, repeatedly, rhythmically, loud. After about half a minute the bolt slid back. Andreno jerked the door open. His livid face immediately went slack when he saw the man with the gold piping.

He looked around. "What are all these people doing out here?"

"If you had attended court like you were supposed to you would know," the man said. "Your grand-uncle has summoned you. And your foreign friend. And that new interpreter who's with you lately."

Adam's gut clenched. Why did the prince want him? He'd never even seen the man as far as he knew.

"Ziegfried is in no state to go anywhere." Andreno opened his door wider.

Ziegfried sprawled in a chair. His hands shook. Deep shadows ringed his eyes. His skin had taken on a gray pallor. And he was drenched in sweat. All of his bodyguards were crowded into the room, most of them rather tired looking and dirty.

"I'll bring Schneider as a representative of Ziegfried," Andreno said.

"Who?" Gold Trim asked.

"The man in charge of Ziegfried's guards," Andreno said. "But since he doesn't speak the language, I'll have to bring the first translator as well. That way the new translator can focus just on whatever Uncle wants instead of working."

"Your risk," Gold Trim said. "Your choice."

"Good thing you dressed nicer today," Strom murmured to Adam. He straightened up quickly when Andreno came and looked them over.

He said to Strom, "Make Schneider presentable. Follow. Be quick." Then he wrinkled his nose at Adam. "Better than what you've been wearing. I guess you'll do."

Adam looked down at himself. Why were they talking about his clothes? Shouldn't Andreno be more worried about what the ruler of the entire country wanted with them?

And what had happened to Ziegfried? He'd been vibrant, energetic, freakishly so after he'd killed that guard. Now he knew what Gerhardt had meant by talking about vampire legends.

When Strom caught up with Schneider, Adam grabbed the bodyguard by the shirt and demanded, "What happened to Ziegfried?"

Andreno turned his head at the name. He frowned and said, "A good servant is silent."

"I am not your servant," Adam told him.

The bodyguard shook himself free. Adam stopped walking. He planted his feet, crossed his arms, and demanded, "Schneider. Explain what's going on. Now."

Scheider gave him a tired glance and continued walking. He threw over his shoulder, "I don't have to explain anything to the likes of you."

"Please don't cause problems," Strom said. He took Adam by the elbow, drawing him forward. "With the prince involved you're going to get all of us in trouble, not just yourself."

Gold Trim had stopped. He glared at Adam, then glanced at some of the guards spaced along the walls. Adam didn't have a right to get others in trouble. He followed.

Gold Trim led the way to a dining room. As soon as they entered, everyone else exited. Except for some of the guards and the old man sitting at the head of the table. He kept eating his lunch, his cutlery delicately tinkling on his plate.

Andreno stepped close. The old man took another bite. Andreno cleared his throat. The old man put down his fork and picked up a crystal goblet of wine. He swirled it around some before taking a sip. He held the wine in his mouth and stared into the goblet.

"You wanted me, Uncle?" Andreno asked.

So this was Sanbralio. He didn't look any more impressive than any other old man Adam had ever seen on a street. And the rudeness of his manners made him even less impressive.

The prince swallowed. He set the goblet down. He picked up his fork again before finally responding to Andreno's question. "Maybe. A long time ago. Not now."

Andreno's shoulders drooped. "Then why did you send for me?"

"The man I set over your bodyguards is dead. Why? Did you kill him?"

"No!" Andreno clenched his teeth. "I should have."

"Why is he dead?"

"He attacked one of my friends," Andreno said with a flick of a glance at Adam.

Sanbralio looked over at Adam, narrowing his eyes, scrutinizing. Adam had to work to try and prevent a look of disgust at being labeled a friend of Andreno's. Sanbralio said, "Your 'friend' doesn't look very agreeable to your claim."

Adam must not have hidden his disgust very well. Sanbralio pushed food around on his plate with his fork before turning back to Andreno. "Did you order your 'friend' to commit murder? Was the guard defending himself rather than attacking?"

Andreno clenched his fists as tight as his jaw. "Why do you always assume that it's my fault whenever someone dies?"

"Figure that one out yourself," Sanbralio said. "Was it your Freedzeeg friend that you ordered to kill him? Where is he? I only see the interpreter here that got attacked. Is he the one you ordered to kill the guard?"

"Ziegfried," Andreno corrected the name. "And no one was ordered to kill that guard. He used his dagger and his fists to try and get inflammatory information about you and Yaquerro and the throne. I told you I didn't trust that man."

Adam frowned as he listened to both the conversation and Strom's translations to Schneider. Strom interpreted exactly what Adam thought Andreno had said. Which was a lie. What Adam didn't know was why. Was Andreno lying because he was being verbally attacked? Or because he was hiding something? Or both?

Sanbralio poked at his food. "You had the guard killed for asking questions?"

"I didn't have him killed." Andreno hunched his shoulders so much he would have bristled if he'd been a dog. "Ziegfried had to kill him as a defensive move."

"And you still haven't answered where he is."

"He's resting." Andreno took a deep breath and regained some of his composure. "He found his friend being attacked with a dagger, bleeding all over the place, and he killed the person doing it. That took a lot out of him. Now he's exhausted. I told him to rest."

Another lie. Andreno added, "I brought the leader of his guards. He can answer for Ziegfried, or take back any message you have for him."

"I'm not interested in speaking to a representative for him." Sanbralio tapped his fork on the edge of his plate and looked Adam up and down. "Where is the dagger? Did Froogzoog take it? That's not tradition."

"No, he didn't take it," Andreno said. "Adam, answer. Where is that dagger?"

"In my room," Adam said.

"Why?" Sanbralio set down his fork again.

Adam opened his mouth to say he didn't even want it. Andreno spoke before he could, "Their people use different weapons. He doesn't know how to use it properly."

"He's going to give it to Zoogfroog?" Sanbralio asked.

"No," Andreno said. "And it's Ziegfried, Uncle."

"Stupid name." Sanbralio pushed his plate away. Adam squirmed, unsure which was worse. Being scrutinized, or Andreno making up stuff about him on the spot. Finally, Sanbralio pursed his lips and said to Adam, "Get lessons."

Adam nodded, keeping silent like so many others always did. Sanbralio dabbed at his mouth with the corner of an embroidered napkin. "On to the next matter, Andreno. I announced in court today that I wish you to marry. You will have a son. You will give that son to Yaquerro to father so he can have an heir."

Andreno went a little slack jawed. "You wish a son of mine to inherit?"

"My only grandson is dead." Sanbralio's voice cracked. He cleared his throat, put his age spotted hands flat on the table and slowly pushed to his feet. "I know I'm not supposed to be sad because he was just a bastard. But I am. My line goes no further through him. No hope for any future noble marriage or heir there. My last remaining son will never have children of his own. Not with his choice in a mate. You will provide one for him."

"Would you like me to use the Brendish tradition of (unfamiliar word, string? Procession? Parade? Strom used the word procession when he interpreted to Schneider)? Or have you already chosen a woman for me since my child will gain your throne?"

Sanbralio stood rigid, gripping the edges of the table. His eyes flicked over to Andreno. The loathing in them startled Adam, breaking his concentration on the new word.

"Surely you have someone in mind," Andreno said. "You wouldn't want the mother of a prince to be a commoner. Or you'd have accepted your second son's choice of mate. And you would marry off Charlass, legitimizing her and making her give Yaquerro an heir. Of course, if you had done that it certainly would have simplified everything in Quillen's case."

"Do not mock me!" Sabralio banged a fist on the table, rattling his plate. Then he turned his back on Andreno's smug face. He stood straight, composing himself. "Speaking of Charlass, her servants have disappeared again."

Andreno smirked. "Who can blame them? In a palace full of nobles, what servant would want to get stuck with her?"

"Some of her servants were last seen with your friend Ziggafee's bodyguards."

"So? They're men who saw pretty women. What's wrong with that?"

"Where did they go?"

"How should I know? I don't keep track of Charlass or her maids. Maybe they were too ashamed to be stuck with her and went to find someone better to serve."

"Find her new servants."

Andreno's smirk vanished. His face reddened. "Why me?"

"Because I don't like the way you talk about her." Sanbralio tugged at the bottom of his shirt, straightening it when it didn't need it. "If they disappear again, I'll hold you responsible."

Adam cringed. Andreno hated being ordered around. Hated not getting anything and everything his way. Would he throw a tantrum right here in front of his uncle? Or would he wait until he got back to his room and take it out on everyone else?

"Why should you even care?" Andreno shouted. "You never even notice when she's in the same room as you."

"I do notice," Sanbralio said. "More than I take notice of you. Her mother was a commoner. She's a bastard. It would be inappropriate for me to show how much I notice, or how much I care. She is still my granddaughter. You would be crazy not to remember that. Nephew."

He spat the word 'nephew'. More of a slap in the face than a term of endearment. A reminder that while Andreno was related he was not Sanbralio's flesh and blood, not as valuable.

Sanbralio left the room, followed quickly by all the guards. Before his nephew could truly work up a proper tantrum. Andreno ground his teeth and balled his fists. He turned to Adam.

"You hit me—" Adam backed up— "and I will hit you back."

"You would not. But Ziegfried would be unhappy." Andreno dropped his fists and stalked out of the room.

"Stupid, stupid, stupid," Adam muttered under his breath. What could possibly have come over him to let something like that slip out of his mouth?

His temper had come over him. That's what. Stupid indeed. He knew better than to act like that.

Chapter 20

ADAM FOLLOWED ALONG as Andreno stormed back to his room. Everyone who saw him scurried out of his way. Once there, he screamed at all his servants and bodyguards to get out.

Ziegfried's bodyguards huddled around him, not moving to leave. If they were staying, so was Adam. He wanted to know what was going on.

One of the people started shooing everyone else away, adding to the noise, yelling at anyone who hesitated, even the people that Sanbralio had sent.

Andreno grabbed the man by the shirt. "Who do you think you are!"

The man crumpled to his knees. "Oh please, strike my face. Do me the honor. I beg you, my Lord."

Andreno let go. "What?"

"Just to be touched by someone of your noble status." The man fingered his shirt where Andreno had grabbed it. "I never thought I would be so worthy."

Andreno backed away. "Are you crazy or something?"

"Prince Sanbralio assigned me to be your personal servant," the man said. "My name is Kurlos. Not that someone as important as you needs my name. I will direct all these people the Prince sent, the tailors, the tutors, the cobblers, all of them, as they prepare you for making yourself as stunning as possible for all the noble ladies looking for a husband. Not that you need the primping. You're perfect just the way you are."

"Stop talking." Andreno backed further away. Kurlos smiled with a closed mouth.

Ziegfried opened one eye half way and slurred. "What's going on? Noble ladies? Husband?"

"Don't worry about it. Go back to sleep," Andreno told him. He kept his face turned to Kurlos, keeping his attention there. "Do I really have to put up with you? Or would Uncle be mad if I tell you to get out?"

"You can tell me whatever you want," Kurlos said. "But if you wish to please your Uncle I'm afraid I'll have to bother you with my presence. And the presence of all those other servants who are inferior to you. I'll schedule everything so you don't have to bother with them too much."

"You're a coordinator then," Andreno said.

"If you wish." Kurlos smiled again. "Would you like me to start by coordinating these filthy Chemwanee to be elsewhere?"

"What Chemwanee?"

Kurlos pointed at Adam and the bodyguards. "Them."

"They're not from the Chemwanitz Mountains."

"As you wish." Kurlos' smile didn't fade. "Would you like them to be somewhere else? Or have you promised them the favor of your superior presence?"

"Favor. That reminds me." Andreno rounded on Adam. "I told you to bring me a favor from a woman. What did she ask?"

Did Adam dare tell him? He was in a state where he likely would try to sabotage what someone else needed. Then again Adam had made a promise. Marietta had to know the risks, else she wouldn't have hesitated. He said, "She wants a job for her sister."

"How old is her sister and what are her skills?"

"She's almost fifteen," Adam said. "She has no skills."

Kurlos lost his smile and put his hands on his hips. "This girl doesn't need just a job. She needs training. That's more than what you asked. And it's better than she probably deserves. What woman asked this of you? One of the whores?"

"One of the whores." Andreno grinned maliciously. "I don't suppose this woman would want a job for herself as well as her sister. And maybe even some of her friends. I know someone who needs some new servants."

Kurlos worked out all the details of assigning whores as servants to the bastard granddaughter of the Prince. That must have worked off the last of Andreno's steam. He turned giddy attention to all the people waiting to pamper and preen him.

Adam didn't know Charlass. But this would be good for Marietta, wouldn't it? Surely serving the granddaughter of the Prince had to be a better position than whoring in the tubs. Andreno had apparently satisfied his petty vindictiveness without putting more burdens on the shoulders of the oppressed in the palace. Adam nearly sighed with relief.

Word spread fast. Within days, the palace swam with noble ladies, all looking for a chance to become the mother of the heir's son. Every one of them had servants who seemed to think that chasing after the men attached to Andreno was some kind of hobby. After a few days of it Adam dreaded even showing up. He entertained the thought of claiming illness, saying he had to stay in bed that day.

Unfortunately, that would likely bring a doctor. Adam got out of bed and donned the clothes that kept mysteriously appearing overnight in his room. With this set he had to go to Strom next door.

Adam held up his right sleeve. "Would I sound like Helmut if I asked you to help me?"

"Not really." Strom chuckled and fastened the buttons at the cuff. "Helmut's never had any problem with buttons as far as I know."

"He's gotten them crooked before."

"And still, he can get them through the buttonholes." Strom finished the last one. "I take it your left hand is still bothering you?"

"It's fine," Adam said.

"So fine you asked for help?"

"If I do anything to strain it, that doctor person harasses me. I'd rather ask for help." Adam turned to head up the corridor.

A page boy met him before he got two steps away from Strom, and held out a note. Adam took it and Strom asked, "Who wants you?"

Adam crumpled up the note. "Andreno wants us both."

"Good thing I'm already dressed," Strom grumbled. The two of them headed in the right direction, Strom complaining the entire way. "He's never called this early before. We haven't even had breakfast yet. What could he possibly be thinking?"

"Of himself," Adam said. "Does he ever think about anything or anyone other than himself?"

"No," Strom said with a snort. "You know, it's half tempting to make him wait and go eat."

Adam stopped to frown at him. "You're the one who's always telling me not to make trouble."

"With your temper." Strom said. "Whenever you get mad you look like you want to hit someone. But this? Come on, tell me you're not tempted."

"Of course." Adam continued on. "Doesn't mean I'd say it out loud. And there are lots of times I haven't hit people who deserve it."

Strom's next snort sounded more like laughter. He swallowed it when they got to Andreno's rooms.

Activity bustled everywhere while Kurlos directed traffic. Servants scurried in and out. The remains of a hurried meal lay half eaten on a side table. Andreno preened in front of a full mirror. He took note of Adam and Strom beside his reflection in the mirror, grinned, and sent everyone out.

"My cousin is dead. Strom, go wake Ziegfried and inform him that Yaquerro's body was found." Andreno tugged at his collar then smoothed his hands down the front of his shirt. "News arrived at the palace just a couple of hours ago. Make sure he's awake enough to understand it. Then I imagine you'll need to go send a message to your Gerhardt. He gets grumpy if we don't keep him informed. Then he takes it out on Ziegfried. Makes them both difficult to work with."

Strom hesitated only a moment, shock on his face, before leaving the room. Andreno turned away from his mirror to face Adam, still grinning. "I'm going up in status now. Important people are going to be paying a lot more attention to me. Make sure to throw in a few foreign words every now and again when you speak to people. Make sure everyone knows how versatile an interpreter I have as a servant."

"I am not your servant," Adam glowered.

"However you want to think of it," Andreno said with a cheery laugh. "I'm generous, kind, and it's a good day. I'll allow you this."

A low growl worked it's way up Adam's throat. He reshaped it into a few mumbled cuss words in languages Andreno wouldn't know.

"Oh, stop." Andreno rolled his eyes. "It's not like you would make a good servant anyway. A good servant is silent, which you certainly are not."

Prince Sanbralio stepped into the room without any warning, startling Adam, and making Andreno stand straighter. His eyes were red and swollen. His nose dripped. His face was mottled and splotchy. His disheveled hair stood up at odd angles.

It made Adam want to reach out and see if he could offer any words of comfort. But everyone at this place played out what Andreno said about servants. The prince likely wouldn't welcome anything Adam could offer in word or gesture or otherwise. So he stayed silent and tried to blend in with the wall instead.

"You're up early," the prince said to Andreno.

"I was told you received terrible news in the night," Andreno said. "I was making myself presentable in case you needed anything."

"Need anything," Sanbralio repeated in a monotone. He ran shaking hands through his hair, making it stick up in more places. "I need my sons. Needed. And their children. If I hadn't made you my ward, I'd have banished you instead of Quillen. I had hoped banishment would protect him from you. Instead…"

Andreno frowned. "I didn't kill Quillen."

"Why should I believe you?"

"If I had any guilt in that matter, the Brendish General would have found it by now. You know how good he's reputed to be in such things."

"Yes." Sanbralio fixed his gaze on a spot on the floor. "I'm tempted to ask his assistance now to investigate the matter of Yaquerro's death. Did you kill him?"

"How?" Andreno asked. "I was here at the palace. He was in the Chemwanitz Mountains."

"Did you arrange it?"

"With who?" Andreno's upper lip curled. "I have no dealings with any Chemwanee."

"What about him?" Sanbralio pointed at Adam. "Light hair, light eyes, light skin, just like a Chemwanee. Your new friends speak gibberish that sounds a lot like what those barbarians speak."

"You haven't heard the Chemwanitz language in years," Andreno said. "That's why you don't recognize the difference. I told you they're from across the sea. They have to use a portal to travel back and forth because it's too far for even an islander's boat."

"Did they use a portal to go up to the mountains and kill my last remaining son?"

"Their magician was too tired to make a portal. Need I remind you, he had to use all his magic to save this man—" Andreno flipped a hand toward Adam— "from getting stabbed to death."

Sanbralio shrank in on himself. "You cover yourself well."

Andreno's volume rose. "You still think I did this! Are you ever going to trust me with *anything*?"

"I'll trust you to hold up a public contract," Sanbralio mumbled. "Sign a contract that when I die you won't turn out Charlass. We'll make it a public declaration that she will always have a home under this roof, in the rooms I have provided for her, with the lifestyle I have provided."

"Why should I?"

Sanbralio raised his face to look Andreno in the eye. "Because if you don't, I will not name you as my heir after Yaquerro is laid to rest."

"Who else is there?"

"As if I'd give you the excuse to kill someone else. You might be surprised at how many people would try to lay claim to the throne if I name no one. They would plot and scheme. They would produce fake documents to back up their claims. Premieres would gather their soldiers to back their favorite person. War would break out. And every contender for the throne would look at you as someone to get rid of."

"You would destroy your own country just to spite me?"

"I would protect my granddaughter, no matter the cost."

"She's not even a noble!"

"She's all I have left." Sanbralio's eyes watered. His chin quivered. His voice cracked. "I'm old. I'm tired. I'm a widower twice. My children are all dead.

My only grandson is dead. She's all I have left. Legally assure her protection and I'll give you everything you ever wanted. A throne. A princess. Children to bear your crown after you. Wealth. Power. The nation's army. Everything."

Andreno looked a little too smug, a little too much satisfaction in his eyes. "I'll do it just to please you, Uncle."

Sanbralio gave no comment to the obvious lie. He simply turned and shuffled back out. One of his bodyguards closed the door behind them. No sooner was it closed then Andreno jumped and whooped and danced about.

Adam backed up, fists clenched. He couldn't hit this man. Even as much as he deserved it. Who in their right mind celebrated a death that so obviously devastated the person who looked after them, paid their way in life? No wonder Sanbralio showed such disgust at having to deal with Andreno. Adam was pretty disgusted too.

He turned away so he wouldn't have to watch. Where he stood, he was now face to face with a tapestry that prominently featured Andreno. Adam grabbed the tapestry, right on the pictured face, and yanked. It came free of its anchor on the wall. He jumped back so it wouldn't crash onto his head.

Andreno stopped whooping and demanded, "What did you do?"

Adam turned to face him. He'd stopped dancing. In fact, he looked a bit alarmed.

Instead of making an excuse or offering an explanation that might deter attention to how angry and disgusted he was, Adam simply said, "Oops."

Chapter 21

I F ADAM HAD THOUGHT women flocked to the palace before, they
came in droves in the days following the news of Prince Yaquerro's death.
With Andreno busy pandering to their attentions, Adam had more freedom
to do what he wanted. So did the servants of the noble ladies. That included
flirting with any male associated with Andreno.

Repulsed by such shallow stupidity Adam, retreated to the window seat
at the intersecting corridors for important guests, especially on the days
when Andreno went outside the palace on the invitation of some nobleman
or other. The window overlooked the main gate and some of the prettier
gardens. Since Adam never went on any of excursions, he entertained himself listening to conversations, taking notes, and watching traffic coming
and going outside.

About midmorning on one of those excursion days a page handed Adam
a summons to Andreno's rooms. He raised an eyebrow at the page, "Are you
sure about this? Andreno is not here."

The poor page got an expression close to panic. He looked around. He
took the note. Re-read it. Then he nodded his head, his eyes showing white
all around. Instead of pushing the issue Adam picked up his belongings and
answered the summons just to abate the boy's unreasonable fear.

Kurlos lounged in Andreno's favorite spot with his feet up and a goblet
of wine at his elbow. He made eye contact with Adam. Then he looked down

and idly shuffled a stack of papers in his lap. He scribbled something down. Shuffled again. Took a sip. Scribbled some more.

Adam cleared his throat. Loudly. Kurlos yawned. He put his feet on the floor and flopped the papers off his lap onto the sofa. He stood, stretched, picked up his wine, and turned to Adam.

"Ah, you're here at last." Kurlos grinned with a hateful gleam. "I suppose I can't really expect someone like you to learn enough manners to come right away."

Adam crossed his arms. "I've been here since you watched me come in."

"When was that?" Kurlos brushed past him to an open bottle of wine. He set the half-full goblet beside an empty one next to the bottle. He spat into the goblet he'd been drinking from.

Someone tapped on the door. Kurlos picked up the bottle and filled both goblets. The door opened from the outside.

"Lady Tabissia," the guard who had opened the door announced just before stepping to the side.

A rather plain looking woman entered. She looked to be in her early twenties, maybe five or so years older than Adam. She walked with her head erect and her shoulders back. Little jewels dangled from her ears and wound around her neck.

Kurlos picked up both the wine goblets. He offered the one he'd spat in to Adam. Adam recoiled in disgust. Kurlos then turned and offered the same goblet to Tabissia saying, "You'll have to forgive him. Chemwanee barbarians don't have any taste for fine things."

"You spit in it." Adam still had his nose wrinkled as the woman took the goblet. She looked down into it then up at Kurlos.

Kurlos smiled like a ferret. "They're also all liars."

Tabissia set the goblet down on the nearest flat surface. "I didn't come here to drink wine. I was given permission to speak with Andreno. Where is he?"

"He's visiting the estate of some noble lady outside the city for the day. I forget which one." Kurlos lied. He knew exactly where Andreno was, what he was doing, and who he was with at any point of any day. "It hardly matters which one. So many of these young noble daughters think they're worth more than they are."

Tabissia's eyes narrowed. Kurlos continued, "I'm sure that's not the case with you. You know exactly how unimportant you are to Andreno. Nevertheless he is kind and gracious. He arranged for you to have some company in his stead."

He grinned again at Adam. Then he leaned over to Tabissia and loudly whispered, "We even made sure he cleaned up and dressed appropriately. You should see what he normally wears."

Tabissia's eyes were hard, glaring holes in Kurlos. "Whatever he wears I'm sure his company is more pleasant than yours."

"Well then I'll just leave you to his limited charms." Kurlos left, shutting the two of them in the room.

Tabissia's eyes went from hard back to neutral. She said to Adam, "You know my name. Give me yours."

"Adam," he said.

She raised one eyebrow but didn't look surprised. "That's not a Chemwanee name."

"I am not from the mountains."

She cocked her head to one side. "Then where?"

Adam gave her the answer he'd been told to give to that question. "Across the sea."

She looked him up and down. "You don't look like an islander."

"Farther."

"The islanders say there is nothing farther," she said.

"We have to use a portal to get here. Ships do not go far enough."

She walked over and sat on the sofa. "With how much people gossip I'm surprised I haven't heard of you."

"Most people do not believe we are not from the mountains," Adam said.

"That I heard," Tabissia said. "That Andreno had made friends with a group of mountain people. I found it difficult to believe. What you say makes more sense."

"You believe me?"

"That you're from someplace so far away no one's heard of it and you have to use a portal?" Tabissia nodded. "Yes. I'm from the north eastern edge of this nation. We border both Brend and the Chemwanitz. I'm very familiar with the accent of the mountain speech. You sound different."

Adam grimaced at the inference that he still had an accent. She asked, "Have I offended you?"

"No," Adam said. "Why?"

"Your face. You wear looks like clothes on your face."

"Say that again?"

"You wear looks like clothes on your face."

Adam mulled over that, repeating the words. He shook his head. "That makes no sense."

She gave him a kind smile and then a description of the phrase. He got it straightened out in his head. It was akin to the phrase 'you wear your heart on your sleeve,' or 'you're as easy to read as an open book.' His emotions showed on his face. Others could easily tell what he thought or felt.

That being the case she figured out very quickly how much he loved talking about languages, vocabulary, phrases, and idioms. Even though he was supposed to entertain her, she ended up treating him as though she were the hostess and he the guest.

He lost all track of time. Someone brought them lunch at some point. Later they had tea and cakes, a tradition very similar to what he knew of the English.

She kept asking about the traditions and culture of his people. He avoided the subject of the war and fed her folktales and ancient mythology.

At a point when they were both giggling over something, the door opened and Kurlos came back in. He saw Tabissia still there and he put on a scowl. Behind him a couple of Andreno's bodyguards entered. Then Andreno himself entered, followed by still others. He saw Tabissia and shot at dark glare at Kurlos.

"Andreno." Tabissia rose from her seat. "I was told I could have a few minutes with you alone."

"Whatever you have to say to me can be said in front of everyone else." Andreno's voice dripped disdain.

"If you insist," she said. "You're looking for a wife. End your search. I'll marry you."

Andreno threw back his head and laughed. He rubbed his eyes, held his belly, and let it go on for a full minute. Then still chortling, he said, "Oh my dear Tabissia. You amuse me."

Tabissia looked completely unfazed by the reaction. She said nothing, just standing there calmly, giving Andreno time to continue. Almost as if she had expected it.

Andreno stopped rubbing his eyes and looked at her with open contempt. "While there was a time I would have jumped on the offer, you have associated with a lower class of people. I no longer have any interest in you."

"You'd better get it back fast," Tabissia said.

"Why?" Andreno asked. "So you can get close enough to slit my throat some night in my sleep?"

"As appealing as that sounds, I think more of other people than myself. Something you don't understand. End your search for a wife."

"I'm not searching." Andreno's upper lip curled. "I'm going through the motions. I already know who I'm going to marry."

"You're going to marry me," Tabissia said. "That will spare whatever poor woman you have in mind, along with a few others if I can help it."

"You just want to get closer to the seat of power," Andreno said.

"Yes, I do, if you're going to be the one on that seat." Tabissia folded her hands in front of herself. "Then maybe I can stop some of the damage I know you'll do."

Andreno puffed out his chest. "You really do want to slit my throat."

"And leave the throne unclaimed? That would start a civil war. I want to prevent damage to our nation, not cause it."

"I'm not marrying you."

"How much support do you think you'll get if certain nasty rumors spread to the district premieres? How many of them do you think will swear obedience to you if they have the word murderer ringing in their ears? You will marry me, or I will start grinding those rumors through the mill that Prince Sanbralio worked so hard to silence."

"No one listened to those rumors before." Andreno paced the floor, so close Adam could have put out a foot and tripped him. "Why would they listen now?"

"Because I'm a high noble," Tabissia said. "As the daughter of a premiere, my word will go farther than Quillin's did. I was there too if you remember. I saw you up in that tree that Sanbralio's youngest son fell out of. I saw you on the boat with Sanbralio's second son. I know you were missing from your room the night your parents were murdered. I know you were present a lot of other times when people died. And now you were in Brend when Quillin was killed. I don't know how you managed to get rid of Prince Yaquerro, but with this many other murders you're connected to, do you really think people will overlook that one? Especially since he was the final block between you and the throne?"

"I didn't kill Quillin." Andreno waved his hands around in the air. "You just want to blame someone because you loved him."

"And I fully blame you." Tabissia remained composed, unmoved by his agitation. "You've had your hand in the deaths of so many others, why should I believe you didn't kill him?"

"I don't care what you believe." Andreno ran his hand through his hair. "I'm not marrying you."

"I'll give you until tomorrow morning to think about what will happen if you don't. How many (killers? Assassins?) your bodyguards will have to protect you from. How many district premieres will go out of their way to defy you. How much trouble I'll make for you. And the rewards if you do. I can give you children. I can give you a head start on some foreign relations. I can give you access to more materials. Yes, I know you've been after them for some reason. I won't ask why. Tomorrow morning, Andreno. Either publicly announce our engagement or I'll start the rumors grinding. Your choice. And in the meantime, I'll be in better company than yours in Charlass' rooms."

She strode past him, brushing him with her shoulder as she clipped by. Andreno steamed, smoke practically curling out of his ears. Adam slunk back into the corner. Who exactly was this woman? She had seemed so nice. She really was a little scary.

"I thought I told you to get rid of her while I was gone," Andreno shouted at Kurlos.

"I tried." He fiddled with a slip of paper like what page boys delivered. "Sanbralio told her she could speak with you and she wouldn't take no for an answer. I thought if she got insulted enough she'd leave. So I gave her that Chemwanee over there to keep her company. I can't help it if he wasn't as rude as most of his people."

"How many times do I have to tell you they're not from the mountains?" Andreno picked up the nearest object, a book in this case, and hurled it at Kurlos. "Tabissia is smart enough to see through any thinly veiled insults as an attempt to get rid of her. What is that in your hand?"

"A summons from your granduncle."

"*You waited to give it to me?*" Andreno screamed.

"I thought maybe you'd want to calm down."

"Unlike you, I do what I'm told by the people I want to favor me."

He stomped out of the room. Adam was half tempted to stay behind just to gain more time without him. Unless Andreno had been called to answer questions about Tabissia. In which case, Adam probably would be called in to answer as well. There was no getting out of that. And really, he was supposed to be tagging along after Andreno anyway.

Just before Prince Sanbralio's chambers, Andreno paused in front of a large mirror. He straightened out his clothes and smoothed down his hair. Then he went and presented himself.

"I came as soon as I received your summons, Uncle," Andreno said.

Sanbralio had gone downhill in the short time since Adam had last seen him. His complexion was ashy and gray. His eyes had a wild look and had sunk in. He sat limp in a chair, his legs sprawled out in front of him, his arms hanging over the sides. His clothes hung baggy from lost weight, which had also left his cheeks hollow.

Again Adam wanted to reach out to him. Maybe offer some sort of commiseration about how miserable a wretch Andreno was? Perhaps tell him his granddaughter was in good hands with Marietta? Again, would the prince accept anything from a common foreigner? Or take offense, making the situation worse? Again, Adam remained silent and let the man suffer alone rather than risk adding to it.

"You haven't been eating, have you," Andreno said.

"Who cares." Sanbralio slurred. He pointed to another man. "The court magician has a request."

"What?" Andreno asked.

"Send away your new friends for a short time," the magician said. This wasn't about Tabissia? It was about the Germans? Adam tilted his head, turning his ears to listen more carefully.

"Why should I?" Andreno frowned.

"The Brendish delegation is on its way for Yaquerro's funeral. Court Magician Jerryck is with them. I would appreciate it if that friend of yours who does magic illegally is not anywhere around."

Andreno rolled his eyes. "It's not illegal to use magic."

The man tipped his nose upward. "Since you never cared to learn anything about my profession, I will inform you that there are guidelines set in place for safety that are controlled by a group that is outside the rule of this nation. All magicians follow them. Your friend does not. Jerryck is easily influenced by bad things, like what your friend does. I don't want them in contact."

Andreno tilted his nose up too, a perfect mockery of the magician. "What does it matter to you?"

"I've always thought of Jerryck as a sort of kid brother," the magician said. "Or a favorite nephew. I feel very protective toward him."

"It's very inconvenient for me to send away my friends just to please someone who has no respect for me," Andreno said.

The magician opened his arms, held out his hands. "Perhaps there is something I can do in exchange."

"I get everything you could offer me from Ziegfried." Andreno looked down his tilted nose. "Everything, and more."

"Even influence with your Granduncle?"

"I have that," Andreno said, though the tilt lowered some and his tone sounded ever so slightly less certain.

"Not the way I do, and you know it." The magician smirked a bit. Sanbralio didn't react at all to them talking about him as if he wasn't in the room. Just how far gone was he? The magician said, "I know Tabissia is in the palace, and not just for the funeral. I can imagine what she has to say to you."

"For your information, I've already seen Tabissia." Andreno lost all smugness in his face. He looked over at a tapestry on the far wall. "And what she said wouldn't interest anyone."

"It interested me a great deal when she came to me for a little chat," the magician said. "I'm certain a lot of others will share my interest."

Andreno jerked his gaze back to the magician, narrowing his eyes. "Did you put her up to this?"

"No," the magician said. "I'm simply using it to my advantage. She came to me concerned that something may happen to her after she spoke with you. And if it did, she wanted me to make certain that what we discussed became public knowledge. Of course, I might be talked out of doing such a thing. In fact, I might even be convinced to talk her out of what she wants from you."

Andreno paled. "She hates you. If she went to you then she went to others as well. How do you think you could possibly stop her?"

"She wants to be closer to the seat of power to try and hold you in check. Just residing in the palace puts her closer. I could convince Prince Sanbralio to ask her to stay with Charlass. He's willing to give her some advantages if she does. I'll do it… if…"

"…if I send Ziegfried away," Andreno finished the sentence.

Adam bit his tongue to keep from smiling. A chance to leave this palace? To get a vacation from Andreno? That was something to get excited about, though it probably wasn't wise to display it.

Sanbralio roused himself a little, shuffling in his seat but not quite managing to sit up straighter. "It won't be for long. And it's not like he hasn't left you for short times before. You don't have to send them all away. Keep that one here in the room. Keep all the rest. Just send that Frigzig fellow away for a few short weeks."

"I'd rather they were all gone," the magician said. Adam almost nodded, caught himself and stopped just in time.

"Compromise," Sanbralio slurred.

"All right," Andreno said. "Make Tabissia one of Charlass' maids and I'll send them all away, including this one here, for a whole month."

"Tabissia's father wouldn't let her stay for that." The magician snorted. "You put her on the same social level as those whores you gave to Charlass and he'll come raging in here crying insult. Tabissia can be Charlass' courtier companion."

"Charlass can't have a courtier," Andreno said. "She's not a noble."

"Tabissia is," the magician said. "She can have the status of courtier to a resident of the palace and the granddaughter of our Prince."

Andreno glowered. "That will raise Charlass in status."

"Only to about what it was before you gave her whores for servants." The magician waved as if swatting away a fly instead of arguing the pros and cons of messing with someone's life. "Nothing lost for you there."

"Agree," Sanbralio said to Andreno. "And I won't ask you to send all your friends away. Just Zizfrizig."

"I'll send most of them away, just keeping this one translator—" Andreno waved grandiosely at Adam— "and the people they use for communication. Just to please you, Uncle, if for nothing else."

Chapter 22

IEGFRIED, HIS BODYGUARDS, AND STROM all left. After that,
Andreno locked down the palace. He claimed it was to protect Prince
Sanbralio from anyone bothering him. Most people complained that
he was flexing his new importance and influence. Everyone treated him as if
he was already legally the heir to the throne even though Sanbralio had yet
to make it official.

Women kept trying to come despite the locked gates. Every time, they
sent a message through to Andreno requesting entrance. Every time, he
denied them. They all had conniption fits, stomping their feet, screaming at
people, waving their hands around. Adam watched them from the window
seat, amusing himself by imagining what exactly they were saying.

Andreno went out visiting someone almost every day. That left Adam
alone a lot. The radio guys holed up in their tower keeping to themselves.
Everyone else he knew was gone. Everyone remaining shunned him. The
nobles considered themselves above him. The servants considered themselves
below him. The guards were mad about the one that Ziegfried had killed. He
ended up at that window seat more and more often, playing solitaire with his
cards in between watching people try and get through the gate.

One day Andreno walked him there making inane small talk. He acted
fidgety, bouncing on the balls of his feet, speaking so fast that some of his

words were unintelligible. Then instead of sitting or relaxing, he kept watch out the window with his eyes glued to the gates.

"Are you waiting for something?" Adam asked.

"Someone." Andreno beamed one of his rare, genuine smiles. "The timing has to be perfect. Then I come out looking like a hero. It makes a good impression. And we must make a good impression. In this case it's everything."

He rambled on some more. Adam only half listened. He made sure to nod in all the right places, making it appear he paid close attention.

Kurlos came up the corridor. "Your Highness, the stable master is asking again when you're coming. He's upset, saying the horses shouldn't be made ready to go and then stand around doing nothing for this long."

"I told you not to call me Highness until it's official." Andreno's smile turned into a gloat of pleasure. "And the stable master can wait. I'll come when it's time and not a moment before."

"He's asking when it will be time," Kurlos said.

Andreno leaned toward the window, catching his breath. The largest group yet approached the gate. There were wagons, a carriage, plenty of horses, and at least a few dozen guards wearing crimson and gold uniforms. They only carried one standard at the head. Every other group had carried two, one for wherever locale they came from and one for the Shontese nation. The Shontese one was absent from this group.

"I'll have the guards open the gate," Kurlos said.

Andreno grabbed him, keeping him from walking away. "Wait."

"Your Highness." Kurlos plucked nervously at his shirt. "We can't keep them out. That's the Brendish delegation."

"I know who they are." Andreno's grin now turned feral. "The timing has to be perfect. Go tell the stable master I'm on my way. I'll take care of getting the gate open."

Kurlos left. Andreno leaned closer to the window, pressing his hands and face against the glass like a child drooling over cake displays in a bakery.

The caravan pulled up to the gate and stopped. The men in front argued with the gate guards. Andreno giggled gleefully and ran down the hall the way Kurlos had gone.

REBEKAH OLSON

Adam watched out the window. The caravan men pointed to their standard. They pointed at the carriage, where Adam assumed the diplomat rode. They grew more and more agitated as the gate guards continued shaking their heads and denying entrance.

The carriage window opened. A pretty girl stuck her head out, then coughed and slapped a hand to her nose. Adam couldn't blame her. The stink of the city outside the walls had been pretty strong when he'd come to the palace. It had to be infinitely worse now in the heat of high summer. The Shontese nobility never paid it any attention. Since this girl did, he assumed she wasn't the actual diplomat. More likely she was just riding in the carriage as the diplomat's servant or something.

Movement inside the walls of the palace grounds caught Adam's eye. Andreno headed out from the stables with the entourage that always accompanied him on his jaunts. They headed for the gate where the pretty girl was jabbing her finger at the guards and yelling at them.

Andreno reached the gate and acted all huffy. The gate opened. He beckoned the caravan to enter. The girl withdrew back inside the carriage.

The caravan rolled in. The guards in their crimson and gold uniforms spread out as everything came to a stop again. A few of them dismounted their horses near the carriage. The girl climbed out of it. No one else came out behind her.

Andreno dismounted too. He walked over to her and bowed low using the grace he reserved only for those he wanted to like him. Was she the delegate after all? Andreno wouldn't react that way to a servant.

Andreno stood from his bow and gave greeting gestures to one of the men who didn't wear a uniform. Adam frowned, confused. Was that the delegate? If so, why had he been on horseback instead of in the carriage?

Everyone acted like the girl was the focal point. The uniforms fanned out with her at the center. Andreno gave her the most attention. He even offered his arm to escort her inside.

Most of his own escorts stayed mounted outside. Some commotion came up one of the corridors near Adam's window. Likely the guests being settled in, since these were some of the nicest rooms. A few minutes later Andreno went back outside. He remounted his horse and left with his escort.

Should Adam move elsewhere? If so, where? He didn't really have any other place to go except holing up in his room. There wasn't much for him to do with Andreno gone. He may as well sit here and play cards or take notes as opposed to anywhere else. Then if he got lucky, he could watch another group come and try to get inside the palace.

About fifteen minutes or so went by. He picked up a lost game and had the deck of cards in his hand when a noisy group approached from one of the corridors. He looked up and saw the pretty girl from the carriage, escorted by several of the uniforms and a couple of the most important servants in the palace. They spoke and acted like they were giving her a basic tour.

Closer up her features were clearer. She was prettier than from far away. She wore small pieces of jewelry, nothing gaudy or flashy, enough to show she had money but didn't care to flaunt it. She wore authority like an invisible cloak yet didn't stick her nose up in the air. As she approached, she made eye contact with him and smiled. It lit up her entire face and turned her from pretty to beautiful. She nodded a greeting to Adam. Then she was passed and leaving through the end of the corridor.

A couple of the guards gave him a closer inspection with much less friendliness. The one with the crooked nose held his hands at the ready like he was prepared to draw a hidden dagger at a moment's notice and use it on the nearest person who looked cross-eyed. The ash haired one had gray eyes to match. He looked mildly curious and half amused. Then they were gone too.

Adam sat for a moment trying to catch his breath. Not one noble had ever acknowledged him on their own. Was she a noble or not? She had to be the diplomat, with that much attention and authority. But a noble? She didn't act like any noble Adam had ever seen here.

He still held his cards. The people passing probably hadn't even seen them. He glanced down at them trying to shake off his stupor, debating whether or not to lay out another tableau.

"What do you think you're doing here?" Someone yelled from the other end of the corridor that the girl had come from. Adam looked up. The court magician bore down on him shaking a finger. "You can't be here."

"Andreno did not tell me that," Adam said. "He sat with me some today here."

"Andreno told me you were staying because you wouldn't bother the Brendish magician. This is too close to his room. You get out of here right now."

"How can I bother him?" Adam asked. "I do not even know which one he is."

"He's the one with the light brown hair."

"There are a few of them with light brown hair," Adam said.

"Only one who isn't a guard. And Jerryck has lighter skin from growing up in a village too close to the mountains. And he has brown eyes that are so light they almost look golden."

"You do not want me near him, so you describe him?" Adam couldn't care less what color eyes the man had.

"Just so you know who to stay away from. Now, go somewhere else."

"Where?" Adam asked.

The magician put his hands on his hips, lowered his head, and sighed with exasperation. Then he lifted his eyes just enough to look at Adam. "If I let you come sit and talk to me will you leave this window and not come back until Jerryck leaves?"

"Why would you want me to sit with you?" Adam cocked his head to one side. "You do not like us."

"Which is why this is so nice of me."

"I do not even know your name," Adam said.

"You haven't asked anyone?" The magician took a half step back with one hand on his chest, so over-dramatic he could play an acting role in the old black and white cinema reels.

"I asked Andreno once," Adam said.

The magician held out the hand he had previously put on his chest. "And?"

"And I should not repeat what he said about you."

"I see," the magician said with a frown. "My name is Masorno. Now come away and let's talk."

Adam slipped his cards in a pocket and stood. "About what?"

"About magic." Masorno led the way up the corridor away from the guest rooms. "What else? That is what I'm best at."

"What is to talk about?" Adam asked. "I do not even know how magic works."

"A person with a strong (unfamiliar word) can use it to (unfamiliar word) the (first unfamiliar word) of whatever they choose if they're (unfamiliar word). Sometimes a direct (unfamiliar word) can be used. Other times an (unfamiliar word) is needed. Why have you stopped walking? Come along."

Learning languages was one thing. Learning jargon was different. It required knowledge of the field it referenced. Adam's brother Matthias used to drive him crazy with it. As soon as Adam picked up some of the jargon Matthias would switch over to lingo just to keep him confused. Then he would laugh like a little maniac at Adam's frustration. Then the kid would go and get into conversations peppered with jargon and lingo with their dad about articles in science journals. Or deep discussions and debates on photos and film developing techniques. Always Adam sat to the side, left out and unable to understand the words.

"I will go find somewhere else to sit," Adam said. "You do not have to give me any more of your time."

"Don't worry about not understanding." Masorno looked somewhat smug. "With someone like Ziegfried for an example there is no way you can possibly understand the finer and more important points about magic. Don't worry about taking my time. It's important that you learn more about this."

Adam shook his head. "If I do not understand a simple explanation, how will I understand finer points?"

"The most important point you should know, but won't think to ask, is just how dangerous magic is." Masorno put an arm around Adam's shoulder and drew him along. "Your Ziegfried has no idea how many different ways he could kill himself and everyone around him. If he did know, he would stop acting so (careless? apathetic?) about it and be more careful."

Killing people didn't seem to bother Ziegfried. Quite the opposite. He had been invigorated after killing that guard.

"The dangers of magic are why the gathering of seats has set down the guidelines they have," Masorno continued.

"Gathering of seats?" That phrase didn't make sense. Did Adam have the interpretation wrong?

"Correct," Masorno said. He let go of Adam but kept walking and talking. "There are nine seats, one for black, one for white, one for brown, and one for each of the other six major colors. The men who live in them (occupy them?) are some of the oldest and wisest magicians known. They make rules and guides (guidelines?) that all magicians follow. It's their job to make sure that all magic used is safe for the commoners (general populace?). Do you understand what I'm saying?"

"I think so." Adam didn't mention the words he struggled with. He had picked up that this gathering of seats was a colloquialism, a phrase used as a title for some kind of governmental body. "Must every magician obey this gathering of seats?"

"Yes." Masorno smiled as good as any politician. "Every man who becomes a magician must first pass tests for them before he's allowed to make his promises."

"And the women magicians?" Adam asked.

"We don't allow women magicians to live." Masorno's smile turned upside down, putting an effected look of sorrow on his face. "Understand, women are very emotional. They couldn't possibly use proper control over magic the way a man can. It's not their fault. It's just the way it is. We have to kill them. For their own protection. And the protection of everyone around them."

Adam stopped. Masorno kept walking and talking, taking him far enough away that Adam couldn't give in to the urge to sucker punch him in the kidneys. Then Adam turned and quietly walked away in the opposite direction.

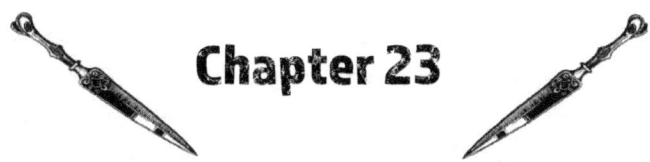

Chapter 23

ADAM ENDED UP MEANDERING ABOUT. Walking off his mad. Cooling his head. He had complete control of his temper again by the time Andreno returned, even though he'd only spent about half the time he normally did for these visits.

The moment Andreno got back he ordered the lockdown ended. He told everyone that if it kept out someone as important as the Brendish delegate it did more harm than good.

The palace gates opened up. Nobles streamed in over the next several days. Andreno used the time to put on public displays of concern for Prince Sanbralio. Meanwhile the old prince babbled and looked more and more disheveled and unhealthy every time Adam caught a glimpse of him.

Every once in a while Adam caught sight of the visiting Brendish. For the most part, the palace staff actively kept him away from them. Several times someone would come whisper in Andreno's ear. He would give Adam some menial task that took him elsewhere. Then someone Brendish would walk in the room just as he was leaving.

That delegate looked prettier and prettier the more he saw her. She was friendly to everyone, even the servants. She looked about fifteen but acted mature enough he would guess her a few years older than that, closer to his age. More and more he put himself in places where he could catch sight of her.

One of the balconies overlooked the area outside the main doors to the throne room. When court let out for the day, usually around noon, the wide doors would fling open and people poured out. The delegate was always among them. Since Adam was supposed to meet Andreno as he came out of court anyway it made the perfect excuse to go to that balcony and watch her.

Others who held their head as erect as hers looked arrogant. She had an air of confidence. Others who walked with those strides did so in a rush. She did it with purpose. Others who smiled like that reminded Adam of politicians. It made her face prettier, even stunning. Others draped themselves in ostentatious jewelry, even the men. She wore only simple and small ornaments.

After several days of watching her from that balcony, her ash haired guard came up. He smiled. Like her, the smile reached his eyes, lighting them up with sparkles of friendly amusement. Unlike her he had the eyes of an old person. There was depth there hiding age and experience Adam couldn't even fathom. And he moved with the liquid grace of incredible strength hidden inside his thin frame.

He leaned on the balcony railing next to Adam. "Been at the palace long?"

"Long enough," Adam said with a shrug.

"Long enough for what?"

Adam looked at him, trying to gauge if he was just joshing or seriously wanted to know. Adam hadn't thought about the phrase perhaps being a colloquialism. He had heard other people speak with such vagueness.

Mischief crinkled the man's eyes somehow enhancing his friendly demeanor. "Long enough to know about the haunted corridor?"

"I know about it." Adam clenched his teeth and gripped the railing with his left hand. It didn't hurt anymore. But that didn't mean he liked the memory.

"Ah, good." The man looked out across the crowd of people below them. "Not everyone does. It's kind of an embarrassment for the Shontese crown. People are discouraged from talking about it. Especially right after another body turns up in there. They send someone through every week, I think, just to check."

Adam wasn't sure whether to believe him or not. No one in the palace had given him this much information about that corridor, not even the talkative doctor. He asked, "Why not just keep it guarded?"

168

"They tried that. The official story is that the guards posted went a little crazy, if they didn't die or just disappear altogether. I think it's just too convenient a spot for the guards to get rid of someone they don't want around so they leave it alone."

That fit Adam's experience. Even the fact that the guards who came to dispose of the body hadn't acted surprised or alarmed at all.

"That's where they'd find your body."

Adam jerked his head to look at the man again. "What?"

"See those men down there dressed like me?" The man nodded his head toward the guards around the pretty delegate. Most of them were staring up at him, and not with friendly looks. "You're making them nervous. There are lots of pretty women here. Why don't you go stare at one of them for a while instead of her?"

"None of the other women are quite like her," Adam said.

"As in... None of the other women's guards are as likely to slit your throat as hers?"

Adam slowly backed away. The man turned to watch him, his friendly smile now seeming more sinister. "Don't worry, they'd make it quick. They wouldn't bother with torture or anything. Just death would be satisfactory enough."

Someone tapped Adam's shoulder from behind just before he backed into them. He whipped around, half expecting to have to defend himself from another crimson and gold clad man wielding a knife or something. But it was just a page handing Adam a note that summoned him to Andreno's rooms. That made the perfect excuse to get away from the ash haired man entirely.

When he got to Andreno's rooms no one was there. Adam sighed, rolled his shoulders, and settled in to wait. He replayed the conversation with the ash haired guard over in his head a few times. He came to the conclusion that he'd been toyed with, when Andreno and his entourage entered.

"There you are," Andreno said. "I sent people out looking for you. You're supposed to be with me just in case I want you."

"Please forgive me, Highness," Kurlos said. "I sent him here without your leave. He was talking with one of the Brendish guards."

"You're not supposed to be talking to any of them," Andreno said. "Otherwise what was the point of me sending the rest of you away? Don't do it anymore."

Adam nodded since it was pointless to say the guard came to him, not the other way around. Andreno passed by him to the room in the back where he always dressed, presumably to change his clothes for lunch.

Kurlos stuck his face in Adam's and glared. "Do you have any idea who those guards with the stars on their collars are?"

"The delegate's protectors?" Adam guessed.

"Those are Brendish Palace Elite. They'll torture you to death without a moment's thought. They'll draw it out. Make it as long and painful as possible. I can't say that wouldn't make me happy. I have half a mind to tell you to go try and make friends with them. But that would upset Andreno. You stay away from them."

Adam stopped looking for opportunities to sneak a peek at the pretty delegate. He actively avoided all of them instead of just letting others do that for him. Still, he couldn't stop thinking about her. She would pop into his head at unexpected moments. He found himself daydreaming about her more and more.

It wasn't much longer before she left to go back to her home. Adam went back to his window seat. The entire caravan escorting her rolled out of the gate, leaving behind the crowd of people who had come out to see her off.

After the Brendish left, so did many others. Group by group, they cleared out of their guest rooms and went back to wherever they'd come from. Adam sat and watched them all. It wasn't nearly as much fun as watching them have fits over a locked gate denying them entry.

Andreno spent every morning in court. Adam still wasn't allowed in, which suited him just fine. He'd only end up losing his temper in there with all those nobles fawning and stroking each other's egos. And it also meant less time he spent with Andreno.

He was sitting in the window seat when Ziegfried, Strom, and the German bodyguards returned. He immediately went down to greet them. Ziegfried rode alone in the carriage. Strom rode on horseback with the bodyguards.

"You know how to ride?" Adam asked in lieu of a greeting.

"Sure." Strom dismounted and tossed the reins to one of the palace servants from the stables. "I've been riding ever since I can remember. My grandfather used to have a tutor just to teach me out at his estate, horses, etiquette, and all kinds of other crap. I used to beg my dad not to make me go out there. He said it was part of my duty, the selfish bastard. Never thought I'd actually be glad for any of those lessons. They seem to work pretty well here."

Ziegfried climbed out of the carriage. He smiled at Adam. "Good to see you! How've you been while we were away?"

"Bored out of my mind," Adam said.

"Splendid, splendid." Ziegfried looked past him. He headed inside. "And how are your lessons going?"

"Lessons?"

"Your dagger lessons. Andreno said he was going to have the palace guards teach you how to use it."

Adam shook his head. Ziegfried puffed out his cheeks a little bit, and said, "I'll take care of that."

Strom hung back, walking more slowly with Adam while the others went on ahead. "What were you really doing with all that time to yourself? Is there a new girl in the baths or something? You had to have entertained yourself with something."

"I wasn't watching the baths," Adam said.

"Oh, come on." Strom rolled his eyes. "Unless you tell me something plausible, I'm not going to believe that anymore."

"While you were gone," Adam said, "the most spectacular girl I've ever seen was here visiting. She out-shined every noble here."

"Aha!" Strom chuckled at him. "You've got that look in your eye. You're hooked! What's her name?"

"I don't know," Adam admitted. "And I don't think I ever will. Her father sent her to represent him. She had her own bodyguards and everything."

"A lot of nobles here do that for their daughters," Strom said.

"They thought I was looking at her too much. They threatened to kill me."

"Wow!" Strom laughed. "You sure know how to pick them. Have you ever taken the easy road? Even once?"

"Not if the easy road is the wrong one to take," Adam said.

"There's no right or wrong when it comes to women," Strom said. "In a woman's eyes the man is always wrong. So for him it comes down to easy or difficult. Some women are easier to please than others. Some are more difficult to get into your bed. That's all. Simple or difficult. There is no right or wrong."

Adam frowned at him. "You really believe that shallow crap?"

"Absolutely!"

They reached Ziegfried's rooms. He wasn't there, just a couple of his bodyguards. Strom didn't even look at them. He plopped down in a seat and kept talking, thankfully changing the subject. "We had a good time while you were here trying to get yourself in trouble. Andreno didn't figure we'd be gone long enough to warrant going all the way to base so he put us up at an estate just outside the city. It was pretty nice, like a resort almost, aside from the lack of electricity and running water. Add those things in and it would have been perfect."

"Yeah perfect," one of the two bodyguards said. "If you want to overlook all the people that kept getting sick."

"Not that many." Strom waved that away. "And it was just some of the lower servants."

"What kind of sick?" Adam asked.

Strom shrugged. "Not sure."

"That's what bothers me about it," the bodyguard said. "Otherwise I wouldn't care. If I don't know what's going around, I don't know who or what to avoid to stay healthy."

"What were their symptoms?" Adam asked.

"They varied," Strom said. "Most of them got a little dizzy. A few threw up. All of them who came down with it got lethargic. I'd have thought they had the flu if any of them had gotten a fever. Instead it was just the opposite. Some of them had to be warmed up because their body temperatures dropped. I gotta admit, that part was kind of weird."

Ziegfried came in with the rest of his bodyguards. He asked Adam, "Where is Andreno? He's not in his room."

"He's in court," Adam said. "I'm supposed to go meet him coming out in another fifteen or twenty minutes. If you'd gotten here much later,

I'd have headed in that direction already and I would have missed you coming in."

"When you see him," Ziegfried said, "tell him that I need to speak with him at his earliest convenience."

"I'll let him know," Adam said.

As it turned out, Adam didn't have to. When court ended Kurlos whispered in Andreno's ear before Adam even got to him. Andreno beamed at everyone fawning on him and said, "You all will have to excuse me. One of my friends has returned to the palace and I'm eager to speak with him."

He went straight to Ziegfried's room, entering without announcement. "You're back."

"And I've had a breakthrough with what you wanted." Ziegfried's smile was almost as wide as Andreno's. His eyes flicked over to Adam and he said, "Oh, and before I get to that, didn't your uncle say Adam needed lessons with that dagger?"

Andreno glanced back at Adam. "I arranged for them."

"He says he's not getting them."

"*What?*" Andreno whirled on Kurlos. "Why not?"

"Prince Sanbralio told him to do it." Kurlos flicked a piece of lint off his cuff. "He didn't tell you to do it for him. I keep telling you these Chemwanee barbarians have no respect for you."

Andreno cuffed Kurlos' ear. "They're not from the mountains."

Kurlos collapsed in a ball at Andreno's feet. "I'm sorry! I'm sorry! I'll arrange it. Please, oh great Prince, have mercy on someone as worthless as I."

"Get up." Andreno rolled his eyes. "Just take him and go do it."

Kurlos scuttled out of the room. Once outside the door he stood and brushed himself off. He smirked at Adam then took off down the hall without looking to see if Adam followed or not.

They went to parts of the palace Adam hadn't been to as yet. They turned a corner and entered an open space arranged like the room of a reception area. Men in red and gray guard uniforms lounged about. Some talked quietly. Others ate or rolled dice on tables. One sat at a table near the entrance with his feet up, reading through handfuls of papers. Kurlos strode right up to him.

"This man." He waved behind him without checking to see if Adam was actually there. "He is to receive instructions on a dagger he acquired. Take care of it."

"We're not teaching him." The guard didn't look up from his papers. "If he doesn't know anything about it he's more likely to kill himself with it."

Kurlos snatched the papers away and slapped them on the table. "This is not a request. This order comes from Prince Andreno himself. Arrange instructions for him. Now."

The guard sneered. "I don't take orders from little Andreno."

Kurlos threw back his shoulders and lifted his nose. "That's Prince Andreno. And you'd better learn to take orders from him. He'll wear the crown after Sanbralio."

The guard picked the papers back up. He flicked them straight and lifted them in front of his face. Kurlos looked around the room. By now all the lounging guards had stopped their activities and were watching them, most of them not with a friendly expression.

Kurlos pointed at one of the guards with a malicious leer. "That one would be the perfect teacher."

The guard at the table lowered his papers just enough to bare his teeth at Adam. "It would be better if he gets himself killed, not if one of us does it."

"I won't kill him." The guard that Kurlos had pointed to set down some dice that he'd been gripping rather than rolling. "I'll just make him wish for it."

The guard at the table put down the papers. "Maybe we can give him lessons after all." Kurlos nodded curtly then spun around and left Adam standing there. The guard at the table looked him up and down. "You think you can handle a knife?"

"No," Adam said. "If I could, I would not need lessons."

"You're asking lessons from the friends of the man you killed. That's kind of stupid."

"I did not ask. I was ordered." Adam dug his nails into his palms to keep calm and focused. They were goading him. Obviously. "And I did not kill that man. I did not ask for help when he attacked me. I did not ask for this dagger. I certainly did not ask to be attacked with it."

"You sound like you're not in control of your own life."

As if any of these guards were truly in control of their own lives. Definitely trying to rile. Adam refused to give him that satisfaction and gave the exact opposite reaction. He nodded agreement. "That is true. So if someone attacks me with a dagger again, I would like to know how to stop them before someone else tries to defend me and kills them."

"You talk so stupid you don't even make sense." The guard leaned back, tipping his chair onto its hind legs. He looked over to the guard that had set down the dice and shrugged.

The other guard said, "You train with knives, you're going to get cut."

"I have already been cut," Adam reminded him.

"Not like you will if you train." The other guard stood, sweeping his arm out to indicate the others in the room. "Every man here hates you right now. We're all looking for a reason to hurt you."

"Then I had better learn fast." Adam refused to give in. They weren't going to get him to give up and quit before he started, not this easily.

"Don't kill him," the guard at the table said.

"I won't," the other guard said.

"Or torture him too much."

"Oh, now that's carrying things a bit far."

"At least not where anyone will catch you."

"One man's torture is another man's training."

"You spend too much time with the Brendish Palace Elite."

Adam flinched. The other guard grinned at that and said, "Leave the dagger in your room tomorrow morning and come to the practice field when court starts. Make sure you wear something you can get dirty and bloody."

"I do not get to choose my clothes," Adam grumped. "And I do not know where the practice field is."

The guard was unsympathetic. "Then learn where it is and get some control."

Chapter 24

STROM BURST INTO ADAM'S ROOM holding up a drab colored shirt with no sleeves. "Here. This should work."

"Why can't I just have my uniforms back?" Adam complained.

"Because you have no fashion sense."

"Who needs that? Why would anyone care about something so stupid?"

"Someone got up on the wrong side of the bed this morning." Strom tossed the shirt at him along with a pair of loose leggings. "Why so grouchy? Did you forget the way to the practice field already?"

"No."

"Nervous?"

"No!"

"All righty then." Strom turned to leave.

Okay, so maybe Adam was somewhat nervous. It wasn't like he knew exactly what he was going to face. It couldn't possibly be anything like basic training. There, he'd learned how to handle guns, march, move in formations, crawl through trenches, recognize enemy equipment, and other such things. The extent of his training with knives was how to affix his bayonet to the end of his mauser and jab. Even if he'd seen actual combat after deployment he couldn't have used his bayonet. Someone stole it the day he shipped out.

He took a couple of deep breaths. He mentally ran through a few vocabulary words. He debated having a smoke then decided not to take the time. Dressed, he made his way out to the tiny corner by the palace walls Strom claimed was called the practice field.

"It's about time," the trainer said.

"I am early," Adam said. "Court has not started yet."

"I don't care," the trainer said.

"What is your name?" Adam couldn't just keep thinking of him by his function, not if they were going to work together.

The man stared at him for several heartbeats, his face as unreadable as his eyes. Then he asked, "You didn't bother to find out?"

Adam didn't need any more guilt poured on that than he already had. "I am now."

"It's Nolrien." The man stared at him silently again. Was he looking for some kind of reaction? When Adam gave none, he asked, "You still want to take lessons from me?"

What was this man looking for? "Yes. I have to."

"Do you know the name of the man your friend killed?"

"Dalrien," Adam said.

"You still want to take lessons from me?"

"What do names have to do with it?" Adam asked.

"Dalrien was born Brendish."

"So?"

"So, I'm guessing you're not familiar with Brendish naming traditions." Nolrien shrugged. "So be it. You've been warned. It's your neck."

Several of the others on the field stopped practicing and ringed around Adam and Nolrien, laughing and jeering. Adam set his jaw. They weren't going to get him to quit this easily. They didn't understand. He'd been given an order. If he disobeyed he would get in trouble. That would cause trouble for his family.

"First thing's first." Nolrien held up a finger. "If you're going to play with knives you're going to get cut. There is no maybe. There is no if. It's when, and absolute. You're going to get cut. End of rule. Don't expect me to be nice to you about it."

Adam shook his head.

"Because of that…" Nolrien picked up a piece of wood carved in the shape of a knife and handed it over, "…all beginners train with practice blades. Not real ones. That will stop me from killing you right away."

"Great." Adam grimaced and accepted the wooden knife.

"Second rule." Nolrien held up two fingers. "Learn how to keep hold of your blade. If you dont…"

He slapped Adam across the face. While Adam stood stunned, Nolrien moved his hands in one fluid motion that forced down Adam's hand that held the blade. He grabbed the meaty flesh just below the thumb. Adam couldn't grip the hilt strong enough to keep hold of it when Nolrien pushed the flat of it out of his hand. The blade dropped.

Nolrien stepped forward, keeping his grip and pushing Adam off balance. He fell over backwards with his teacher looming over the top of him. With one sweep of the arm, Nolrien plunged the wooden dagger straight at him. Adam hadn't even seen him pick it up. The knife stopped just short of stabbing him through the eye.

"…anyone with a little experience can take it away and use it on you." Nolrien finished the sentence he'd left incomplete. He tapped the flat of the blade on Adam's cheeks, just hard enough to sting a little. Humiliating.

Everyone laughed. More joined the crowd. Nolrien stood and held out a hand, offering help up off the ground. Adam stared at the hand. Could he count this much as a lesson and say he obeyed? Should he even risk it?

Aside from that, Nolrien had a point. He had the dagger. Just like any other weapon, if he had it in his possession without learning proper use and care, that was negligent and irresponsible. He took the hand and stood facing his teacher again.

Nolrien gave him the practice blade. Then knocked him over and took it away again. Instead of stopping the oncoming thrust of the blade, this time Nolrien jabbed Adam with it a few times it the stomach. That was going to leave some bruises.

Everyone laughed again. Adam stood again. He accepted the returned practice blade again. This time Nolrien punched him in the gut, disarmed him, threw him to the ground, then kicked him. Adam got back up.

Over and over and over. Disarm. Knock down. Strike. Get up. Repeat.

Adam's temper flared. He cussed in several different languages. Nolrien wasn't teaching him anything except how to take a beating and get laughed at for it. He tried to hit back. Or kick back. Anything to get Nolrien to stop making such sport of him. Every time, Nolrien blocked the strike and hit him. Hard. He got a bloody nose. He bit his tongue. And his lip.

The ground started swaying and the world spun. Nolrien knocked him down once more, this time with a feather light brush. He didn't offer a hand up. Adam got as far as his hands and knees on his own.

Nolrien stepped back. "That's enough."

"Court's not out yet," one of the sideline men piped up. "You can keep going."

"He's making this too easy," Nolrien said.

He walked away. Everyone else clucked their tongues in disappointment or loudly protested, calling Nolrien back to do more beating. Eventually they all wandered away. By that time the world had stopped spinning enough that Adam regained his feet and headed back to his room.

Strom was there. He said, "Ziegfried wanted me to wait for you. You look terrible. Did you learn anything at all? Or did they just beat you?"

"I learned the guy giving the lesson hates me." Adam's words slurred across his sore tongue.

"That's it?"

"I also learned that if I play with knives someone will take it and kill me. I got killed a lot today. I lost count how many times or different ways."

"Maybe this isn't such a good idea. You should quit."

"I'm not quitting."

Strom looked at him like he was crazy. "Why not?"

"Because." Adam wasn't going to give an explanation. Strom did what he wanted no matter what the rules. He'd as much as stated he didn't care if his family was in danger. He wasn't going to understand Adam's motives.

Besides, Adam wasn't really sure. He told himself it was for his family. What if he really hoped to learn something? The prospect certainly came with a bit of a thrill. Or possibly he was just pigheaded and stubborn.

"I'm getting you a doctor," Strom said.

179

"For what?" Adam asked.

"You just got beat up."

"I did not."

"Oh, for the love of… Forget it! You know what? Forget I ever helped you. You never listen to anything I say anyway." Strom yanked the door open to leave.

"All right!" Adam held up his hands in surrender. "Listen, I'm sorry!"

Strom paused. He glared over his shoulder at Adam. Then he shrugged it off and turned to leave again, saying, "I'll get you the doctor."

Adam sat on his bed, leaning his back against the wall. Before long, he got a visit from the same doctor that had treated him before. He looked Adam over, and said, "Most of these are just bruises or shallow injuries."

"I really am fine," Adam said. "My friend just got you because he was upset. I am sorry you had to come all the way here. You can leave now if you want."

"It's really not a problem." The doctor dabbed from his dark colored bottle, the one that made the sting on cut flesh. "You'd be surprised how many times I'm called into this corridor. I'll tell you the same thing I tell every other man. Be more careful next time in your choice of women. Some of them out in those baths can get pretty rough."

Adam opened his mouth to ask for clarification. He quickly closed it again, realizing the doctor thought he'd gotten his injuries from harsh bedplay. He blushed at the very thought.

"It's nothing to be embarrassed about," the doctor said. "It happens to everyone."

"I got these injuries practicing with one of the guards," Adam said.

"Ah, I see. Which one? I'll have a talk with him."

"Nolrien. And please do not talk to him."

"He's going through a rough time," the doctor said. "Losing his father the way he did… I'm surprised he didn't do more damage to you."

"Why me?"

"Did he say anything to you about his father? At all?"

"Mostly he just beat me. Before that he said something about names. Nothing about his father."

"Do you know anything about Brendish naming traditions?" the doctor asked.

Adam sat back slightly. This again? He obviously had missed something. He said, "Please tell me."

"Nolrien's father was Brendish." The doctor said, packing up his medicine bottles. "There, the first daughter is given a name similar to her mother and the first son is given a name similar to his father."

The pieces clicked into place for Adam. "Oh."

Nolrien, son. Dalrien, father, the guard who had attacked him and been killed. When the doctor left Adam put his face in one hand and swore softly. If he'd been in Nolrien's shoes he'd want to do a whole lot more than beat someone.

So now what? He couldn't back out of the lessons. At the same time he couldn't just stand there and take beatings day after day either.

Nolrien had to have some presence of mind. He hadn't tried to seriously harm Adam. Every injury was superficial and would heal within a week or less. No broken bones. Nothing that would leave any scars. And he'd pulled his punches. He hadn't even hit hard until Adam tried to hit him back.

Perhaps a peace offering was in order? An acknowledgment? Adam hadn't killed his attacker but maybe some sort of apology was appropriate anyway.

Chapter 25

ADAM TOOK THE DAGGER with him out to the practice field. Nolrien frowned at him. "You came back for more?"

"I learned Brendish naming traditions," Adam said. He ignored the men already gathering around to watch and held out the sheathed dagger. "Among my people something like this would go to the son. If you want it then it is yours."

Nolrien stared at the dagger for a moment, not moving. Then he swallowed and turned his back. "It's yours."

Adam took a breath to insist. Nolrien leaned over and picked up his water jug. "We're not among your people. Here, if a man dies while attacking someone, the weapon he uses goes to the one he attacked."

"I did not kill him," Adam said.

"No." Nolrien took a swig from the jug, set it down, and straightened back up. "If the tradition were that the weapon went to the killer, the dagger would belong to Ziegfried."

"I understand you being angry at me because of him," Adam said.

"Do you?" Nolrien turned around to look at him, fire in his eyes. Anger, the first real emotion Adam had seen from him. "Is your father dead too?"

Some of the men on the sidelines snickered. Adam ignored them and said to Nolrien. "Not that I know of. Maybe. Things are bad at home. He might die no matter what. If I do the wrong thing, people will kill him. But as far as I know he is still alive."

The anger melted out of Nolrien's face back to neutrality. "You don't know."

"Messages from home are not allowed," Adam said.

Nolrien glanced at the dagger one more time. Then he turned to the crowd of men ringing them. He waved his arms and swung at a couple. "Don't you all have something better to do? Get out of here. You lazy bunch of (unfamiliar phrase)."

They scattered. Nolrien closed Adam's hand around the dagger. "It's yours. Put it down. Get the wooden one and tell me when you had your last knife training."

Adam put the dagger down by Nolrien's water jug and picked up one of the wooden practice blades that lay there as he said. "Yesterday."

"The one before that," Nolrien said with a droll tone.

Adam stood. "Never."

"Really?" Nolrien cocked his head at him. "I didn't show you how to hold it. You do that well."

"Then how to you keep taking it away so easy?"

"You're not (unfamiliar word) enough."

"I do not know that word," Adam said. He repeated it slowly.

"You don't attack right," Nolrien said. "Fight back effectively. Don't just try and defend. Or hesitate while deciding whether or not to attack. Be (same word)."

Strategically aggressive. Or on the offense. Combative maybe. In the context, Adam would lay bets on aggressive. Never in his life had anyone ever accused him of not being aggressive enough.

He repeated the word a few times. He ran it through a few other languages ending with a mental note to double check with Strom.

"That was interesting," Nolrien said. "How many languages was that?"

"I did not count."

"I've never heard those languages before," Nolrien said.

"They are from my home," Adam told him.

"You also have no accent," Nolrien said. "That other guy does. What's his name? Shtrome?"

Adam pronounced it correctly for him. "Strom."

"Have you been learning this language longer than him?"

"No." Flattered as Adam was at being told he had no accent, he wasn't going to get all braggart about it. "I keep having to ask him about words. He knows much more than I do."

"Then how is it you speak so much better?"

Adam took a step back, leaning away. "Why the compliments? Are you trying to confuse me?"

"No." Nolrien smiled slightly. This one reached his eyes. Another emotion.

"Are you going to teach me?" Adam asked, not trusting this new side of the guard. "Or beat me more? I really do want to learn how to use this weapon. Or at least defend against it."

"Of course you do." Nolrien smiled. A much bigger one than before. Except this one didn't fill his eyes. He looked around the tiny yard they used for a practice field. Some of the men who had scattered now stared at them from the other side of the small space. He made some sort of gesture at them, Adam guessed a rude one by their reactions. Then he said, "Let's get to work."

Adam gripped the dagger and braced for Nolrien to take it. The corner of Nolrien's mouth quirked. Standing his ground, he drew a finger in the air vertically down the front of Adam's body. "Have you ever heard of a center line?"

"No." Adam braced harder. He wasn't going to be distracted this easily.

"Think of a line down the center of your opponent's body. Now, If I turn like this—" Nolrien stepped back with one foot, putting his body at about a forty-five-degree angle to Adam's— "It narrows my center line from what you see. It makes it harder for you to hit me and easier for me to defend myself. Do it."

Adam stepped back a little with one foot. Nolrien said, "Now you're a smaller target."

"If I want to be a smaller target—" Adam turned more— "should I not be sideways to you?"

Nolrien stepped forward with his hind foot, putting himself right behind Adam, and slapped him right in the kidneys. When Adam flinched Nolrien simply said, "No."

He stepped back again. Adam mimicked his angle. Nolrien said, "Go back to sideways. You saw how easy I hit you. From sideways, you try and hit me."

"So you can hit me back?" Adam stepped sideways again.

Nolrien smirked with almost a chuckle, real emotion again. "I won't hit you for it. This time."

Adam stepped forward with his back foot just like Nolrien had. Except it didn't put him behind his opponent, just to the side. Adam swung anyway. Nolrien swiped his elbow across Adam's swinging arm, completely deflecting him. At the same time, he stepped, turning so that he was again facing Adam at a forty-five-degree angle.

"Easier to attack. Easier to defend." Nolrien said. He bounced a little and slapped his thighs. "Also, bend your knees some. Don't keep them straight."

One of the other guards sauntered up to them. "Hey, Nolrien!"

Nolrien took a swing at him. "Busy."

The guard skittered back. "You said you're doing your father's job now. Who else am I supposed to go to?"

"Say what it is and leave," Nolrien snarled.

"A magician from down south just arrived." The other guard stayed out of arm's length. "He's with Masorno asking questions about the Brendish Court Magician."

Nolrien's shoulders dropped. He sighed and muttered under his breath. He asked the guard, "Anything else?"

"No." The guard skipped back, putting more distance between them.

"I have to go check on this," Nolrien said to Adam. He looked around at everyone else still watching them. "Don't stay out here without me. Leave before I do. I'll show you more tomorrow."

Adam set the practice dagger back down and picked up the real one. He took it back to his room. Someone had already laid out different clothes for him. He rolled his eyes. Why couldn't he just keep what he had on?

Changing clothes in the middle of the day was stupid. Especially in the heat of summer. Now instead of stinking up one set of clothes with his sweat, he would make more work for the laundry personnel by stinking up a second set for no good reason.

Regardless, he made sure to put on the other clothes and go out just before Court was scheduled to end. He went to the balcony above, waiting with several others for the doors to open. Some of them looked eager. Others looked as bored and indifferent as Adam.

One of them nudged Adam. "Hello. You're that language servant of Andreno's, yes? Tell me what he—"

"I am not a servant," Adam snarled. He left the balcony and headed down to the floor.

The court magician stormed into the large, open space there. Nolrien followed him. He saw Adam and made discreet shooing gestures.

"You!" Masorno pointed his finger at Adam and stalked over to him. "You and your friends. Get out. All of you. Leave this palace immediately!"

Several heads turned at the magician's shouting. Some people whispered behind their hands to others. A few giggled softly.

The doors to the throne room opened. Everyone outside straightened up. Those inside poured out. Masorno pushed his way in against the crowd, loudly demanding, "Where's Andreno? Get him out here. He and I are going to have a talk."

Kurlos headed him off. "You don't demand to speak with a prince."

"Don't you sass me." Masorno stood nose to nose with Kurlos. "Get me Andreno. Do your job. Now!"

"Put your request in writing and I'll check to see if the Prince has time for you," Kurlos said.

Andreno came up behind him. "Don't be ridiculous. I always have time for someone as important as Uncle's court magician. Let's take this to my chambers."

Andreno swept out of the crowd with Masorno and the usual entourage in his wake. Nolrien said to Adam, "You probably shouldn't be here. Masorno is nervous. Having you or any of your friends around won't help."

"I am assigned to Andreno," Adam said. "I have to follow him. That is my job right now."

"Of course it is." Nolrien's voice was as blank as his face.

As soon as they got to Andreno's quarters he gave Masorno his fake, politician smile and said, "Tell me how I can help you."

"I don't need help." Masorno crossed his arms. "I need you to get rid of your bad, magic using friend and everyone connected with him."

"I already did that for you once." Andreno's smile remained plastered. "He just got back. Why should I immediately send him away again?"

"Because now my life is at risk," Masorno said. "Not Jerryck's."

Andreno's smile slipped. "What are you talking about?"

"I have a visitor," Masorno said. "He's the messenger for the gathering of seats. If he finds out there's a man here using magic illegally and I haven't done anything about it, they'll kill me. I ignored Ziegfried for you. You owe me for this."

"I am a Prince." Andreno's smile turned into a sneer. "I owe you nothing. You owe me everything. I'm not sending him away. He's in the middle of getting a project started for me."

"I'll do the project for him," Masorno said.

Andreno laughed. "I don't think so. Just go manage your guest. Instead of me getting rid of someone who treats me the way I deserve, you go get rid of your guest."

Masorno wrung his hands. "I can't ask him to leave, not with his connections to the gathering."

"I didn't tell you to ask," Andreno said. "Find out what he wants. Give him something close to it that makes him look in a direction away from you. A direction that gets him to leave. You've been a member of the court long enough. You should know how to handle that."

"I can't give him anything close to the information he's looking for without possibly putting Jerryck in danger."

"Who cares?" Andreno shrugged. "I thought you were concerned about your own life. Let the Brendish court magician take care of himself."

Chapter 26

NOLRIEN KNOCKED THE PRACTICE BLADE out of Adam's hand and sucker punched him in the stomach. Adam doubled over clutching his abdomen, unable to suck air into his lungs.

"I shouldn't have to keep telling you." Nolrien towered over him. "Protect your middle. Just because you're the one with the weapon doesn't mean you can be stupid."

"Nolrien!" A guard approached, the same one that had told about the magician's visitor the day before.

Nolrien muttered, "Speak of stupid and he comes like a summons."

The guard skidded to a halt beside him. "A courier to the Brendish Palace left this morning."

"I'm aware of that," Nolrien said. "Go away."

"Did you tell them about the gathering visitor who headed their direction this morning?"

"Why should I?" Nolrien shrugged. "As if it's any of your business."

"I promised your father I'd help you if anything ever happened to him," the guard said. "He told me that was the best way to learn to do what you do. So I thought—"

"No you didn't," Nolrien interrupted. "That's your problem. You don't think. If you did you'd realize that a magician who uses magic to travel will get to his destination long before any message I send."

"Unless you have a magic means of sending it," the guard said. "I know you have ways. And good connections with Brend. I want to help."

"Then why don't you start by not spouting off anything you think you may or may not know in front of people who don't need to know?"

The guard's eyes widened and he flicked at glance at Adam. He blanched and said, "Oh."

"Oh. Stupid. Get out of here." Nolrien followed up the command with a swipe at the guard's head. He ran off.

By this time Adam had regained control of his lungs. He pulled himself back to his feet. Gerhardt had said he wanted contact with Brend. Perhaps the means stood right here on this practice field.

"You have good connections with Brend?" Adam repeated what the other man had claimed.

"I trained there for a while," Nolrien said. "My father wanted it. And I'm useful to them."

"Do you think we could be useful to them?" Adam asked.

"*We?*" Nolrien cocked his head. "As in you and your comrades? I guess they could use you for target practice. Maybe. That may be a bit beneath them though, unless you do something to directly irritate them."

"We just want to trade."

"Just trade? Nothing else? Nothing else at all?"

"What else would there be?"

"Oh, I don't know, a few things. But honestly, I've looked at the amounts you people are trading with Andreno. You're paying him stupid high prices for a piddly amount of goods."

"Piddly?" Adam raised his eyebrows. Either he didn't have the word right in his mind, or he was on a completely different train of thought.

Nolrien gathered up his belongings, his water jug and extra shirt. He swiped the practice blade from Adam and snagged the extras he kept on the side. "Lesson's over for today."

"Wait." Adam followed him as he walked off the practice field. "What do you mean by what you said?"

"Strom claims your people are at war," Nolrien said. "And what Andreno trades you helps supply your army. True?"

189

"That is what I have been told."

"Then either you have a stupid small army, so small you can't really wage an effective war, or you've been lied to. Which do you think it is?"

Adam said nothing. Nolrien stopped, turned, and stared at Adam.

Adam still said nothing. If word got out that he believed the government and his commanding officers had lied to him and everyone else, what kind of pressure would they apply to ensure his compliance?

"Have it your way," Nolrien said. He broke eye contact, turned his back, and went inside the castle. Adam followed since Nolrien kept talking. "But if you think that kind of silence will work with the Brendish, be prepared to pay the price."

"There is a price to pay if I say something," Adam muttered.

He said it in German so Nolrien wouldn't understand. Regardless, Nolrien stopped and swung his elbow. Adam jumped back to keep from taking it right in his solar plexus.

Nolrien glared at him over his shoulder. "Just because I don't understand the words doesn't mean I don't know the tone of a complaint."

A few people ran past them and up a corridor. Adam thought maybe they'd been alarmed by the sudden violence. Then someone else ran inside from the same door he and Nolrien had used and ran the same way as the others.

Nolrien watched them go with a frown. Adam asked, "Is something going on?"

"Not sure," Nolrien said. He headed the same way they had gone. Adam followed.

A page ran their way. Nolrien snagged him by the shirt. "What's going on?"

The page leaned close and whispered something to Nolrien. Then he ran off. Adam asked, "Anything I should know?"

"Prince Sanbralio is ill," Nolrien said. "Collapsed in the throne room during court. Go change."

"Why?" Adam asked.

"Because Andreno is going to strut around with his entourage, showing off pretend concern," Nolrien said. "He'll want everyone around him to look the part, not like someone who sweated a training session with a guard."

That made sense to Adam, more sense than just changing for the sake of wearing different clothes. He went to his room.

The closer he got, the more he had to dodge people running and scurrying pell mell through the place. Some of them strode by with purpose in their step, intent expressions on their faces. Many of them jabbered with each other, speculating on how this occurrence might affect whatever lord they were associated with.

In the hall, a couple of women that looked like they were from the baths scooted out of rooms half dressed as if they'd been expelled in a hurry. Adam rolled his eyes. The corridor for those with the ears of important men indeed. Adam couldn't get out of there and away from them fast enough.

Unfortunately, that put him in the position of shadowing Andreno. Which meant exactly what Nolrien predicted. He preened. He showed off. He bragged about how worried he was. And whenever he thought no one was looking, he strutted and smirked.

The only relief Adam had was when Ziegfried and Andreno locked themselves away with no one but Ziegfried's bodyguards. Not even Andreno's were allowed in.

Adam wasn't released to leave at supper time. After a while, people drifted off to bed. And still Adam wasn't released. About halfway through the night, when Andreno finally retired, Adam figured enough was enough. He left and went to bed hungry.

He woke in the night to Marietta shaking his shoulder. The candle was lit, and Nolrien leaned against the closed door. Adam groaned and mumbled to himself, "Don't get enough of hitting me on the practice field? You have to come in here too?"

Adam didn't see Nolrien move. He just was suddenly yanked half out of his bed with his face pushed to the floor. Marietta pushed Nolrien without getting him to let go. She said, "Stop it!"

"I know the tone of a complaint," Nolrien said the same thing he'd said the day before.

"That's not what we're here for." She took his arm and peeled his hand off of Adam.

He sat on the edge of the bed, now fully awake. "What do you want?"

"Have you had a chance to hear anything Andreno is talking to your Ziegfried about?" Marietta asked.

"No," Adam said. "You woke me up in the middle of the night just to ask that?"

"It's not the middle of the night," Nolrien said. "It's near dawn. Toughen up."

"Has Ziegfried said anything about Sanbralio's illness?" Marietta asked. "Anything at all?"

"Not to me," Adam said. "I hardly see him anymore, let alone speak with him. Why?"

"Just a hunch," she said. She patted Nolrien on the chest. "Someone is very (unfamiliar word. Afraid? Paranoid? Suspicious?) when it comes to Ziegfried. Not that I blame him. But nothing's been proven. So…"

The way she touched Nolrien almost absent mindedly, along with his lack of reaction, made Adam think the two had more than a passing familiarity between them. Which led him to wonder if his treatment of her had more to do with Nolrien forgiving him than offering up the dagger.

"If that's all," Adam said, "can I go back to sleep now?"

"No," Nolrien said. "We can get an early start today on your training. Since you're up."

"Be nice," Marietta told him.

"I am." Nolrien put on his creepy, blank eyed smile. "He's still breathing, isn't he?" He looked at Adam then pointed to the clothes on his little table that kept mysteriously appearing there every night when he slept. "Get dressed. Come out. We'll make up for quitting early yesterday."

Marietta tipped her chin down, smiled, and batted her eyes. "Want me to help you get dressed?"

"No!" Nolrien answered before Adam could say one way or the other.

"Aww," Marietta turned her coy face to Nolrien. "You didn't even give him a chance to turn me down."

"That's not what we're here for," Nolrien said.

Instead of taking offense at having her own words thrown back at her, she snickered and left. Nolrien pointed his finger at Adam. "Take too long and I'm coming back in here."

Then he left too. Adam made a rude gesture at the door, the same one he'd seen Nolrien use many times now. It didn't satisfy. Maybe because Adam still hadn't figured out exactly what it meant.

While dressing, he found he had bruised up pretty good where Nolrien had punched him the day before. He was a bit stiff from that. But at least it was in a place people wouldn't see and ask about as long as he kept his shirt on.

He went out into the hall where Nolrien was waiting for him. Adam said, "Could I at least get something to eat first?"

"Sure," Nolrien said with a flat tone. "It'll make it that much more fun to hit you hard if you puke from a full stomach."

"I haven't eaten since breakfast yesterday morning," Adam said.

Nolrien's eyes fluttered in almost a roll. But he led the way to the mess hall where a few of the earliest risers were already getting some food. Adam took only a little, anxious that Nolrien really would hit him hard enough just to be sadistic.

Out on the practice field, Nolrien ran him through a few exercises he claimed were designed to train someone to keep their hands up while defending. When others trickled out to the field, he had them square off with Adam. Supposedly that would give more experience since everyone had their own style. Adam figured it just gave more people a chance to hit him.

Adam drew the line when Strom came out to the practice field. He shook his fist at his fellow interpreter and said, "If you join this line to try and hit me, do not expect me to hold back."

Strom laughed. "How about I take you away instead? Ziegfried wants you. And I imagine Andreno will too."

Adam turned to tell Nolrien the practice session was over for the day. The guard who had asked about Nolrien sending a message to Brend was running up waving his arms.

"Nolrien!" the guard shouted, skidding to a halt in front of him. "That magician is back. The one from the gathering that went to Brend yesterday. He's back! Already! You want me to go ask him why?"

Nolrien's upper lip curled. "No."

"But—"

"You can go away," Nolrien said. "Adam is going with me to go meet him."

"I am?" Adam asked.

"Ziegfried wants him," Strom said.

Nolrien's face went flat, his eyes cold. "Adam is definitely going with me then. Tell your little Ziegfried he can go and (unfamiliar phrase)."

The guard who'd delivered the news dropped his jaw. "You're not supposed to talk that way about a nobleman's guest."

Nolrien stepped in, hooked a leg behind the guard's ankle, and shoved. The man flipped down to the ground flat on his back. While he lay there looking stunned, Nolrien grabbed Adam by the shirt and marched him off the practice field.

"So um…" Strom called after them. "I'll just… er… I'll tell Ziegfried you'll come when you have a chance."

Adam waved acknowledgment just before Nolrien pulled him inside. He tried shaking himself loose. Nolrien kept hold and pushed him ahead.

"I can walk on my own, you know," Adam told him.

Nolrien said nothing, his mouth flat, his lips nearly gone he'd pressed them so close together. But at least he let go. Adam followed him rather than risk him getting irate.

He went to Adam's room, told him to clean up from the training session, and waited for him. Then he said nothing more as he led the way to where Andreno and Sanbralio's rooms were.

At the end of that corridor he climbed a wide set of stairs. At the landing at the top he pushed through a heavy door off to the side that let into a circular room with more stairs curving up the round wall and disappearing above the ceiling.

Servants ran around packing luggage bags. Masorno paced the floor looking as excited as a kid on Christmas. He talked with a dark-haired man of olive colored skin who sat half reclined on a sofa.

"I'm just glad it's finally happened." Masorno waved his arms in the air. "Now, Gintario, don't you worry about whoever it is they picked to approve. I'll take care of him."

"I'm not saying you can't handle him," the visitor said. "I'm telling you to take care. I approved this arrangement. He knows a lot. He's not going to be as easy to impress as some random person out in a crowd of commoners."

194

"I'll take care of him," Masorno repeated. His pacing brought him to face Nolrien and Adam. His shoulders hunched forward and his face pinched with anger. He stormed over at them. "Out! Both of you! Now!"

"Give me information," Nolrien said.

"Out on the landing!"

Nolrien gestured to the door. "You first."

Masorno stomped out. As soon as Nolrien and Adam had both come out, he slammed the door shut. He shook his finger at Nolrien. "If you ever—"

"Save it," Nolrien said. "I'm not in the mood."

"Why did you bring him?" Masorno tilted his chin at Adam.

"Why is your visitor back so soon?" Nolrien asked. "And why are your servants packing?"

Masorno now shook his finger at Adam. "Don't you ever enter my tower again without my leave."

"Adam," Nolrien said. "Go inside and introduce yourself to the visitor. Tell him all about Ziegfried and what kind of magic he does."

"No! No!" Masorno leaned his back against the door, spreading his arms out and blocking the way. "You set one foot in there or say one word to him and I'll set your hair on fire."

"Not if I punch you in the throat first," Nolrien said. "No talking, no spell casting. No hair on fire. Gintario finds out everything. He tells the gathering. They kill you. Or you could just cooperate and answer all my questions."

"He's back because he fulfilled his mission already," Masorno said. "He's that good. He went to the Brendish palace yesterday, did what needed done, and came back this morning to tell me how it went so I could be the first one."

"The first one to what?"

"To go to Brend to apply to be Jerryck's mentor," Masorno said. "Officially he still needs two more weeks. Of course, it's all just a formality at this point. But then he can go and get his license like he should have done a decade ago."

"Jerryck?" Adam asked.

"The Brendish Court Magician," Masorno said. "The one I told you about when he was visiting after Prince Yaquerro was killed."

"The one Ziegfried had to leave for," Adam said.

"Yes." Masorno smiled. "That's the one."

"What was that talk about someone having to approve?" Nolrien asked. "Approve what?"

"If I tell you," Masorno said, "do you promise not to tell Ziegfried? I don't want him trying to get there first."

"Don't be insulting," Nolrien said. "Or I'll just punch you in the throat and take Adam in there to introduce him myself. Answer the question."

"Anyone who wants to apply to be Jerryck's mentor has to meet the approval of a certain third person," Masorno said.

"Who?" Nolrien asked.

"Who cares?" Masorno shrugged.

Nolrien stared at Masorno a few moments, a muscle twitching in his jaw. Masorno shifted his weight and looked away. He cleared his throat, glanced at Nolrien a couple of times, then stared at the floor. "I know it's not the king. Some guard or something. Probably one of their elite ones, I'd imagine. Beyond that I really don't care, so I didn't ask, so harassing me isn't going to get you any more information. Will you take him—" he pointed at Adam— "and leave now? Please?"

Nolrien nudged Adam back down the wide stairs. Then he led the way into a side corridor. Adam dogged his heels saying, "You used me."

"Yes," Nolrien said, his tone as flat and emotionless as ever.

Chapter 27

ADAM RESISTED THE URGE to punch Nolrien in the kidneys like he deserved. It probably would only get him beat to a bloody pulp. For all the times he'd been hit on the practice field, never once had he successfully hit back no matter how many times he tried.

He turned around and went back. Staying with Nolrien only made it that much harder not to hit him. Unfortunately, Nolrien followed. "Where do you think you're going? This morning's training isn't finished."

Adam didn't stop. "Then why did I clean up?"

He re-emerged into the corridor with the private rooms of the nobles. There was a lot of activity by Andreno's, a lot of servants coming and going. Almost as many as ran up and down the stairs at the end with Masorno's luggage.

Nolrien grabbed his arm, pulling him to a stop and saying, "If you'd smelled, Masorno would have used that as an excuse to get rid of you instead of giving me the information I was after."

Adam jerked his arm away. He stayed where he was, refusing to look Nolrien in the eye. Using a quiet voice he said, "I do not like being used."

"No?" Nolrien's tone remained flat. "Then why are you a soldier in a war? Hmm? Why are you here for Andreno to use as a decoration?"

"I am his interpreter," Adam said.

"And how often does he use you for that?"

Adam clenched a fist, the temptation to hit Nolrien growing stronger with every passing second. Then Tabissia entered the corridor with a stately woman about the same age and about as pretty, along with Marietta and a couple of other women dressed as maids.

Marietta caught Adam and Nolrien's eyes as they passed. She smiled. Nolrien's flat look softened into something more human. Then they were gone, entering Sanbralio's rooms. Nolrien continued looking in their direction.

Adam took the chance to walk away. The closest place to escape to was Andreno's rooms. Not ideal. But close enough Nolrien might not try and stop him again to harass him about going back to the practice field.

When he walked in, Andreno grinned at him. "There you are. Did you finish talking with Ziegfried already?"

That reminded Adam that Ziegfried had wanted him. He quickly made up an excuse. "I came to you first. Then I'll go see what he wants."

"Ah, how very respectful." Andreno slapped Kurlos on the arm. "You see? He's learning manners. I told you he could."

Kurlos looked down his nose at Adam. "We'll see how long it lasts."

Adam looked around at everyone scurrying around, far too reminiscent of Masorno's room. "Why is everyone packing?"

Kurlos' sneer turned smug. "That didn't last long."

"Oh, stop," Andreno said with a laugh. He came to Adam and put an arm around his shoulder. Adam did his best not to cringe at the unwanted touch while Andreno talked at him. "Now don't be too disappointed, but I'm leaving for a while. It'll only be for a few weeks. Then you can have me back."

A page ran in with a note. Kurlos walked over and took it, drawing Andreno's attention. That not only spared Adam from having to respond, but it got Andreno's arm off his shoulders. Good thing too, because the only response Adam could think of was to shove him away.

Kurlos read the note then handed it to Andreno saying, "Your granduncle wants you."

Andreno laughed. "Sure he does. Wants me gone maybe. I'm sure it's just to bid me farewell."

He left the room motioning for Adam to join him. In the corridor he talked as he walked to the other end. "You'll have to occupy yourself while I'm gone, what with most of your people being away except the communication people."

Adam started in surprise. "What are you talking about?"

"I'm talking about Ziegfried going back to Gerhardt," Andreno said. "It's been three months since the last trade with your country. Time to trade again. Normally I go with him. Except last time. And this time. This time I'll be in Brend."

"Like Masorno?" Adam asked.

Someone cleared their throat. Adam looked over. Nolrien was still following him and now was shaking his head.

"What was that about Masorno?" Andreno asked. They reached Sanbralio's rooms. He said, "Hold that until I finish in here. Then tell me."

The guards posted at the door didn't move. They didn't stop him or bar the way. But they didn't open it either. He stood there for a moment. Then he put his hands on his hips and said to them. "Well? Open the door and announce me."

They looked away. One of them stuck his finger in his ear and wiggled it around as if he'd suddenly gone deaf. Kurlos clucked his tongue with disgust and reached for the door handle.

The guards blocked him. One of them said, "He's spending time with Lady Tabissia and Charlass. Don't interrupt."

Nolrien cleared his throat again. The door guards glanced at him. He said, "Andreno has been summoned. Let him in."

The door guards stopped blocking. One of them glared at Adam. "The filthy mountain barbarian should stay out here."

Kurlos smirked at that and opened the door. Andreno frowned, not looking so amused. He said, "Just for that, I'm bringing him in. You don't get to order me around. And he's not from the mountains."

Kurlos opened the door and loudly announced, "Prince Andreno for our Esteemed Leader Prince Sanbralio, as summoned."

Andreno gave Adam a push across the threshold of the room. Then he swept past him and opened his arms wide. "Uncle! How are you feeling this morning? Better I hope."

Sanbralio sat limp in a chair in front of a blazing fire. The stately woman with Tabissia stood by him, her hands folded in front of herself, her eyes downcast. Tabissia stood by the fire. She curled her upper lip at Andreno. "You should practice that little speech in front of a mirror until you don't look and sound so excited that he's ill."

Andreno pointed at the stately woman. "What's Charlass doing here?"

"I enjoy her company," Sanbralio slurred as he spoke. He looked up. His glassy eyes looked past Andreno to Adam. His lips spread in a small smile and he pointed. "You. Come closer."

Adam swallowed. Wary, he obeyed, stopping one step to the side and behind Andreno. Sanbralio said, "You're with Andreno a lot. And I've heard you stand up to him. You must be a nobleman's son. Who's your father?"

"Uncle," Andreno said. He put out his arm, gesturing for Adam to step back. "He's a foreigner. An interpreter. Remember? The one you ordered to get dagger lessons?"

"That's ridiculous. I don't order things like that," Sanbralio said. He beckoned Adam closer again. This time Adam didn't move. Had the old prince gone mad? Sanbralio shifted until his slouch leaned him slightly in Adam's direction. "Are you looking for a wife?"

Adam shook his head, backing up a couple more steps. Maybe Sanbralio was drunk. Adam looked around the room. There were no cups or goblets. No wine bottles, empty, open, or otherwise. No kegs. No signs at all that he'd been drinking. Not even the smell of alcohol in the room.

Sanbralio took the stately woman by the hand and said, "My granddaughter Charlass is free to marry. She has a guaranteed place in this palace. If you take her for wife, you can live here too. And then you can speak rudely to Andreno whenever you want and he wouldn't have the ability to toss you out. Doesn't that sound wonderful?"

Charlass stiffened and gently removed her hand from the old man's. Tabissia said, "Highness, that's tactless. You shouldn't try and set people up like that."

"Yes!" Andreno lifted his chin. "Not just tactless, but plain rude. Did you summon me just to show me how you're trying to undermine my future rule of this country?"

"I was talking about it being tactless to him." Tabissia pointed to Adam. "And I sent the summons. I want to know why you're packing. Where do you think you're going?"

"You don't get to summon me," Andreno said.

"You're going somewhere?" Sanbralio sat up slightly.

"To Brend," Andreno said. "You told me last spring when I came home early that I could go back when the princess had her birthday gala this fall."

"Oh, by all means, leave," Tabissia said. Her eyes narrowed. "Run away when your Prince is ill. Show how much concern you truly have for him by abandoning him. Prove to everyone that you didn't cause his illness by going to a celebration."

Andreno balled his fists. "Who told you I caused his illness?"

"You made me sick?" Sanbralio slouched further down and stared at the fire. "Figures. Easy to get rid of me that way."

"I didn't make you sick," Andreno shouted. He snarled at Tabissia, "Who's saying I did? Are you the one spreading this rumor?"

"No," she said. "I don't have to spread it. Others are doing that quite well without me. And when you leave, I also won't have to spread rumors that you're running to create plausible deniability if the worst happens and you end up ascending the throne."

Adam backed away further, closer to where Marietta and a couple of the other women stood. She was still smiling, looking the last few feet at the door where Nolrien stood just inside the room. He wasn't looking at her. He was watching Andreno, his face as blank as ever.

Sanbralio halfway smiled at Andreno. "Leave. Yes. Go. I'll be happy to help spread rumors that you ran to hide because you made me sick."

Andreno glowered at Tabissia. "You arranged this well, leaving me without much of a choice."

Tabissia smirked and batted her eyes. "Why, your high and mightiness, whatever do you mean? Surely you must know I'm only looking out for your reputation, letting you know what others are saying behind your back."

"Denying me any pleasure," Andreno added when she stopped.

"Oh, silly me." Tabissia's tone went as flat as Nolrien's usually was. "I had thought your granduncle's illness had already done that."

"So," Sanbralio said. "How soon will you be gone?"

Andreno tucked his chin down, turning his voice into nearly a growl. "Apparently I'm not going anywhere."

"Oh." Sanbralio sank back down into his seat and stared into the fire. "That's too bad. I had thought to be rid of you for a while. Oh well. It is what it is. Tabissia my dear, I should talk to you about marrying Andreno. He needs a wife. And I like the way you talk to him. I think you'd be perfect."

Tabissia grinned with a closed mouth, almost making it look like a feral leer. Her eyes glinted with malice as she turned that leer on Andreno.

Andreno turned and stalked toward the door. The women with Marietta watched his every move. Andreno changed course and went to them with a hand raised. "What do you think you're staring at?"

He smacked the first one he reached. All three of them yelped and jumped back. He followed, raising his hand again.

Adam jumped between them, shoving Andreno back. Andreno skipped a couple of hopping steps, eyes wide with shock. His mouth worked open and closed. As soon as he stood stable he snapped his fingers at Nolrien, speaking in a squeak of a voice. "You, do something!"

Sanbralio laughed. He had turned sideways in his chair. Both his arms hung over the side. He clapped his hands, still laughing. He said, "Yes. Do something. Do that again. Push him harder so he falls on his butt!"

Andreno stomped over to the door. Nolrien opened it for him. He stomped out into the hall. Adam followed, making good his escape from the crazy prince Sanbralio. After what happened, Adam could almost feel bad for Andreno. Almost.

The door closed. Andreno whipped around, swinging his fist at Adam's face. Adam blocked without even thinking. When Nolrien grabbed his other arm, he realized he'd also raised his fist to hit back.

Andreno backed away, eyes smoldering. "You were going to hit me."

"I told you," Adam said. "If you hit me, I will hit you back."

Someone coughed. Andreno glanced at the noise. It was one of the door guards. He had a hand over his mouth and looked more like he was trying to hide laughter, not a cough.

Andreno looked back to Adam and said, "You need to cool your temper. Switch places with Strom. You go back to Gerhardt. He gets to stay here with me. That should give you some time to remember your place."

Chapter 28

ADAM WENT DOWN one flight. So did Nolrien. Adam did his best to ignore it and went to Ziegfried. No one barred the way, though he was half hoping they would. It would be a good excuse to hit someone. Either that or he could get back at Nolrien by telling them to keep him out.

Ziegfried looked over when Adam came in. He said, "There you are. I just sent a page looking for you. We need to make arrangements for the next few weeks."

"Because you're going back to base," Adam said. "There's been a change of plans."

"No, no." Ziegfried waved that away with as grandiose a gesture as Andreno or Sanbralio ever had. "This is scheduled. I have to be at Far Base every third month."

"You've been hanging around the noble snobs here too long," Adam said. "I wasn't talking about that. I was talking about Andreno staying here and—"

"Actually, he's not." Ziegfried held up a finger. "And I don't appreciate you taking that tone with me."

"What tone?"

"Stop interrupting." Ziegfried folded his hands behind his back and lifted his pudgy chin to look down his little nose. "Andreno is going to visit an important noble near the border of Brend, just like the last portal opening.

Or he'd be going with us to base as normal. Either way, you're going to be here at the palace with just the two radio operators."

"Andreno isn't going anywhere," Adam said. "That's part of the change in plans. The other part is he wants Strom to stay here, and me to go to base."

Strom stood from a seat in the corner where he sat with a woman. "Really?"

"That's ridiculous," Ziegfried said. "He doesn't order things like that."

Adam threw his hands in the air. "Why do people keep saying that? This isn't something I'd make up."

"I certainly hope not," Strom said. "Because it sounds like a great plan to me."

"It's not your decision," Ziegfried said.

"And it's not your decision either," Adam said.

"Of course it is," Ziegfried said. "I'm the one who's here."

"I'm going to the radio tower to talk to Gerhardt about this." Adam turned and walked back out.

Nolrien still followed him. At the base of the tower Adam turned on him. "Leave me alone!"

"No," Nolrien said.

"Don't you have anything better to do?" Adam asked. "Like scare small children or pick on the elderly?"

"Or make sure no one beats on you for touching Andreno," Nolrien said.

"Who?" Adam asked. "Sanbralio laughed. And the guards don't seem to like him much. Or respect him."

"Doesn't mean they won't hurt you for it," Nolrien said. "Just because they don't like Andreno, don't think they won't do their job and protect him. Or obey him if he decides to make you suffer."

"As if you would stop them from hurting me," Adam muttered.

"As long as I'm following you around," Nolrien said, "they'll think you're being escorted and watched. They're more likely to leave you alone thinking that if you needed punished, I'd do the dirty work."

"Which you would," Adam said.

"Absolutely I would." Nolrien's tone was as flat as ever. "So don't do anything else that earns you punishment."

There wasn't any point in arguing further. Adam climbed the stairs to the radio room. He was so annoyed he didn't bother with any courtesies like knocking and waiting for permission to enter.

The guy currently on shift and manning the com equipment jumped up with a start and a guilty expression. He quickly slapped shut a thick book and whipped it behind his back.

"New message for the Oberst," Adam said. "Andreno is staying here because Sanbralio is sick, and he wants Strom to stay with him instead of me. I'm going back to base with Ziegfried for the portal opening."

"Right. Of course. I'll get right on it." The com guy stuffed the book under a stack of papers before turning to the equipment.

As the guy fiddled with his dials and switches and went through the protocols of raising base, Adam sidled over to the stack of papers. Did this guy have a forbidden book too? Unable to get the better of curiosity, Adam lifted the stack just enough to get a glimpse.

It was a Bible. Not forbidden. Rare on this side of the portal but certainly not forbidden. Then Adam caught sight of the name 'Gruber' etched on the bottom right corner. Jorgan was the only 'Gruber' Adam knew, and he certainly had lost a Bible.

Adam yanked the book out from under the papers. That got the radio guy's attention. He jumped out of his chair, lunging to grab at the Book. "Put that back!"

Adam held the Bible back, out of the man's reach. "Does Hauptmann Gruber know you have this?"

"He's a religious man. He's supposed to forgive. He'll understand."

"You *stole* a Bible?"

"No! Give it back!" The man lunged again.

Adam pushed him away. "You stole a *Bible*!"

"I'm taking good care of it." The man doubled his fists, stepping back in. Adam shot out his hand, flat open, smacking the guy in the nose. He grunted and bent forward covering it with his hands. His eyes teared up. "Ow! That smarts!"

"Serves you right. Stealing a Bible. How depraved can you get?"

"I didn't mean to." The man's words were muffled by the hands on his nose. "I borrowed it, and it sort of didn't get put back."

Adam backed to the door, nearly running over Nolrien. "It's getting put back now."

Whoever was on the other end of the communication transmission was squawking, demanding to know why there was no response. The com guy glanced at it and said, "You can't leave until this is done. What if they want to talk to you? Or ask you questions? Or issue different orders?"

"Handle it." Adam backed the rest of the way out of the room and started down the stairs.

The com guy called down to him, "Tell Gruber I'm sorry."

"Tell him your damned self," Adam growled up at him.

He left the tower and stomped all the way to his room. Nolrien still followed. Then he stuck his foot in the way when Adam tried shutting the door in his face.

"Leave me alone," Adam told him.

Instead of answering, Nolrien pushed his way in. "Those were good moves you used. But I somehow doubt that's normal procedure for your method of communicating."

"It is not a matter that concerns you." Adam pulled his sack out and stowed the Bible with his language dictionaries.

"That book is different than the others you have," Nolrien said. "Why?"

"Because it is a different book."

"And why are you so riled over it?"

"He stole it!"

"Ah, I see." Nolrien nodded. He leaned his shoulder against the wall. "And because you took back stolen property you're not worried about getting in trouble?"

Adam froze. He hadn't thought of that. Nolrien said, "Or are you now that you're calmer?"

Adam looked up at him. "I have to give this book back to the man it belongs to."

"Who is that?"

"My friend. His name is Jorgan."

"Hauptmann Jorgan Gruber. I remember him. I still think you people are strange, wearing three names and all. You're what, Loitnint Adam Vise?"

He pronounced it as terribly as everyone else here. Out of habit, Adam repeated it correctly. "Leutnant Adam Weiss."

Nolrien shook his head. "Marietta said you told her everyone in your family wears the name Weiss. What is the Leutnant name?"

"My rank in the military." Adam closed his bag with hands that were slightly shaky. Now that he had released some of his mad he could think more clearly.

"That makes more sense," Nolrien said. "You're always so worried about getting in trouble. You think you will for all this?"

"I may very well get in trouble for hitting him."

"Explaining about the stolen property won't help?"

"No, not really," Adam said. "Not if Jorgan doesn't want people to know he has it."

"Afraid someone else might steal it?"

"Uh…" Should Adam explain that some books were forbidden, and others were frowned upon? Then he thought of something else. He put a hand over his eyes.

"Now what?" Nolrien asked.

"I will have to explain why Andreno wanted me to leave," Adam said. "Which will bring up that he was mad because he is not going to Brend, which will disappoint Gerhardt. He wants contact with Brend."

"Will you get in trouble even more for missing an opportunity there?"

"I do not know." Adam hung his head. He put his sack back under the bed. Then he just sat there. "Maybe."

Nolrien remained quiet until Adam pulled himself off the floor to sit on the bed. Then Nolrien asked "What if I help you out there?"

"Why would you do that? And why?"

"A few reasons," Nolrien said. "Admittedly, some of them are self-serving. But if it works, we'll both benefit."

"If what works?"

"I can write you a letter of recommendation," Nolrien said.

"Who would I take it to?"

"You don't. I send it directly to the Brendish General. If he decides to look into the recommendation he'll find you and test you for qualification. If you pass, he'll offer to train you for a minimum of five years."

"I cannot train with another General," Adam said. "I am already in the military for my country."

"That's where some of the benefits come in," Nolrien said. His voice was animated for once. No flat tone here. "During those five years, and after if you want, I imagine he'll train you to work as a link between his country and yours. That's how I was trained. They'll test you for other skills as well."

"When would this qualification test happen?" Adam asked.

"That I don't know," Nolrien said. "First, I'd send with you a letter for your Gerhardt asking permission to send that recommendation. The General won't accept men under another's command without their permission first. Then, there's really no telling. And if he tests you, it's unlikely you'll recognize it as a test until it's over and he tells you whether you passed or failed. You may not even meet him first if he sends someone else to check you out and test you instead."

"And why would you do this for me?"

"First, you have the courage you'd need to work for him, proven by the fact that I couldn't drive you away from dagger lessons." Nolrien held up fingers as he ticked off his points. "Second, I respect you risking getting in trouble to help your friend. Third, I appreciate what you did for Marietta. Fourth, the Brendish are always after me for information. If you're stationed here after being trained by them, they might bug me less. And if you pass, then I get credit for finding you, which comes in the form of money."

Adam sat there, stunned silent. He could understand the part about getting a finder's fee. But Nolrien could have just said that part and left off everything else.

"Well?" Nolrien held out a hand, palm turned up. "Do you want the letter asking Gerhardt's permission or not?"

This might just earn Adam enough favor that Gerhardt would overlook his temper flares today. Adam nodded. "Yes. Absolutely."

"Do you want to hand deliver it?" Nolrien asked. "Or would it be better if I sent it right away?"

Perhaps opening that door ahead of time would soften the news of Adam's behavior. He said, "You can send it now."

Chapter 29

ADAM'S DISMISSAL TOOK EFFECT IMMEDIATELY. Since he hadn't received orders to attend Ziegfried, and neither he nor his bodyguards seemed to care, Adam avoided them. He still had to go to dagger lessons in the mornings. After lunch, he was free to do as he pleased. And he pleased to return to his window seat, enjoying the conversations buzzing around him and watching the comings and goings from the front gate.

Nolrien still hung about like a shadow. But he didn't interfere, didn't interact. So Adam ignored him rather than trying and failing to get him to go away.

When Andreno paced up and down the wide corridor calling for doctors to come tend his uncle he wouldn't even look in Adam's direction. Which was fine. Then no one else looked at him either. They carried on their various conversations as if he wasn't there and he listened in, drinking in the variations of their accents and speech patterns.

Come to think of it, that pretty girl from Brend had used a completely different accent. All the Brendish had. The Shontese talked mostly using the front of the mouth and the tip of the tongue. The Brendish talked slightly further back than that, not quite in the middle of the mouth. It flattened out some of the vowel sounds. In comparison, it was like an American accent as opposed to a Spanish one. If he went to Brend for whatever person Nolrien wanted to recommend him to, he would have to make sure to alter his accent and pronunciation of the language. If no one could tell he was a foreigner by his speech patterns, he had the language perfect.

Charlass passed by the window seat with Tabissia, Marietta, and a couple of others, on their way to Sanbralio's rooms again. They all looked Adam in the eye. And they smiled as they did so. Conversations continued around them as they did around Adam, as if they didn't exist. He had to wonder if they listened in as much as he was. Then he dismissed the notion. What reason would they have for that? It wasn't like they were studying their own language to learn how to speak it better.

After almost a week of sitting in the window seat being generally ignored, some of the talk in the corridor turned to talk of Andreno's foreign friend packing to leave. That was the same day Masorno returned. All the talk shifted to speculation on why he'd returned before the Brendish Princess' birthday gala, a topic he wouldn't elaborate on.

From there, it turned to predictions of which magicians Masorno would bring in to diagnose and possibly heal Sanbralio. Some talked about Masorno being close friends from someone sitting in a white seat, whatever that meant. Everyone else seemed to know what it meant and talked like it was significant and could be extremely beneficial to Sanbralio.

That was the day Andreno finally stopped ignoring Adam. He walked right up to the window seat with his stupid, politician smile and said, "Adam. There you are."

Adam just looked at him, trying to keep his expression as flat as Nolrien's. If focusing on that kept him from talking, then he wouldn't have to bite his tongue to keep from mouthing off. Andreno had walked by Adam many times in the past week. He couldn't possibly not know where he was, so the pretense was idiotic.

"Oh, now don't look at me like that," Andreno said, so Adam's efforts to keep his expression flat must not have worked. "I've sent you away for your own good, and you know it."

"What do you want?" Adam asked.

"I want you to let Ziegfried know that he should leave a day or two early, like this afternoon or tomorrow morning," Andreno said. "The weather scryers are predicting rain within a week, and it'll make the roads difficult. The sooner he leaves, the better for his journey."

"I'll deliver the message," Adam said.

Andreno nodded once. Then he left without any further acknowledgment. Adam rolled his eyes and looked out the window at the latest batch of people coming in through the front gate.

A couple of minutes passed. Then Nolrien asked, "You're not running off to deliver Andreno's message?"

Adam shrugged. "Ziegfried won't leave this afternoon. If he even bothers to notice I'm around. I'll tell one of his bodyguards at supper this evening. Maybe we'll leave sometime tomorrow."

Nolrien said nothing more. A group of giggling women passed up the corridor, gossiping about who would be best to marry Andreno and become the next Shontese Princess. Another group out the window left through the front gate. Then Masorno came to Adam.

"You need to leave," he said. "You and your magician and you people. All of you. Leave. Aren't you supposed to go back to that castle about now anyway?"

"Yes," Adam said. "Ziegfried is packing now to leave."

"Good," Masorno said. "See if you can get him to leave this afternoon. I'm contacting a close friend of mine, the white seat of the gathering, and you all have to be gone when he gets here."

"So he doesn't find out about Andreno's 'bad magic using' friend that you allowed to stay here?" Adam asked, thinking Masorno might backpedal, not remember that he'd used those words himself.

"Yes!" Masorno didn't even hesitate. "The white seat is the best healer I know of since our mentor died. I need him to come figure out what's ailing Sanbralio and heal him. Aside from that, I need to speak with him concerning Jerryck's behavior while I was in Brend. And you all have to be gone by the time he gets here. If you're not, I'll have to take action. Which means I'll kill you all."

He stalked away, as if he thought the threat was enough. Adam shook his head and looked out the window again. Nolrien muttered, "Interesting."

"Not really," Adam said.

"Certainly it is," Nolrien said. "It's a very rare occasion that Andreno and Masorno are in agreement on something. Especially when that something is the whereabouts of Andreno's associates. Masorno has taken great pains to keep Ziegfried's presence from being known. And now it appears that Andreno is as well. Exactly how many jobs has Ziegfried done for Andreno that magicians wouldn't approve of, I wonder."

"I have no idea," Adam said. "Why does that even matter?"

Nolrien regarded him for a few moments, his face flat, eyes blank. Then he said, "I guess I'll have to recommend you either be passed for training on information gathering, or taught the importance of noticing nuance. Come. I'll go with you to get your Ziegfried moving. Masorno wasn't kidding about his threat to kill you."

"As if he could," Adam said.

"Don't rely on your superior long-range weapons to save you," Nolrien said. "He'd use magic, not might. And I doubt you know how to defend against that. Come."

Andreno had been right about the weather. For the first two days of the journey the sky was clear. Then the clouds blew in and it rained during most of the rest of the trip from the palace to Far Base. They struggled to move the wagons down muddy, rutted roads, pulled by animals that bit or kicked at every opportunity. No fire stayed lit. That made all of the meals cold travel rations. The nights carried the chill of approaching autumn. Almost everyone acquired sniffles and coughs before the trip was halfway complete.

When they finally rolled in through the gate to the base, Adam nearly cheered. He grabbed his sack from under the tarp that protected the contents of the baggage wagon. All the Brass met them, droning words of insincere welcome at Ziegfried. Other men in important jobs lined up in perfect rows, looking like they'd done a spit polish before come out to get drenched in the pouring rain. Kiefer was absent. Jorgan smiled. Doc Lieber began immediate examinations of all the coughs. Helmut bounced around in muddy boots and a grin from ear to ear, waving at everyone arriving.

"Where's Kiefer?" Ziegfried looked around with a little bit of a pout.

"In my office," Gerhardt said.

"What for?" Ziegfried asked. "For how long?"

"For insubordination," Gerhardt said. "For however long it takes me to get back there and give him an appropriate reprimand, which should be just long enough to tell him he's confined to quarters. And before you ask, no, you may not visit him during confinement."

Ziegfried pouted more. "Why does he always manage to get into trouble just when I'm around?"

"I assure you—" Gerhardt said, "—it's not just when you're around."

Adam went inside and up to the second floor. He walked into his room there and caught his breath. Every inch of vertical space had been wall-papered with Helmut's drawings.

Jorgan came to the doorway. "Oh, no. Helmut must have come back in here after I went to bed last night. I made him take most of these down."

"It's okay." Adam smiled. "I like his drawings. Did he ever figure out how to bind them into a book?"

"Yes." Jorgan opened the drawer in Adam's little bedside table, showing a leather-bound book Adam hadn't ever seen before. "Don't tell him I showed it to you. He wanted you to find it and be surprised."

"Speaking of a surprise book—" Adam dug into his bag, drawing out the Bible. "I have one for you."

Jorgan's mouth dropped open. Then he closed it and swallowed. He reached out and took it with all the reverence Kiefer had handled Adam's forbidden book. He held it sandwiched between both his hands and stared at the closed pages.

Adam broke the silence. "The guy who had is said he's sorry."

"I don't care who had it," Jorgan's voice was nearly a whisper. He opened it, flipping through the pages until they stopped on a photograph of a pretty lady, exactly like the Helmut-drawn picture on his wall. Jorgan smiled. His eyes filled. "She's still here."

Kiefer came to the doorway. He saw the Bible and the picture. Saying nothing, he motioned Adam to come out to him in the hall.

Adam stepped out of the room. "I heard you were in trouble again."

"As always." Kiefer smirked. "I'm supposed to go to my room. On my way, first, I'm supposed to tell you that Gerhardt wants you and some dagger you acquired in his office as soon as possible. Second, where did you find that?"

He pointed back into the room at Jorgan, the Bible, and the photo. Adam said, "One of the guys stationed at the palace had it."

"And he gave it to you without a fuss? Who was it?"

Jorgan stepped out into the hall with them. "Doesn't matter."

Helmut entered the corridor and barreled toward them with outstretched arms. "Adam! I missed you!"

Adam stood there, allowing Helmut whatever greeting the big man wanted to give. Helmut wrapped his meaty arms around him, lifted him off the floor, and squeezed the breath out of him.

Kiefer laughed. "Stop, Helmut. Put him down. You're going to crush him, you big galoot."

"I fixed up your room special just for you." Helmut put Adam back on his feet and released him. "Do you like it?"

"It looks great," Adam gasped. "Thanks."

Helmut tugged at him. "Come on in. I'll show you which ones I like best."

Jorgan headed him off. "You like all of them best."

"And he doesn't have time right now anyway," Kiefer said. "Ernest wants to talk to him."

"Oh." Helmut looked down at the floor, crestfallen. Then he brightened and looked up again. "I'll show *you* which ones I like best."

"You've already shown me," Kiefer said. "Every single one of them is your favorite. And I have to go to my room."

Helmut cocked his head. "Are you in trouble again?"

"Of course I am." Kiefer winked at him. He said to Adam, "You better get going."

Adam nodded. He had the dagger on him so he didn't even have to go back into his room to fetch it. He made his way across the castle to the room Gerhardt used as an office.

"Sit," Gerhardt told him as soon as he entered. The Oberst didn't even look up at him. He dug through a drawer and produced a piece of paper with writing in the native language. He said, "This came. Do you know about it?"

"Is that the letter from Nolrien?" Adam asked.

"Yes," Gerhardt said. "Keifer translated it, so you can expect him to ask you about it. What have you been doing in those dagger lessons you're getting?"

"Getting knocked around mostly." Adam picked up the letter and read it.

OBERST ERNEST GERHARDT
A CORRESPONDENCE FROM GUARD NOLRIEN
BRENDISH PALACE ELITE SENIOR RANK
AT STATION IN SHONTESE PALACE OF QUEXIN

Greetings,

You have under your command one Loitnint Adam Vise. I am his tutor for handling a blade he acquired. He is an exceptional student, one of the best I have ever had. He would do well to train with another who can teach him more. I ask your permission to recommend him to my associates. If tested and accepted he will go to Brendish Palace of Coraline for training.

"Wow." Adam set the letter back on the desk. "That's... um... wow. That's pretty terse. And he spelled my name wrong."

"Kiefer said it's transliterated, spelled the way it sounds when the natives pronounce it," Gerhardt said. Adam frowned. Nolrien had spelled Gerhardt's name and rank correctly. Gerhardt asked, "Is this his handwriting?"

"I haven't seen him write, so..." He trailed off. "He never said anything to me about being ranked among the Brendish Palace Elite. He just said he trained there for a while."

"But you knew he would send me this letter?" Gerhardt asked.

Adam nodded. "He asked me."

"Show me the dagger," Gerhardt said. Adam laid it on the desk, sheath and all. Gerhardt's eyes barely even flicked to it. "You were instructed to wear it at all times?"

"Most of the time. I don't take it to those lessons."

"Where you mostly get knocked around?"

"Yes, sir."

"Have you learned a lot?"

"Some."

"Do you show talent? Eagerness? What?"

"It's a little hard to be eager or talented while I'm picking myself up off the ground and counting all the stars floating in and out of my vision."

"You had to have said or done something that made an impression. Think."

"I keep coming back for the lessons?"

"I doubt that's it." Gerhardt leaned forward, interlacing his fingers on his desk. "What did he say when he asked to send this?"

"He said he's doing me a favor," Adam said, almost in a mumble. "To try and help me stay out of trouble."

Gerhardt narrowed his eyes. "What trouble?"

Adam spilled it. All of it. Everything that had happened that day. He recounted it as if he had been called in for a debriefing. When he finally finished, Gerhardt leaned back in his chair. His interlaced fingers now rested on his stomach.

"You found Jorgan's Bible?" Gerhardt asked.

Adam nodded. His throat was closing up while he hoped he didn't get in trouble after all. Gerhardt said, "And your teacher doesn't want you to get in trouble because you're one of his best students?"

"I think he's lying about that part," Adam said. "I think he's having a fling or something with a woman I helped there at the palace."

"You're not in trouble." Gerhardt picked up the letter and filed it back in his drawer while Adam held back a sigh of relief. "As for the radio operator, you hitting him over this theft is much more lenient that what Velig would have done. I'm not pleased that you upset Andreno, but considering his nature it was bound to happen sooner or later."

"I'll apologize to him as soon as I return," Adam said.

"He'll get over it if he's distracted enough in the meanwhile. Don't bring it up if he doesn't." Gerhardt steepled his fingers. "You know I've been looking for an opening to a line of communication with Brend."

"Yes, sir."

"Do you have anything against this arrangement, going there to train with someone else?"

"No, sir."

"Good. Then I won't have to order you to do this. I'm writing a letter back to Nolrien and giving permission for him to send that recommendation."

Chapter 30

A SOLDAT CAME UP THE HALL. "Is Hauptmann Jorgan Gruber available?"

"No." Adam leaned against the wall outside Jorgan's room. Keifer stood in his open doorway nearby, their conversation interrupted. "Go away."

"How much do you need?" The Soldat drew close, glancing back and forth between Adam and Kiefer. "To let me through, what do you want? I can get my hands on a lot of stuff."

Adam just stared at him. Did he think they would take bribes or something? Was he going to start naming specific contraband items next? Just how far would this guy go? How much would he risk?

"Listen." The man nearly whispered now. "Someone's got to get a message through to the other side. The supplies that are fueling the war machine back home, they're not coming from here. We're not sending back enough."

"Noticed that, did you?" Kiefer rolled his eyes. "And what exactly do you think that means?"

"We're here for some reason other than supplies. Because those have got to be coming from someplace else. There has to be some other world out there somewhere, like this one."

"That's not what it means, moron." Kiefer laughed, short and sharp. "It means that's one of the reasons they said no communications to home. What do you think they would do to the good Hauptmann if he tried to pass that message on through? He's not stupid. It's not going to happen."

"No, there has to be other worlds," the man insisted. "I figure that's why they made us remove all our symbols. In case we run into someone from another world who doesn't like us, or is against the cause of the Fatherland."

"You'd best leave," Adam said. "Before Gerhardt learns what you're trying to do."

"Before Hauptmann Gruber comes out here and catches you," Kiefer added. "He's a stickler for rules. If you talk to him, Gerhardt will absolutely find out. You'll have burning duty for the entire next year."

Jorgan's door opened. Kiefer gasped, exaggerating the gesture with a jump and a hand to his breast. Milking the moment further, he grabbed the Soldat and ran back down the corridor with him. "Quick! Run! Save yourself!"

"What was that?" Jorgan asked.

"Kiefer taking advantage to laugh at some idiot," Adam said.

They went down to the first floor to the same rigmarole as before. They waited outside the locked doors to the mess hall, listening to the crackling fire within. One of Ziegfried's bodyguards came and told them it was safe. Gerhardt unlocked the door. They all went in. Jorgan went through the portal. Crates on hand trucks were exchanged. Adam and Kiefer double checked the crates with native writing. A dozen or so men crossed through to their side, some of them rather wobbly. Jorgan came back. The portal was shut down.

Gerhardt started the same welcome speech as last time. He got about halfway through when the wobbliest of the new men bent over and puked. Doc Lieber took the situation in hand. Gerhardt finished the speech as if nothing had happened. Jorgan and Helmut went off to count inventory. The new men were filed out. Everyone else put the room back in order. Grippe told Adam to go make sure he was ready to leave with Ziegfried for the palace first thing in the morning. And all that took up most of the day.

When the call for supper sounded a couple of hours later, Kiefer and Adam walked down the hall together heading for the main stairs down to the mess hall. They got as far as the landing where Kiefer stopped dead in his tracks.

221

Ziegfried stood there, rosy cheeked, back straight, and wide awake. Jorgan was behind him, looking confused. Ziegfried pointed at Kiefer, crowing triumphantly. "Aha! You see, Jorgan! He's free. We can have supper together after all."

"You're awake." Kiefer stared at Ziegfried the way he might have looked at a picture painted with poop. "Does Gerhardt know you're awake?"

"What does that matter?" Ziegfried tipped his nose up in the air. It reminded Adam of Prince Sanbralio before his son died. "I'm not inviting him. I'm inviting you."

"Aren't you tired at all?" Jorgan tapped him on the shoulder. "Maybe you should rest a bit just to be certain. At least until Helmut finds Gerhardt and we can talk to him."

Ziegfried flicked Jorgan's hand away with a sneer of disdain. He put an arm around Kiefer's shoulders. Kiefer cringed as though a slimy, human-sized slug had just wrapped around him.

"Now, now," Ziegfried said. "Don't you worry. I don't mind touching you. That's not going to sully me. And you can rise above your blood, I assure you. Especially now that you don't have any family holding you back and weighing you down."

Kiefer turned and kicked Ziegfried right in the crotch, his face twisted with rage. Ziegfried squeaked and doubled over clutching his family jewels. As his face went down, Kiefer raised his knee to meet it. The two connected with a loud whack. Ziegfried flipped over backwards.

Adam shook off his shock enough to grab Kiefer, locking arms around him from behind and pulling him back. Kiefer squatted down just enough to get out of Adam's grip, turned around, and swung at him. Adam angled himself back and swiped Kiefer's fist away. He was a lot easier to deflect than Nolrien.

Helmut burst out of the command corridor with Gerhardt behind him. He looked down at Ziegfried, bloody nose, still squeaking, still holding himself, crying and rolling around on the floor in a pudgy little ball. Helmut's mouth opened in a little 'oh' shape, and he looked wide eyed at Kiefer. "What did you do?"

"Not enough!" Kiefer turned back to Ziegfried. He raised a foot over his head. "I'll kill him!"

Gerhardt stepped between the two, pushing Kiefer back. "We need him."

"I don't care if we're stuck here forever." Kiefer pushed back, but put his foot down on the floor. "I don't care if we never get another portal open ever again. I hate him!"

"You're going to strip family from every man here?" Gerhardt took Kiefer by the arm, hauling him roughly back into the hall, but speaking kind and gentle. "You want to explain to Jorgan why he'll never see his wife again? You going to do that to him?"

Jorgan peeled Ziegfried off the floor and supported him while he hobbled toward the infirmary whimpering. A few men had gathered at the bottom of the stairs that led up to the third floor. Every one of them gaped.

"What are you all staring at?" Adam shouted at them. "Get down to supper or skip it."

They thundered past at a dead run. That left Helmut and Adam alone on the landing. Helmut trembled, biting his nails.

"Kiefer is naughty," he said.

"Gerhardt will take care of him," Adam told him. "Don't you worry. Let's get you something to eat. It might make you feel better."

He took Helmut down to the mess hall. Several tables fell silent when the two of them came in. Whispers hissed across the tables as they passed. Adam got Helmut eating then went back upstairs. With the lump in his stomach the very thought of food didn't settle well.

Kiefer's door was shut. Gerhardt's voice rumbled quietly inside. Adam when to his room. He dug out some paper and scribbled on it, doodling by writing out several different words for anger, their synonyms, their homilies, their translations. He'd only filled about half the page when Jorgan came.

"Ziegfried wants you," he said.

Adam scribbled some more. "Ziegfried can go to hell."

"He wants your company for supper. I'll be there too so deal with it."

"I'm not hungry."

"Me neither." Jorgan reached over and plucked the pencil from Adam's fingers. "Let's go."

With a sigh, Adam followed Jorgan to the parlor Ziegfried liked so much. His nose was swollen and he walked like his private parts were made of glass.

His little nose pointed up with a snoot, and he stood in a posture that again reminded Adam of Prince Sanbralio. Other than that, he acted like his usual, talkative self as he expounded on his cleverness and many virtues.

Jorgan didn't bother grunting or responding in a way that made it seem he listened. He put an elbow on the table, rested his chin on his hand, pushed uneaten food around on his plate, and looked thoroughly bored.

Since Ziegfried didn't seem to notice Jorgan's lack of response, Adam didn't bother with it either. He used his fork to pick threads out of his napkin, imagining how long it would take Ziegfried to cry like a little baby if he plucked every hair one by one out of the pudgy little man's head.

Gerhardt came in about halfway through the meal. He looked down on Ziegfried. "What's changed?"

"Apparently nothing." Ziegfried daintily plucked up a forkful, chewing carefully and swallowing before saying anything more. "I had hoped Kiefer would get over the past by now. Not to worry. I'll give him more time. I won't hold this against him."

"I meant with you," Gerhardt said. "Usually you're out cold after a portal transfer. This time you're awake."

"Oh that!" Ziegfried beamed with pride. "I tried a little experiment and it worked. I've been storing up extra energy in a charm. It worked quite well for this portal opening."

"Stay away from Kiefer."

"I can handle him," Ziegfried said. "I understand he loses control and goes a little animalistic at times. He can't help it. I'll just—"

"Stay away from him," Gerhardt repeated.

"I appreciate your concern for my safety, but—"

"You got what you deserved." Gerhardt rocked back on his heels. "Say something like that to him again and I'll beat you myself. I won't be as kind about it, though. This order has nothing to do with your safety. It has everything to do with Kiefer not having to put up with your callous stupidity. Stay away from him."

Ziegfried said nothing more for the rest of the meal. Adam and Jorgan left at the first possible excuse. Jorgan went to check on Kiefer. Adam went straight to bed anticipating a miserable trip the next morning.

Chapter 31

A SOLDAT ROUSED ADAM before sunup. The sky was murky with rain. He peered out the window at the outline of the hill, barely visible in the gray, pre-dawn drizzle. He still wanted to climb it to the top. He turned from the window and made one last check in his packed sack.

"Adam?" Kiefer came to his doorway.

"Morning." Adam closed his sack. "Didn't realize you were up this early."

"I asked to be wakened. I wanted to apologize for trying to hit you yesterday."

"Not a problem," Adam said.

"Yeah. It is. You're my friend. I don't have many of those."

"And it gave me a chance to try out what I've been learning," Adam said. "It's one thing to practice it over and over and over. It's something else to actually have it work when someone really is trying to hit you. So, honest, it's not a problem."

Leaving the awkward talk behind, Adam took his sack outside to the dirt yard between the wall and the castle front. While most of the base still slept, the wagons were packed and ready. The animals were hitched. Everyone going to the palace had gathered. Everyone except Ziegfried.

They waited for him while he dawdled. First the men got restless and fiddled with the baggage and their gear. No one wanted to make the journey, but the sooner they got started the sooner it would be over.

Then the animals got restless and the drivers had to work to keep them calm in their harnesses. An hour after the sun rose and the rest of the base woke, one of the native drivers demanded Adam go find out what the hold-up was or he would unhitch his animals.

Adam headed for the door to go inside and look for Ziegfried just right as he finally emerged with Gerhardt pushing him from behind. Adam strode up to him. "What's taking so long? Everyone's antsy and the natives are threatening to abort."

The smell of rinsed soap hit Adam's nose. He took a closer look at Ziegfried. "Why is your hair damp?"

"I had to have a bath," Ziegfried said. "It was my last chance before that filthy road."

"And you took the time to dry your hair instead of just dumping a bucket of water for a rinse and coming out?"

"I had to have breakfast after the bath." Ziegfried sauntered across the yard. "If I don't eat it throws off my blood sugar."

Gerhardt dogged his heels. "You don't have blood sugar problems. Hurry up."

"I'll end up with them if you don't stop hurrying me through meals or try to make me skip them altogether." Ziegfried circled the carriage, bending over to examine each wheel. Then he bent further to look underneath.

"What are you doing now?" Gerhardt asked.

"Inspecting," Ziegfried said. "I can't make a long journey without making sure of the quality of the vehicle."

"I already inspected," Gerhardt said. "So did a few others. There's no reason for you to. Stop delaying and get going."

"Hmmph," Ziegfried grunted, sticking his nose up a little. He opened the door to the carriage and put one foot inside. Then he put his foot back down on the ground. "Wait. I can't leave without saying goodbye to Kiefer."

Enough was enough. Adam grabbed his arm and shook him. "I am about two seconds from picking you up and tossing you in that carriage."

"Sir!" One of the radio men ran toward Gerhardt from the castle waving a piece of paper in the air.

Gerhardt read it over. He stared suspiciously at Ziegfried for a few moments. Ziegfried put a hand on his forehead looking a little bit too concerned. "Oh, my. Has something happened? What is it?"

"Unpack," Gerhardt called loudly to the entire caravan. "You're not going anywhere."

"Why not?" Ziegfried now looked a little bit too surprised, enunciating his words a little too well, as if rehearsed. "What's going on?"

Gerhardt ignored the question, calling for a meeting in his war room with everyone at the base with a significant job. Adam figured that included him.

Adam grabbed his sack, ran upstairs, chucked it onto his bed, then headed to the war room. Jorgan met him on the way, "What's going on?"

"Not sure," Adam said.

Others came in behind them. Jaws flapped in a speculative buzz. Everyone quieted when the Brass entered. Gerhardt waited until all attention was on him.

"Prince Sanbralio died late yesterday afternoon," he told the room. "He was sick. He took a nap and never woke up. His body was discovered after sundown. Since sundown cuts radio communication, they contacted us first thing this morning. The palace is locked down. Therefore so is this base, until we assess how this change in leadership will affect our situation here."

"The caravan is leaving, though," Ziegfreid said. "Right?"

"What part of locked down is unclear to you?" Gerhardt glared at him. "No one comes. No one goes."

"What about Andreno's gold?" Ziegfried's concern began to look a little more genuine.

"He'll get his gold once the lockdowns are lifted," Gerhardt said. He looked around the room at everyone else. "I expect all of you to inform everyone in your charge. You'll be informed when something relevant changes. Until then, dismissed."

People filed out. Ziegfried lingered. Irritated, Adam leaned over to him and muttered, "If you were so concerned about getting Andreno his gold maybe you shouldn't have dawdled. We'd already be gone."

"I didn't know the base would be locked down too," Ziegfried complained.

"Too?" Gerhardt asked. "Like you expected the palace to be locked down? Did you have prior knowledge this would happen? Or did you somehow have a hand in it?" Anger leaked into Gerhardt's face. He stepped in Ziegfried's way, keeping him from leaving while the room cleared. Then he said, "Tell me exactly what experiment you did that kept you awake after the portal yesterday."

"I already told you," Ziegfried said. "I've been storing up energy in a charm."

"Did you figure out how to draw energy from people without touching them? Is that how you had extra to store up?"

"No!" Ziegfried let out a laugh that sounded a little forced. "Absolutely not. Why would you think such a thing? That's ludicrous. I've told you before. It can't be done."

"Like opening a portal can't be done?" Gerhardt didn't look convinced. "And magic isn't real? And other worlds don't exist?"

Ziegfried crossed his arms with a scowl. "You're being unreasonable."

"Weiss," Gerhardt turned to Adam. "Has anyone at the palace showed any signs that he'd drained them? Anyone he hasn't touched?"

"Not that I'm aware of," Adam said.

"It wouldn't necessarily look like when he killed that guard that attacked you," Gerhardt said. "They might lose color in their skin, act like they're fighting a cold or the flu, get chills. What did Prince Sanbralio look like when he first took ill?"

"Just weak," Adam said. "Lethargic maybe? A little pale but not gray like that guard. He didn't lose all color in his skin, he still had some."

"Besides," Ziegfried said, turning up his nose. "I was here when he died. As impossible as it is to do what your claiming, what's the chance I could do it over this much distance? And even if by some miracle I did pull this off, what are you complaining about? This could be very beneficial for us. Andreno will have complete control over the country now. Including their military."

"Then he can stop asking me to go on a campaign for him," Gerhardt said.

Campaign? Andreno was trying to get Gerhardt to go on a campaign. Adam narrowed his eyes, wondering if that was what all those meetings were between Andreno and Ziegfried, the ones where they locked the door and shut out Adam and all of Andreno's bodyguards.

"No, no." Ziegfried chuckled and shook his head. "We should still go on that campaign. He now has control of the forces that could occupy land after we clear it out."

"I'm not taking anyone up into the mountains to murder innocent people." Gerhardt turned absolutely stony. Adam nearly swallowed his tongue to keep from asking what they were talking about. If Gerhardt didn't think Adam already knew, he probably wouldn't be talking this candidly. Good thing Adam hadn't said anything thus far.

"It's not murder," Ziegfried said. "This is war. It's collateral damage."

"Those people in the mountains are not at war with us." Gerhardt said. "It's murder. And an unnecessary risk to my men."

"What risk?" Ziegfried raised both his hands, palms up. "No one here can withstand our weapons."

"You don't know very much about military campaigns. Anything that can go wrong, will go wrong. Weapon superiority is never the ultimate factor on who will be the victor. It's just an advantageous edge," Gerhardt said. Then he said to Adam, "Weiss, go inform the palace guards that escorted you here of the death of their prince and the lock down. You'll need to be the go-between for them while they're stuck here."

"Yes, sir," Adam said, glad for the permission to leave the room.

The Brass put Adam on a rotation schedule. Every few days he had to take a turn keeping Ziegfried away from Kiefer. Other days, he had to keep Kiefer busy and away from Ziegfried. And every day between those duties he had to make time for the palace guards. That included practicing with his dagger with them. After only one practice he figured out that while Nolrien was harsh, his lessons were far superior.

The palace lockdown lifted after only a couple of days. It remained in force at the base. A few weeks passed. The days turned almost as chilly as the nights while radio communications informed them that nobles gathered at the palace from all over the country and beyond. Adam had a passing wish that he was there. If that pretty girl from Brend came again on her nobleman father's behalf, he was missing a chance to catch a glimpse of her.

The closer they got to the next scheduled caravan to bring in goods for the next portal, the more antsy the men got for the lockdown to lift. Finally, the brass held a meeting with key personnel that everyone hoped would be it. Gerhardt announced to them, "Andreno wants us to have more of a presence in the palace."

Ziegfried perked up. "I'll return immediately!"

"More than that," Gerhardt said. "If he just wanted representation, Strom and the radio personnel currently there would suffice. He wants command."

Ziegfried shrank in on himself a little. "Which means you?"

"Grippe's in charge of this base." Gerhardt pointed at individuals as he named them. "Velig keeps discipline and training in order here. That leaves me. Andreno wants us there as soon as possible. The coronation is today. We go there tomorrow."

"I'll open a portal," Ziegfried said.

"I thought portals were only for going between worlds," Grippe said.

"I can do it for quick travel to other places on the same world." Ziegfried puffed out his chest. "As long as I keep it to only a few people. Me, my bodyguards, Gerhardt, and of course Adam. Andreno will want him back. Everyone else will have to travel overland."

"And Hauptmann Gruber," Gerhardt said. "You can handle one more. Jorgan has made himself invaluable to me. I'll need him."

"How many times have you opened a portal that doesn't cross between two different worlds?" Grippe asked Ziegfried.

"I used to do it all the time back at home," Ziegfried said. "How do you think I convinced our Fuhrer that magic is real? He wanted me to use it for troop movements, until I convinced him that wasn't feasible with the numbers required."

"How many times have you done it here in this world?" Grippe asked.

"Not now," Gerhardt cut off the line of questioning. "Kiefer, inform the natives of the plans. Everyone else, get ready for tomorrow's departure."

As soon as the meeting ended, Jorgan went to his room to pack without so much as voicing his opinion on the matter. Adam pitched in to help him sort out all the odds and ends that had collected in his room over the past couple of years.

After a few hours of sorting, Helmut paced up and down the corridor, calling out, "Jorgan? Jorgan?"

"Ah, man," Jorgan said. "I was hoping to put this off longer."

"Jorgan?" Helmut stopped in Jorgan's doorway. His jaw dropped. His eyes widened in horror. "Oh no! Don't pack! It's not true!"

"What's not true?" Adam asked.

Helmut sniffled and swiped his nose with his sleeve. "Someone said Jorgan is leaving."

"I need your help, Helmut," Jorgan said.

"With what?"

"Kiefer needs someone to look after him."

Helmut stuck out his lower lip. "You look after him just fine."

"Gerhardt also needs someone to help him," Jorgan said. "And he's leaving for the palace."

"Is Adam leaving again too?" Helmut looked at him mournfully.

"Yes," Jorgan said. "But Kiefer is staying here. He and Gerhardt are going to be in two different places, so I can't keep an eye on both of them. Which one do you think I should stick with?"

"I think... I think..." Helmut sniffled again. "I want you all to stay here."

"He has to go," Jorgan said. "I can only help one of them. You and I, we're a team. Right?"

Helmut nodded and said, "Yes."

"We look out for Kiefer and we help Gerhardt. Right?"

"Yes," Helmut said again, without the nod this time.

"One of us has to go with Gerhardt," Jorgan said. "And one of us has to stay with Kiefer. Which one of them do you think needs me more?"

Tears dropped down Helmut's broad cheeks. "You should go with Ernest Oberst Gerhardt."

"Okay," Jorgan said. "I'll do just what you said. Thank you for helping me figure that out."

Helmut left, sobbing. His door slammed. Jorgan sat on his bed and drooped, looking like he'd just had to kick his favorite puppy.

Adam patted his shoulder. "You handled that a lot better than I would have."

"Doesn't make it good," Jorgan mumbled. "But thanks."

Chapter 32

NO ONE GOT DIZZY from going through the portal to the palace. Except Ziegfried. His bodyguards caught him as he stumbled through, held him up while he shut it down. Once that was complete, they were all greeted by a representative of the palace, backed by Nolrien and several other red and gray clad palace guards.

Strom took them to their quarters, which had moved to a corridor parallel to the one used by noble guests. That suited Adam just fine. Good-bye old quarters. Good-bye view of the baths. Good-bye temptation. Good riddance.

"You're in here, sir," Strom said to Gerhardt, opening a door to a guest room for him. "Jorgan, Adam, and I will share the room next to you. The palace is rather crowded right now, but Andreno made sure we had these rooms despite how many people were fighting for them."

Gerhardt barely glanced inside the room. "When does Andreno want to meet with us?"

"Tomorrow afternoon," Strom said. "That was the soonest he said he could fit us into his new schedule without raising a lot of questions. He's taking pains to make it look like we're just some representatives of foreign, wealthy businessmen. Thus the appropriate rooms. It's also the reason for the escort guards. They'll stick around while we get settled in. Eventually they'll disappear, hopefully by tonight."

Gerhardt eyed the uniforms tagging along behind them. He said to Adam, "I want to meet the man you're taking dagger lessons from."

Adam pointed to Nolrien. "That's him."

"Very good," Gerhardt said. "Go put your bag in your room. Then bring him back and introduce him properly."

When Gerhardt went into his room Strom relaxed, letting his shoulders drop. Then he took Jorgan and Adam next door. The new room was quite a bit larger than Adam's previous quarters. It had its own separate washroom with a private toilet. Curtains hung on the windows. And the only showcase outside was kitchen gardens, not bathing lewdities.

Nolrien told the other native guards to stay in the corridor while he followed them in. He said, "I've been told to inform you that if any of you do anything that harms the reputation of our new Esteemed Leader you will quietly disappear."

Adam picked a bed and tossed his unopened bag onto it. "Did Kurlos tell you to say that?"

"Yes," Nolrien said. "Now that's done and out of the way, how soon can I get back to beating you? Tomorrow morning?"

"You'll have to ask Oberst Gerhardt," Strom said. "He wants to meet with you."

Nolrien gave him his creepy, blank eyed stare. "I guessed that when Adam pointed at me."

"What's going on?" Jorgan got more and more of a frown with each passing sentence. "What's he saying?"

"He gave us a standard behave-or-else threat," Strom said.

"Is he one of the ones who actually means it?" Jorgan asked. "Or did he just say it because he was ordered to?"

"Both," Adam said.

"I guess behaving should go both ways," Jorgan said. "Take him to meet Gerhardt like you were told."

Adam and Nolrien went next door. The room was identical, but had only one bed, some tables, chairs, and a desk arranged like some sort of work area. Gerhardt's face was as expressionless as Nolrien's. The two eyeballed each other for a bit. Then the Oberst said, "Show me how he teaches you."

"Can't I just describe it?" Adam asked.

"You already did," Gerhardt said. "Now I want to see it."

"Here?" Adam pointed at the floor under his feet. "Right now?"

"Here," Gerhardt said. "Right now. You have the dagger on you. Show me how he teaches you."

"I don't use it for lessons. We use wooden practice blades. And I don't have any here."

"Don't make me get Strom in here to tell your teacher to give me a demonstration," Gerhardt said. He waited a few heartbeats while Adam fought the urge to squirm.

"What's going on?" Nolrien asked.

"He wants a demonstration of how you teach," Adam mumbled to him. Nolrien broke out his emotionless smile. "Draw."

"I told him we don't have any practice blades."

"Use the real one," Nolrien said.

"What if I hurt you?"

"Think you can?" Nolrien asked.

"What if you hurt me?"

"That's more likely," Nolrien said. "And the longer you take, the more I'll make it hurt."

Adam sighed and grit his teeth. He reached for the hilt of the dagger on his belt. Before he had his fingers around it, Nolrien grabbed his forearm and yanked it up. That put his elbow almost by his ear, forcing him to bend sideways.

"Why aren't you resisting?" Nolrien's grip was a steel vice, leaving Adam no room to maneuver. "You have two hands. Use the other one."

Adam reached for the dagger with his left hand. Nolrien's weight shifted. He kicked Adam's foot holding most of his weight out from under him. He fell onto his left arm, pinning it. Nolrien leaned in, holding him down.

"Reaching for your dagger with your opposite hand wasn't what I meant," Nolrien said. "Why didn't you pivot and use that arm to attack?"

"You were holding me," Adam said.

"With my arm lifted, leaving my ribs wide open," Nolrien said. "If you'd led a pivot with your hips or your legs, you would have had the leverage to counter my grip. Also, why aren't you using your left arm now?"

"I can't!" Adam bared his teeth. He wriggled and kicked, trying to gain just a couple of inches for space to maneuver that arm.

"You could if you weren't laying on it." Nolrien pressed in harder the more Adam struggled, keeping that steel vise grip on his right arm. "Why are you laying on your free arm?"

"You tripped me!"

"So?"

"So I landed on it."

"Why?"

"Because you tripped me!"

Nolrien let go and his weight lifted. Adam scrambled a few feet away into a crouch. Nolrien looked a bit disgusted. He said, "What are you supposed to do when someone trips you?"

"Uh…" Adam tried to think. "Take them down with you?"

"Slap the ground!" Nolrien demonstrated by whapping the whole of his forearm and palm on the floor. "Are we going to need to go through another day of drilling this over and over again? Have you been practicing at all while you were gone?"

He stood and launched into his normal lecture on the topic. "If you slap the ground when you fall, it does two things. One—" he held up a finger— "it breaks the fall, helps you keep from hitting your head or breaking ribs without damaging your arm or wrist by landing on it wrong. Two—" he held up a second finger— "it extends that arm, which prevents it from getting pinned under your own bodyweight, leaving it available for use. Come, get back in the position we had. I'm going to trip you again. This time, do it right."

Adam glowered, still in his crouch. Nolrien said, "Get over here."

Gerhardt asked, "Is that all? Or is there more? So far, it doesn't look like you learned anything."

Adam sighed. As annoying as it was to get beaten repeatedly, he had held his own quite well while practicing with the guards during the stay at Far Base. That wasn't something he could have done before Nolrien taught him. He stood and said, "Not done yet."

He stepped over and allowed Nolrien to put him back in the same awkward, arm bent, high elbow position. Nolrien said, "Remember to tuck in your chin too."

This time when Nolrien swept his foot out, he extended his arm horizontally. Just before his torso hit the floor, he tucked his chin to the top of his sternum and slapped his arm down. His head stayed off the floor and his arm remained free.

"Good," Nolrien said. "Now you have the opportunity to gain yourself enough leverage to take space."

Adam drew his arm along the floor over his head, bending his elbow. That gave him a pivot point. He drew up his right leg and pushed his foot on the floor, rolling his torso back. That pushed Nolrien's weight. With that, Adam shifted directions with a roll, slipping out of Nolrien's grip and away from him.

"Good," Nolrien said. He stood and almost smiled. Almost. His mouth remained flat. It was his eyes that gave it away. "Very good. Next we should go over how to pivot while you're on your feet so you don't get tripped."

"Impressive," Gerhardt said. "Though you kept hesitating. Are you afraid of him? Or are you just not aggressive enough?"

"Both?" Adam suggested. "It's hard to be aggressive enough with him when he scares the bejeebers out of me. He could beat me any time he wants to."

"Good. Keep that in mind," Gerhardt said. "How soon will you resume regular lessons?"

"He asked about tomorrow."

"Perfect," Gerhardt said with a nod. "Ask him if he received my response to his letter, and if he's acted on it."

Adam relayed the question. Nolrien said, "I got the message. I sent the recommendation. It should have gotten there by now."

"When do you think you'll hear back?" Adam asked.

"I won't hear anything back," Nolrien said. "If he acts on it, I'll hear whether or not you passed whatever test he decided to throw you through. I'll warn you now, he's a mean whelp of a troll when it comes to testing."

"What if I change my mind when the test starts?"

"Who are you going to tell?" Nolrien asked. "You probably won't even know you're being tested. He's damn good at this. If he can't use a real situation to test you, he makes one. Or he sends someone else who makes one."

"That's a lot of words for what should have been a simple answer," Gerhardt said.

Adam relayed what had been said. The Oberst looked completely at ease with the information. He simply said, "Very well. Work hard. Continue learning what you can from this man. I want you ready for whatever his associate will use for a test. I want that opening for relations with Brend. Next question. I know the court magician here doesn't like us. Do you know if he's ever taken any actions to keep us away from other magicians?"

"Yes, he has," Adam said. "He doesn't just not like us, he hates us. He says if some other magicians ever found out he was this close to Ziegfried for this long, they'd kill him."

"I see." Gerhardt frowned. "I don't suppose your teacher knows how to quietly contact a magician who isn't afraid of what others think of him?"

Adam asked. Nolrien said, "I don't mess with the affairs of magicians. And neither should you. Magic can be dangerous if used wrong. If I was allowed, I'd kill your Ziegfried myself."

Adam told Gerhardt, "He doesn't trust magicians, doesn't associate with them, and hates Ziegfried."

"Understood," Gerhardt said. "You're dismissed. Send Strom in. Tell him he's giving me details on the happenings here over the last few weeks, so he better bring in the report he's supposed to have written up."

Chapter 33

ANDRENO HAD MOVED to the rooms Sanbralio had resided in. When he wasn't there bragging about how much better everything was now with him in charge, he spent most of his time in meetings. He closed himself in with people Adam didn't know, leaving him to loiter in the corridor with others not given leave to participate.

Adam had kind of hoped that Strom would continue acting as Andreno's interpreter. No such luck. Andreno claimed Adam's attitude was more entertaining and a break in monotony. Which reduced him from a tool to an amusing toy as far as Adam was concerned. Insulting.

More insulting, Adam's uniforms disappeared again. New clothes appeared by his bed every night while he slept. Then again during his morning training sessions with Nolrien. Those training sessions took place indoors now that the weather had turned cold and rainy, more and more so with every passing week.

The biggest change was that Andreno wanted Ziegfried and Gerhardt at his supper table. That meant at least one person, or more, associated with them had to stand attendance. They didn't have to do anything. Just stand there by the wall and watch everyone eat while their own stomach growled.

Ziegfried wasn't always there. At least once a week he locked himself in his rooms and refused to come out. Then when he did, it was to go down into the dungeons. When Gerhardt asked why, he said he was doing his job, that sometimes criminals would share information that others wouldn't and maybe he might find some clues for things that could help the German operation.

Adam learned to situate himself off to the side, or in a corner. Not just with the meals, with everything. People tended to ignore him there and he could amuse himself by catching them doing things they weren't supposed to, like making rude gestures at Andreno behind his back.

Sometimes after supper Andreno would call people in to talk with him. By that time, Adam was released, so he couldn't care less. Until one of the evenings when Ziegfried didn't attend supper. Andreno called him and Gerhardt into a meeting room afterward, along with Adam and Strom to interpret.

"As if Ziegfried needs an interpreter with that spell he uses," Strom groused.

"Gerhardt does," Adam reminded him.

"Ziegfried could act as interpreter." Strom's stomach gurgled. "Then we might be able to snag some supper before all the food is gone."

He stopped grousing when Gerhardt arrived with Jorgan. Andreno arrived next and seated himself at the head of the table that dominated the room. He mumbled some generic greetings, then laughed about how silly such protocols were since they'd just eaten together. Neither Adam nor Strom bothered interpreting all that.

Ziegfried shuffled in, leaving his rooms for the first time that day that Adam knew of. His arms hung limp. Dark circles shadowed his droopy eyes. He slumped into a chair, put his hands on the table, and rested his chin on them.

Gerhardt frowned. "Where are your bodyguards?"

Ziegfried mumbled, barely audible, "I don't need them everywhere."

"Don't evade," Gerhardt said. "Tell me where they are."

"In my rooms," Ziegfried said. "Andreno came to me last night with a training scenario he wanted them to go through this morning. They're tired now. I left them to rest."

Gerhardt said, "I didn't authorize any training scenarios. Strom, tell Andreno he's not to use my men this way without my permission."

"They're *my* men," Ziegfried said.

"No, they're not," Gerhardt said. "They're your protectors, under my command."

Andreno cleared his throat. Loudly. Everyone looked at him. He smiled. "Now that you're paying attention to me, as you should, let's get this started. Ziegfried, thank you for informing him of how you assisted me. That takes care of the first item I wanted to address."

Strom interpreted to Gerhardt and Jorgan. Adam stood back. The less he interacted with Andreno the better.

"The next topic," Andreno said. "Now that I can do things however I want, you'll run your operation from here at my palace."

Gerhardt said, "I'm not moving my men out of that castle."

Andreno didn't wait for an interpretation. He kept talking as if Gerhardt had said nothing. "From here, the transfers between our worlds will be much more convenient. Safer too, since my gold won't have to travel halfway across the country. I've already arranged for the monthly caravan shipments to come here instead. And then when you finally agree to mobilize for me—"

Gerhardt stood as soon as he heard the interpretation of that sentence, and headed for the door. Andreno surged to his feet. "I didn't give you permission to leave."

Strom started the interpretation, then stopped when Gerhardt held up a hand to him. Gerhardt said, "Tell him he already has his answer. I'm not mobilizing my men to take care of his petty desires to expand his territory. I would resist doing that even if I had permission. Which I don't."

Strom bit his lip. Then he said, "I don't want to tell him that. He tends to throw tantrums when he gets news he doesn't like."

Adam wrinkled his nose at Strom. Then he said to Andreno, "We are not mobilizing for you. We are not your military, not your invasion force, we take no orders from you. We are not going to war for you."

"Why not?" Andreno asked. "You're already at war. What's a little more fighting? Especially since it's a sure win. The enemy won't be able to defend themselves against your weapons."

"That is not the point," Adam said. "And aside from that, he does not have permission to do such a thing for you."

Andreno sat back and pouted. Gerhardt left the room with Strom and Jorgan. Ziegfried slowly hauled himself back to his feet saying, "Don't worry,

Andreno. I'll work at getting permission from our home. Then he'll have less of an argument to stand on."

"You do that," Andreno said. "I'll look for another incentive for him."

Not everyone made rude gestures behind Andreno's back. Some people kept themselves carefully controlled and difficult to read. Some remained aloof. Others fawned on him. Those were the ones he usually surrounded himself with. The few times he sent them away were when he was behind closed doors with Ziegfried, some of his military commanders, or Gerhardt.

Adam usually was there when Gerhardt was called in, even though Strom acted as the main interpreter. The meetings tended to follow the same pattern. Every third or fourth day Andreno would summon Gerhardt. He would demand to know if Gerhardt was willing to mobilize yet. Gerhardt would refuse. Andreno threatened to withhold trade items. Gerhardt warned that would cut his gold payments.

Then came the day that Kurlos interrupted while Andreno waited for Gerhardt to answer the summons. Kurlos gave Adam the evil eye, as usual. Then he leaned close and whispered in Andreno's ear. Andreno looked a bit surprised. "Already? It's sooner than I expected."

"Absolutely certain, Highness," Kurlos said. "You want me to have the mountain barbarians removed from your palace now?"

The skin around Andreno's eyes tightened. "You're not still telling people that, are you? Because if you are, that could mess up some of my plans."

"I… um…" Kurlos stuttered a bit. "They certainly act as barbaric as the mountain people. And you know very well this won't change Gerhardt's mind like you want. Which is just proof that—"

"It might." Andreno sniffed and tilted his nose up. "It might very well if he's reasonable enough."

"And if it doesn't?" Kurlos asked.

Andreno thought for a moment. His eyes slid over to Adam and stayed there. Adam said, "Do not look to me. I have no answer for you."

"I might have an answer for myself, though," Andreno said. "Kurlos, let's set another plan into motion just in case. Send me Charlass. Then tell Ziegfried I'm coming to see him after that."

Gerhardt arrived with Strom then, cutting off any reply Kurlos may or may not have had. Andreno waved Kurlos away, presumably to do as he'd been bidden, and faced Gerhardt. "Are you ready to mobilize for me yet?"

Before Strom even finished the interpretation, Gerhardt shook his head. He looked bored, and said, "You don't have to interpret everything, Strom. Just let me know if he says anything different. If not, give him the same reply as usual."

Andreno also didn't wait for interpretation. "I just received word that one of my villages near the border with the Chemwanitz Mountains has been raided. Have you received authorization to mobilize yet? And if not, how soon can you get it now that this has happened?"

Strom's mouth opened. He blinked a couple of times. Andreno frowned at him. "What are you staring at? Interpret already."

While Strom did that, Adam said, "He is not going to get authorization to mobilize over a village on your border."

"Then I'll have to cut the supplies." Andreno swiped his hand through the air. "No more threats. Consider it done. And I don't want to hear any nonsense about the gold being cut. You people being at war yourselves, I had thought you would understand this kind of thing."

"We do," Adam said. "All of our villages are affected. Not just one. Just one is not a reason to attack a nation."

By now Strom had finished interpreting. He even interpreted what Adam said. Then Gerhardt responded. "How do we know exactly who did the raiding? What kind of investigation has been made to ascertain exactly who the perpetrators were and why they did it?"

After the interpretation, Andreno said, "It's kind of obvious who did it. Most people aren't even going to ask."

Strom interpreted. Gerhardt said, "I'm not most people. I'm asking. And we're not mobilizing."

Andreno's face darkened with anger when he heard that response. Adam bit his tongue to keep from saying 'I told you so.'

"What is it going to take?" Andreno snarled. He balled his hands into fists. "Why are you so stubborn about this?"

Strom opened his mouth. Adam said in German, "Don't interpret that. It's not worth it."

Gerhardt tipped his chin down at Adam. "How about I be the judge of that?"

"You know what?" Andreno kept going. He opened one fist just enough to point at Gerhardt. "I don't want you at my dinner table anymore."

"I doubt he will think of that as punishment," Adam told him.

Someone knocked on the door. Kurlos opened it from the outside and said, "Prince Andreno, Charlass has arrived as you summoned."

"We'll leave you," Adam said.

"Why?" Andreno laughed. Charlass entered and he said, "It's not like this is a private meeting. I reserve those for important people. In fact, Kurlos, leave the door open so I can get rid of her that much faster."

Charlass said nothing in her own defense. She kept her gaze on the floor and took such mincing steps her skirt didn't even move. It made her look like she just sort of floated across the floor while her shoes clacked along.

"Where have you been during the evening meals?" Andreno demanded.

"In my rooms, Highness," Charlass said.

"That's not showing proper gratitude," Andreno said.

A few people congregated at the open doorway, some craning their necks to see in. Adam bit his tongue to keep from lashing out in front of them. Or in front of Gerhardt, who was listening to Strom's quiet interpretations. Andreno glanced at them, then at the people in the door. He smirked as if enjoying people watching him berate his bastard cousin.

"My granduncle took you in," Andreno said to her. "Cared for you. Protected you. Even took pains to make sure you were cared for after his death. And you're so ungrateful that you don't bother to show yourself at his table?"

"It's your table now, Highness." Charlass spoke in a voice as flat as Nolrien often did. "It was suggested that you would not want to be bothered with my presence."

"If I have to let you leech off of me, you have no right to try and hide it," Andreno said. "Show yourself at your customary place at my table for the evening meals. That way, everyone can see my generosity, even to someone as unworthy as you."

Adam couldn't hold it in any longer. "Andreno, you are the one who told her not to come, that you did not want to be bothered with her."

Andreno laughed. Everyone in the doorway laughed in response. After Strom interpreted, Gerhardt shook his head and said, "Weiss, that was not smart."

"It's true," Adam told him.

"I like you," Andreno told Adam. "You're funny. If you weren't already working for someone else, I'd offer you a position as my official comedian. Tell you what, since Gerhardt isn't going to be at my table, how about you take his place."

Adam suppressed a shudder before remembering his manners. "No thank you."

"That wasn't a request," Andreno said.

Chapter 34

ADAM PACED THEIR ROOM. Jorgan sat writing notes on the little table in the sitting area by the door. Gerhardt watched Adam from one of the chairs there while Strom laid shirts out on Adam's bed.

"Are you sure you can't get me out of this?" Adam asked.

"Why would I?" Gerhardt retorted.

Strom lumped shirts in groups. Then he picked and draped them all over his arm. "These are more for impressing willing women, which I doubt you'll find much of at the dining table."

"Why can't I just grab the top one?" Adam reached for the closest one.

Strom slapped his hand away. "I might ask which one you want if you weren't so stupid when it comes to clothes."

"I'm not stupid," Adam said.

"You are about clothes," Strom said with a snicker. "What color are your freaky eyes tonight?"

Adam threw his hands up and snarled. "Who cares?"

"Green then," Strom said, turning back to the shirts.

Adam growled. If he just grabbed every stack there and tossed them in the fireplace and lit them that might solve a lot of problems. Unfortunately, it would also create others, such as irritating Gerhardt.

"Run this by me again," Jorgan said. "Word for word as close as you can remember, everything Andreno said."

"Why?" Adam demanded.

"Something isn't adding up." Jorgan lifted his pencil. "The timing is off, and there's too much. You said Andreno sent for Charlass after Kurlos interrupted with a message and while Gerhardt was already on the way?"

"Yes," Adam said.

"And you don't know what exactly the message was?"

"I told you," Adam said. "He told Gerhardt he just got word that the village was raided."

"But did you hear Kurlos say that?"

"Not exactly," Adam admitted.

"And then Andreno said for Ziegfried to come after he was done with Gerhardt and Charlass?"

"Yes," Adam said.

"Did he say for Ziegfried to come?" Gerhardt asked. "Or for Ziegfried to be brought? Or for someone to come for Ziegfried?"

"Aren't those all the same thing?" Adam asked.

"Not exactly," Gerhardt said. "And I ask because sometimes the tiniest details matter."

Jorgan's eyes went out of focus. He rolled his pencil between his thumb and fingers. "Why would he send for Charlass?"

"That's what I wondered," Adam said. "And then pretend he hadn't told her to stay away from his table."

"That was his sick way of playing a game," Gerhardt said. "He has power over her. He can tell her to stay away, then shame her when she obeys, then punish her for showing up because she was shamed. Which was why it wasn't smart for you to point it out. Because it showed you're naive to those kinds of machinations, and therefore vulnerable."

"But what's the game?" Jorgan asked, his eyes still unfocused and distant. "He has a tendency to manipulate circumstances so timing portrays a certain illusion. I should go to the dinner."

"Good," Adam said. "You can take my place."

"No he can't," Strom said. He brought over two shirts, one in each hand. He held them up, looking back and forth between them and Adam's face while he talked. "Andreno basically called you his court jester. He wants you there, not any of the rest of us."

"I thought he said official comedian," Adam said.

"Directly translated, yes," Strom said. "A better translation would be a trickster. The colloquial meaning of the phrase he used, he called you a court jester."

"I don't think I'm that funny," Adam said. "I don't run around telling jokes and singing songs."

"No, you're blunt about pointing out hard truths," Strom said. He tossed one of the shirts at Adam. "This one."

"You made that decision look a lot more painful than necessary," Adam said.

"Only because you're stupid about clothes." Strom smirked. "You need help putting it on? Or do you know how to dress yourself?"

"Enough," Gerhardt said. "Jorgan, you're going to go have a chat with Ziegfried. Weiss, hurry up and get going."

Adam hurriedly changed into the stupid clothes, not just the shirt but an entire outfit. Strom had tried foisting off on him pants that glittered and sparkled. When Adam had put his foot down and utterly refused to even touch them, Strom had made an entire production out of selecting a shirt that matched a more acceptable pair of pants.

When they got to the dining room, it was mostly full already. The chair Gerhardt was normally seated in was occupied. Kurlos directed Adam to one all the way on the opposite end of the table from Andreno's seat at the head.

"As amusing as my Esteemed Leader find you," Kurlos said, "the dinner table is not the time nor place for barbarians and their antics. I expect you to behave here, no matter how difficult you may find it to do so."

He was seated at the corner, right next to Charlass already at the foot of the table. Adam said to Kurlos, "I think I can manage. The company at this end of the table is probably nicer and more polite than at the other end."

"Spoken like a true barbarian," Kurlos said with a sneer. Then he went to seat a couple of the last stragglers. Nevermind that servants were already guiding them to chairs.

"You're funny," the man directly across from Adam said to him. "Bold too. Not many would have the guts to speak that way of anyone at the other end of the table."

The man next to him laughed. Then the two dove into conversation as a few cubes of cheese were put on everyone's plate. They went through introductions, why they were at the palace, how little hope they had that their petitions to the throne would be granted, etc. The man seated right next to Adam joined in with them at some point. They threw a couple of questions Adam's way, as if trying to draw him in to talk with them. Never once did they even glance at Charlass, let alone try and include her.

She ate daintily, keeping her eyes down, nibbling away. And she seemed to pay no heed to any of the talk all around her. Even when the talk turned to the news of the village that had been raided, and speculation on what exactly had happened, she showed no reaction and drew no attention.

Adam waited impatiently. How long did it take to eat three cubes of cheese? As hard as it was to wait on the side while everyone else ate, he found this more difficult. Maybe there really was something to the notion that nibbling at something small whet the appetite, because he was hungrier than usual now.

Finally Andreno finished off his appetizer, or Hors d'oeuvre, or whatever they called it here. Servers swept away the miniature plates for the cheeses and replaced them with cup sized bowls of soup with some kind of lentil.

Andreno was served first. After his first slurping bite, Charlass received hers. He looked at her across the length of the table. Adam shuddered at his expression. It was the one he used when he anticipated a reaction from something he'd done. Was Jorgan right? Was there more to the timing of everything than Adam knew?

Charlass didn't meet his eye. She kept her gaze down. She sampled the soup. Everyone else ate. She raised her spoon again. No reaction. But Andreno was smiling. More like leering actually, so he must still be anticipating something.

Strom leaned in and whispered at Adam, "If you don't eat along with everyone else, they'll take it as insult."

Adam ate. Even though everything in him screamed warning, that something was wrong. He was hungry. And even though the soup was as bland as every other food dish here, at least it would help fill his belly. Then maybe he could figure things out better.

Charlass dipped her spoon back into her soup, hesitating before raising it again. The man sitting next to her across from Adam cleared his throat, then kept talking. Charlass frowned, setting her spoon down. She put a hand to her chest, her breathing getting shallow.

"Are you…" Adam's throat tightened up. He cleared it, swallowed a couple of times, and tried again. "Are you all right?"

She looked at him. At first he thought it was because he sounded a little hoarse. Then he realized all the color was leeching from her face, draining away as he watched.

Seeing how shallow her breathing was made his own chest feel heavy in sympathy. The heaviness put a tickle in his throat. The two men across from Adam also breathed shallow, setting down their spoons and pushing away their bowls. The man next to Adam took out a handkerchief and coughed into it, sounding phlegmy.

At that noise, everyone stopped eating and turned to look. Andreno stood, his eyes glittering with malice. "What's going on down there? Is my table not good enough for a commoner woman?"

Charlass said nothing. Still breathing shallow, her hand on her chest shook. For the first time that Adam knew of, she met Andreno's eyes. And there was just as much hate and malice in her gaze as there was in his.

Adam leaned back and away. His hands shook too. Andreno shouted, "Answer me!"

Adam opened his mouth to tell him to back off and leave her alone. Instead he coughed. It sounded just as bad or worse than the man next to him. And it hurt.

He held his breath, trying to get it under control. He stopped coughing after a few moments, but didn't dare take in more than a trickle of breath for fear that it would start up again.

The man across the table stood. He swayed a moment and grabbed onto the table, stabilizing himself. He said with a voice gone raspy, "Please, Highness, excuse me. I must leave. I fear I'm ill."

"I get ill when I get too close to her too," Andreno said with a laugh. For once, no one joined him.

Charlass waved a shaking hand at one of the servants. They helped her out of her chair. Andreno said, "I didn't give you permission to leave."

Then she collapsed, going straight down like her knees buckled while she tried to stay upright. The servant caught her, supporting her weight.

Most of the diners jumped to their feet. Someone screamed about poison. Servers rushed in to snatch away the bowls of soup.

Most of it sounded far away to Adam. Like he was watching it on a cinema reel in a dark theater. Pressure built up in his head, making everyone sound like he listened to them under water. Someone touched his arm.

It was Strom, leaning close again. "Adam, you all right?"

Adam shook his head. He tried to say he was dizzy, he needed to go lie down. Instead, a coughing fit wracked him all over again.

"Let's get you back to the room," Strom said.

He called over one of the servants and together they hauled Adam out of his chair to his feet. His legs didn't want to support him. If they didn't already have a good hold on him, he'd have collapsed like Charlass.

They took him back to the room. No one else was there. Strom told the servant to get Adam to bed, then told Adam he was going to go find Gerhardt and Jorgan.

Adam managed to peel off the stupid shirt that Strom had made such a fuss over before the servant stuck him between his sheets. He shivered, pulling the covers higher. They had somehow become heavier, so heavy he strained to cover himself.

He lay there under them for several moments, his chest growing heavier and heavier with every breath. Gerhardt came in and pulled the blanket back. Adam's teeth chattered. He reached to try and get them back. Gerhardt put a hand to Adam's head and said, "Good God, you're burning."

"Cold," Adam managed while he shivered. Then he coughed.

"No," Gerhardt said, keeping the blankets away. "You're hot. Too hot. You need to cool off. That much I know. Strom is getting Jorgan and the doctor. Just hold tight. They should be here soon."

The coughing eased up. By then, Adam was so weary he didn't even have the strength to complain about a doctor coming to see him.

Chapter 35

ADAM SHOULD NEVER HAVE LEFT HOME. He should have stayed there. If he hadn't fought with his dad so much, if he'd listened instead of being so naive, he might never have gone and voluntarily enlisted. Then he wouldn't be sick.

Great shivers wracked his body. His teeth clacked so hard from chattering he gave himself a headache. And people kept putting cold things on him. Not that he had the strength to push them away, or even pull on a blanket for that matter.

Even if he did get sick at home, it would have the comfort of familiarity. His brother Matthias would tease him for hit. That would irritate their dad, who would give Matt extra chores for it. His mother would pamper him. She'd make chicken soup with garlic and onions and prop cushions and pillows around him on the couch. Then she'd turn on the radio for him to listen to. She might even surprise him with a new dictionary. That was always his dad's suggestion, even though she picked them out. His dad didn't know Adam knew, but Matthias had snitched and their mom hadn't denied it.

The chills eventually subsided. A bit. The people who had been sticking cold things on him stood around somewhere out by the periphery of his awareness. Somebody said something in the Brendish language about how many hours a fever reducing spell lasted. Somebody else said the same thing in German. People talked a bit more, words floating around that Adam didn't have the strength to pluck and derive their meanings.

Gerhardt's voice cut through the brain fog so sudden and loud it was like a spike driving into Adam's skull. "That's not acceptable!"

Then he was gone. Everyone was gone. Adam floated. Still miserable. Not quite as bad as before. People came back. Hands touched him. People talked. Voices came and went. Some stayed longer than others.

Doc Lieber, from the base, wandered into Adam's dreams. "I want them all in here."

"One of them is a woman," Strom said. "A socially unacceptable woman. People aren't going to like her lying in here with other's she could infect."

"I don't care what people will like or dislike," Lieber snapped. "I care about curing anyone who's affected by this. That's easier to do if I don't have to go hopping and skipping up and down corridors and flights of stairs to their separate rooms. Get them all in here. Now!"

Jorgan sat in a chair someone had pulled over to the bed. "I think you woke him up."

This wasn't a dream. How had Lieber gotten to the palace? He had to have been here for a while. Adam had an IV needle stuck in his arm. The glass bottle rigged on a stand next to his bed was half empty. Pillows had been stacked behind him, propping him into nearly a sitting position.

Lieber came over to him. "Adam?"

"What are you doing here?" Adam asked. His voice rasped and scratched his throat.

"Figuring out what happened and how to heal you from it," Lieber said. "Unless you meant how did I get here. That was through a portal opened by Andreno's court magician. Let me check your vitals again while you're awake."

He stuck a thermometer in Adam's mouth. Adam sighed, too weak to resist. Too lethargic to pull his arm away from the pressure cuff Lieber wrapped around his upper arm and pumped air into. He cooperated fully, without even jerking his wrist away when Lieber counted his pulse.

Lieber took the thermometer and studied it, rolling it between his fingers to view the mercury level. "Are you hurting anywhere?"

"I'm fine," Adam croaked.

"You say that to me one more time and I swear the next time I take your temperature it'll be rectally."

"You've said you're fine almost a dozen times just since he's gotten here," Jorgan said. "You may not remember, because of that potion they gave you to ease the coughing. You weren't exactly very cognizant. But you have. And You're driving us all crazy with it."

"Now that you're responding proper, I expect a proper answer." Lieber shook the thermometer down. "What's hurting? Your head? Your throat? Your chest?"

"All of them," Adam said. "Mostly just my chest. Only a little."

"Liar." Lieber tucked the thermometer away in its metal case.

"I am not," Adam said. Lieber flicked him on the head with his fingertips. Adam flinched. "Ow. What was that for?"

"For a demonstration. That's only a little hurt. The other patients have described great weights on their chests, making them ache. That's not a little hurt."

"I guess it's more than a little," Adam admitted. "It does feel like weights, right over my lungs."

"That's more like it." Lieber put the stethoscope hanging around his neck into his ears. "Let me listen. Roll onto your side."

He didn't have the strength to roll by himself. Lieber and Jorgan both had to help him. Then the cold circle of the stethoscope chilled his back.

"Take a deep breath," Lieber commanded.

Adam tried. A coughing fit took control, sending his entire body into spasms. The stethoscope moved around on his back as he drew in air and coughed repeatedly.

Lieber pulled the stethoscope away. The coughing continued. He said, "Jorgan, fill that bowl with hot water again. We'll do another steam treatment."

"It'll make him silly again." Jorgan moved away. Water splashed, pouring from one container to another.

"I'll fix that." Lieber fiddled with the bottle the IV tube was attached to. "He needs more sleep. Save everyone's sanity at the same time."

Adam couldn't protest. The coughing prevented him from speaking. And it hurt. Whether he wanted to admit it or not, it hurt. It hurt his chest. His throat. His belly. His head. He ached all over.

Jorgan set a bowl of hot, steaming water close to Adam's face. He put a cloth over it, holding open one side and venting the steam in Adam's direction. Lieber added a few drops from a dark colored vial. It smelled something between menthol and the chamomile tea his mother used to force on him. Two scents he would never have associated with each other.

"Breathe that in good and deep," Lieber said.

It certainly warmed like menthol. With that comforting burn Adam's chest muscles relaxed. The coughing eased up then let go. Lieber stuck the stethoscope on his back again. "Try now to take deep breaths. We'll see if this works better this time."

Adam breathed in the steam. This time it worked. No coughing. The warmth from whatever was in it left him sleepy and drifting. Or was that from whatever Lieber did to the IV? He had no idea. At the moment he didn't really care.

He left himself drift. Dreams replaced reality. Most of them were disjointed splashes of sensory input mixed with emotions caused by events long passed. Some of them were more coherent.

He ate his mother's sausages. Those turned into the apple strudel the crazy cat lady down the street always made. That turned into the snickerdoodles the bully of the block's mother always brought to dinner events.

His mother sang folk songs in this world's native language. He talked to her in several other languages. She had always understood him but never responded other than in German. In his dreams she not only responded, she held entire conversations with him.

Slowly she morphed and shifted into that pretty girl from Brend who had come as a delegate when Prince Sanbralio's son died. She spoke to him in all those different languages too. She laughed like his mother. She cooked like his mother. She had a much prettier smile. She put a blanket around his shoulders. She felt his forehead. She removed her hand and put a cool, wet cloth there instead.

Again, he wasn't dreaming. The cool cloth brought him back to awareness. It wasn't that pretty Brendish girl. It was Marietta.

"Sorry," she whispered leaning in close, the room in near darkness. "I didn't mean to wake you."

"It's okay." His voice was still raspy.

"Shh." She put a finger gently to his lips. "Most everyone else is asleep. Your doctor said to let everyone that's sick sleep as long as they need to."

Jorgan stepped over to the bed, also speaking in a whisper. "You're awake. How are you feeling? And don't say you're fine."

Adam turned his head away saying nothing. Jorgan poked his arm. "Hey, are you going to answer?"

"You said not to tell you I'm fine," Adam rasped. He refused to admit how lousy he felt. It might bring the doctor back. Charlass slept in the next bed over. He glanced back to Jorgan and smirked, covering his current wretched state. "You tell your wife there's another woman sleeping in your bed?"

"Ha, ha, very funny." Jorgan didn't look amused. "Strom and I both have temporarily moved next door, sleeping on cots in Gerhardt's room. We're still spending most of our time in here though, taking care of all of you."

"All?"

"You, the lady, and the three other guys." Jorgan pointed to Charlass in his bed, the man who occupied Strom's bed on the other side of that, and across the room where two others lay in cots. All of them slept.

"What time is it?" Adam asked.

"Early, early morning," Jorgan said.

One of the other men mumbled. Strom lifted his head from the table where he sat and went over to the man. He blinked groggily, shuffled his feet like he was half asleep. The man said nothing more, and Strom didn't bother him. He did turn to glare at Jorgan.

"Keep it down," he whispered. His eyes flicked to Adam. "When did he wake up?"

"A couple minutes ago," Jorgan said.

"Did you get Lieber?" Strom asked.

"Not yet," Jorgan said. "You do it."

Strom somehow managed to stomp quietly on his way out. Jorgan rubbed his eyes and sat in the chair still by Adam's bed. "And I thought you were grumpy at times. You're nothing compared to him when he hasn't had enough sleep."

He went on rubbing his eyes and yawning. Marietta leaned over, changing the cool cloth again. She gave him a cheerful smile. "I think your friends need more sleep. They were up most of the night."

"They are acting grumpy," Adam said.

She snickered. She dipped another cloth in a basin of water, wrung it out, and put it on Charlass' head. She said to him, "Did you know you talk in your sleep?"

"What was I saying?"

"I don't know. It wasn't a language I recognize. At first I thought you were just mumbling, until you kept repeating some words."

Adam used German to ask Jorgan. "Was I talking in my sleep?"

Jorgan quit rubbing his eyes. "Yes."

"What was I saying?"

"I don't know," Jorgan said with a shrug. "It was some other language. Russian, or Italian or something."

"Which one?"

"How am I supposed to know?"

"Because those two languages sound completely different."

"So? You expect me to know what other languages sound like when I don't understand any of the words? Don't be ridiculous."

Lieber entered the room, Strom behind him still stomping quietly. The door shut without either of them touching it, so there had to be someone out there in the corridor. Strom went back to the table, sat, and laid his head on his arms.

Adam endured Lieber's attentions, getting what he claimed were vitals. Adam was alive. He breathed. His heart beat. What more vitals were needed than that?

"You're doing better." Lieber retrieved his precious thermometer from Adam's mouth again. "Lungs don't sound the best, better, still not well. Fever's down some."

"I still don't know what happened," Adam said. "I've never in my life gotten this sick this fast."

"We're working on that." Lieber stuck the thermometer back in. Adam frowned, biting a bit too hard. Lieber shook a finger at him. "You bite hard enough to break that and I'll break your teeth. I only have a few of those left and I have no idea if they're going to send me any more from back home or not."

He wrote on a clipboard by Adam's bed. Adam asked Marietta, "Has anyone figured out what happened?"

"Don't talk with your mouth full." Lieber didn't even look up from what he was writing.

"Not exactly," Marietta said. "Not yet. Everyone at your end of the table fell ill. Most people just have a few symptoms, and they get milder they further they sat from Charlass' spot. It seems to have started there."

"And I sat right next to her," Adam said.

"All four of you did." Marietta waved her hand to indicate the other three sleeping men. "No one else is quite this bad. They're functional, and it didn't look like they might die within hours, so your doctor didn't fight to get them moved her like all of you."

"Die within hours?" Adam asked, earning him another evil eye from Lieber.

Marietta nodded. "It was a little scary. Your doctor is healing you, but no one knows how you all got this sick this fast. Some people swore only magic would do that. So Andreno has the court magician working with your people's magician to try and figure some of it out. No one thinks they'll find anything. Neither of them has a reputation for healing illness."

Lieber took the thermometer back. Marietta smiled at him. "He doesn't act as nice to you as he does to the others. Do you irritate him? Or does he just not like you?"

"I think I irritate him," Adam said. "I am not sure why."

The man who had stirred earlier began to rouse. Lieber went to him and called Strom over to interpret. Marietta changed the cool cloth again. Did the same for Charlass again.

For once the sounds of a different language held no fascination for Adam. His head hurt. His chest ached. His throat was on fire. And his arms and legs

259

had turned into jellied preserves. He tuned everything out and let it all turn into droning in his ears, grateful that at least no one was talking about him dying within a few hours.

Chapter 36

ADAM SLOWLY RECOVERED. He slept a lot. Partly because he was still lethargic and tired. Partly just because he was bored.

Lady Tabissia brought in entertainers, storytellers and singers mostly, what few who were willing to come into the room even after it was proven the illness wasn't contagious. That cut down the complaints from the other victims, including their dislike of being stuck in the same room with Charlass. They left the room the moment Doc Lieber allowed, inviting Tabissia to come to their new location and continue entertaining them. She laughed right in their face and told them Charlass was better company.

Since Adam slept at odd hours, he also woke at odd hours. Sometimes it was during a meal, when Marietta or her sister or one of her friends were serving everyone. He preferred Marietta or her sister. The friends sometimes got a little flamboyant and flirty.

Sometimes he woke only when Lieber was practicing his annoying habit of checking what he called vitals. At one point he woke because Jorgan and Strom were arguing over something. They were quiet about it, whispering over in the corner with the table. He couldn't make out most of what they were saying, something about making accusations against Ziegfried and if something he'd done was detrimental to the operation or not. They stopped as soon as they realized Adam was awake, and they wouldn't tell him what they'd argued about.

Another time, when Adam was beginning to feel much improved, almost healthy, he woke in the middle of the night to whispers in the Brendish language from Charlass' bed. She said, "That's why I'm begging you not to tell him. He'll pull me out of here, and risk exposing himself to do so."

"He asked me to protect you." Nolrien was there too.

"And he wouldn't be thinking straight," Charlass said. "If he pulls me because Andreno failed to kill me, what will that do to his intelligence gathering here? If he lacks that, how much harder will it be for him to keep his job?"

"They're not going to kick him out for losing a contact, especially if it was because the contact was in danger," Nolrien said. "And what do you think he'll do to me when he learns about this from somewhere else?"

"He won't."

"Of course he will."

"Think about it. Part of the reason I can collect information to pass to him is because I'm practically invisible. They all talk around me because to them I don't exist. No one's going to talk about this incident. You can't tell him."

Adam lay perfectly still, his back to them. Who was Charlass passing information to? Someone Nolrien wasn't? He obviously knew who she was talking about.

"What about the other men that took ill?" Nolrien asked.

"They were too minor in status," Charlass said. "That's why they were at my end of the table. No one's going to talk about them either."

"Charlass…"

"Here's something else you may not have thought of," she said. "If you tell him about this incident, word will also reach him about Adam and his people."

"I already sent them a lead that opened a door to contact with Adam," Nolrien said.

"You did *what*?" Charlass sounded incensed. "How could you do that? Everything we've done to hush up them being here will be wasted. They'll get in contact with the gathering. They'll find their magic weapon. They'll trade their weapons for that knowledge. And what do you think the gathering will do with that?"

"They're going to find out eventually," Nolrien said. "You can't prevent it forever. And if we help direct the contact, say, through a king who hates the gathering and employs a magician who defies them, don't you think that minimizes the damage it could do?"

"Whether he defies the gathering or not, he's still a magician."

"Charlass, I have to give them something," Nolrien said. "I'm due to send my report tomorrow, and I've spent the last several days doing nothing but guard the door to this room. I haven't gathered any information other than this sickness."

"Tell them about the wasting disease in the dungeon," Charlass said.

"I already did," Nolrien said. "They weren't very interested. And don't you think that could also lead to exposing these foreigners, since it gets worse every time Ziegfried goes down there?"

"No one is talking about it," Charlass said. "At least, they weren't a few days ago when I was healthy and out listening to conversations. Ask Tabissia or Marietta if that's changed at all. If not, send it, tell them it's still ongoing and no one's figured out the cause."

"I still think Ziegfried is the cause."

"You can't prove it," Marietta said. "And you can't suggest it without telling people he's here."

Nolrien let out his breath. It wasn't quite a sigh. It sounded more like frustration, or annoyance. After a moment, he said, "I'll consider it. I'll let you know before I send it. Now, get some more rest."

There was no noise of him walking away. Everything just went quiet. Adam barely heard the door when Nolrien left.

That left Adam lying in the dark, reeling with information. He replayed it in his head over and over as best he could, trying not to lose any of it. Good thing his brain wasn't as foggy as it had been the past several days.

After a while, Charlass' breathing slowed into the rhythmic pattern of someone sleeping. Adam stayed awake, not nearly as tired or lethargic as he had been lately. And after what he'd heard, there was not a chance of getting any more sleep tonight.

When the window brightened slowly with the gray light of pre-dawn, he sat up. Charlass was sound asleep. Jorgan had his head down on the table by the door, apparently asleep that way instead of lying down in the cot he claimed had been moved into Gerhardt's room for him.

Gravity took hold of Adam's bladder. He turned and put his feet on the floor, wriggling his toes on the soft rug. Sitting felt good.

He tried standing. That felt good too. He took a few slow, experimental steps. That worked without making him dizzy or anything. Moving slow to make sure he stayed balanced, he crossed the floor all the way to the privy.

After relieving himself and washing up, Adam came back out into the main room. The morning sun had risen, splashing the room with light. Jorgan was sitting up and blinking groggily. He quietly said, "I did hear you moving around. I thought maybe it was my imagination until I saw your bed empty. You okay?"

Adam nodded, shuffling slowly over to sit with him at the table. Jorgan said, "You still look like death warmed over."

"Feeling better though," Adam said. He sank into the chair and leaned heavy on the table. "Still feel weak. Moving feels good, but walking across the floor just now made me exhausted."

"It can take a while to kick lethargy after an illness," Jorgan said. "Take it easy. If you overdo it, Lieber will nail your hide to the wall. Maybe you should get some more rest?"

"I'm tired of resting," Adam said. "I woke in the middle of the night to Nolrien and Charlass having a whisper conversation, then couldn't get back to sleep."

"What were they saying?"

"A few things. One of the last ones was something about a wasting disease in the dungeons that gets worse every time Ziegfried goes down there."

Jorgan's jaw dropped open and his face went slack. "That's how he's doing it."

"Doing what?"

"Ah, man!" Jorgan shook his head. "I wish I was better at gathering up information pieces. I can put them together really well. I can figure out the big picture with less pieces then most. I just can't find the pieces unless someone hands them to me."

"What are you talking about?" Adam asked.

"His charms," Jorgan said. "That's how he's storing up energy. Gerhardt thought maybe he was just siphoning off his own energy to store up for later use. Which would explain why he's always tired. I told him that doesn't have the right feel, that something else was going on. You just handed me the piece I was missing."

"You think he's draining the prisoners in the dungeon?"

"Yes, I do," Jorgan said. His eyes went out of focus. "Of course, now we have another mystery. The reason Gerhardt thought he was siphoning off his own energy is because he so often looks like he's recovering from heavy magic usage. If he's filling his storage charms from draining other people, then what's he using his own magic for?"

"No idea," Adam said.

"They didn't mention anything else about him?"

"Uh…" Adam tried to replay the conversation in his head. It was gone. All he had left was impressions. "I think maybe my head is still a bit foggier than normal. It just feels clear in comparison to the last few days."

"It's all right," Jorgan said.

"I think they were talking about what happened at the dinner table," Adam said. "I think? Did the magicians ever figure it out?"

"It was hostile magic," Jorgan said. "Masorno is horrified and wants us expelled, as if that's a change. Ziegfried is all kinds of giddy about it, trying to figure out how to replicate it in a way that can be controlled."

"Controlled? Why control magic that makes people sick?"

"We're at war. With both sides trying to develop weapons that give them an edge over the other. Why do you think Ziegfried would want that?"

Adam rubbed his forehead. "I kind of don't want to think about that right now."

"Probably for the better," Jorgan said. "Anyway, it was a spell that attacked the lungs, placed on the lentils in Charlass' soup bowl. Thing is, what's making Ziegfried most giddy is that it spread. It jumped from the lentils in her bowl to the other bowls closest to it, and then on from there. Which is why other people showed symptoms, but more mild the farther they sat from Charlass' bowl. Also, it took hold so fast people stopped eating, some of them before the magic spread to their bowl."

"Like the people at Andreno's end of the table," Adam surmised.

"Exactly," Jorgan said.

The door opened from the outside. Marietta entered with a covered tray. She smiled at Adam as she set the tray on the table and said, "Good morning. It's good to see you up. Feeling better?"

"Some," Adam said. "I'm tired enough I could go back to sleep now. I just don't want to walk back to my bed."

She grinned. "So sleep in the chair. After you eat something."

She uncovered the tray revealing a steaming pot of porridge and a few bowls. Jorgan stood and took the bowls, helping to dish them up. She smiled at him and asked Adam, "Is he claimed?"

"Claimed?" Adam asked.

"Does he have a woman who claims him as hers?"

"He has a wife," Adam said.

"How disappointing," Marietta said. "Good for her. Disappointing for the rest of us. I have a few friends who would *love* to have a man who isn't afraid of helping out with chores. It's so sexy!"

Adam swallowed. He'd never heard any girl describe him that way. Wouldn't it be nice if that pretty girl from Brend thought of him that way? No, she didn't even know he existed. Better not to think about it. He shook his head. "I don't want to hear anything about him being sexy."

"Because he's your friend? Or because you're embarrassed thinking about it?" Marietta asked. Adam turned his face away. She leaned over until her grin was in his line of sight. "You're blushing."

Chapter 37

ADAM WENT BACK to boring routine. At first Nolrien went easy on him in the mornings, walking him through some defensive moves without actually hurting him. At first. Then Adam irritated him, or he woke up on the wrong side of the bed, or something. Everything went back to normal.

After court every day Andreno spent hours going over reports of continued raids on villages, at least one every couple weeks. He consulted with nobles and military commanders. They organized and planned a retaliation campaign for the next spring. He ignored any attempts to get him to investigate these raids to ensure the actual culprit. He ignored any attempts to draw his attention to more domestic problems, like the plights of the poor in his nation, or even the wasting illness in the dungeon under his own feet in the palace.

Disgusted, Adam retired every evening to the room he shared with Strom and Jorgan. There he got out his dagger and drilled all the moves he learned from Nolrien. Back and forth across the floor he went, ducking, dodging, sidestepping, sweeping, parrying, thrusting, all against an imaginary Andreno.

Until the night Jorgan was there with papers spread all over the little table by the door. The moment Adam went into his routine of taking out his frustration on an imaginary offender, Jorgan said, "You get too close to me swishing that blade around and I'm smothering you in your sleep tonight."

"No you wouldn't." Adam stopped swinging and sauntered over to him. "You always follow rules. And murder is illegal."

"Self-defense is perfectly legal." Jorgan didn't even look up while he wrote on the paper currently under his nose.

"What are you working on, anyway?" Adam looked over all the papers. "Stats and flow plans? For what?"

"The portal opening," Jorgan said. "I have the pattern down pat at base. Here, I have to redo all the logistics so that everything gets transferred within the duration of time Ziegfried is able to keep the portal open."

"There's a time limit?" Adam hadn't thought of that.

"Oh, yes," Jorgan said. "One time early in the operation we hit the limit. The portal collapsed before we got our supplies. Ziegfried was unconscious for a couple of days. And when he woke he accidentally killed the nearest person. Which is why now I'm tasked with finding the most efficient procedure."

Adam glanced down at his dagger. Perhaps sometimes he should be imagining Ziegfried as his pretend opponent instead of always Andreno. Then he shrugged it off. It wasn't like it made much difference. It was just for stress relief anyway.

He retreated to the other side of the room away from Jorgan, hoping that would be enough distance to keep from disturbing him. Then he asked, "Why are you working on portal stuff already anyway? The next one isn't until winter, isn't it?"

"Did your illness addle your sense of passing time?" Jorgan held up a calendar, tapping his pencil on the month of December. "We're in winter."

"It's not that cold," Adam said. "No snow. I thought we were reaching the end of autumn."

"It doesn't snow here much," Jorgan said. "I'm told we're too far south, too mild a climate. They get snow more to the north. Here it mostly just rains."

Adam sheathed his dagger and returned to the table to take a closer look at the calendar. "You have my birthday circled."

"Oh, is that your birthday? That's the day the portal is due to open."

Adam dropped the calendar back down on the table. "I guess it wouldn't be a good idea to ask for that day off then."

"Not a good idea anyway." Jorgan shuffled through a few stacks of papers until he pulled out lists of numbers. "Only kids celebrate their birthdays in this country. If you ask for it off, they'll think you have the mentality of a child."

"Not even birthdays that mark a decade?" Adam asked. "I'm going to be twenty."

"Not even those," Jorgan said.

Adam went back to the other side of the room to continue drilling. He didn't even get two moves complete before Strom sauntered in with a big grin. He took off his shirt, grabbed a new one and thrust his arms in the sleeves.

"Why are you changing your shirt?" Adam asked.

"To confuse you." Strom buttoned up the double-breasted front.

"There was nothing wrong with what you had on," Adam said. "It doesn't look dirty, or ripped, or anything."

"See?" Strom laughed. "It worked."

Gerhardt burst in the room. Strom swallowed his laughter and looked away. Gerhardt bore down on him, grabbing his shirt and shaking him. "You are one slippery fish when you don't want to report. I am about this close—" he held his thumb and forefinger about an inch apart— "to beating it out of you."

"There's nothing to report." Strom shrank, his shoulders hunching up making his neck shorter, his back arching away from Gerhardt and lowering his own height.

"Are you even trying?" Gerhardt let go and Strom nearly toppled onto his butt. "How difficult can this be?"

"When they disappear, it's in the middle of the night." Strom took a couple steps backward, putting distance between him and Gerhardt. "By the time I get there in the morning, the door's locked and they won't let me in. They won't tell me what they're doing or where they go. There's nothing more I can do."

"You can report it to me when they disappear," Gerhardt said.

"I do," Strom said.

"Immediately!" Gerhardt's volume rose so loud Adam flinched. "Not later that evening. Or whenever you think it's convenient. Immediately."

"All right!" Strom threw up his hands. "Fine. I'll wake you up next time. Just don't yell at me when I do."

With that, he stomped out. No dismissal. No salute. Not even a yes, sir. And Gerhardt didn't demand the protocols. He simply let Strom go. Adam stood on the far side of the room, not daring to move, not even enough to pick his jaw up off the floor until Gerhardt also left.

Then Adam found his tongue. "Who keeps going missing?"

"Ziegfried's bodyguards," Jorgan said. "Three weeks out of the past four, they've disappeared for most of a day. Looking back, I think it's been going on even longer. I don't suppose Andreno has said anything about it?"

Adam shook his head. He went back to drilling until he finally exhausted himself enough to sleep. Then over the next few days he paid more attention to every word said by and around Andreno. There was nothing about Ziegfried's bodyguards.

When Andreno wasn't talking about taking revenge on the mountains over the villages he was doing nothing to help, people were talking about Ziegfried's scheduled portal opening. That talk was about the Germans in general, not specifically the bodyguards.

Adam half waited for someone to ask him about his own people. Or even realize they were talking about his people in front of him. None of them did. He mentioned that to Jorgan.

"Think about it," Jorgan said. "If they talk to you about our people, who are so far away that the only way of traversing back and forth is through a portal, then that shatters the rumor that we're from the Chemwanitz Mountains, which are close enough to travel to overland."

"I still don't know why that rumor keeps going," Adam said. "Since every time Andreno hears it he insists it's not true."

"Which shows what people think of Andreno's opinions and assessments," Jorgan said. He bent back over all the papers he still worked on. "Now, leave me alone. I have to finish all these figures."

Since Adam couldn't help, he left Jorgan alone to work and just did the best he could to try and gain the information that would ease Gerhardt's angst. By the time his birthday dawned, the day the portal opened, he still had nothing.

Strom lounged in the room while Jorgan donned his dress uniform. Adam said, "I still think it looks odd without any patches or symbols on it."

"Bruises and marks of a beating would look more odd if he put symbols or patches back on," Strom remarked. "That's what happened to the last person who didn't have them all removed before coming here."

"I still don't know why we had to remove them all," Adam said.

"It's not like it matters." Strom used a droll tone, as if bored.

"It kind affects some of the way we operate here," Jorgan said.

"Only if you're correct," Strom said.

"You know why?" Adam asked Jorgan.

"It's not like it matters either way," Strom said. He pointed a finger at Jorgan. "And you don't know for sure either. You can claim superior deductive powers all you want. No one has confirmed your theory one way or the other."

"This isn't the only place different from ours," Jorgan said. "Other worlds are populated too. Some of them recognized the symbols we use in the rise of the Third Reich and they put an absolute halt to the operation. So now we remove the symbols."

"If that's true," Strom said, "then why do we still wear the same uniform?"

"Others use the design?" Jorgan said, straightening the straps and the cut of the cloth of said uniform. "It's just different enough that it's not recognized as easily as the symbols? I haven't quite figured that one out yet."

Strom snorted, scoffing. Jorgan scowled at him. "At least I'm trying. Have you made any progress at all in figuring out what you're supposed to?"

"I figured out that Ziegfried's bodyguards didn't disappear this week." Strom rolled his eyes. "That should please Gerhardt. Maybe they stopped whatever it was they were doing."

Jorgan stood frozen, staring at Strom. Tension slowly straightened his back and shoulders as he stiffened. Adam asked, "What is it?"

"Nothing," Strom said. "That's what it is. Jorgan thinks he's figured something out again. But again, he has no verification for whatever it is he's thinking. No proof. So it's nothing."

One of Ziegfried's bodyguards came then, telling them it was almost time. Strom strode out ahead of them, leaving them to come on their own to the large room Andreno had made available for them. Adam asked Jorgan, "Is he mad at you or something? Or is he just irritable because Gerhardt is on his case?"

"Kind of both," Jorgan said. "He's had to do all the interpreting with the natives to set this up the way I want it to run here at the palace. That's another advantage of Far Base. We don't have to go through interpreters."

"I could have helped with that if someone had told me," Adam said.

"Not while Andreno wanted you to just stick around him," Jorgan said. Then he smirked. "Besides, it's good for Strom to actually work once in a while."

Many native workers stood around outside the door to the room. Some of them complained about not being able to go inside and get the job over with. Their complaints ceased when Andreno approached with Masorno.

Jorgan grumbled under his breath, "What's he doing here?"

"The prince or the magician?" Adam refrained from using the names so the respective people wouldn't know they were being talked about.

"The magician," Jorgan said. "I already know what the brat... er... I mean the prince..."

"I know what you meant," Adam said.

"Why is everyone standing around out here?" Masorno demanded. "I thought you said the portal is opening in the room already."

"We wait until my friend sends a messenger saying it's safe," Andreno said.

"If he has a proper containment shield up, it should be safe enough." Masorno put his hand on his hips. "Doesn't your friend know how to do even that much?"

He stalked over to the door and put his hands on it. After a few whispered words he went stone still. Gerhardt asked Adam, "What are they saying?"

"Their magician is confused why our portal opener isn't using a method safe enough for us to be in the room with the magic," Adam said.

"Interesting," Gerhardt said. "I didn't know there was a safer method."

"I'm pretty sure there's a faster method," Jorgan said. He looked over at Strom, far enough away he wouldn't hear what they were saying. "I think Ziegfried is opening portals for his bodyguards to use."

"A portal every week?" Gerhardt frowned.

"It lines up with him going down into the dungeons to leech energy off of the prisoners there," Jorgan said. "You pointed out if that was the case then he was either storing up a lot more energy than he claimed, or he was using it. I think he's using it."

"To open a portal every week," Gerhardt said. "Next questions are why and to where?"

"Shouldn't we report this back home?" Adam asked.

"So the regime learns that they can have magicians leech energy off of people and store it up in charms?" Gerhardt asked. "No."

"Do you have any idea what that would do to the people trapped in POW and concentration camps?" Jorgan asked.

"Concentration camps?" Adam asked. "What are those?"

"Forget he mentioned it," Gerhardt said, scowling at Jorgan. "Like magic, it's one of the things that's being hidden from the public eye."

"Dangerous to talk about, got it," Adam said.

"Besides that," Gerhardt said. "If the regime decides that whatever Ziegfried is pursuing is beneficial to the operation before I find out what it is, then there's no way I can figure out if it actually is beneficial or detrimental, and put a stop to it if it's the latter."

Either way, it was more of a reason for Adam to help figure it out too. Maybe he could ask Nolrien for help. At the very least he could ask how best to collect information people were trying to keep secret. Which meant all he had to do was wait through the rest of the day then talk to Nolrien in the morning during training.

"This is very sloppy work." Masorno took his hands away from the door. "Even I could do better. And I'm not very good at portal making."

"Could you make it as far as this is going?" Andreno asked with a smug look.

"No," Masorno said.

"I thought not," Andreno said.

"It's just to the mountains," Kurlos mumbled in Andreno's shadow.

Andreno whirled around and cuffed his ear. He turned into a sobbing puddle on the floor. Until Andreno turned away. Then he smiled and picked himself up without even a sign of any tears.

Adam looked away. He repeated in his head to just get through the day. That was all he had to do. Just get through the day.

One of Ziegfried's bodyguards came and said, "It's ready."

Gerhardt opened the door. The portal stood right in the center of the large, warehouse-like space, as mesmerizing and beautiful as ever. Masorno wrinkled his nose at it. "Sloppy. Very sloppy work."

"And yet," Andreno said with a laugh. "You admitted you'd couldn't do as much. Why do I keep you on?"

"Because I keep your contacts with Kemetulla and the gathering friendly," Masorno said.

That shut Andreno up. Which made Adam smile. As much as he didn't care for Masorno, anyone who could stick it to Andreno couldn't be all bad.

Jorgan nudged him and whispered, "Hey, every once in a while someone slips me a little something while I'm on the other side. It's never anything important. Usually a pen, or some matches, or a candy, or something stupid like that. If it happens this time, you want it since it's your birthday?"

"Aww, aren't you a nice guy." Adam poured as much friendly sarcasm as he could muster. "Thanks. But I'm fine. Really."

"Suit yourself," Jorgan said.

With that, he stepped through the portal. The transfer began. It didn't go nearly as smooth as it did at base. Strom ran up and down the line, interpreting instructions to everyone working the flow. He was stuck with doing that alone, since Adam was stuck double checking the writing on the crates.

Only about half the crates went home than the last time. After the gold came Adam watched Andreno, half expecting him to throw a fit over how much less there was because of it. Instead, he laughed and joked and mocked.

The supplies from home came through, about half the amount as last time. Then the new men. That number was the same. A few of them staggered. One of them stumbled off in the wrong direction and fell over.

"How odd," Masorno said.

"Someone always reacts badly to it," Andreno said.

"What? That man? That's not what I was talking about," Masorno said. "Quite frankly, I'm surprised more of them didn't collapse. This portal has sucked energy from every person who's stepped through it, except that first man who went in. I've never seen anything like this."

Adam told Gerhardt, "Ziegfried is sucking energy from people crossing through again."

"As always," Gerhardt said.

He stared at the portal. Strom shuffled the new men off to temporary quarters until they could be shipped with the goods to Far Base. The natives worked at setting the room to rights around the portal. Andreno yawned, made excuses, and left. Eventually one of Ziegfried's bodyguards came and asked what was taking so long.

"Hauptmann Gruber isn't back yet," Gerhardt said.

"Should we send someone back through to see what the hold up is?" the bodyguard asked. "Ziegfried isn't going to be able to keep this open much longer."

"They know that," Gerhardt said.

The bodyguard paced. Jorgan wasn't actually trying to get a little something for Adam, was he? Gerhardt continued staring at the portal. Finally Jorgan came back. Wearing a red welt on his left cheek he gave the cut off signal, sending the bodyguard running back to relay the message to Ziegfried. Then he handed over the package he always carried to Gerhardt.

"They weren't happy with the amount of supplies that came through," Jorgan said.

Gerhardt thumbed through the papers Jorgan had given him. Then he tilted his head, looking at Jorgan's cheek. "I can see that. Did you say what I told you to?"

"Yes, sir," Jorgan said. "That's when they made the amendments you see on the papers. They still weren't pleased."

"So Wattenberger smacked you?"

"That wasn't Wattenberger," Jorgan said. "That was someone I didn't recognize."

Chapter 38

ADAM WENT TO PRACTICE EARLY. He didn't mean to. It just happened after a chain of irritating events.

Jorgan had risen grumpy that morning. The welt on his cheek had bruised over. And he complained about all the work he now had to do to compensate for the shortage of supplies sent from home, and how to get everything and the new personnel overland to base.

Strom woke grumpy too. Strom arose grumpy any time he slept in his own bed. Probably because that meant he wasn't in some woman's bed taking advantage of her. Of course, he had to make a remark about Jorgan's bruise. "Did someone finally get tired of you and whack you for it? Or did you see someone breaking a rule and it hurt your eye that much?"

Adam quickly dressed and slipped out of the room to escape the argument that comment incited. Since he was early to breakfast there was no line. He got his food faster. He seated himself faster. Thus, he finished and went to practice sooner.

Nolrien was already there. He was off in a corner talking quietly with someone. It could have been one of the workers that helped with the portal the day before. Then again, maybe not. Adam had seen so many faces in the palace some of them meshed together after a while. Both that guy and Nolrien watched Adam come in, approach, set his water down. Neither said a thing, not even to each other.

"Did you stop talking because I am here?" Adam asked.

"Yes," Nolrien said. "You're early. Why?"

"Just because I am." Adam didn't feel like getting into details. "I do not see why it matters. And I wanted to talk to you anyway."

Nolrien crossed his arms, staring at Adam with that blank look he used. The other man moved off. Nolrien said, "You're here early, and don't want to talk about why, because you want to talk?"

"All right, fine," Adam said. "I am early because I left my room early because Jorgan is grumpy."

"Grumpy because someone hit him yesterday?" Nolrien asked.

"Close enough," Adam said.

"Was it someone he could hit back?" Nolrien asked. "Or is there nothing he can do about it?"

"Why does it matter?"

"If it's the second one, that would make me grumpy too," Nolrien said.

"Even if he could hit them back," Adam said, "And he probably cannot, he is not that kind of person. Satisfied?"

"More than you know," Nolrien said. "What did you want to talk about?"

"How do I go about figuring out what someone is doing when they are trying to hide their actions?"

"Like who hit your friend?"

"Like what Ziegfried's bodyguards are doing and where they go when they disappear for a day."

Nolrien stared at him for a moment. Then without giving an answer, he turned away, picked up the practice blades, handed one to Adam, and said, "Let's get started."

Adam glowered. "If you are not going to help me, the least you could do is tell me no."

Nolrien ran him through some of the first warm up exercises before he said anything more.

"I don't figure things out," Nolrien said. "I just collect pieces of information to hand to others to figure out."

Like Jorgan. Adam said, "I could do that."

"You don't even know when you're giving information away," Nolrien said. "How are you supposed to gather up information dropped by others if you don't even recognize when you drop it?"

"Maybe if I learn how to pick it up I will stop dropping it," Adam said.

"That would make my job harder," Nolrien said. "You're not giving me any reason to help you with this. Now, stop talking and get to work."

With that the lesson began. If a lesson is what it could be called. They had revisited drilling how to fall properly. Then they had gone over how to keep from being tripped. Now Nolrien claimed he was teaching Adam how to not get grabbed by the arm and put into an awkward position in the first place.

To Adam it was more of an excuse to humiliate him. He was supposed to draw while either fending Nolrien off, or getting his weapon out before Nolrien grabbed him. He tried side stepping. He tried ducking. He tried feinting. Nothing worked. So he went on the attack instead.

He tried pushing. That worked at first. Then the second time, Nolrien tripped him instead of grabbing for his arm. Adam jumped back to his feet full of temper and took a swing with a fist.

Nolrien blocked Adam's right swing with a left hand on his forearm. Before Adam could react to that, Nolrien slid his left hand down to the wrist and grabbed hold. At the same time, he shot his right arm around Adam's right shoulder and twined around his elbow. That bent him forward and sideways, his entire side exposed.

"Now what are you going to do?" Nolrien asked.

Adam lurched to the left, trying to yank his arm free. Nolrien held fast and said, "There are so many things I could do to you in this position. For instance, I could break ribs by lifting my knee."

Adam tried hooking his foot behind Nolrien's leg. If he could trip him, maybe that would force him to let go? Unfortunately, Nolrien simply lifted his foot out of the way. "Oh, you want to play it that way. Very well."

The next thing Adam knew, he was on the ground again. And he still couldn't get his arm free. For all the effort Adam was exerting, Nolrien didn't even sound winded when he said, "You're making it worse for yourself. Don't just lash out. Stop and think. You're pinned. What are you going to do now?"

Adam bent his left arm at the elbow, attempting to hit him in the kidneys. He had no leverage. And as soon as he moved, Nolrien shifted again, putting his knee on Adam's upper left arm and pinning that too. He said, "Worse and worse. Now what?"

Adam was out of options. Straining did no good except to wear him out. Retaliating brought no success, and only made Nolrien restrain him more tightly. The only limbs he had left to strike with were his legs, and he couldn't maneuver them into position to do so. Worse and worse indeed.

"You could ask for advice," Nolrien said.

"I did," Adam said. "You told me no."

"You asked advice on something I can't teach," Nolrien said. "Not for this."

Adam was out of options. And he was too tired now to keep struggling. He went limp. Nolrien let go.

Rolling away, Adam sprawled on the floor and lay heaving until his lungs had their fill. Nolrien sat a couple of feet away, saying nothing. That allowed him the space to just gather himself and calm down.

One of the other guards edged over to them from watching another sparring match. He looked at Adam and said, "Nolrien, did you finally kill him for us?"

"Get out of here before I rearrange your face," Nolrien snarled.

Instead of leaving, the man chuckled like he thought it was a joke. He held out his hand to Adam and helped him back to his feet. Then asked, "Are you joining us for the Winter Festival this year?"

"Festival?" Adam hadn't heard anything about this.

"How can you have been part of Andreno's entourage and not heard about our Winter Festival?" the man asked.

"Andreno never helps with that," Nolrien said. He actually sneered instead of maintaining his normal flat expression and tone. "He's always left the work of planning and preparation to everyone else. He just wants the advantages as if he's still a child."

That got laughs out of several within earshot. The man said to Adam, "You won Nolrien's approval. You're with us now. You're joining us at the Festival."

"I will see if I have permission," Adam said.

Strom stood in front of the door of their shared room, blocking it with both arms out. "You are *not* going wearing that! What happened to the clothes I gave you for this?"

"I already changed once today after sparring," Adam said. "And only because I was sweaty and stinky. I'm not changing again. That's stupid. These clothes are clean enough."

And the clothes Strom had told him to wear looked stupid too. Adam didn't figure he should say that part. For a week now, since he'd told them some of the palace guards wanted him to join them, Strom had been bugging him about this. He looked over at Jorgan, sitting at the table and pretending to read his Bible while staring at the picture of his wife instead.

"Help me out here," Adam said.

"Nope," Jorgan said. He leaned back and grinned. That was a bit of a relief. This was the first time, even since the bruise on his face began fading. "I'm actually with Strom on this one. I've had to listen to you complain this entire time, when he's the one who knows what attire would be appropriate for this. Look, he's dressed up, and without complaining."

"He changes clothes every time he turns around," Adam said.

"And right now, you're going to change too," Strom said. "Everyone knows I pick your clothes. And I'm not going to let you damage my reputation by wearing... this." He flicked his fingers at Adam's shirt. "Not to a festival."

"Besides," Jorgan said. "Out of the two of you, he's the one who's been to this festival before. Even if you weren't stupid about clothes, I'd trust his judgment on what's appropriate to wear."

"Fine!" Adam stalked over to his bed where Strom had laid out the stupid change of clothes. He yanked off what he was wearing. He must had pulled a bit too hard, because one of the sleeves ripped at the shoulder seam.

"Careful!" Strom still wouldn't move from blocking the door. "My favorite seamstress gets irritated when you do that."

Growling under his breath, Adam wadded the shirt up into a ball and threw it on the bed. He yanked on the other one. "That's what happens when you make me do stupid things like change clothes for no good reason."

As soon as Adam had fully changed, Strom stomped over and grabbed up the shirt. He opened it, holding the rip close and examining it. Adam took the opportunity to escape out the door.

He stood in the hallway a moment, not even sure where exactly to go. Not wanting Strom to come out and harass him further, he headed for the nearest area where people tended to congregate. Before he got there, he met Nolrien coming his way.

"There you are," Nolrien said.

"Sorry if I am late," Adam said.

"Late?" Nolrien looked at him quizzically, a nice change from his customary blank expression. "This is a holiday. No schedule. I just wanted to catch you before Andreno decided he wanted to show off to the people he normally surrounds himself with."

He turned back the way he'd come. Adam followed. Nolrien said, "We'll have to put in an appearance for all the other guards. Then we can move off somewhere a little quieter if you don't mind. Marietta and her friends asked for you."

"I don't..." Adam hesitated. Should he say he didn't want to spend a holiday with women who had recently been prostitutes? Would people think he was using them inappropriately? Then again, he also didn't want people thinking he had no interest in women. So if he refused...

"Marietta told me everything," Nolrien said. "You don't have to worry about anyone bothering you that way. It's just a party."

They reached the open area where Adam had first met Nolrien when looking for a teacher. The noise volume increased exponentially. Men laughed raucously, took bets on arm wrestling at tables, danced around to a couple of musicians in the corner Adam couldn't even hear.

Several women mingled around, not all of them fully dressed. They cussed and laughed and ate and drank as much or more than all the men. One of them spotted Adam and sauntered over with an ear-splitting grin.

She had to raise her voice for Adam to hear her. "Did you bring Strom?"

"No," Adam said.

"Aww." She pouted. "I was half hoping you would. He always gives the nicest little presents."

One of the guards normally seen during practice shoved a mug at Adam. "Finally you join us!"

The woman brushed up against the man's side. "Did you bring me one?"

The guard grinned wider, put an arm around her waist, and handed her the mug he'd been drinking out of. She laughed and emptied it. Adam sniffed at his. It smelled faintly of watered-down ale. He wrinkled his nose.

"Drink up," the guard said. "What's the matter? Too used to Andreno's wine?"

"I prefer other drinks to wine," Adam said. He sampled the dark liquid in the mug. It tasted worse than it smelled. He grimaced.

Several guards around them laughed. One of them called out. "Not used to a good ale?"

"This is not good ale," Adam said. "My people make good ale. This is terrible."

They all laughed again, some of them agreeing as they did so. Someone handed Adam a plate of food. It was just as bland as always. He set it aside, eliciting more laughter from the men. Then one of them snagged a passing woman and said, "Let's say we try for an announcement next winter festival?"

She slapped his face so hard she left a mark. As she stalked off, back stiff, everyone around him hooted and jeered. Adam leaned to Nolrien and asked, "What was that about?"

"Birth and pregnancies that have happened during the past year are announced publicly at the winter festival," Nolrien said.

"Then he deserved to get slapped," Adam said. "Bad drink. Bad food. Bad mannered people. I have put in an appearance. Can I be done now?"

"We can go," Nolrien said. "Slip out while I distract them so they don't stop you. Head for the practice field. I'll find you."

"I don't want to go out to the practice field," Adam said. "It's cold outside. And raining."

"You won't get that far. I'll find you first." Nolrien made a shooing gesture. "Go on."

Adam didn't question any further. He left. No one stopped him, so Nolrien must have distracted the others as promised. Also as promised, he caught up before Adam got outside. He directed Adam up a narrow set of back stairs saying, "This is the shortest way to Charlass' rooms."

"Can I only just make an appearance there too?" Adam asked. "I would rather just go back to my room."

"She probably has something to give you," Nolrien said. "It won't be much, because she doesn't have much. Maybe some sweet biscuits or something."

"This is sounding more and more like a festival my people have in the middle of winter," Adam said.

"Oh?" Nolrien went up another flight, this one just as narrow. "Do you celebrate with the first snow like they do up north? Or with the solstice like us where we don't always get snow?"

"Around the solstice," Adam said. "We call it *Weinacht*."

"And you do birth and pregnancy announcements?" Nolrien asked. "Some places also do marriage and engagement announcements. Around here that's more the nobility than the commoners."

"We have other traditions," Adam said. "Like *der Weihnachtsmann*. He brings gifts for well-behaved children."

Nolrien left the stairwell and strode up a wide, but unkept, empty corridor with frayed carpeting and dust everywhere. "And if the children aren't well behaved?"

"Then they get a visit from *Belsnickel* who gives them a beating," Adam said with a shrug. "Or *Krampus*, or *Knecht Ruprecht*, it depends on what area you grow up. *Krampus* is more northern. *Belsnickel* is more southwestern."

"Different areas, variations on similar traditions," Nolrien said with a nod. "Just like here. Human nature is human nature no matter where you go."

He stopped in front of a wide door, his hand hovering just over the latch. Then he pulled it away. "Before we go in, I have something for you."

"I have no gifts to give in return," Adam said.

"If you want an exchange," Nolrien said, "then I'm the one returning. And I'm returning a poor exchange at that. You gave Marietta, her sister, her friends, you gave them a life. All I have is my father's other dagger."

He crouched and pulled up a pant leg. Buckled around his angle was another dagger exactly like Adam's, only smaller. He took it off and said, "The one you acquired was half of a matched set. There were supposed to be more, but he didn't have the money to pay for them. So there were only these two."

He stood with the sheathed weapon. He put it in Adam's hand. "Marietta means a lot to me. So what you did means a lot. And I thank you."

Nolrien opened the door, striding inside and leaving Adam standing there trying to pick his jaw off the floor.

Chapter 39

E VERY EVENING, ADAM USED THE ONLY OPEN SPACE in the room he shared to go over the dagger moves he'd learned from Nolrien. He still didn't know how to use two at a time, but that didn't stop him from playing with two now that he had them. Maybe if he practiced enough then someday he wouldn't get beaten so badly in the mornings.

During those times, Jorgan sat with his open Bible. The red mark on his face healed enough it was completely gone. His mood had not fared as well.

About a week after the winter festival, during one of the evening sessions, he groused at Adam. "Remember that night I threatened to smother you? I meant it. You get any closer to me while you're waving that thing around and I'm going to suffocate you in your sleep."

"I'm nowhere near you." Adam completed another move. "Besides, how are you going to suffocate me in my sleep when you keep me awake with your snoring?"

"I don't snore," Jorgan grumbled.

"How do you know. You're asleep. You don't hear yourself."

"I don't snore." Jorgan's eyes didn't move across the words of The Book. The photo of his wife lay on the page, right in front of his nose.

Adam lowered his dagger. "You all right?"

"I think I know why I was sent here."

"Really?"

"There was an SS officer on the other side of the of the portal this last time." Jorgan closed his Bible over the photograph. "My wife's maiden name was the same as his, and I could see a family resemblance. He's the one who hit me. He never even said anything. He just glared, like he was angry, or hated me for something."

"You think he's a relative of hers?"

"Pretty sure of it," Jorgan said with a nod. "And it adds up. It would explain the timing of my conscription. If an SS officer is mad that I married his niece, or cousin, or whatever she is to him, he might take whatever steps he could to separate us. It also stands to reason that he's pressured her into getting that annulment I'm so terrified of."

Adam sheathed his daggers. "If he's still mad at you, wouldn't that mean she hasn't done it?"

"Maybe. The only thing I really can't figure out is why he'd be so opposed. It's not like I couldn't provide for her. I'd just started a well-paying job. I had a nice house in a good neighborhood. And it was in Neuberg, the least hit city in the entire war."

"You're from Neuberg? That's where I'm from! My parents' house is on the southern outskirts, about a mile from that park with the big fountain."

"I don't know that part of the city." Gruber shook his head. "I lived across the river to the west, closer to those hills at the foot of the mountain. The few times the city has taken hits, it was nowhere near our neighborhood. I'd have kept her as safe as she could be in this damned war. But one of her relatives pulling strings is the only thing that makes sense. I took preventative steps to keep from getting conscripted. At least, I thought I had. If there was one thing I could have gone back and done differently, maybe I should have tried harder to meet her extended family."

Adam waited, making sure Jorgan's ramblings had petered out. He asked, "You really think it would have made a difference?"

"I'll never know now," Jorgan said with a shrug.

"If there was one thing I could go back and change, I'd have gone to work for my dad like he wanted me to." Adam put his daggers away in his drawer. "I wish I hadn't fought with him so much, that I'd listened to him instead of running off to enlist."

"That's right. I forgot. You said you volunteered. I forget why."

"I thought I could make a difference." It sounded pretty stupid now as Adam said it.

"One person? In this war? That's a little naive."

"I know that now," Adam said. "And if I'd gone to work for my dad instead, I don't think he'd have gone looking for that forbidden information that got him in trouble. It's the kind of thing he'd do, dig up proof to give me that he's right. My family wouldn't be under threat. And I wouldn't have been sent here."

Jorgan smiled a little. "But then you wouldn't have had the pleasure of meeting me."

"True."

"And you'd still think that magic was only in fairy tales." Jorgan ticked off the points on his fingers. "And you'd be stuck with learning only the languages of our home world. And you wouldn't get to spend all your time in Prince Andreno's company. Wait... Maybe it would have been better for you to stay home after all."

Adam laughed. Strom walked in just then. He had a smile from ear to ear plastered on his face. "Hey, no laughing and having fun without me."

"Then we'd never have any fun," Adam said. "You're never here. Besides, how do you know we're not having fun at your expense."

"Proves you're both jealous of me." Strom smiled at them. He changed his shirt. Then he headed for the door again. "Don't wait up for me."

"As if we ever do," Adam said once Strom was gone. "Why does he come in and change his shirt like that? The ones he changes out of are never dirty. What? Why are you giving me that look?"

"He changes into something more fancy." Jorgan said it like Adam was a complete moron. "He's dressing to impress."

"Who'd be impressed by a stupid shirt?"

"It was a very nice shirt. Not a stupid one. The kind that the wealthy women here seem to be attracted to."

"It was a shirt. A shirt is a shirt is a shirt."

"No wonder Strom chooses all your clothes for you. You're a complete dunce." Jorgan said. "I suppose you also haven't noticed he has pretty good taste."

"Taste in clothes?"

"Yes, you idiot." Jorgan gave him a droll look. "He makes it so you don't stick out like a sore thumb among all the nobles hanging around with Andreno. That's the important thing. And if you're too dumb to do it, that's why your uniforms were taken away and someone else chooses what you wear every day."

"How'd Strom get to be good at picking clothes?" Adam put his hands on his hips. "I thought that was a girl thing."

"His relatives are one of the old noble families," Jorgan said. "He's always been overly conscious of what other people think of him because of it. He takes pains to look good, even to people he doesn't like. And to him, that includes learning about clothes and favored fashions."

"He said he's not that close to his dad."

"He's not," Jorgan said. "Which might turn out good for him. As of the last portal, Gerhardt has a list of the names of men whose families will get harassed and punished if we don't get the raw materials back up to demand by the next portal opening."

"Strom's name was on it?"

"It was one of the names that got crossed off, probably because he's one of our few interpreters. The government hates the old noble families. They'll use whatever excuse they want to make examples of them."

"Was mine on it?" Adam's gut clenched at the very thought.

"No."

"Yours?" Adam asked.

"No."

"Helmut's?"

"Helmut was raised in an orphanage," Jorgan said. "He doesn't have any family to threaten."

"What about Kiefer?"

"There's nothing they can do to Keifer." Jorgan's face darkened. "His family is dead. All of them. What little good behavior we get from him is out of sheer respect for Gerhardt, nothing else."

"Were they killed because he misbehaves so much?"

"He misbehaves partly because they were killed," Jorgan said. "Most of us, we get the option to behave and keep our family safe. Kiefer didn't get that choice. They were killed after he got here, and before he had a chance to do anything wrong. He found out when he heard Ziegfried laughing and making jokes about it."

That explained a lot. And it left Adam with a sour taste. His desire for conversation died for the rest of the evening. It seemed to have helped Jorgan, though. His mood lifted after that. He went back to reading his Bible at nights, instead of stopping to stare endlessly at the photo of his wife. He ceased complaining about Adam practicing with his dagger. He even exchanged cheerful banter on the few occasions Strom made an appearance. Perhaps he had just needed to let off some steam.

Andreno's mood lightened too, despite continued reports of village raids. He found out that villages in Brend were also being raided, and that nearly made him giddy. Until he did a bit of correspondence with the Brendish King. Then he went back to taking his temper out on his servants.

Other than a few childish fits now and then, he generally remained in a good mood. He entertained guests. Sometimes in his private chambers. Sometimes he took time for them out of his military planning sessions. Most often, he simply ate lunch with them.

It was during lunch one day about a month after the winter festival, while Adam's belly grumbled at him about being empty, that Ziegfried staggered into the room, ashen faced, stumbling like a drunk. He babbled, "They knew. They were prepared. They were warned. Some of the men are injured. They had to retreat."

"What are you going on about?" Andreno rose to his feet, his face flushing. "What's wrong with you?"

"My men." Ziegfried huffed and gasped for breath. "You know they went this morning. It was a disaster."

"Oh." Andreno said. He smiled at his guests. "I'm terribly sorry. I have to take care of this. Perhaps you can all join me for the evening meal instead."

With that, Andreno took Ziegfried by the arm and led him from the room. His usual cadre of servants, bodyguards, and officials followed him. He snarled at them, "Leave us alone!"

The servants and officials hung back. The bodyguards followed them to Ziegfried's chambers. Andreno allowed them that far, then said to them, "You wait out here. Give us some privacy."

Adam tried to step into the main room behind Ziegfried. Andreno held out a hand to stop him. "You stay out too."

Adam pushed away Andreno's hand. "If Ziegfried needs help, why should I stay out here?"

"You don't question me!" Andreno shoved Adam away and slammed the door shut.

Adam went straight to Gerhardt. He and Jorgan had papers strewn all over a large table. They were bent over them, their foreheads nearly touching. Both looked up at him when he entered.

"I think Ziegfried's bodyguards went somewhere again today," Adam told them. "Ziegfried looks like he opened a portal. And the way he's acting, things went sour for his bodyguards."

Gerhardt and Jorgan left the paperwork immediately, following Adam to Ziegfried's chambers. Andreno's bodyguards made halfhearted attempts to stop them from going in, doing little more than sounding bored while they said that Andreno wanted privacy. Gerhardt didn't even wait for Adam to interpret. He simply threw open the door and strode in.

Ziegfried's bodyguards were all there, all out of uniform. Some of them were half naked, binding up shallow wounds, or propping up swollen append-ages. The ones fully clothed wore furs and skins. They stood over the injured, holding bandages and tonics. All of them had paint on their faces, making them look like they wore costumes of American Indians right out of a western flick in the cinema.

"You're not the medic!" Andreno snarled. He yelled out the door, "Where's that medic I sent for!"

"What is going on here?" Gerhardt roared. No one answered him. All the bodyguards stood in frozen horror, staring at him with the fearful expressions of a child caught with their hand in the cookie jar. Gerhardt shouted again. "Explain this!"

"Well… um…" Schneider, the man in charge of the bodyguards stuttered with a cracking voice. He cleared his throat and tried again. "It's all rather embarrassing, sir. It started last fall."

Gerhardt crossed his arms. "What started?"

"Andreno was telling Ziegfried about the barbaric practices of the people who live in the mountains to the east." Schneider got his tongue working, but his voice still cracked once in a while. "And Ziegfried said it sounded like what he knew of the American Indians. Andreno said he'd like to learn more about some of their tactics. Then his military could do training exercises to practice fighting. Ziegfried has us dress up like Indians and do mock drills. We pretend to attack soldiers, who pretend to be villagers."

"I don't believe you." Gerhardt waved a hand around at all the men. "These kinds of injuries aren't from any damned drill. This looks like it was a real fight. Not a mock one."

"Things got a little carried away today," Schneider said. "They tried a new tactic. They had some kind of alarm set up. It alerted the defenders to our oncoming attack. We were rather annoyed by it, because no one told us they were going to do anything like that. So we really hit them with our weapons, instead of pretending. So they really hit us back."

"This is between me and Andreno, anyway," Ziegfried puffed from the chair where he sprawled.

"These are *my* men," Gerhardt barked at him. "Not yours! I've assigned them to protect you. Not serve you. And as for you, you're in enough trouble as it is. Explain why you look like you just opened a portal."

"Because I did." Ziegfried mustered up enough strength to stick out his chin a little bit. "All right? Are you satisfied? I open portals for them to go to these mock battles every week or two. Then when they get back, I go get a refill and put some of it into my charm. This isn't going to affect my ability to open the portal to home when the time comes. What's your problem?"

"You have no right to do this with my men."

"You think that international relations are just a matter of trading gold for some raw materials?" Ziegfried frowned. "You have to also please the leaders of the other nation. If they want it, you have to try assisting them in studying military tactics."

"Don't you lecture me on diplomacy," Gerhardt said. "You didn't even broach this with me."

"I'm a civilian," Ziegfried said. "I don't have to. I'm not subject to your orders."

"You're a civilian," Gerhardt repeated with his lips peeled back baring his teeth. "You're not a military commander with the authority to give orders to military men, or send them on any kind of op. These exercises are shut down. I'm assigning you new bodyguards. These men are all going back to base to face reprimand for acting out of line with the chain of command."

"Now wait just a damn minute." Ziegfried tried to sit up. He made it almost halfway.

"What's going on?" Andreno had been watching, his head turning back and forth between the two men as if watching a tennis match. "What's he saying now?"

"He's trying to take my men away from me," Ziegfried said.

"My men," Gerhardt corrected.

"We can't allow that." Andreno sniffed haughtily. "Tell him I demand they stay. You, Adam, you're supposed to be my interpreter. Tell him I command this."

"Your commands are why he is angry," Adam said, trying to think of another way to put things so that Andreno would be agreeable rather than indignant and difficult. "He is responsible for these men. If they are injured protecting Ziegfried, they have done their job. If they are injured doing extra things he gave no permission for, you have dirtied his reputation."

"Oh, I hadn't thought of that." Andreno blinked. "In that case, tell him if he's willing to leave them here with Ziegfried, and allow them to continue helping me, I'm willing to compromise with him on some things."

When Adam told Gerhardt, he said, "He already knows what I want."

"He can't give you all those resources right now," Ziegfried said. "He's using them. He has to use them. Because you keep refusing to help him."

"I don't have the authority to do what he wants any more than you have the authority to send my men on an operation." Gerhardt narrowed his eyes at Ziegfried. "Besides, his excuse for this stupid campaign he's cobbling together is flimsy at best."

"Those Chemwanee attacked his villages." Ziegfried managed to sit up a little bit more. "He has every right to invade their land."

"The set up makes me think they're scapegoats," Gerhardt said. "He was trying to get me to attack them before the raids started. And if he wasn't so hell bent on this, he'd have the resources to trade us. Get me them. Or you're getting new bodyguards."

"I'm not going to dictate to him," Ziegfried said.

"Pack up." Gerhardt ordered the men. "You're all being transferred to Far Base for disciplinary reviews. No matter the outcome, the least all of you can expect is burning duty for the next year. Jorgan, go have the radio men raise base to prepare for incoming. Tell Grippe to select men to send as replacements. And Schneider, if I find out there's more going on than you admitted to, you're a dead man."

"WAIT! Wait! Wait." Ziegfried deflated, dropping limply back into the chair. "Can we please at least try to work this out? Privately?"

"Fine, but it better be good." Gerhardt hiked his thumb back over his shoulder, his eyes roving over every person in the room except Ziegfried and Andreno. "Out! All of you. Out."

Chapter 40

EVERYONE SLOWLY WORKED through the bottleneck of the door. When they had all gotten into the corridor, Gerhardt closed them out just as a medic approached. The man saw all the injuries and started triaging. All of Ziegfried's bodyguards glared at Adam.

"Why did you have to go and tattle?" one of them asked him.

"Why did you have to go and do stuff you weren't supposed to?" Jorgan challenged in Adam's defense.

"I had no idea you were doing that other stuff." Adam had no need for anyone else to stand up for him. "All I knew was that Ziegfried came to Andreno saying some of you were hurt. They wouldn't let me in to see how bad you were, so I went to the man responsible for you."

"Like you should have done," Jorgan said. "That's not tattling. That's looking out for your welfare, even if you're too stupid to do it yourself. And where's Strom? He should have gone to Gerhardt with this too."

"He gets a day off when we do these exercises," Schneider said.

"Why?" Jorgan asked. "Plausible deniability?"

"Strom is a little high strung," Schneider said. "He needs a break sometimes. We give him one on a day when Ziegfried won't need him anyway."

"If Strom is high strung—" Jorgan said— "I'm a monkey's uncle."

"You're a monkey's friend." Schneider sneered. "It's disgusting how nice you are to that ape you call Kiefer Fritz."

Jorgan flew at him, fists swinging. Schneider flicked away every one of them, making it look as easy as when Nolrien did it to Adam. Andreno's bodyguards stepped away, giving room, not doing a damn thing to stop it. The rest of Ziegfried's bodyguards laughed. Adam grabbed his friend, pulling him back.

"Stop it," he hissed in Jorgan's ear.

"That's right." Schneider leered. "Hold him back before I have to hurt him."

"Shut your mouth!" Adam snapped. "That includes slander about Fritz!"

Schneider narrowed his eyes. "You're going to defend that ape too?"

"I shouldn't have to defend any German assigned here." Adam pushed Jorgan behind him. He stepped forward, getting in Schneider's face. "Not to anyone. Especially not to you."

"Back off." Schneider poked him in the chest. "Or I'll hurt you."

"Go ahead." Adam inched closer. "I'll let you. I won't even fight back. See what happens. I'll use that to make certain you're removed from your position."

"You don't scare me," Schneider said.

"Then hit me," Adam challenged.

They stood toe to toe for a few heartbeats. Adam's pulse sung through his ears. Then the man looked at Andreno's bodyguards, even though they hadn't closed in when Adam stopped Jorgan. Schneider blew out his breath, backing off a step, mumbling, "You're pathetic. Not worth it."

The door to Ziegfried's rooms opened. Andreno pointed at Adam. "You. Get in here and interpret."

"Ziegfried can interpret," Adam said, adrenaline still surging through his veins.

"Do as I tell you, servant," Andreno said.

Adam refused to budge. "If you are the master, go interpret for yourself."

"Weiss, get in here," Gerhardt called from inside. Adam entered. Gerhardt stood by the chair where Ziegfried looked like he had passed out. "Why did you hesitate?"

"I'm through answering to spoiled brat princelings and their petty demands," Adam said. "The next time he hits someone over nothing, I swear I'm going to hit him back."

"Choose your battles carefully," Gerhardt said. "Put that one aside for now. We have bigger problems on our hands than your ego."

"Now then." Andreno stood up tall, straightening his back and shoulders. "Let's begin again. Due to the fact that your reputation is in question, I'm willing to make some exchanges. I will take over responsibility of these men. Any injuries they may or may not receive in the future will be on my hands, not yours."

Adam interpreted. Gerhardt snorted. "I'm not going over all that stupidity again. Tell the spoiled brat princeling I don't appreciate him wasting my time."

"I'm not finished," Andreno wouldn't let Adam tell him Gerhardt's answer. "I will do this only if you agree to make another trade with me. I'll give you all the resources you want for the next portal opening to your home if you also promise to help me in my upcoming campaign in the mountains."

Gerhardt responded to the interpretation with, "I'm not going back over that again either."

"I know, I know, he already gave me his answer." Again, Andreno didn't let Adam tell him what Gerhardt said. "He doesn't have permission. If I meet the demands for supplies, would he be willing to allow Ziegfried to seek permission for him to go on a campaign?"

"He wants to trade all the supplies we want—" Adam said— "for Ziegfried attempting to gain permission from home for you to carry out a military campaign."

"Permission?" Gerhardt asked. "Or an order to proceed?"

"He said permission," Adam repeated.

"I'm willing to trade on that." Gerhardt nodded to Andreno. "But that's a large compromise. And the bodyguards are another matter entirely. Did Schneider or any of the others happen to mention Strom's location during all this hullabaloo?"

Adam did tattle now. "They said he takes a day off when they go on these outings."

"Is that so." Gerhardt sounded more droll than surprised. "Then if they want to keep these men as Ziegfried's bodyguards, I need someone to keep an eye on them for me. Inform the brat Princeling that I'm willing to let them stay if you and Strom exchange places."

"*What?*" The very notion left Adam incensed. As much as he would love to leave Andreno, switching to Ziegfried wasn't an improvement. Not in the slightest.

"Actually," Gerhardt said. "I'm exchanging the two of you even if they don't agree and I have to assign new bodyguards. But they don't need to know that."

"Well?" Andreno demanded. "You two have done enough talking back and forth. Tell me if he agrees to my compromise."

Adam grit his teeth while he interpreted. Andreno lit up like a Tannenbaum, until Adam got to the part of the personnel exchange. Then he grimaced and said, "As much as I prefer you to Strom, I have to say this is a fair trade, as long as these men continue to help me study the battle tactics of barbarians."

"He wants them to keep doing the mock battles," Adam told Gerhardt.

"Only as long as I give permission for each individual practice," Gerhardt said. "I have to be informed. And no one comes back hurt again. I want the battle plans ahead of time. I want the safety guidelines. And I want detailed written and verbal debriefings of every one of them, from every person involved. That includes the defenders, not just my men."

Adam interpreted the terms. Andreno gave his winning, white teeth smile. "Done!"

"Weiss, I need a word with you." Gerhardt took long strides to the door. Adam followed. Out in the corridor, Gerhardt said, "Jorgan, go find Strom. He and I need to have a chat. Schneider, you too. Come."

Schneider clenched his jaw and followed. Gerhardt went to his room. He told Schneider to wait in the hall and took Adam inside.

"Sit." He pointed to a chair by the table he now used for a desk. "The main reason I'm exchanging you and Strom is because I need information."

"Information, sir?"

"Ziegfried is up to something." Gerhardt leaned on the table with his fists. He didn't speak again for a few moments. He clenched his jaw a few times, not looking Adam in the eye. Finally he said, "We're supposed to find magic that can be used as a weapon against the allies."

"Sir?" Adam wasn't sure he wanted this information.

"Ziegfried opens a tiny portal every month." Gerhardt looked at him now. "He keeps command informed of our efforts in that regard. If it doesn't appear that we're making enough effort, they demand more supplies. That's our measuring stick. They figure if we don't have enough influence to get more supplies, then we won't be able to get information on weaponizing magic either."

Adam couldn't fit that together in his head. "How is that comparable?"

"It's not." Gerhardt shrugged. "But it's the military. We do a lot of stupid, inane things. That doesn't change our situation. We have to at least have the appearance of progress. Which we're not getting in Shontarra. And every attempt I've made at extending our contacts, to try and find a magic user elsewhere, has been stymied or blocked. At first I thought it was Andreno doing it, because he likes the gold we pay him and wants to keep it for himself. But lately I've suspected Ziegfried is in on it and I don't know why."

Weaponized magic. Adam suppressed a shudder. The war was bad enough already. Could he continue to help this pursuit in good conscience? Even for the sake of his family?

"Permission to speak frank?" he asked.

"Are you going to tell me that weaponized magic is a horrifying concept?" Gerhardt asked. "Because if you are, don't. I already know that. If we find it and give it over, innocent people will die. If I don't at least look, innocent people will die. What would you do?"

"I'd make it seem like I was looking and put off finding anything for as long as I could," Adam said.

The side of Gerhardt's mouth quirked upward momentarily. "Smart man."

"Is that what you're doing?"

"I'm not confirming or denying that." Gerhardt's mouth went right back to a frown. "Especially not to someone who could be punished just for me telling him about all this."

"Why are you telling me then?"

"You need to know what to watch for with Ziegfried." Gerhardt pushed off the table and clasped his hands behind his back, facing Adam directly. "He may or may not suspect I'm putting up the facade of looking. He may have decided to run searches using his own methods, such as dragging our people up into the mountains to capture one of their magic users and force them to capitulation. I need you to gain his confidence enough that he'll open up to you. Stick with him. Don't stray from his side without my leave."

"Sir, I can't be with him every moment of every day."

"No. And that's why when you're not with him, Jorgan or I will be. That'll give you another advantage. He's more likely to do whatever it is he's doing with you around than with either of us."

"I'll do what I can, sir. Do you also want me to discontinue the dagger lessons while on this assignment?"

"No," Gerhardt said. "I would like you to try and change the time to after supper rather than in the mornings during Andreno's court sessions."

That was a big relief. "I'll speak with Nolrien about that."

"Also," Gerhardt said, holding up one finger. "That monthly correspondence portal, he has a tendency to let Andreno know about the results before me. Make sure to alert me when it's happening. Jorgan and I will come immediately, before he finishes if we can manage it."

"Yes, sir."

There was a knock on the door. Gerhardt said, "Answer that."

Adam went and opened the door. Strom stood there looking slightly disheveled and very unhappy. Jorgan poked him in the back and he stepped inside. Gerhardt said, "Weiss, shut the door on your way out."

Adam spared a glance for Schneider, looking at ease leaning against the wall. Except for the clenched jaw and the tightness around his eyes. Gerhardt's distinctive rumbling came from the other side of the door. His voice was raised just enough they knew he was yelling, not enough to make out the words. Schneider's eyes narrowed. He blew out a puff of air, and turned his head to look up the corridor away from everyone.

Jorgan went next door to the other bedroom. Adam followed. "You found him pretty fast."

"Not that hard," Jorgan said. "I know where the hookers hang out looking for customers."

"Does he know what our actual mission is?" Adam asked. "Or that Ziegfried does a communication to home every month?"

299

"Are you crazy? Of course not. How do you know?"

"I'm supposed to come get you and Gerhardt next time Ziegfried does the monthly correspondence," Adam said. "I assume Ziegfried's bodyguards know about that?"

"I don't know if they've been informed or not." Jorgan sat down at his table and picked up his pencil. "I think they at least suspect, if they don't know for certain. It's not a regular, scheduled time, and he does it in private. It could be any time during the month. No predicting when exactly it'll be. Just whenever he has energy for it."

Chapter 41

ZIEGFRIED AND HIS BODYGUARDS gave Adam the cold shoulder. Not that it hurt his feelings any. It just made him bored. He sat in the corner of the room, watching them go about their daily routines. That seemed to amount mostly to loafing around and goofing off.

Zeigfried's level of energy slowly and steadily rose. He ate like a pig, slept more than twelve hours a day, and after a little more than a week, he went down into the dungeons. The palace guards wouldn't let anyone in with him. He came out practically bouncing with energy. Adam reported that to Gerhardt.

The next day Ziegfried rose about midmorning, rather than noon. He announced to the bodyguards, "You should all take the rest of the day off."

"Is it that time again?" Schneider asked.

"Yes, it is. Go enjoy yourselves," Ziegfried said. The bodyguards got excited and left. Adam stayed. Ziegfried narrowed his eyes at him. "You too. Take the day off."

"Sorry, sir." Adam made sure to put as much respect as he could muster into his voice. "I can't do that."

"Are you my babysitter now?" Ziegfried demanded. "If I do anything Gerhardt doesn't like, you'll run off and tattle to him?"

"Like reporting that your energy is at more acceptable levels again?" Adam asked.

"Like tattling on the activities I send my bodyguards to perform!"

"Sir, you came staggering to Andreno obviously unwell, worried about your men. I wasn't allowed in to make sure you were okay or if there was anything I could help with. What would you have done in my shoes?"

Ziegfried sighed. "I suppose I would go to the next person in authority that I knew would be concerned enough to help."

"Exactly," Adam said. "Part of my job is to make sure you're safe and healthy. I have no idea why your bodyguards aren't taking their job seriously. Maybe they should be replaced after all."

"I appreciate your concern." Ziegfried eyed him with more kindness now, the hostility gone. "Truly I do. Please understand. Once a month I seclude myself for a day. It's nothing you need to worry about. Gerhardt is aware that I do it."

"Are you talking about when you make the monthly correspondence with home?"

Ziegfried's face went slack with surprise. "You know about that?"

"Yes."

"Oh..." Ziegfried paused, then stammered a bit. "Oh... well... um... then I suppose it's all right. I guess. I still need you to leave the room, though. I can protect myself from the opening process, just not anyone else. In fact, you should probably go let Gerhardt know about it, so I don't have to worry about that part later while I'm exhausted."

"I can do that," Adam said. "As long as you promise no one else will come or go from this room. Why don't your bodyguards post themselves outside your door when you do this?"

"They don't need to. I lock the door."

Adam nodded and left. Once outside and away from Ziegfried he did the same thing he always did now. He took a deep breath of fresh air untainted by the little man's slimy demeanor and his need to insult his integrity by catering to it.

He went to Gerhardt and told him the correspondence was occurring. He and Jorgan were both sent back to sit outside Ziegfried's door to await completion.

It was a long wait. They tried entertaining themselves. Adam attempted to teach Jorgan some phrases in the native tongue. He couldn't pick up on them. He posed some riddles to Adam, who couldn't figure out the answers. They ended up just playing with Adam's cards.

It was nearly supper time when they finally heard the lock click back. The door didn't open. Adam inched it ajar and peeked in. He saw no one. He opened the door farther and entered.

"Ziegfried?" he called softly. No response. He scanned the room turning full around. Behind the door Ziegfried slumped against the wall. Adam reached out to him. "Are you okay?"

From the doorway Jorgan said, "Be careful."

Ziegfried grasped onto Adam. A wave a dizzy, breathlessness slammed into him. All the air was sucked from his lungs. Sure that he had somehow started bleeding his life out of every pore of his body, Adam reflexively arched backwards.

"Whoa!" Jorgan grabbed Adam and pulled. "Let go! Ziegfried! Stop it! Let go!"

He kicked Ziegfried a few times. Ziegfried released. Adam gasped for air, filling his lungs as desperately as a drowning victim taking his last breath. The sudden rush of oxygen deepened the dizziness. He went from suffocating to hyperventilating. The blurry form of Jorgan leaned over him, just as darkness closed in.

It only lasted for a moment. The darkness receded. Jorgan hadn't moved. Still lightheaded and dizzy Adam lay on his back with the floor swaying under him like a cradle. It had to be just him. Jorgan wasn't moving with the rocking of the floor.

"Easy," Jorgan said. "Take deep breaths. Slow down."

"I'm sorry," Ziegfried slurred. "I thought you were someone else. I didn't mean to."

"Shut up a minute," Jorgan said over his shoulder.

"Go get Strom," Ziegfried said. "He knows what to do."

"If I go get anyone—" Jorgan snapped— "it'll be Gerhardt."

"Yes, get him too," Ziegfried said. "An important message came through for him. Marked urgent."

Jorgan pointed at Adam and told Ziegfried, "Don't touch him."

"I won't." Ziegfried was a little petulant, a little indignant. "I said I'm sorry!"

"Listen," Jorgan said to Adam. "I'll be right back. Stay here. Okay?"

Adam managed to nod his head. Jorgan left. Ziegfried started talking. For some reason all the words blurred together. Adam couldn't follow them.

Goose pimples popped up on his skin. He rolled onto his side, curling up, conserving body heat by wrapping his arms around himself. He shivered anyway.

He tried running the word 'cold' through other languages. His brain froze up. The words and their translations got stuck in ice and simply wouldn't come. His teeth chattered.

Ziegfried moved, slowly crawling across the floor saying something about a blanket. Good idea. A blanket. Adam should go find one. He struggled to stand.

He may as well have done leg presses with a few hundred pounds of weight. It might have been easier than getting to his feet. He swayed some. Just standing took his breath again. Was he anemic or something? Maybe that explained why he was so cold. The sooner he found something warm, the better.

The weather was chilly enough several people should have hearths going. Perhaps if he wrapped himself in a blanket by a fire with a hot cup of coffee that would penetrate the cold. No fire burned in the hearth in this room. Best to go find one. Ziegfried called to him, something about staying.

Moving around generated body heat. The more he walked, the more the dizziness cleared. The shivering eased. A cup of coffee still sounded good. Then he could ignore the people he passed, talking with words that wouldn't sort themselves out in his head.

Wandering aimlessly, he lost himself. What had he been looking for? Coffee? Was there any coffee around? It had been a long time since he'd had a cup. He leaned against a wall trying to remember when that was.

He shivered. Not coffee. He was searching for warmth. He looked around. He was in a corridor similar to the one where Andreno's room was. Not quite as fancy. Or was he just remembering wrong? This one looked vaguely familiar. He must have been here at least once. Everything was screwy in his head. Nothing fit right.

Getting warm would help. He opened the door to Andreno's rooms. Surely there would be a fire in this hearth. Someone had constructed a parlor in front of the main room. Andreno had changed the furniture and decor to a softer, more feminine look. Flowers on the rounded coffee table. Lace doilies on the chair backs. Vases with potted plants. In fact, this reminded him of the one time he'd been to Charlass' rooms where Marietta now worked.

There were voices on the other side of the curtained doorway that led farther in. Some of them sounded familiar. None of them were Andreno.

They were talking about someone named Quillen. A woman called him her brother. Then there was a man. Listening to his voice, the roll, the cadence, the tone, Adam knew this man. Nolrien! What was he doing in Andreno's rooms?

Adam stumbled along, aiming for the curtain. He tripped over his right foot, caught himself on one of the chairs, wrinkling the doily over the back and knocking over the potted plant on the floor beside it.

The curtain flicked aside. Nolrien came out, "What ... you doing ...?"

Adam was missing words. He heard them. He just didn't understand them properly. He put his shaking hands to either side of his head. Why weren't the words working right? What was wrong with him? And why was he so cold?

"I don't know where I am," he tried to tell Nolrien. "Something's wrong."

"... you... ... drunk ... ...?" Nolren stepped close and sniffed.

"Drunk?"

"You ... not smell ... you ... drunk," Nolrien said. "Why ... you ... words mixed ...?"

"... he ... ... okay?" Marietta stood in the curtained doorway. Charlass right behind her. For some reason, that pretty Brendish delegate came to mind. These ladies were nice, but not as pretty as her. Although she had good enough taste. She probably would like this room where he now stood. Wait, was this Charlass' rooms?

"I … … care … him," Nolrien said. He took Adam, guiding him from the room. "Come … … … you … you friends."

"Friends." Adam knew that word.

"You … … cold," Nolrien said. "… …?"

There was no way to answer a question Adam couldn't even understand. Nolrien didn't ask again. He simply led Adam along. He had no idea where they were going until they reached his own room.

"There you are!" Jorgan jumped up from his paper strewn table. He ran over. "Everyone's looking for you. Why did you leave Ziegfried's room?"

"I don't know," Adam mumbled. "I don't remember. Something's wrong."

"I know," Jorgan said. He and Nolrien led Adam over to his bed. Jorgan threw a blanket around him, wrapping him tight. "You'll be okay. You just need some rest. Tell Nolrien to go to Ziegfried's room to let everyone know he found you."

"I can't," Adam said. "The words aren't working. I can't get them right."

Jorgan sighed, passing a hand across his eyes. "I should have suspected this might happen."

"Stay." Nolrien shook a finger at Adam as he backed to the door. "Stay … …"

"You're still shivering." Jorgan yanked the blankets off both his and Strom's beds and put them on Adam. "I hope your friend is going to go get someone. I don't dare leave you alone again."

"Friend? Nolrien?" Adam laughed. "I'm just a punching bag to him."

"I don't think so," Jorgan said. "Or he wouldn't have brought you straight to us. And when you were sick, he wouldn't have stood guard over you so much. We couldn't get him to go away. I started to think the man never slept!"

When Nolrien returned it was with Gerhardt, Strom, and a servant who was laden with a warming pan and hot water bottles. They packed that delicious heat around Adam. Soon his teeth stopped chattering and the shivering ceased.

With the warmth came drowsiness. Adam might have run a marathon with how tired he felt. He closed his eyes, unable to keep from drifting. Others talked. There was Gerhardt and Jorgan. Strom said something with

Nolrien in the native tongue. The voices melded and fuzzed together down into sleep where he dreamed it was that pretty Brendish girl who packed heat and warmth around him, not a Shontese servant.

Chapter 42

WHEN ADAM WOKE it was a long, slow, and luxurious process. Reminiscent of a lazy Saturday morning promising an easy day free of responsibility. No chores. No school. No rush to hurry it along. He dozed intermittently. In between those periods he stretched. He yawned. He scratched. He rolled over a few times.

When he finally opened his eyes for good it was late morning, judging by the angle of the sunlight through the window. Nolrien sat across the room watching him. He stood and went to the door. Just before he left, he shook his finger at Adam and said, "Stay."

Once alone Adam sat up and stretched again. He was still in the middle of it when Nolrien returned followed by Jorgan. He asked, "Feeling better?"

"I'm fine," Adam said.

Jorgan rolled his eyes. "I didn't ask if you were fine. I asked if you were better."

Nolrien silently went back to watching from his chair. Jorgan asked, "Hungry?"

"Yeah," Adam said. He was closer to being famished. Sometime during his sleep, ravenous hunger had replaced the icy cold.

"Food's on the way," Jorgan said. "Other than that tell me how you really are. Don't say you're fine."

"Are you going to get the doctor?"

"You'll need one if you give me the wrong answer. Tell me how you are."

"I'm not sure," Adam admitted. He swung his legs over the side of the bed setting his feet on the floor. "I still feel kind of weak, almost anemic."

"That's expected," Jorgan said.

"Am I mixing up my words?"

"No."

Adam turned to Nolrien and tried repeating the question in the Brendish language. Nolrien gave him a confused look and raised an eyebrow. Adam grit his teeth. He shook his head and scrubbed his face with his hands.

"I can talk to you," Adam said to Jorgan. He gestured at Nolrien. "Why can't I talk to him?"

"I don't know for certain," Jorgan said. "Maybe it's because German is your first language and his language is one you had to learn? German is the first language that Kiefer started understanding again."

"This happened to Kiefer?"

"Uh…" Jorgan cleared his throat. "…yeah. Don't tell him I told you. When we first got here, Ziegfried had to set up his translation spell. He drew the ability from Keifer. It was bad. A lot worse than what you're going through right now. He couldn't understand any of us for weeks. German was the first thing he started understanding and being able to speak again."

"Is that another reason he hates Ziegfried so much?"

"Another one of many, yes," Jorgan said. "It's also because Ziegfried acts like a jerk, even if he hasn't drawn from anyone in a while. When he draws from someone else who acts that way, he's intolerable. After drawing from you he threw a few temper tantrums last night and this morning."

"I don't throw temper tantrums."

"You probably did as a little kid," Jorgan said. "You may have learned how to deal with your short temper and keep it in check since then. He hasn't."

"So, how long did it take Kiefer to pick up the native language. I really don't want to wait weeks."

"The day after he started understanding German again," Jorgan said. "Even before he picked back up the other languages he's learned, like Spanish and French. He came out of that period fluent in the native language here.

Some of the natives at the base took care of him. Since he couldn't talk, they didn't feel it was inappropriate to talk around him. We think he must have picked it up as he regained his abilities."

"And that explains why he's so friendly with the natives at the base."

"Yeah. That's exactly why."

Food arrived. Nolrien checked the servant bringing it. He checked the food. He checked the dishes. He checked the tray used to carry everything. He checked the hallway outside the room while the door was open.

"Is he being paranoid?" Adam asked as Jorgan cleared some space on the table for the food.

"According to Strom, oh, how did he put it?" Jorgan said. "He's being protective of his student to ensure health so he can continue to beat on him sometime in the near future."

Adam glowered. "How encouraging."

His stomach growled. The smell of food set his mouth to watering. He risked his feet. He was steadier than he'd thought he'd be. He made his way over to the table, his hunger increasing with every step, as did his weakness.

He fell on the food like a ravenous winter wolf on a hare. He shoveled it in so fast he didn't even taste it. Within two minutes he'd eaten all of it and still hungered for more.

"Don't worry," Jorgan said with a laugh. "Lunch will come in less than an hour. You can eat again then."

"Good," Adam said. With the edge taken off his appetite he looked at all the papers spread out on the table. "This is just as much paperwork as you did for the portal opening."

"More," Jorgan said. "All of this is just spill over from Gerhardt's room. He received orders to assist Andreno in a military campaign to obtain the raw materials they want."

"Not permission? An order?"

"An order. He was hoping they would hem and haw, throw up some bureaucratic red tape, and create a bunch of flaming hoops for Andreno to jump through before they even thought about giving permission. Instead we have to throw everything together and make it happen."

Adam sat back, sobered. The palace was annoying. The food was bland. The company was less than desirable. He missed his family. But at least people weren't dying in the numbers that heated battles would cause.

The fighting at home was bad enough. Now it was spreading to here. He'd joined the army with the delusion that he could make things better. Things had done nothing but get worse. For everyone.

Adam was given a couple of days to recover. At first, he thought it unnecessary. Then he ended up sleeping through most of it. When he wasn't sleeping, he ate. He didn't see much of anyone else except Nolrien. The guard hung around, a lurking shadow of a nightmare that wouldn't shake off.

Ziegfried recovered from the small portal for the communication. Andreno still locked himself away with his military leaders. Gerhardt now locked himself away too. Jorgan was busy helping with logistics and running messages back and forth between the Oberst and the radio guys up in the tower. Strom was busy writing translations.

Since Gerhardt had insisted on written debriefings from the exercises, Andreno provided them. In the native language. Strom complained long and loud that he shouldn't have to sit and write out something so long and boring. Adam tried to help. The words on the page turned into nothing but squiggles that he could no longer make sense of. He tried referring to his own notes. His own handwriting was the same, unintelligible gobbledygook.

After about a week, Gerhardt called a meeting. He began with the statement, "The interworld portal opening next month will have to take place at Far Base, not the palace."

"No! No! No!" Ziegfried pounded the table. "That interferes with Andreno's schedule. You can't do that. He won't allow it. And neither will I."

Gerhardt glared. "Since when do I take orders from you or Andreno?"

"Andreno is going to a lot of trouble right now to get you the materials you want." Ziegfried rose up out of his chair a little. "You would do well to show him respect."

"I'm risking my men as a spearpoint in his campaign," Gerhardt said. "That's respect enough."

"What risk?" Ziegfried snorted with derision. "We have guns. They don't."

"Sit down." Gerhardt waited until Ziegfried obeyed, then said, "The superiority of our weapons doesn't negate that in battle, the unexpected happens. The enemy will always have tricks up their sleeves that you're unable to anticipate. People are going to get hurt. Our people. It's inevitable. I'll coordinate with Andreno as much as possible. But I have to go back to base to tie up loose ends and get the main force of our men underway."

"You'll have to wait to go back until after the portal opening," Ziegfried said.

"Not possible. Andreno is leaving to head up his occupation force after the portal opening. If he wants us to spear-point, we have to have our main force already on the way up there to clear things out."

"My bodyguards have three more mock battles scheduled. They have to be here for those!" Ziegfried slapped the table with both hands.

The more temper he displayed, the more it disgusted Adam. He didn't really act that way, did he? Short temper, sure, but this was ridiculous. He got up to pace back and forth along one wall of the room, letting off some nervous energy to try and keep himself from doing something he would later regret.

"I can't be in both places at once." Gerhardt took the minor tantrums in stride. "Unless you're able to open another portal immediately to get me to Far Base the same day, it's going to happen there. Not here."

"I have to be here." Ziegfried repeatedly tapped the surface of the table with a stiff finger, as if frantic to poke a button that wouldn't depress.

"We can go back and forth on this as much as you please," Gerhardt said. "It doesn't change facts. Certain things need to happen that require my presence at the base. It's not optional. There is, however, the option of whether or not to cut off these drills your bodyguards are doing for Andreno."

"No!" Ziegfried stood again, fully this time. "There isn't. That's not an option at all. They've already been scheduled. He's expecting them. The men have already prepared. They're looking forward to them."

"I don't care."

"Can't you figure something out?" Ziegfried pushed away from the table. "That's your job."

"My job is to follow orders, run this operation, and keep my men safe," Gerhardt said. "These mock drills have already caused minor injuries, so they're rather low on my priority list. If you want them to take place, figure it out yourself."

Ziegfried slammed both his fists on the tabletop. "This is unacceptable!"

Adam was passing within arm's length. He reached out and slapped the back of Ziegfried's head, exactly as his father had always done to him any time he'd ever shouted at his mother. Then the words of his father spilled out of his mouth before he could stop them. "Keep wagging your tongue with that kind of sass and I'm going to reach in there and rip it out with my bare hands. You don't speak that way to someone who deserves your respect."

By that time, Adam's brain caught up with his actions. He swallowed the next couple of words that would demand apology. Everyone stared, several of them with jaws hanging open. Except Gerhardt. He pursed his lips, holding his face tight, not breathing.

"Why did you... What... How could you..." Ziegfried stammered a couple of times. Then he looked directly at Gerhardt. "Do something."

Gerhardt shook his head, his face getting tighter, still not breathing. Ziegfried drew himself up with an indignant huff. He stalked to the door, yanked it open, and left. A couple of the bodyguards snickered before following him. Schneider gave Adam a lopsided smirk and said, "That was pretty ballsy."

He was the last of the bodyguards to leave the room. As soon as they shut the door Strom giggled. Then Jorgan chuckled. Then Gerhardt let out a belly laugh, like water bursting out of a broken dam. Adam shifted from foot to foot. Were they laughing at him? Or at Ziegfried?

Gerhardt wiped his eyes, still laughing while he spoke. "Adam, to be responsible I have to tell you to never do that again."

"Yes, sir," Adam said. "Sorry, sir."

Gerhardt took a deep breath, stopping his laughter. He still smiled as he said, "Don't be sorry about putting people in their place when they need it. Just find more appropriate ways to do so in the future."

"Yes, sir," Adam repeated, this time accompanying it with a nod.

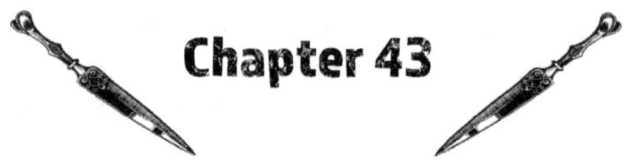

Chapter 43

ADAM SAT OUTSIDE the locked door. Ziegfried had been in there with Andreno for most of the afternoon. He still could only understand about half the words spoken by the natives. He couldn't even stave off the boredom by listening to their conversations.

Ziegfried's bodyguards no longer gave him the cold shoulder, not that the change in behavior gave him any desire to get to know them better. He got his cards out to pass the time. When they asked to join him, he told them they couldn't because solitaire was exactly that, single player.

Gerhardt strode up the corridor to them. Adam jumped to his feet, swiping his deck of cards behind his back. The bodyguards snapped their spines straighter, appearing more alert. He relieved Adam, sending him to get supper, telling him to take some to Jorgan as well.

Eating didn't take long. Adam had found that the best way to deal with the blandness of the normal fare was to just swallow it and get it over with, much like military chow. Then he grabbed a serving for Jorgan and took it to their room.

Jorgan sat at the table poring over reams of papers. Strom was also there, saying to him, "Come on. It'll be good for you. You could use a little rest and relaxation."

Adam set the plate in a spot that didn't look in immediate threat of burial in a paper avalanche from the nearest teetering stack. Jorgan didn't even glance up. "Thanks."

Strom asked Adam. "Gerhardt finally cut you loose?"

"Finally," Adam said. He flopped down on his bed. "End of shift took forever to get here today. I'm bored out of my mind."

"No dagger lessons still?" Strom asked.

"Not until I can understand my instructor again," Adam said. He muttered, "That's taking forever too."

"We told you it'll take at least a week," Jorgan said, still writing. "It hasn't been a week yet."

"Close enough." Adam frowned at him. "How do you write and talk at the same time?"

"Practice," Jorgan said, still moving his pencil. "Lots and lots of practice."

Strom snatched the pencil from Jorgan's fingers. "Which is exactly why you need to get out and have some fun. You work too much."

Jorgan lunged for the pencil. Strom held it just out of reach. Jorgan said, "I'm not going to go sleep with strange women just because you think I need fun. I'm a married man."

"So what?" Strom shrugged. "She'll never know."

"I'll know." Jorgan swiped the pencil back. He sat back down and wrote while he spoke. "Besides, I find myself comparing every woman I see to my wife. And quite frankly, none of them measure up to her."

"You're hopeless," Strom said, throwing up his hands. "How about you, Adam? You haven't been out to play much lately."

"I have to be available in the wee hours tomorrow morning," Adam said, shaking his head. "The next mock drill is scheduled and I'm supposed to be there to watch the bodyguards go and come back."

"So?" Strom shrugged. "Entertain yourself until it's time. That way you're sure to be awake."

Adam tried a different excuse to back out. "Jorgan described my situation."

They both gave him a confused look and Strom said, "You're not married."

Adam pictured that pretty Brendish girl, her smile, her hair, the way she walked. "I compare every woman to a certain other one, and they don't measure up."

"You have got to be kidding," Strom said. "You don't even know her name."

"Why are you pushing so hard for this?" Jorgan asked. "Did some woman say she wouldn't have anything to do with you unless you brought a friend or something?"

"You two are both hopeless," Strom said. "No wonder you're friends. Enjoy your dull evening together." He stomped over to the door, yanked it open and left.

"That's a yes." Jorgan snickered and bent over his paperwork again. "So, Adam. Tell me, any indication yet that Ziegfried has figured out his little conundrum?"

"He looked smug when he went into the meeting with Andreno this afternoon," Adam said. "Nothing more."

"With Ziegfried that's enough," Jorgan said. His pencil scratched away. "I'm probably working out all these figures for nothing. If I were a betting man, I'd lay odds he got Andreno to order his court magician to open a portal for us to use to get to base after the transfer with home."

"How do you figure that?" Adam asked.

"Simplest solution," Jorgan said.

"Then why didn't you suggest it?" Adam asked.

"Ziegfried makes enough problems he can figure his way out of some of them himself," Jorgan said. "Serves him right if he can't. He can suffer a little of what he makes others go through. Besides, I don't want to do it here because—"

Gerhardt burst into the room. "Jorgan, have you started on the food requirements for the trip back to base?"

"Not yet," Jorgan said. "I should be able to get on it tonight or tomorrow morning."

"Belay that," Gerhardt said. "Change of plans. Andreno's bullied his court magician into opening a portal to base for us after our portal transfer with home, so that'll take place here. Get on that instead."

"I have the system already in place for it at base." Jorgan grit his teeth. "Doing it here is about ten times the amount of work."

"Which is why I tried talking him out of it," Gerhardt said. He sifted through some of the stacks of papers. He picked up an entire stack, cradling it as it shifted and threatened to spill from his arms. "I'll take these and finish them for you. Get on the new figures and work out that old system you tried before we were given Far Base to use."

When he left, Jorgan threw his pencil down and shoved a couple of the paper stacks off the table onto the floor. Adam waited for cussing to follow. Instead, Jorgan took a few deep breaths, then sat down, picked up his pencil, pulled several fresh sheets of paper close, and scratched away at them with new writing.

After a few moments, he said, "You better get some sleep if you have to be up halfway through the night."

"Right," Adam said. Leaving Jorgan to work, he got ready for bed as silently as he could before slipping between the sheets.

Adam was dragged out of bed sometime after midnight. He had to carry a candle to light his way through the sleeping palace to Ziegfried's rooms. Schneider and the bodyguards had already prepared for the mock drill. They were dressed up and wore paint on their faces. They bounced around riffing each other, acting giddy with anticipation.

When the portal was safe, they went through. After about three hours they returned acting more like men who had been put through the paces by an officer running exercise drills. The portal closed. Adam returned to his room and went back to bed.

Over the next couple of days, the words of the Brendish language came back to him. Hour by hour he understood more and more. Then one morning he woke up and it was like someone had flipped a switch in his brain. He understood everything as before.

That was the day Andreno got troop movements underway. He had been sending out smaller groups here and there. Now, the bulk of his army moved. Everyone talked about it an all it affected. Merchants came to the palace striking deals concerning supply lines. Nobles came striking deals concerning troops passing through their territories. There were even a couple of traders that offered translation and interpretation services between anyone Shontese and the Chemwanee. Adam wanted to talk to them more. Unfortunately, they disappeared before he could talk to them. When he asked, he was told Andreno had turned them out personally, as he had no intentions to talk to the people who had raided his villages.

As for the Germans, Gerhardt was constantly climbing up the tower with the radio to coordinate with base. He sent out scouts, small teams of five men to the foothills of the Chemwanitz Mountains. They were to make their way uphill, getting the lay of the land and its people.

When the bodyguards left for their next scheduled mock battle, it came almost as a surprise. As bored as Adam was now that he was assigned to Ziegfried, everyone had been so busy it was hard to believe an entire week had passed already. While the bodyguards went through the paces of anticipation waiting for the portal to be usable, Adam struggled to stay awake without yawning.

"Have you done every single one of these at night?" he asked.

"Every single one of them," Schneider said. "This is supposed to be a simulation of how the mountain barbarians attack. Remember? So we do our mock attack in the earliest hours of the morning, anytime between midnight and dawn."

The portal opened. The men went through. Adam sat back and waited thinking maybe he'd take a nap. Last time it had been about three hours. Ziegfried was in the back room with the door closed. He wouldn't know either way. Gerhardt was probably still up. He had so much work to do he'd been averaging about two or three hours of sleep in the morning when he couldn't stay awake any longer. On the off chance he showed up to check on them, Adam decided to stay awake. He took out his cards to entertain himself enough to do so.

In half the expected time, the bodyguards fell back out of the portal in a tumble. All of them sported injuries of varying degrees of severity. The acrid stench of burnt flesh filled the room. They dripped blood with every step they took.

"Get a doctor," Schneider gasped at Adam. "Quick!"

Adam ran. It was still dark. Most people were still in bed. He didn't know where the doctors resided, so he went directly to where the pages congregated between tasks. He sent one to fetch a doctor. He sent another with a written note to Gerhardt. Then he went back to Ziegfried's rooms.

The portal shut down. Ziegfried stumbled out of the other room. "Why are you all back so soon?"

He stopped just inside the room, leaning against the wall. Without looking at the state of the men he sniffed the air. "Why does it smell like burnt bacon in here?"

"Burnt humans," Schneider said. "Burnt hair. Burnt flesh. Not bacon."

"What happened?" Ziegfried asked.

One of the unconscious men woke up just enough to moan painfully. Schneider had to raise his voice a little to be heard. "I think we ran into another alert."

Adam was incensed. "You think!"

"The portal opens half a mile from our target," Schneider snapped at him. "Far enough away that if there's an alert, we can't hear it. All I know is that everyone was awake and waiting for us."

"What did they do?" Adam bared his teeth. "Did they throw torches at you or something? This isn't sounding like any kind of drill I've ever heard of."

The doctor arrived with the page and dove immediately into triaging. He sent the page back out with a list of medicines, supplies, and the names of other doctors to send immediately.

Gerhardt clomped into the room. His eyebrows furrowed together. The corners of his mouth pointed down. Dark storm clouds gathered in his eyes. He said nothing, looking over everyone in the room, taking in the injuries, the blood, the charring.

"I can explain," Schneider said quickly.

"Where is Gunter?" Gerhardt asked.

Everyone in the room froze momentarily. The bodyguards that were conscious looked around at themselves. Adam silently counted them. Sure enough, they were one short.

Gerhardt folded his arms, glaring as Schneider. "You said you could explain."

"We were all in pairs in case we were doing another scenario where the defenders were alerted," Schneider said. He asked the others, "Who was paired up with Gunter?"

Several fingers pointed to the half-conscious, moaning man. Gerhardt said, "While you explain how Gunter got left behind, fill me in on everything else. Feldmann's arm looks broken. You're moving like you have broken ribs. These men have blunt trauma wounds. I see blade cuts and stabs. All of you have burns of varying degrees."

"The defenders had a magician with them. He was flinging little fireballs at us like bullets," one of the men said. He closed his mouth again when Schneider shot him a warning glance.

"A magician," Gerhardt said. "This doesn't sound like anything close to the safety protocols that were laid out for me. Explain why the defenders weren't adhering to the protocols if this really was just a mock scenario."

"You'd have to ask Andreno that," Ziegfried spoke up.

"I'm asking all of you," Gerhardt said.

"Andreno is the one in charge of the strategies that the defenders use," Ziegfried said.

"I don't believe you," Gerhardt said.

More doctors arrived with more supplies. Gerhardt stepped out of the way for them. Strom and Jorgan also arrived, hanging back in the corridor.

As the doctors moved about deftly attending the injuries, Ziegfried sagged into a chair. He passed a weary hand over his face. "I need a refill."

Gerhardt grabbed his shirt and hauled him into the other room. He slammed the door. The lock clicked.

"Oh, boy." Strom ventured into the room, Jorgan trailing just behind him. "I wouldn't want to be in his shoes right now."

"What does he do when he's this mad?" Adam asked.

"I don't know," Jorgan said. "I've never seen him quite this mad."

The doctors moved the worst injured to the infirmary one by one. The palace stirred. People moved about tending to their daily tasks. Breakfast was served. The doctors had food brought in to those healthy enough to eat.

Adam couldn't eat. He had too big a lump in his stomach. Most of the bodyguards fasted too.

A medic inspected Schneider's ribs. Two of them were cracked. The bruising from that caused him the most pain and discomfort. Or was it?

He sat with a grim expression, his eyes glued to the locked door to the back room.

When the worst of the men were cleared out, the doctors stitched, salved, and bandaged those that were left. Servants cleared away breakfast, eaten or not. A page came and handed Strom a note.

"What is it?" Jorgan asked.

"Andreno wants me." He tucked the note in a pocket and headed out. "I'll make sure he knows what happened here."

He wasn't gone long before Andreno came striding into the room, his bodyguards left out in the hall, Strom desperately trying to assure him that everything was under control.

"Where is Ziegfried?" he demanded. Adam and Strom pointed to the other room. Andreno tilted up his nose. "Fetch him. I want a word."

"The door is locked," Strom said.

"Get the key," Andreno yelled. "If you don't know where it is, pound on the door until they answer."

"Begging your pardon," Strom said. "I don't dare disrupt Oberst Gerhardt right now."

Andreno's face went slack with shocked incredulity. "Are you refusing to obey me?"

"I keep telling you," Adam said. "We are not your servants. We obey Gerhardt. And right now he is angry. Very, very angry."

"Because he didn't train his men well enough for them to keep from being sloppy enough to get little injuries again?"

"Big injuries," Adam said. "And one is missing."

"*What?*" Andreno jerked himself straight. He shook a fist at Schneider. "You left a man behind? You fool! How could you do such a thing?"

Despite the language barrier the tone was clear. Schneider cringed, shrinking in on himself. Still his eyes never strayed from the locked door. Beads of sweat popped out on his forehead.

He blanched when the lock clicked. The door opened. A drooping Ziegfried shuffled out. He didn't move fast enough. Gerhardt gave him a hard shove from behind, sending him sprawling on the floor.

He looked around the room. "Where is everyone?"

"The doctors took the worst to the infirmary," Adam said.

Gerhardt nodded. He locked eyes with Andreno for a moment. Then he grabbed a fistful of Schneider's hair and dragged him into the other room. The door closed and locked again.

"What did you say?" Andreno asked Ziegfried.

"He was going to shoot me." Ziegfried sobbed on the floor. "I had to tell him. He was going to shoot me in the feet, my hands, my knees, any place that wouldn't kill me until I told him."

A gunshot punctuated from the other room. Andreno jumped about a foot. The lock clicked again. The door swayed gently open. Gerhardt came out spattered with blood, luger in hand. Behind him Schneider lay face down in a growing pool of blood and gray matter, a large hole in the back of his head.

"Schneider has been relieved of duty due to negligence, gross insubordination, and treason," Gerhardt said. He pointed the gun at Ziegfried's head. "And if you ever cross the line again, I'll relieve you as well."

Chapter 44

"**L**ET'S EVERYONE CALM DOWN." Andreno held up his hands in a placating gesture, drawing Gerhardt's gaze. His eyes flicked to the gun. He said, "Adam, tell him to calm down. Whatever he was told, I'm sure it was a mistake. Everything can be explained."

"Weiss," Gerhardt said before Adam could interpret anything. "Tell his royal pain in the ass that he's going to immediately set a recovery operation underway to bring me back my missing man. He's going to search for a magician who can open a portal to our home in case Ziegfried becomes unfit, or is killed. And he has one week to provide you with a teacher for the Chemwanitz language. If he refuses, or doesn't come through, I will pull the rug out from under his finances so fast he won't even have the time to get dizzy in his fall."

Adam told Andreno, "He will calm down if you find another magician to open portals for us, if you get someone to teach me the language used by the people living in the mountains, and—"

"I already told him those things are useless!" Andreno sneered. "No self-respecting magician around here will talk to any of you. They're too afraid of the gathering of seats. And the Chemwanee are barbarians. They have nothing of value to say to anyone."

"They might have something of value to say." Adam wasn't giving up a chance at a new language that easily. "If we capture one trying to cut our supply lines, or scouting us, or trying to direct a counterattack, or—"

"Fine! Have it your way!" Andreno threw up his hands. "I'll find you a stupid teacher. I'll have Masorno come talk to Gerhardt. Be happy with that."

"You did not let me finish the demands," Adam said. "You have to find the man that got left behind."

"Of course, stupid." Andreno crossed his arms. "I don't want him out there loose and uncontrolled any more than you do. I'll send people to coordinate that with him."

"He'll do it," Adam told Gerhardt. "For the most part. I think the magician may be problematic. He'll send his court magician to talk to us."

Gerhardt holstered and secured his luger. He left the room calling for Jorgan to follow. Andreno's bodyguards peeked into the room, saw that Andreno was still safe, and parted to let Gerhardt pass. Kurlos did more than peek. He stepped into the room.

"Everyone out!" Andreno ordered. "I need a word in private with Ziegfried."

"Your highness," Kurlos said. "Court is due to start in a few minutes. You don't have time to waste with these foul people."

"Court waits for me." Andreno tilted up his nose. "Not the other way around. Now, get out."

He practically shoved at everyone to get them to leave. Outside in the corridor Kurlos paced back and forth in front of the door. Every once in a while, one or two people would come and ask what the hold-up was. The more time that passed the more frequently they came.

When Andreno finally emerged, he looked as prim as ever. He flicked a finger at a page. "Send for Masorno."

The boy ran off. Andreno looked around at all the people. He raised his voice. "One of my foreign friends executed a man who was trying to betray me. That should satisfy all your curiosity. Now, where is that merchant who makes runs up into the mountains and speaks that barbaric language? The one that was bothering me last week."

"You sent him away," Kurlos said. "When he offered to teach the language to your military and some of your foreign friends, you threatened him with—"

"Don't be ridiculous," Andreno interrupted him, avoiding eye contact with Adam and Strom. "You must be thinking of someone else. Get him back. My friend Adam needs to learn that language."

"There's no need to trouble yourself," Kurlos said. "Your friend Adam I'm sure already speaks that language, since that's where he's from."

Andreno slapped him so hard his head snapped sideways. "Every time you say that you may as well accuse me of lying."

"I'm sorry. I'm sorry." Kurlos dropped to his knees. "Please forgive my weakness. You're such a greater man than I. Please, allow me to learn. I beg you. Don't send me away from your side."

"Oh, all right." The anger drained out of Andreno's face. "Do as you're told and I'll forgive you."

"Of course," Kurlos said. "I'll do anything you say. I'll have that merchant brought back right away."

"I'm going to go hold court now," Andreno announced loudly.

With grandiose strides he stepped past Kurlos. Most people followed him toward the throne room, Strom included. Kurlos stood, brushing himself off.

"Barbarian." He gave Adam a look of hatred. Then he acted like he spat, though nothing but the sound came out of his mouth. He stuck his nose so high in the air he couldn't possibly see where he was going as he left. Adam rolled his eyes. The man was pathetic.

The few German bodyguards that were left trickled back into Ziegfried's room. Adam followed them. Ziegfried sat limp, barely awake. One of the men said to Adam, "Go get him someone worthless that he can draw energy from."

Adam planted his feet and stood his ground. "I'll do no such thing."

"I gave you and order!" The bodyguard came at Adam, swinging his right fist.

Adam pushed the swing inside with his left hand. He grabbed the man's wrist with his right hand and pulled. With his left hand he pushed down on the back of the man's shoulder, putting him on the floor.

It was a move Nolrien had used on him countless times. It was a move he had tried over and over with an imaginary opponent in his room in the evenings. It was a move he had never done successfully on Nolrien. This man, this trained bodyguard, went down as easily as Adam did. For a split second he didn't know what to do next.

The bodyguard used the hesitation, grabbing Adam's right leg and yanking it out from under him. He would have fallen over backward if another of the bodyguards hadn't grabbed him from behind and pulled him back.

Adam raised his left foot and swiped the edge of his boot down the shin of the man behind him. The guy yowled in pain and his grip loosened. Adam went limp, slithering down and out of the hold.

That put him at the level of the man he'd pushed to the floor. He grabbed Adam's right arm, yanking it away from him, pushing his back to the floor and pinning him with a right knee to the chest, left knee on Adam's upper right arm.

"Settle down," one of the other bodyguards said. Rather lame, and rather late.

"If he hadn't tattled none of this would've happened!" The man pinning Adam drew his walther. "Schneider would still be alive!"

For the second time in his life Adam looked down the barrel of a gun. It wasn't any more pleasant than the first time. Except now he knew that talking the person down wouldn't work. He grabbed the barrel with his left hand, swerving it away from his head, pointing it at one of the other bodyguards.

The man jumped out of the way. "Whoa! Hey! Watch where you're pointing that thing."

Adam and his attacker struggled over control of the gun. More of the bodyguards jump out of the line of fire. Adam's options flashed through his mind. Unable to draw his own walther with his right arm restrained. Unable to wrest the gun out of his attacker's hands. Unable to use any of the disarming techniques Nolrien taught without relinquishing his grip on the weapon. Adam brought the man's hand closer to his face, raised his head, and bit his attacker's hand hard enough to draw blood.

"Yeaagghh!" The man screamed, letting go of the weapon. Adam also let go, since he couldn't use it by gripping the barrel. One of the other bodyguards quickly swept it out of reach with a foot.

"Knock it off!" The man who had grabbed Adam now grabbed the attacker. "We're in enough trouble as it is."

"And it's all his fault." The attacker shook his bleeding hand at Adam's face, splattering him. He elbowed the man trying to pull him off, dug his knee into Adam's chest, making breathing difficult. Using his injured hand, he grabbed Adam's throat.

Adam drew his dagger with his left hand. He stabbed it into the meat of the thigh pinning his chest.

"Aagh!" The man screamed again. This time he jerked away. Adam kept hold of his dagger, yanking it out of the flesh. The man screamed a third time, scuttling back across the floor whining and whimpering.

Strom entered the room, Nolrien and a couple of other guards close behind him. They looked around the room, at the blood, at the drawn weapons. Strom held out his hands. "What the hell?"

The attacker pointed at Adam. "He attacked me!"

"We heard some scuffling and shouting when we came near." Nolrien stepped over to Adam and held out a hand to help him off the floor, the same as he did during training. "Looks like your practice has paid off some. They were stupid enough to attack you?"

"What's he saying?" the wounded bodyguard demanded.

"He says it looks like you attacked Adam," Strom said. "Not the other way around. How stupid can you be? Schneider is dead. Gerhardt is about an inch away from executing Ziegfried."

"No way he'd do that," the bodyguard said. "He'd never get another portal open."

"And that may be the only reason Ziegfried is still alive," Strom said. "He doesn't need you for that. He may still decide to kill you all. Are you trying to make sure of it?"

The bodyguard held his injured hand close to his chest. He pointed at Adam with the other. "If he hadn't tattled on us, none of this would have happened."

"His tattling didn't cause your burns and injuries," Strom shouted. "He didn't make you leave a man behind. Your own stupidity got you in trouble."

"I didn't bite my hand or stab myself in the leg. He attacked me."

"If you pulled your gun on me, I'd stab you too," said the bodyguard who had grabbed Adam from behind. "Strom, I tried to break it up. I did. They kept going at each other. You'll tell Gerhardt this wasn't all of us, right? He's the only one who'll be punished for this?"

"How should I know?" Strom said. "Gerhardt's mad enough he might use any excuse at all. Even if he had to make one up."

"Gerhardt doesn't make things up just to dish out punishment," Adam said.

"Not this time he certainly didn't," Strom said. He looked each of the bodyguards in the eye. "You've all been temporarily relieved of duty and are to be confined until you can be transferred back to base for disciplinary actions."

One of them pointed to Ziegfried, passed out and prostrate in his chair. "Who'll watch out for Ziegfried when he's like this?"

"Some of Andreno's guards for now," Strom said. "That's why these guys came with me. Andreno wants him taken down to the dungeons where he can get a refill. There are more guards out in the corridor to escort the rest of you down there."

"I'm not going to be locked up in that nasty dungeon." The attacker stood on his good leg. "Tell them they're taking me to the infirmary."

"Everyone who was taken to the infirmary has been transferred down there," Strom said. "You'll be treated there along with them. And you'd better go, because they have orders to kill you if you don't. And if you think they'll hesitate, think again. Andreno told everyone that Schneider is dead because he was plotting against the throne. The guards think you're all guilty by association until proven otherwise."

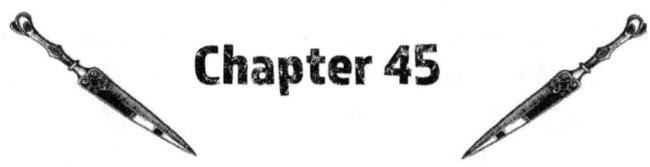

Chapter 45

ERHARDT CALLED ADAM to his room before the day was done. Just as Adam arrived, Ziegfried pushed his way in. He addressed the Oberst by his first name as if they were friends. "Ernest, enough of this foolishness of keeping me away. You need to let me explain this to you."

Gerhardt drew out his luger and placed it on the table. "Explain where you want a bullet. Knees? A hand? That one sounds good. You're right-handed. You don't need your left one."

Ziegfried cupped his left hand, hiding it from sight. "I know we can smooth this over."

Gerhardt fingered the luger. His voice dropped to a near whisper. "Get out."

Ziegfried now wrung his hands as his tone turned whiny. "If you'd just listen."

Gerhardt picked up the luger and aimed at Ziegfried. "You have until the count of three."

"Be reasonable."

"One."

"Now, Ernest…"

"Two."

Ziegfried fled, leaving the door flapping behind him. The entire time, Adam hadn't dared utter a peep. Now, alone with the angry Oberst, his stomach clenched and his breath shortened with fear. Gerhardt took slow measured steps to the door. Adam didn't move. The door clicked closed behind him. Gerhardt's footsteps trod heavy on the floor on his return.

He circled Adam like a shark smelling blood. "Ziegfried's bodyguards. You worked with them. You sat in the same room every day. You listened to all their conversations. How could you not have picked up on this disaster?"

"They only ever talked about mock drills," Adam said. "If I tried to get more out of them, they changed the subject, evaded, or got threatening."

"I put you in that position specifically to figure out what they were doing," Gerhardt said. "You failed. And now people are dead. A lot of people. They were the raiders attacking the outlying villages."

The floor dropped out. Adam's soul plunged into icy water that filled him from the inside out. He choked on it, terrified that if he came up for air he would hear his commanding officer telling him that his family was as good as dead.

And eye for an eye. A tooth for a tooth. A life for a life. He couldn't deny that he deserved to lose them. And more. Still, it tore him to pieces.

Gerhardt smacked him on the shoulder. "You have nothing to say for yourself?"

Adam heard words come out of his mouth. "There is no excuse for my lack of action."

"You're damn right there's not." Gerhardt backed off, going over to his desk. "And that's without addressing the number of people yet to die. How many innocent villagers do you think they killed? We'll start with that. Then you try and think about how many innocent people will die in those mountains, because these raids were used as an excuse to order me to go there and fight."

"I can do nothing for the dead." Adam's numb lips moved somehow. The words left his mouth without him feeling them. "What can I do for those in the mountains?"

"That's not the end of it," Gerhardt said. "They were raiding villages in Brend along with Shontarra. Both times they ran into resistance it was in Brend. And this second time they left a man behind. If he's taken captive and they figure out he's connected with us, what are our chances of ever opening up friendly channels of communication? Let alone trade with them?"

The last shred of hope Adam held for his family slipped away. A leaf in a storm. His father would be executed as a traitor. His mother and brother would be imprisoned, brutalized, and worked to death. They had warned Adam not to screw up. Even once. He'd more than done it with this.

"If we weren't so short on interpreters, I'd pull you so fast it would make your head spin." Gerhardt leaned his hands on his desk. He wouldn't even look at Adam. At least his luger was back in its holster. "I'm putting you back on Andreno because I know you hate him. And when he leaves to meet up with his army and go occupy those mountains, you're going with him so you can see firsthand all the devastation we're going to wreak up there."

A tentative knock on the door interrupted them. Strom timidly stuck his head inside. "You wanted to know immediately when the Shontese court magician arrived."

"Do we have the maps I need?" Gerhardt demanded. Strom opened the door wider revealing several paper rolls in his arm. He brought them in and laid them on the desk. Gerhardt said, "Show me the exact spot."

As Masorno sauntered into the room, Strom partially unrolled the maps until he found the one he wanted. He laid it flat and tapped a spot with his finger. Gerhardt put his finger on that spot and said, "Strom, ask Lord Masorno if he can open a portal near this spot so we can send someone through to get word about, or possibly extract, our man that was left behind."

When Strom interpreted, Masorno let out a short bark of a laugh. He said, "No. Not if next week you still want me to get you to that castle you people are using."

"Does he know anyone else who can do this?" Gerhardt asked.

"I'm not exposing any of my colleagues to you people," Masorno responded. "Andreno said those men were plotting against him. If one of them is still there, good riddance. I hope he's captured. The Brendish will torture him to death. I'm not helping you beyond getting you out of this palace and away from here!"

Strom summed it up for Gerhardt. "He can't help us."

"There were more words than that," Gerhardt said.

"I'd rather not tell you the rest of what he said." Strom grimaced. "It wasn't flattering. It boils down to he can't help us."

"Can't?" Gerhardt glared at him. "Or won't?"

"Both," Strom admitted.

"Weiss!" Gerhardt shouted. "Can't, or won't?"

"Both," Adam said. "He can't open a portal and still get you to base next week after the transfer with home. He won't assist us with any other magicians or any other methods to get Gunter back."

"You want me to report on everything Andreno's doing to find Gunter?" Strom asked.

Gerhardt stared coldly at Strom for a moment without answering. Then, as if the question hadn't even been asked, he said, "Tell Lord Masorno I thank him for his time and apologize for any inconvenience."

Strom did as ordered without even complaining that Gerhardt had double checked his interpretation. From that point on he accompanied Gerhardt everywhere, from person to person, meeting to meeting, organizing and arranging things. Adam was well and truly stuck with Andreno, who continually shut him out of any meeting with his military officers or national officials.

Adam ended up hearing bits and pieces of things later from Jorgan. A couple of Andreno's scouts had been dispatched to try and get information on Gunter. People coming and going in anticipation of Andreno's campaign made organizing the portal transfer difficult. Ziegfried's former bodyguards were escorted by Shontese soldiers back to base where they'd be disciplined. Adam didn't bother asking what form that discipline would take. He didn't want to know.

The entire time, Gerhardt never once had a single word for Adam. He wouldn't even look at him if they were in the same room.

Andreno gloated and bragged. He encouraged people to shower him with adulation through a farewell celebration. He planned to leave to meet up with the bulk of his army the day after the portal exchange.

During Andreno's court sessions Adam went back to his window seat where he could see the front gate. All kinds of people came and went. Not that they captured his interest. The rooms lining that corridor filled with people coming to try and get a few minutes with Andreno before his departure. As long as Adam stared quietly out the window, they all left him alone.

While Andreno was at supper in the evenings Adam was supposed to still go practice with Nolrien. He skipped all the sessions claiming weariness and need for sleep. The few times Nolrien forced him into practice he didn't resist any of the humiliation or beatings.

Nolrien badgered him, demanding details of exactly what had happened between him and Gerhardt. Every time he did that it just reminded Adam that his family was gone. His throat closed up. All his strength left.

The day before the portal opened, Gerhardt gathered every German currently in the palace to brief them on the occasion. Everything would operate as normal until after the portal to home closed. Then Magician Masorno would open a second portal to base. Whatever personnel came through in the transfer would go immediately to base. Strom and the radio personnel stationed at the palace would remain at their posts.

A Medic Thoel, a couple of radio operators, and half a dozen soldiers from base would come through that second portal to accompany Adam and Andreno to the main camp of the Shontese army. Gerhardt, Lieber, Jorgan, and everyone else currently there would go back to base. Most of them would be there just long enough to turn around and leave the next day, moving out with the bulk of their men. They would travel faster than Andreno or his army, bypassing them and going up into the mountains. If everything went as planned, they would start the actual attack about the same time Andreno arrived at his camp.

The next morning Jorgan put on his formal uniform. The portal opened. He went through it to the other side. Andreno remained true to his word, supplying every item that had been on the demand list from home. It went through crate by crate. Supplies came back in return. About fifteen soldiers came through in transfer. After them, six men came through wearing civilian clothes and toting suitcases rather than the standard rucksack of a soldier. They jabbered excitedly among themselves, pointing at everything like wide-eyed tourists.

Gerhardt frowned. "What the hell?"

Jorgan returned. He carried about twice the normal amount of paperwork. He handed it all over to Gerhardt and gave the cutoff signal. Strom sent a page with a message for Ziegfried to shut down the portal.

Gerhardt pointed at the civilians. "What is this?"

"Magicians." Jorgan eyed them skeptically. "Supposed to be, anyway."

"Of all the times to send..." Gerhardt cut himself off. He worked a muscle in his jaw. "Was is specified what they're here for? How much do they know how to do?"

"I wasn't given a lot of details," Jorgan said. "Just that they're supposed to learn everything they need to from Ziegfried."

Gerhardt raised his voice loud enough to address the civilians. "Stop setting down your suitcases. We're not staying here."

They stopped pointing at all the native decor and picked up their belongings again. Masorno entered the large room where they all lingered. He watched the closing of the portal with an upturned nose. "You all make quite a mess. I'll be glad to get rid of you."

Gerhardt didn't ask for an interpretation. He still wouldn't make eye contact with Adam. He held all the new paperwork and watched Masorno open a portal right there in the room with all of them present. Ziegfried was brought in on a stretcher.

Masorno had a portal open in about a quarter of the time it usually took Ziegfried. It wasn't nearly as pretty. The colors of the swirling spiral were rather anemic in comparison. Gerhardt sent the supplies through first, leaving the crates of gold for Andreno. He sent all the personnel leaving the palace. Then he waited for Thoel, the two radio men, and the five soldiers coming from base. He spoke quietly with them for just a few moments, making sure they had their orders and equipment straight.

He looked Adam in the eye then. Without a word he shook his head and turned away. He stepped through the portal and was gone.

Masorno shut down the portal. It must not have drained him as badly as it did Ziegfried. He didn't collapse or have to be carried out of the room. He stomped out all by himself saying, "Good riddance."

The newcomers all looked to Adam. He said nothing. He did nothing. They all looked to Strom.

"Let's get you all situated for the night." Strom led them out of the room.

Servants and workers cleaned everything up, leaving no trace of all the activity. Then they left too. Adam was alone.

He slowly meandered around the palace. He passed people that gave him no heed. He passed servants and workers who turned their faces away. Eventually people moved toward the dining hall to eat supper. No one came and told him to eat. That was fine. He wasn't really hungry anyway.

He went back to the window seat. He studied the pane of glass instead of looking out at the grounds as they darkened in the sunset. Andreno had once pressed his face against this glass in giddy, child-like anticipation, awaiting the culmination of one of his schemes. The Brendish diplomat had come then. That pretty girl. What would she think if she knew Adam had allowed villagers from her nation to be attacked by his inaction?

He turned away from the window and the memories. He hung his head, shuffling his feet toward his room. Just his now. Jorgan was gone. Strom never used it anymore. Alone.

Nolrien waited for him in there. He wore his customary blank look, his voice as neutral as ever. "You skipped supper again."

"So?" Adam shrugged. He started across the room to the privy in the back. He didn't need to use the toilet. It just made for a good excuse to continue his isolation.

"You haven't been wearing your dagger," Nolrien said. "Either of them. Where are they?"

Adam pointed to the drawer. Nolrien grabbed him by the shirt, whipped him around, and slammed his back against the wall. Before Adam could move or say anything, the tip of his dagger touched his throat.

"You sure?" Nolrien's voice remained neutral, his eyes blank.

"If you cut my throat," Adam said, "you will get blood all over yourself."

"You're right." Nolrien lowered the dagger. A smoldering wisp of anger crept into his eyes.

He grabbed Adam again, jerked him away from the wall, and stepped behind him all in one move. He kicked the backs of Adam's knees, driving him to the floor. As Adam went down, Nolrien wrapped an arm around his throat, locking his head in. He squeezed, cutting off all ability to breathe and squeezing the arteries in his neck.

Adam went limp. His body screamed for air. His pulse pounded through his head. That was easier to bear than the guilt. His consciousness slipped away. The last thought in his head was that he deserved this.

Chapter 46

THE NEXT THING ADAM KNEW he was lying flat on his back, sprawled on the floor, breathing normally. Nolrien knelt beside him, leaning over, watching him revive. His eyes smoldered with anger rather than giving their normal, creepy blankness.

"What is wrong with you?" Nolrien's voice still remained neutral, despite the flames behind his eyes. "You haven't reacted to anything that you normally do. And now you're not even going to fight for your very life? Why? Do you think you deserve to die?"

Adam turned his face away. Nolrien sat up straight, moving to the edge of Adam's peripheral vision. Some of the anger leaked from his eyes into his voice. "I can guess some of what happened between Gerhardt and the rest of you. What I don't understand is why you're taking this so hard."

"People died," Adam squeezed out the words.

"What people?" Nolrien asked. "The man Gerhardt killed? Other people? Strangers? Someone close to you? I still don't understand. Your nation is at war, isn't it? People die in war all over the place. Why is this so different?"

"My fault," Adam said.

"How?"

"I did not..." Adam's throat closed. Memories of his family played behind his vision, loved ones he would never see again. He stammered and stuttered, "I was supposed to... I did not... My father... Maybe..."

"You're going on a maybe?"

Adam turned his face back to look at Nolrien. "You do not understand."

"Your right. I don't." Nolrien rose to his feet. "You're broken up over a maybe. I *know* my father is dead."

He flicked the dagger. It twirled end over end a couple times, biting into the floor to stand vertical on its point by Adam's ear. Adam didn't flinch. "You did not kill your father by not doing what you were supposed to."

"You sure?" Some of Nolrien's anger drained out of his face. He scrubbed all expression off with his hand. His eyes dulled and went blank. He yanked the dagger out of the floor and replaced it in the drawer. He held out a hand to assist Adam back to his feet. "Come."

Adam didn't take the hand. "Where?"

"I need a drink." Nolrien reached down and pulled Adam to his feet anyway. "And so do you."

He led the way to Charlass' rooms. He went inside her parlor and called for her. Marietta burst through the curtained doorway to the main room with a delighted grin. "Nolrien!"

She pulled up short when she saw Adam. Her grin faded, replaced with an expression somewhere between pity and concern. Before she said anything more, Tabissia came into the parlor from the main room. She was followed by Charlass, who said, "You brought us a guest."

"He's leaving tomorrow with Andreno," Nolren said. "He could use a taste of that brew you claim doesn't exist."

Charlass turned back to the main chamber with a smirk. "If I never see it, I can't confirm its existence."

Marietta ran back into the main chamber as well. Tabissia came further into the parlor. She said to Adam, "You look upset."

"I am fine," Adam said.

"No you're not." Tabissia gave him a droll look. "I told you before, you wear your heart on your sleeve. It makes you easy to read. Right now, you're upset. You're leaving for a war zone tomorrow. You need your head in the right state to—"

"Do not lecture me on the right state of mind for war," Adam cut her off.

"Ah, a little temper." Tabissia smiled. "That's more like it. More like you. That puts my mind at ease."

Marietta returned with a bottle and three small glasses. Tabissia laid a hand on Adam's cheek and said. "You take care out there."

She turned and went back into the main chamber. Once the curtain had swished back into place, Marietta set the glasses on the low centerpiece table. She poured a couple fingers of dusky gold liquid into each.

"Charlass is letting Adam use her glassware." Marietta grinned. "Are we getting him drunk?"

"No," Adam said.

"Not even just a little?" Marietta's eyes glinted with mischief. "Some of my friends want to test what I keep telling them. And if you're drunk, it's a good opportunity."

Alarm sirens went off in Adam's head. "What did you tell them?"

"That you're the perfect gentleman," Marietta said. "Do you know what kind of drunk you are? Mean? Feisty? Impish? Funny? You have been drunk before, right? I've never heard of any of your people touching any ale here."

"I touched your ale," Adam said. "Once. It tasted terrible compared to my people's ale."

"This isn't ale." Marietta handed him one of the glasses. "I make it myself. My mother taught me. You probably don't want to know what she used it for, so I won't tell you."

Adam stared at the glass in his hands. He might never learn anything from his mother ever again. His gut tightened. He set the glass down on the table. He stepped toward the door to take his misery elsewhere, away from people he might affect poorly.

"Oh, no you don't." Marietta grabbed his arm and steered him to sit on a sofa. "Don't drink, if it offends you so much. Stay anyway. We like your company."

"Drinking does not offend me," Adam said.

"Reminding you of family is what disturbs you right now." Nolrien plopped into a seat of his own. He picked up one of the two remaining glasses and downed the contents. He winced and cleared his throat. "Reminding you of that 'maybe', because you didn't act. You're not as alone as you think. My father died because I didn't act."

"Your father died because Ziegfried murdered him," Adam said.

"He wanted me to gather more information about Ziegfried's men and their activities." Nolrien poured another couple of fingers into his glass. "I was never as dedicated to that part of the job as he was. What information I bothered to get, I didn't always pass on as soon as he liked. I still don't. So I didn't get what he wanted, when he wanted it. So he took you into that corridor to try and get it for himself. I didn't act. Now he's dead."

He swirled the dusky liquid inside his glass, staring into it rather than drinking. Adam looked at his glass. Maybe he should down it after all. It might ease this new guilt that was creeping in over the top of what was already there. He really wasn't alone. Nolrien lived with this every day. No wonder he always kept his face so blank. It masked the agony and guilt that had to be screaming at him from the inside.

"Can you explain something to me?" Nolrien still stared into his glass. "If your family is so far away, how would what happens here affect them? Surely your leaders are too busy running a country and fighting battles to bother with the family of one interpreter."

"My leaders are..." Adam didn't know the word in the native language. He didn't want to think about it anyway. He picked up his glass and downed the contents. It burned, erasing whatever taste it might have had. The warmth radiated out to his limbs. He blinked, his eyes watering.

"Wow." Marietta poured him another. "Most people choke on that the first time they try it."

"My people..." Adam's words came out wheezy. He cleared his throat and tried again. "My people are very good at making drink. It has good flavor. This stuff is strong."

"That's understating it." Nolrien downed his second glass. He reached for the bottle and poured more into Adam's. "What exactly did you do that's so terrible that you're worried for the lives of your family?"

"The same as you," Adam said. He hadn't eaten. This alcohol was going to pass through his stomach straight into his intestines. The drunk would come immediately. He downed his second glass.

"With Ziegfried's men?" Nolrien asked.

"They are not Ziegfried's men," Adam corrected him. "They are Gerhardt's. And they were doing something bad he did not give permission for. I was supposed to find out what."

Marietta refilled both their glasses. "Do you have any training for gathering information?"

"It does not matter," Adam said.

"Yes it does." Nolrien set his refilled glass down rather than drinking it. "Training gives you tools. You think a tailor can make clothes without a needle and thread? You think a baker can give you bread without flour and an oven? An information gatherer has to have tools of the mind. Without them, you're useless."

"That does not matter." Adam drank his third glass. "I still failed."

The others looked at him funny. Had he spoken in their language or his? He was definitely slurring his words, whatever language he had used. He repeated what he said, careful to put it in their language. They poured him another glass.

Everything got fuzzy after that. His memory blanked. He woke up on the sofa with a pillow under his head, a blanket wrapped around him, and a monster headache and no idea how much he'd told them or anything else that may have happened. Light stabbed into his eyes like daggers into his brain.

"Good morning," Marietta whispered into his ear. Feminine laughter tinkled in the main room. He glanced at the curtain. Marietta cocked her head toward the laughter. "My little sister is getting her lessons, along with some of my friends who now work as Charlass' servants. I should let you know, they all took a try at you."

"They what?" Adam bolted upright. His head immediately threated to explode and nausea punched him in the gut.

"Don't worry." Marietta chuckled at him. "You proved me right. Even drunk, you remain the perfect gentleman. They did ask if you had a wife, or were interested in getting one. But all you did was go on about how pretty some Brendish woman is. You couldn't even remember her name."

She picked up a tin cup from the low table and pushed it at him. He refused to take it and asked, "What is this?"

"Something to help your head," she said.

"I need water and food for that," Adam said. "And maybe a drink not as strong as what you gave me last night. Mostly, I need water."

"Water?" Marietta asked. "For a headache after drinking too much? Are you going to try to wash it away?"

"I drink it," Adam said. "The headache is mostly from being too dried out. At least, that is what my mother always told me."

He looked down at the floor. He still didn't want to think of the peril he'd put his family in. Maybe he should just endure the pain in his head. He certainly deserved it.

Something in the other room clattered, stabbing into his headache. The feminine laughter resumed with gusto. Marietta gazed at the curtain, her face softening with affection.

"I know you're worried." She gently pulled Adam to his feet. "There's something you should know. You saved us. Me. My sister. Some of my friends. Charlass. Tabissia. And in a way, you saved Nolrien too. He thought about killing himself for a while, until you needed lessons with that dagger."

Adam hadn't done all that. Not really. Other people had put the women in their positions with Charlass. And he hadn't saved her either. Doc Lieber had saved her when she was sick. As for Nolrien, Adam hadn't done anything there. Other people had thrust them together.

"Whatever happens to your family, you can always come back to us." Marietta put the tin cup in his hand. "You drink that. And when you go out there to the war, look for more people you can save. It won't bring back your family if the worst has happened. But it will give you a new one."

He raised the cup and sniffed at it. It smelled of honey, dandelion, and ginger all mixed together with a few other things he couldn't quite identify. He downed it quickly. The bitterness of the dandelion was strongest, despite the honey taking off the edge. Still, he'd had worse.

"You come back to us as soon as you can." Marietta took the cup and primly swished through the curtain to the main room.

Taking that as dismissal, Adam left. The palace buzzed with activity, people running about, trunks and boxes being packed and carried around. He navigated through the controlled chaos to his room.

Strom was there stuffing things into Adam's sack. One of Adam's uniforms was laid out on the bed. Strom said, "I hope you don't mind I packed for you, since you were busy. Why do you have so many books?"

"I only have half a dozen," Adam said. "They're dictionaries."

"Some of them don't use any letters I recognize." He held up the books for Mandarin and Hebrew.

"Other languages use different letters." Adam plucked the books from Strom and carefully stowed them in the sack. "You should know that just by the letters used in the native language here."

"Of course I do," Strom said. "I was kind of hoping you'd tell me what language they are."

"Doesn't matter." Adam said. "No one here speaks them. And if I never get home I'll probably never use them."

"You never did tell me exactly how many languages you speak."

"Not as many as I'd like to," Adam said, avoiding giving him an answer.

"Whatever." Strom shrugged, not really hiding his disappointment. He picked up the clothes on the bed and held them out to Adam. "Here, you can have your uniforms back. And you're supposed to wear the dagger with your walther, not stuff it in the drawer. And where did you get a second one?"

"A gift to go with the first one." Adam peeled off the clothes he'd slept in. Strom opened the shirt and held it out like he expected Adam to slip into it. Adam grabbed it and yanked it on. "I can dress myself."

"Whatever," Strom said again. He tossed the rest of the uniform back down on the bed. "Have fun last night?"

"I, uh, what?"

"I'm glad you finally got out," Strom said. "This was your last chance for who knows how long. I heard you were in Charlass' room with Marietta and some of her friends. That's good. They're a lot of fun."

"Sure." No way was Adam going to admit he couldn't remember.

"Your eyes are a little bloodshot," Strom said. "Marietta give you some of that rot-gut she calls alcohol?"

"Yeah."

"Good stuff! Powerful strong. Not like that dirty water the soldiers try to pass off as ale. How much did you have to exchange her for it?"

Adam yanked on the last of his uniform. "She didn't ask me for anything."

"Really?" Strom's eyes widened. "Wow. She must really like you."

Adam changed the subject. "Do you know who I'm supposed to be answering to on this little outing? Gerhardt didn't tell me."

"He told those new guys they're all answering to you." Strom stuffed the last of the books into the top of the sack. "Honestly, I think Gerhardt wouldn't talk to you because he was afraid he'd be too harsh and then regret it later. The only reason he was talking to me was because he already worked through that part of his mad. I'm still likely to get more of the brunt of punishment than you."

"I'm the one who screwed up," Adam said. "I'm the one who didn't find out what they were doing."

"I didn't even try." Strom shook his head a little. "I know I said that I didn't care what happened to my father. Now that I'm actually facing the possibility…"

"It's different than you thought," Adam finished when Strom tapered off.

Strom nodded, keeping his eyes averted. He swallowed hard. Adam clapped Strom on the shoulder, not really knowing what to say.

Strom tied the rucksack closed and picked it up. "I'll walk you outside. We're in one of those hurry up and wait situations. We all have to be ready to go at a moment's notice, for when Andreno's ready a few hours from now. If we're lucky."

Chapter 47

A WAGON TRANSPORTED THE GERMANS and their equipment. Adam didn't tell them that others in the convoy jeered at them for not knowing how to ride horses. Nevermind that most of those jeering walked on their own two feet. For the most part his comrades left him alone to brood. Probably they were just happy he wasn't ordering them around the way some people did with their first command.

When they reached the encampment, the convoy was engulfed by the size. The Germans were given a tent near the edge. The radio men asked Adam, "You want us to set up and update Gerhardt on our arrival?"

"Uh, sure," Adam said. "How soon can you get that done?"

"It'll take some time to set up," one of them said. "We'll try and get it done by sundown. If not, we'll have to wait until morning to transmit. Do you have any idea how far away he is?"

"Does it matter?"

"If he's close enough, we might be able to use ground waves." The man went into the jargon that annoyed Adam so much. He glanced up from the foothills where they had stopped. "Though I wouldn't recommend that unless they're behind us. Aerial would work for the terrain ahead, and we've got a vertical for it. Though if he's inside one of the bounces—"

"Okay! Okay!" Adam refrained from sticking his fingers in his ears and humming to blot out the words that flitted just beyond his understanding. "Just, do whatever you need to do."

"Set call time is dawn," the other radio man said. "I'm sure they know where this encampment is, so if we set up now and just wait for their signal that might be easier."

"Whatever works," Adam said. "So long as he gets the message."

One of Andreno's military commanders approached them with a man who didn't wear a uniform. The Commander focused on Adam and said, "Good afternoon."

"Are we needed?" Adam asked him.

"Not by Andreno." The commander clasped his hands in front of himself. "I know your name is Adam. I don't believe I've ever had the chance to properly introduce myself. My name is Mirvian. I'm the military representative and Commander from the Garham District."

"Isn't that the district we're in now?" Adam double checked.

"Yes." Mirvian nodded. "My District Premiere would have been here to greet Prince Andreno himself if he wasn't so busy dealing with all the logistical problems created by a large group of men encamped in his territory."

Adam raised an eyebrow. "And you're not with Andreno trying to explain away the snub?"

"I was, until I was given a menial task as punishment for my Premiere's absence." Mirvian smiled happily. "Andreno's been doing that ever since his visit to Brend a year ago. He claims their King does that sometimes. Now I must leave the presence of our grand prince, however much that may or may not pain me, and introduce you to my friend here. His name is Chouthan. He knows the Chemwanitz language."

Excitement pricked Adam for the first time since the fiasco with Ziegfried. "Are you my teacher?"

Chouthan spat on the ground. "You look stupid."

"Now, now." Mirvian waggled a finger at Chouthan. "Just because Andreno smacked you around and tried to get you to quit before you started is no reason to take it out on your student."

Adam ignored the angry glare Chouthan now gave Mirvian and asked, "When can we start?"

"Later." Chouthan turned around and stalked away.

Mirvian's happy smile turned to one of amusement. "You'll have to excuse him. Everyone's been giving him a rough time. The only reason he stayed to teach you is as a personal favor to me."

"You did that for me?" Adam asked. "Why?"

"As you can see, my district borders the Chemwanitz." Mirvian waved a hand, taking in the peaks rising immediately to the east. "I've been telling Andreno this entire winter that we ought to send someone up there to talk to the people and straighten out this entire mess."

"I cannot imagine he liked that," Adam said.

"No." Mirvian's smile faded, and his eyes veiled some. "I told him the reports from the attacked villages didn't match the normal procedures and methods used by the mountain warriors. He's pretty determined. And he has other Commanders calling for blood. I'm out of favor at the moment."

"I know what that feels like," Adam muttered. He kept it in the native language. The others didn't need to know the man they answered to was under judgment.

"Is that why you've been assigned back with Andreno?" Mirvian smirked. Then he shook his head. "Don't answer that. Instead, you should go to his tent, make sure everyone knows you're here and you have access to him. Then you'll hear interesting things."

"Like how he plans to kill women and children in those mountains?"

"Like how a small group of important Brendish men are on their way here. They're traveling rapidly, especially compared to Andreno's sluggish pace. They're expected sometime tomorrow."

"You are just giving me this information?"

"Nolrien asked me to look out for you, since he couldn't come do it himself. He trusts you. And that's not something he does easily. Besides, if I bring you in, then Andreno's more likely to let me stay."

Adam glowered. "You're using me."

"Only when it also gives you an advantage," Mirvian said. "Would you rather I lie and deny it?"

"No." Adam sighed. He switched to German and told his comrades, "Finish setting up. I need to go do some things."

None of them questioned him. They simply continued with their work. People around stared at the antenna the radio guys were raising. Thoel shuffled around inside the tent, presumably organizing his meager stash of medical supplies. The soldiers that weren't pretending to do busy work just loafed.

Adam left them and followed Mirvian to the large, multi-roomed tent in the center of the camp. It's splash of bright colors striping up the walls and over the roof gave it a garish look compared to the drab canvas of every other tent. Mirvian led the way inside. Most of Andreno's military commanders were in there. A couple of them sneered at their entrance.

"Adam!" Andreno beamed. "How respectful of you to come without making me send you a summons. I have some good news. Have you contacted your Gerhardt yet? He'll need to know about this, I'm sure."

"We are working on that," Adam said. "What news?"

"A group of Brendish are coming." Andreno practically bounced on the cushion where he sat. "Two of them are on the King's central staff. I'm hoping to talk one of them into going up into the mountains to the forward camp to meet with your people's magician. I think they'd work well together. Gerhardt will need to know he's going to have a visitor."

"He may not want visitors up there," Adam said. "And Ziegfried is in trouble."

"Yes, yes, we all know about the tiff between the two men." Andreno waved that away. "Honestly, they fight like cousins over their grandfather's inheritance. He'll like this visitor. He'll set Ziegfried straight on several things. He may even be amenable to teaching you people everything he knows about magic if you treat him right."

Adam didn't resist getting in a dig. "Does he know how to find missing people?"

The enthusiasm in Andreno's voice and demeanor vanished as fast as a match in a gale. "I have no idea."

Adam should have taken more time to mentally prepare himself. He was in trouble enough as it was. If he riled Andreno too much, it would only make things worse.

"You should have people serving you who do their jobs well." Adam attempted to placate the bratty ruler. He had to grit his teeth as he forced the words out. "The people you sent should have found the one their looking for by now."

"It's possible they may have." Andreno relaxed, leaning back on his arms, looking appeased. "We just may not have heard back yet. Our communications system isn't nearly as fast as yours."

"Is this Brendish man coming just to work with us?" Adam asked.

"Not specifically." Andreno grinned impishly. "I'm still unsure if they even know you exist. He's coming because it's appropriate for King Terrance to send important men to me. After all, his villages were attacked by the barbarians too."

Adam clenched his jaw. "By the barbarians."

"I'm so glad to have you back instead of Strom." Andreno chortled. "He acts more like one of my minor nobles. You're much more fun."

"Great." Adam couldn't muster up any enthusiasm for the word.

"As I was saying." Andreno waved a flippant hand. "Terrance is sending two men from his central staff. That's the highest station a minor noble can get to in Brend, almost as important as a high noble. I sent the King an invitation to join me in the invasion. I'm hoping these men are bringing me a positive reply."

"He hasn't moved any troops toward the border," Mirvian said.

"You just love being sour." Andreno frowned at him. "Don't even try to pretend you know Terrance's intentions any more than I do."

One of the other commanders snickered. Everything went downhill from there. A couple of them berated Mirvian, even using insults with words Adam hadn't completely grasped yet. Andreno watched it all like an entertaining cinema flick playing out solely for his amusement. Eventually, Adam had enough. He slipped out. No one stopped him. He couldn't tell if anyone even noticed.

The sun was setting. Food sizzled over cook fires. Despite how bland and terrible the food probably tasted, the smell set Adam's mouth to watering and his stomach to growling. On the road, he and his comrades were always one of the first groups served after Andreno and his commanders. Hoping that would continue here in the encampment, he headed back to their tent.

The nearest Shontese still openly stared. The radio tower was now complete, as far as Adam could tell. He didn't ask after its status in case it set the radio guys off on another jargon filled description.

After supper they retired early so they could rise before dawn. When the sun came up, they turned on all the radio equipment. The operators worked with dials and frequencies and whatever else they did. They listened to squeals, static, and whines, adjusting here and there, until they received a scratchy voice on the airwaves.

Adam grit his teeth, listening to all the rigmarole of the initial contact, the verification, the jargon, the lingo, and slang. He was supposed to be in charge, so he resisted the overwhelming urge to either walk away or smash all the unintelligible equipment to tiny pieces. Then they decided that he needed to talk too.

He relayed the information that two important Brendish men were on their way, due in sometime that day. Gerhardt asked, "Did Andreno specify who or for what reason?"

"No, sir," Adam said. "He acted blatantly ignorant about the reason. He said he's hoping they'll say their King will assist with the invasion."

"Have any of his military commanders expressed reason for him to believe that?" Gerhardt asked.

"Most of them said nothing," Adam told him. "Especially after he got really annoyed with one of them for pointing out lack of Brendish troop movement."

"Stick close to Andreno without drawing attention to yourself," Gerhardt ordered. "When those visitors arrive, I want you right there if you can possibly manage it."

There was a short pause on the other end of the communication. Adam strained to hear through all the fuzz coming through the speaker. Finally, Kiefer came on, identified himself, and spoke in American. His accent through the static made it even more difficult than normal to understand. "Have you asked for information about the status of our missing man?"

"I asked," Adam replied with the same language. Gerhardt must not want anyone else to know about it. "No word yet."

"When the visitors from the north get there…" Kiefer's voice scratched out in the middle of the sentence.

One of the radio men fiddled with the equipment. Some of the static cleared. Then he asked Kiefer for a repeat of the last transmission. Kiefer still used American English. "When the visitors from the north get there try and find out what they know. If possible, set up a route of communication back to their leader."

"I'll do what I can," Adam said.

Chapter 48

AS IT TURNED OUT, Adam couldn't have missed the arrival of the foreigners if he'd tried. Late morning, the entire camp went into a flurry of activity. Every idle person, soldier and civilian alike, suddenly found a chore they could busy themselves with. The foreigners were escorted through all the hullabaloo to a tent not far from Andreno's.

They came in a wagon. Adam counted four men with six guards. The guards wore crimson and gold uniforms with gold stars at the collars. All of them had three flat stripes on the upper arms of their sleeves. Of the other four men, one slept in the back of the wagon. He was barely visible with the way they had him covered. The Brendish court magician was one. A third one looked vaguely familiar with ash gray hair and eyes. The last was completely unfamiliar to Adam.

When they stopped, they refused to allow any Shontese servants help them carry anything into the tent. They moved everything themselves. And the sleeping man didn't stir when they shuffled him inside along with their parcels.

Adam drifted with some of the onlookers back into Andreno's tent. The spoiled princeling paced around inside, bouncing with every step, talking so fast some of his words were garbled. He had servants prepare lunch. Then he called for his foreign guests to be brought to him. Three of the civilians, the ones not sleeping, and three of the guards came. The guards wore that same cold, stony look they had worn in the palace.

"Welcome to Shontarra." Andreno put on his winning smile and opened his arms to them. He made eye contact with the court magician, "Jerryck, I'm so pleased you've come."

This was the man that Masorno had been so adamant that the Germans stay away from, especially Ziegfried. This was the man that everyone had shuffled Adam around specifically to avoid. Up close, there didn't seem to be anything special about him. In fact if anything, he looked a bit shaggy and slightly unkempt.

"Sinchet, good to see you again." Andreno greeted the next civilian, the unfamiliar one. Then he turned to the ash haired man. "You must be Tajor, the new priad. It's a pleasure to finally meet you."

Jerryck opened his mouth like he was going to say something. Sinchet shot him a warning look and he stopped. Tajor smiled. Laughter danced in his gray eyes, tickling at Adam's memory without bringing up anything solid. He'd met far too many people over the last year.

"I know it's a bit early for the midday meal." Andreno didn't seem to notice the individual reactions of his guests any more than he noticed anything other people did. "But I also know that while you're on the move it can be difficult to get the time to sit down to a decent meal. Please join me."

Adam rolled his eyes. Andreno hadn't had any difficulties sitting down to eat on the road. They'd made very slow progress because every time he'd wanted to eat, they'd had to stop and set up all the accoutrements he insisted on.

Tajor made eye contact with Adam. There was a brief moment of recognition. Then the man's attention flitted elsewhere.

As the food was served Andreno went into the routine of talking empty pleasantries. Sinchet and Tajor responded the way most people did, by spouting empty pleasantries of their own. Sinchet did it better. Tajor kept looking away and smirking. Jerryck was stiff and completely non participatory.

"Jerryck," Andreno got his attention. "I haven't seen you since you came to the palace that time with Nita. How is she getting on?"

Adam's ears pricked up. If they were referring to the pretty girl who had been the delegate, he now had a name to attach to her lovely face. That almost made it worth putting up with Andreno.

"She's fine," Jerryck answered.

"I hear that the processions have started for her," Andreno said. "How is that going? Has she shown interest in any of the young men in particular?"

Tajor answered that one. "Not as yet."

"It's good that she's cautious," Andreno nodded.

He scowled at a servant dishing him a second helping of the main course. Adam twitched, holding back instead of jumping to pull the servant away. He dug his fingernails into his palms as Andreno cuffed the servant on the ear hard enough to knock her sideways to the ground.

Jerryck focused in, paying very close attention to the action. His eyes narrowed. His brows drew together. His gaze followed the servant's scramble to get out of the way. As usual Andreno kept on talking like nothing had happened. "Someone in her position can't afford to show that they've taken a liking to anyone if they're not appropriate for the position they'll be marrying into."

Marry? That pretty girl was looking for someone to marry? His girl was looking for a husband. Why was it so disappointing that he wasn't even close to being a candidate?

She wasn't his girl. She didn't even know he existed. Besides, he'd never given much thought to marriage. That had always been his mother's venue.

Gloominess swamped him. His mother might never have the chance to push another girl at him.

Adam did a mental shake. He forced himself to put that aside, to pay attention to what was going on around him. Sinchet was still chatting emptily with Andreno. The uniformed Brendish guards had faded in with all the other guards and the few Commanders who had stayed to observe the meal. Their eyes darted to and fro, taking in everything. Tajor somehow looked at everyone, everything, and still participated in the conversation. The magician was staring at each of the servants one by one, and looking more and more upset each time.

"Jerryck, do you not like the food?" Andreno asked. The magician didn't respond. He kept staring at the servants. Andreno waved at him. "Jerryck?"

"Huh?" Jerryck snapped his attention off the servants and onto Andreno. "I'm sorry. What did you say?"

"I asked if the food wasn't to your liking," Andreno said. "You've stopped eating."

"I apologize." Jerryck looked down at his full plate. He turned slightly green around the edges. "The food is fine. Very good in fact. I'm not hungry. I think I need to rest more than I need to eat."

"Then you should go back to your tent and rest," Andreno said. Jerryck jumped out of his seat and ran out of the tent. Andreno raised a skeptical eyebrow. "Tired, huh?"

"Our apologies," Sinchet said. "The court magician is well known for displaying odd behavior at times."

"At times?" One corner of Tajor's mouth twitched upwards. "How often would you describe as 'at times'?"

"Do you really have to do that here in front of our host?" Sinchet scowled. Tajor laughed.

"It's quite all right with me," Andreno said. "Your priad is reputed to ask annoying questions as much as your court magician is reputed for being slightly odd."

"Slightly odd or not," Tajor said. "Jerryck is very good at his job."

"I have no doubt of that," Andreno said. "His reputation covers his skills as well as his oddities. Tell me, is it true that he had to step in to assist my court magician in front of your king?"

"Yes," Sinchet said. "There was wind whipping all over the place until Jerryck took control."

"What exactly was Masorno doing?" Andreno asked.

"He was putting on a demonstration to try and impress Tajor," Sinchet said.

"Why would he do that?" Andreno asked. "He told me he was going there to work with Jerryck and teach him."

"No one can do that unless they first impress Tajor," Sinchet said. "It's been made an official proclamation that even the gathering of seats has agreed to."

"Why?" Andreno asked.

"He wants to annoy other magicians by exposing them to me?" Tajor shrugged. "Isn't it said that a lot of them have been annoying him for several years now?"

"I doubt that's his reason." Sinchet let out a rather tense sounding chuckle. "Although, you can be rather annoying at times."

"Rather?" Tajor smirked. "At times?"

"Also," Sinchet ignored him. "Tajor is gaining a strong reputation for being very knowledgeable on the subject of magic. Jerryck knew this ahead of time. That's why he specified that Tajor had to be the one who was impressed. So far, none have succeeded."

"Why is that?" Andreno asked.

"Is it not the job of an adviser to poke holes in theories and propositions in order to point out what is incomplete?" Tajor asked.

"I suppose," Andreno said.

"Why should I not then also poke holes in claims magicians make that their work is impressive?" Tajor asked.

"I begin to see why you rose to the position you did," Andreno said. "The King of Brend chose well, I think. I hope he also chose well when it comes to whether or not he'll be joining me in the mountains?"

"You don't want to wait until tomorrow when we have an official meeting to discuss these things?" Tajor asked. Andreno made an attempt at a coy shrug, something he hadn't perfected. Tajor said, "Then I suppose I could tell you that King Terrance sent us to bring his regrets. He will not be joining you in your military campaign into the Chemwanitz."

Andreno bared his teeth. "Weren't his villages attacked by the raiders this winter?"

"Yes," Sinchet said, "But—"

"—but," Tajor cut him off. "He has decided to use diplomacy."

"That's it?" Andreno threw down his napkin. "What about that letter I got stating that you were coming here to deliver information you had obtained about the raiders?"

"Yes," Tajor said. "The information is that there is not enough evidence to declare war against the Chemwanee people."

"Not enough evidence." Andreno surged to his feet. "His villages were raided the same as mine. What more evidence does he need?"

"Why don't you write him a letter and ask him?" Tajor asked. "Would you like us to take it back to him for you?"

"What about that other man that's with you?" Andreno pointed vaguely in the direction of their own tent.

Tajor's face was as blank as Nolrien's usually was. "What other man?"

"In your tent," Andreno said. "I was told there was another man that you brought with you. Someone no one recognized. He had the skin tones of a Chemwanee."

Tajor's blank look disappeared, replaced by an exaggerated look of realizing what Andreno was talking about. "Oh, him. He's sleeping."

"Tell me who he is," Andreno said.

Sinchet opened his mouth. Before he could speak, Tajor said, "He's a man."

"And?"

"And what?" Tajor went back to his blank expression. "He's a man."

"Where did he come from?"

"Most likely his mother," Tajor said with a smirk.

Sinchet squirmed uncomfortably. "Tajor, please."

Tajor's smirk widened. "Although I'm sure his father had a part in that as well. I wouldn't advise you ask me who they are. I would have to tell you I have no idea."

Andreno clenched his fists. "That's not funny."

"Did I claim it was funny?" Tajor asked. "You didn't like the answer to your question?"

Andreno's face reddened with anger. "You didn't answer it."

"Didn't I?" Tajor asked. Beside him, Sinchet put his face in his hand. Tajor kept going. "If he didn't come from his mother and father, then where do you think he came from?"

"I meant what country?" Andreno threw his hands up in the air. "What land? What people?"

"What about them?"

"Which ones did he come from?"

"That's a good question." Tajor tapped his chin and looked away momentarily, as if thinking. Then he looked back to Andreno. "Shouldn't you be asking him rather than me?"

"You said he is sleeping," Andreno said.

"Is? Or was? Those are two different things. If he was asleep, do you think he could have awakened with all your shouting? Is that the 'is' you're referring to?"

Adam had to turn away. He couldn't hold the grin off his face any longer. He had to bite the inside of his cheek to keep from laughing out loud as the conversation continued on. If one could call it a conversation. This seemed more like some hazing episode a clever soldier would give an idiot recruit new to a post.

Most people cowered when Andreno got this mad. Tajor just kept prodding. They went round and round. Every once in a while, Sinchet would make a feeble attempt to get Tajor to stop. Andreno got more and more frustrated. Tajor kept evading and tossing out useless information, or asking diverting questions that turned everything on its ear. He posed riddles, gave half answers, and still remained polite and respectful.

Eventually Tajor and Sinchet left, going back to their own tent. After that Andreno geared up into a regular tantrum. Adam ducked out.

Before he got five steps away, Andreno's screaming rant cut short. That was a first. Adam looked back. A page sprinted out and headed for the visitors' tent.

The guard at the entrance poked his head inside. Then Jerryck came out. With many a backward glance he shuffled his way to Andreno's tent.

Everyone else exited the garrish tent, as if Andreno had demanded privacy with the magician. Most of the servants went off in one direction. The few military commanders went in another. Mirvian and another quietly argued about something, too quiet for Adam to hear.

Adam kicked himself for leaving too early. Now he could only make guesses. What was Andreno up to? Jerryck would know a lot about magic. He must, to hold a position of court magician. Was that who Andreno had referred to when he talked about sending someone to work with Ziegfried?

Adam's stomach clenched into a knot. He went to his comrades and said, "Get on the radio. Raise Gerhardt. I think we may have a problem brewing."

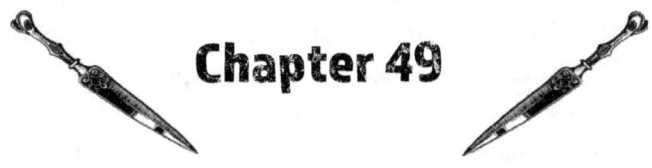

Chapter 49

"I'LL DO WHAT I CAN." The man nearest the radio equipment flipped a few switches. He pointed up to the sky. "No guarantees."

Adam looked up. There were a few dark clouds to the east. No threat of rain at the camp.

The page that fetched Jerryck came running in their direction. He fumbled with a pen, trying to write on a scrap of paper as he moved. Adam snapped at the young man. "Just tell me!"

"Prince Andreno summons you and your doctor," the page said breathlessly. "He says to come immediately and bring your sleeping medicines."

Adam clenched his jaw. There wasn't enough time to think of a way to tell Andreno no and get away with it. The radio crackled and spit static. They weren't going to get through to Gerhardt in time for him to ask either.

What was the medic's name again? He'd met too many people. Oh yes. Adam called, "Thoel!"

The medic crawled halfway out of the tent. "Yes?"

"Get your sedatives," Adam told him. "Andreno wants you and I."

"I'm not supposed to use those unless absolutely necessary."

"Just do it," Adam said.

The doctor disappeared back inside the tent. After a few moments he re-emerged with a leather satchel and a scowl. They went to Andreno's tent.

Jerryck was seated on a cushion, straight backed, stiff, obviously uncomfortable. Andreno was behind him. Both the men looked up at the entrance.

"I was told you wanted us," Adam said.

Andreno jumped on Jerryck, holding him with one arm, clapping the other hand over his mouth. "Use your sleeping medicines! Quick!"

Adam stood there unable to make himself comply, unable to flat out refuse. Jerryck twisted and writhed, struggling to get free. His voice worked, not that any of his words were understandable.

"Is this really necessary?" Adam found his voice. This wasn't happening. It couldn't be. Not even Andreno would stoop to attacking a foreign dignitary. Would he? More than that, if the Germans assisted it would further sever any chance they had to open any kind of peaceful communications. But if they didn't assist, it could anger and alienate their only source in this land.

"If he talks, he could use magic against us." Andreno's muscles bulged and strained. "I can't hold him long."

Adam stated the simplest solution. "Then let him go."

"Don't disrespect me!" Andreno yelled. His eyes flicked to the doctor. "Tell him to do it or I'll have Ziegfried send a letter of dissatisfaction to your authorities. Your family will be as good as dead."

Except Adam's family was likely already as good as dead. The threat didn't mean much to him. But what would it mean for the medic? Adam hadn't learned anything about any of his men aside from their jobs, not even if they had families that could be threatened.

"Sedate the victim," Adam ordered Thoel.

"But..." Thoel started.

"I know, you're not supposed to," Adam said. "You don't know everything going on here. I need time to think. I need to talk to Gerhardt. For now, just do it."

"I don't suppose you know his approximate weight." The medic knelt, setting down his satchel and opening it. "I'm guessing about 195, maybe 200 pounds? What do you think?"

Adam had no idea. "Sure, sounds about right."

Thoel filled a syringe with clear liquid from a labeled bottle. When he approached Jerryck with the needle, the magician's eyes rolled in panic. His collar was pulled back and the shot administered in the muscles of his shoulder.

Andreno whispered something in his ear. Jerryck sucked air through his nose in a sudden gasp. His back arched and his entire body shuddered. Then he went completely limp. His eyes rolled up. His breath slowly released.

"I've never seen this reaction." Thoel leaned over Jerryck with a frown, peeling back his eyelids one by one, revealing dilated pupils.

He took out some more tools. He took blood pressure. Counted pulse rate. Listened to breathing, lungs, and heart. He did other things Adam didn't care to know details about. Medical personnel seemed fond of doing things he tried hard to ignore.

"I don't understand." Thoel examined the eyes again. "He shouldn't have gone under that fast. I can't find anything else abnormal. I need better equipment, more thorough examination procedures."

"Is he conscious or not?" Adam asked.

"He's out," Thoel said. "As much as anyone I've ever dosed with this."

"He sleeps," Adam told Andreno.

"Good." Andreno finally let go of his victim. "Next time I tell you to do something, do it immediately. This is your last warning."

He stood, blew out his breath, and shook his arms. He rolled his head, popping his neck. Then he called loudly for the guards always stationed outside his tent. When they entered, he bounced on the balls of his feet while he gave them orders. "There's a man I suspect is being held as a prisoner in the Brendish visitor's tent. Bring him here along with Priad Tajor. Kill all the rest."

"You cannot do that!" Adam burst out. It didn't stop the guards from leaving to carry out the orders.

"You think you can tell me what I can and can't do?" Andreno laughed at him. "This is all part of my plans."

"Your plans." Adam snorted in derision. "Like how you planned to cause a war in the mountains?"

"And how I plan to start one with Brend," Andreno said. "Don't you worry. I can stop it. I'll give them an exit when—"

"I hate war." Adam clenched his fists. "Too many people have died."

Andreno waved that away. "I told you I have it all planned. As soon as they've had enough of a taste of your people's weapons, I'll offer them a peace treaty through marriage."

"You will not get Gerhardt to help you attack Brend," Adam said. "He already does not like that he is in the mountains."

"Get out," Andreno snapped at him. "I tire of you."

Adam snagged Thoel and ushered him out. He protested, pointing at Jerryck. "I should stay with him. The drugs will only keep him under for a few hours."

Adam forcibly pushed him along. Andreno called for his servants. They scurried in. Adam kept the medic going, despite his continued protests.

The sounds of fighting came from the visitors' tent. Clatters and shouts. The screams of dying men. Thoel gasped and stiffened. He turned in that direction.

"No!" Adam yanked him back toward their own tent. "There's nothing you can do except get yourself killed. I'm trying to straighten this out. Don't make it worse."

The struggle could be heard from the Germans' tent. The static of the radio hadn't changed, no progress there. Both the radio guys and the half dozen soldiers stood around facing the screams and the clashing.

"Who's fighting?" they asked. "What's going on?"

"Bad things." Adam sent Thoel inside the tent. He asked the radio guys, "Have you made contact yet?"

"No."

"How much longer will it take?" Adam asked.

One of them pointed at the clouds in the east. "I'm not sure we'll get through at all."

"Keep trying."

Adam paced. He fisted his hands in his hair. The fighting quieted down. Then shouts of alarm rose off to their right a few tents away, still close to the perimeter of camp. There was the screech of metal on metal, a few grunts, a scream of pain, then feet pounded away from the camp at a dead run.

Thoel jumped out of the tent, staring off in the direction of the new tumult. "I don't suppose you'll let me help there either."

"Let me check it out first," Adam said. He walked away giving a parting order to the radio guys. "Keep trying."

He passed the few tents to their right. Almost a dozen men had gathered there. A couple of the Shontese doctors had already arrived, tending a few men lying wounded on the ground. One of them still had a knife between his ribs. A couple of others were obviously dead.

Adam drew close enough to hear the men talking as one of the soldiers said, "I'm not going after Brendish palace elite."

The man he'd spoken to wore insignias of a low command. he punched the soldier in the face then kicked him in the gut. He looked around at the other gathered men. "Anyone else want to disobey my orders?"

Despite the corporal punishment, another protested anyway. "They'll kill us all!"

The officer drew a sword. All the others scattered, running off in the direction the pounding feet had fled from camp. His eyes met Adam's. He shouted, "You're not supposed to be here! Get away!"

Adam went back to the German tent. He told Thoel, "It's already being taken care of by other doctors. You're not needed."

The man's eyes flicked toward the center of the camp. Adam turned that way. Two of Andreno's servants approached. One of them clutched his ribs and limped. The other supported him, helping him walk.

"Will you help us?" the unhurt man asked Adam. "We've heard your doctors don't care if someone is just a servant or not."

Thoel passed Adam, latching onto the injured servant. "Don't tell me not to help him. It's an order I'll disobey."

Adam followed them inside the tent then asked in the native language, "What happened?"

"Andreno is angry," the unhurt servant answered. "It's very difficult to please him when he's angry."

"Why is he angry?" Adam asked. "He was happy the last I saw him."

"Something went wrong, I think," the servant said. "He ordered some of the guards to be whipped. I think someone died who wasn't supposed to, and some who were supposed to die got away. At least, that's what it sounded like to me."

Adam strode out of the tent. Thoel called after him, "Where're you going? I need interpretation for the patient."

He didn't answer. He caught the surprise on the faces of the radio guys as he flashed by them. He went straight to the tent of the visitors. It was a bloody mess. Almost a dozen Shontese soldiers were dead. Three of the Brendish dead wore the crimson and gold of their elite guards. Sinchet was dead. The mysterious sleeping man lay still covered, now in a pool of congealing blood and a sword pinning him to the ground through his torso.

Adam wiped his mouth with the back of his hand. The stench made his stomach roil. One of the soldiers pacing around the tent put out a hand to him. "Stay back."

He pushed the man aside and picked his way over to the body of the sleeper. He pulled the cover off the head. There was Gunter.

"You can't be here." The man who had tried to stop him grabbed his arm and hauled him away. "You have to leave."

Adam shook the man off. He went to Andreno's tent. He didn't ask permission to enter, let alone wait for it. He just pushed aside the flap and went in.

"I knew you'd show up." Andreno glared at him, seated on a cushion, encircled by all his commanders, their aides, and several servants.

"What have you done?" Adam demanded, striding over to him.

"Don't you dare raise your voice to me." Andreno jumped to his feet. He raised a hand to strike. Adam stepped back. He clutched the hilt of his dagger with his left hand. His right hovered over his walther. Andreno hesitated.

"We will not help you fight a war with Brend," Adam said.

"That's not your decision," Andreno said. "Get out."

"Fine." Adam headed back toward the entrance. "Then when the sleeping medicines wear off and the magician wakes up, do not expect me to come running to your rescue when he makes you pay for all this."

Andreno paled. "How long before the medicines wear off?"

"How should I know?" Adam stopped just before the entrance. "I am not a doctor."

"Go get your doctor," Andreno said. "Bring him. Now."

Adam stuck out his chin. "You will have to wait."

"I do not." Andreno stamped a foot. "I wait for no one. I'm a prince!"

"My doctor is treating someone you injured." Adam matched Andreno's volume. "You have to wait because of your own actions. I will bring him when he is finished fixing what you did. Not before."

He stepped outside before he could say anything else that was stupidly belligerent. Andreno shouted, "Get back in here! You don't leave without permission!"

Adam looked at the guards hanging about the tent entrance. One of them looked away and yawned. Another shrugged and said, "I didn't hear an order for us to stop anyone leaving, or to bring them back in if they tried."

Adam walked away.

Chapter 50

ADAM TOOK SEVERAL DEEP BREATHS of the cool air, trying to clear his head. The days were still short. The sun was dipping closer to the horizon. According to the radio operators, that would cut off any chance at contacting Gerhardt.

He went back to the German tent. They still hadn't gotten through. They still pointed to the clouds in the east, blaming them. Adam paced. How was everything spiraling out of control so quickly?

Spotty contact got through. Everything was broken and unintelligible. No message was clear in either direction. The only thing they really understood was when the other end asked them to repeat what they'd said. The sun slipped below the western horizon. The speakers spit white static.

"That's it then," one of the operators said. They shut everything off.

Adam went inside the tent. Thoel had wrapped the injured servant's ribs and ankles. He'd also splinted the man's left arm and put it in a makeshift sling. Adam surveyed it all. "That much damage?"

"A couple of cracked ribs," Thoel said. "A wrenched elbow. The ankles are weak, look like old injuries. I wrapped them to give support, nothing more."

"When you're finished, Andreno wants you to come check on the guy he attacked in his tent." Adam hiked his thumb toward the center of the camp. "He asked how much longer the sedatives will last."

"There's a little time yet," Thoel said. "Not so much that another dose would be too overly detrimental if they want him to stay under. I'm finished here. I should go check on him anyway."

Adam took him back to Andreno's tent. Andreno reclined on a cushion again, looking amused while watching Mirvian arguing back and forth with another commander. Everyone else had left except for a couple of servants slinking in the corner and the guards at their posts in a ring around the outside of the tent.

Andreno waved his two commanders silent and frowned at Adam. "Could you have taken any longer?"

"Yes," Adam said.

Andreno stood. "I don't think I like this attitude you've gotten lately."

"Tell me about it," Adam said. "Give me every detail. Take your time. You have plenty to spare before the magician wakes up. Yes?"

Andreno's eyes flicked to the medic and his leather satchel. He turned to the back of the tent and lifted the flap to his sleeping room. Inside, the magician lay on a pallet, still unconscious. On the other side of the little room Priad Tajor sat on another pallet, his hands shackled at the wrists in front of him, his face blank.

Adam snarled at Andreno. "Abusing one important person was not enough for you?"

"Just tell your doctor to do his job and leave," Andreno said.

Adam hesitated. They were already in too deep. How could he do anything without causing more damage? He couldn't do what Andreno wanted. Not without further harm to their chances with Brend. At the same time, he couldn't just demand the release of the two men and honestly expect to be obeyed.

"Do whatever you need to," he told Thoel. What other option was there at the moment?

Thoel went into the back room. He knelt by the magician and opened his satchel. He took out a pressure cuff and stethoscope. After that Adam averted his eyes.

The two commanders watched. Adam narrowed his eyes at them. Could he trust either of them? Mirvian? Maybe. The other? Certainly not.

"Is all that really necessary?" Andreno pouted, watching the doctor. "I don't want him waking up and able to talk. Tell your doctor to just put the medicine in."

"No," Adam said.

"Do what I tell you!" Andreno snapped.

Tajor spoke up. "If you're not careful with those kind of medicines it could affect him badly."

Andreno sneered at him. "How would you know?"

Tajor mirrored the expression perfectly. "You think I got my position by being ignorant about a great many things?"

"You don't have anything to say that I feel like hearing," Andreno said.

"Does that mean you'll send me home?" Tajor asked. "Does that include Jerryck?"

"You're one of the most annoying people I've ever met," Andreno said.

"It's a little late for you to try flattering me." Tajor tilted his nose up and sniffed, as haughty as any nobleman. "After all you did today, compliments will get you nowhere."

"That wasn't... I mean... I didn't..." Andreno grit his teeth and fisted his hands. "Stop it!"

Thoel nodded his head toward Tajor while he administered another dose of sedatives to the magician. "Is that man injured? Does he need anything from me?"

"Are you injured?" Adam asked Tajor.

"He's fine," Andreno said.

Tajor glared at the syringe the doctor was putting back in the satchel. "I have no injury other than my pride."

Adam interpreted into German. "He's insulted but unharmed."

Thoel nodded, then asked, "Are they going to let me stay with my patient this time? Or make me leave again? The dosage this time was slightly weaker to avoid adverse effects since he already had some still in his system. I probably should stay and monitor."

"I'm not staying," Adam said. "And you're not staying here without me. If the man wakes up and blasts his kidnappers to hell, so be it. I won't say they don't deserve it."

"Very well." Thoel sighed. He packed the rest of his tools back into his satchel and closed it up.

Tajor watched the medic while saying to Adam, "I don't suppose your friend has anything in there to help Andreno with his crazy head?"

"Don't think I won't have you beaten," Andreno threatened.

"Aww…" Tajor smirked. "Did I hurt your feelings?"

Andreno answered a little too quickly. "No!"

"Do you *have* feelings?" Tajor asked.

"That has nothing to do with this."

"Did your papa not give you enough hugs as a little boy or something?" Tajor asked

"Be quiet!"

Tajor whispered. "Is this quiet enough?"

"Close your mouth and stop talking."

"For how long?" Tajor went back to speaking normal. "Is five seconds long enough?"

"AARRGGHHH!" Andreno raised a fist toward Tajor.

Adam stepped between the two. Maybe he should stay after all. It would please Thoel at the very least.

"Get out of my way!" Andreno bared his teeth at Adam. "I'm going to teach this (unfamiliar word) to respect his superiors!"

Tajor leaned over to peer around Adam. "If you really were superior, I would give you respect. You want to go ask Terrance how much respect I give him? I'm sure he'd be happy to take you in as a, um, guest."

"I cannot leave." Adam stood his ground. "The doctor needs to watch the magician. He was very unhappy he could not stay last time. He stays, I stay. And as long as I am here, I will not allow you to hit anyone. If you so much as strike even a servant, I will hit you back."

Andreno clenched and unclenched his fists at his sides. Behind him the servants all turned their faces away. Mirvian kept his face carefully blank. The other commander started spitting and fuming. "You can't threaten our prince."

"I didn't hear any threats." Tajor smirked. "I heard a warning of impending danger. Why didn't you warn your beloved prince of that danger? Are you hoping he'll get hurt? Do you hate him that much?"

369

Andreno pointed at Tajor and shouted at his commander, "Get him out of my tent."

"Good idea." Tajor said. "Separate your prisoners. Make it twice as difficult to keep us guarded. Why didn't I think of suggesting that?"

Adam laughed. "Because it is stupid."

"You want your doctor to keep watch on the magician." Andreno glared at Adam. "Then you people can damn well guard them both. You're not doing anything else except eating my food and taking up space anyway. Make yourselves useful for once."

"They're on the edge of the camp." The other commander frowned. "That may not be such a good idea."

"Now who's questioning the sanity of our prince?" Mirvian said. "It's perfectly resourceful, putting idle people to work. A wise decision, Prince Andreno."

"Of course it is," Andreno said.

Adam told Thoel, "Go get the other guys. We're taking charge of the prisoners so you can keep an eye on them."

"And so they can possibly escape?" the doctor asked.

"You shouldn't say such things," Adam said. "You don't know how much of our language anyone has picked up over the couple of years this operation has been in progress. Go get the others before he changes his mind. Hurry!"

Thoel ran out. Andreno demanded, "Where's he going?"

"To get the others of my country." Adam still didn't know the best native word for comrades. "They have to be here to help move these two if you want us to get them out of your tent."

"I'll have the tent next to yours emptied for you to put them in." The other commander left too.

"In the meanwhile," Tajor said. "You might want to have your servants go ahead and get your nighty night things ready so you can sleep as soon as we leave. You're being a very grumpy little boy. Do you need your favorite dolly to cuddle with? Or do you just suck your thumb?"

Andreno clenched his teeth. "It's beneath me to respond to that."

"You saying that wasn't a response?" Tajor asked.

Andreno tensed up so much he trembled. Adam took a step in the direction Tajor leaned, putting himself between them again. He crossed his arms and tried to look intimidating.

Mirvian put his hand gently on Andreno's shoulder. "Let it go. Please. You said it's beneath you. Let it go."

Andreno turned around and slapped Mirvian, leaving a red mark on his cheek. Adam uncrossed his arms. Mirvian held up a hand, stopping him from hitting Andreno back.

Andreno gave him a smug glance. He walked over to the few servants and kicked one of them in the stomach. Adam just about lurched forward. Mirvian stopped him again.

Chapter 51

THOEL RETURNED ALMOST BREATHLESS. He had to have run
to be back so fast. The others he brought weren't so winded. Adam
said to Mirvian, "We need something to carry the magician."

"He's on a litter laid over the pallet," Mirvian said. "You just can't see it
because of the blankets."

Adam pointed to the two prisoners and told his comrades, "Take these
two men. A tent next to ours is being emptied for them."

Two of them lifted the blankets enough to find the handles of the litter
under the magician. They lifted him easily and carried him out. Tajor didn't
resist coming along. Mirvian came with them too.

A cadre of Shontese guards escorted them all. Adam tried a bluff to get
them to keep their distance. "If any of you set one foot in that tent, I will
shoot the prisoners and be done with them."

"Andreno wants them alive," Mirvian said. "Or they'd already be dead."

"At the moment," Adam said, "I care very little for what Andreno wants."

"Back off," Mirvian told the soldiers. They stopped several paces away
from the tent. Mirvian said, "Farther. Give some privacy. Stay only close
enough to hear if you're called."

The soldiers backed off, melting into the shadows between the neighboring
tents. Mirvian whispered to Adam, "I'll keep them far enough away so you
can make whatever plans you need with those two. If they escape, you'd best

make sure they hurt you in the process. And have them send my apologies to their king from my premiere."

Adam nodded once. He entered the tent where his comrades were trying to settle the two prisoners. Tajor remained on his feet refusing to sit. When they set Jerryck down he stirred slightly.

"That's not right," Thoel said.

"Your doctor looks concerned," Tajor said. "Tell him not to worry. The medicine will affect the magician oddly because he cast a spell on himself."

"He did?" Adam should have thought of that. "When? Before he went to see Andreno?"

"Does it matter when?" Tajor countered.

"What does it do?" Adam asked.

"How much I tell you depends on your plans for us."

"Well…" How to go about what Adam wanted?

"I heard what the commander whispered to you," Tajor said. "I have very good hearing."

The magician stirred again. Thoel leaned over him, checking him out. "He shouldn't be waking up. This isn't right."

"Don't worry about it for now," Adam told him. "I said before, I'm fine if he wakes up. Gerhardt wants good relations with their country. Helping to abduct them isn't the way to go about getting that."

"What if we help them escape?" one of the radio guys asked.

"That might be a little difficult while surrounded by men loyal to their abductor," one of the soldiers said.

"We're close to the edge of camp." Adam waved toward the perimeter. The magician groaned and stirred some more. Adam said to all the men, "Go outside and pretend you're patrolling around out there. Make sure no one stops them if they incapacitate me and crawl out under the back of the tent."

All of them went out, even Thoel. That left Adam alone with Tajor and Jerryck. Tajor asked again, "What exactly are your plans?"

"If you hit me," Adam said, "I may not be able to stop you if you leave."

Tajor's expression darkened. "You don't want me to hit you."

"Either that, or you stay and find out what Andreno wants with you," Adam said.

Tajor jerked his hands apart, snapping the shackles as easily as if they had been made of paper. He repeated, "You don't want me to hit you."

The magician pushed himself into a half sitting position. He opened glassy eyes and looked around. He fixated on Adam. He mumbled something unintelligible.

Tajor waved his hands at him. "No! No!"

Adam stepped forward to have a word with the magician, intending to explain things. One of Tajor's waving arms struck him in the stomach. He might as well have swung a policeman's billy club. Or a rod of iron rebar. For a moment Adam was sure Tajor's arm went right through him and out the back. He fell to his knees completely devoid of breath and unable to take another.

Fire erupted from the magician's hands. It shot up in two streams like duel flame throwers. Adam threw himself the rest of the way to the ground. Tajor face planted right beside him.

"Stop!" Tajor shouted at his friend.

The fire died on the magician's hands. Too late. The roof of the tent dripped flames. Still unable to breathe, Adam rolled to the entrance and scrabbled outside.

"Fire! Fire!" The shouts went up through all the surrounding tents. "Water! Get shovels! Fire!"

Adam's stomach muscles spasmed, trying to draw in breath after all the movement he'd done. Thoel grabbed him and dragged him away from the burning tent. Other hands took hold and helped. Still he struggled to get air into his lungs.

The edges of his vision started to darken and blur. His chest ached for air before a tiny trickle seeped in. He wheezed, sucking in what little he could get. Only then did his stomach start to hurt.

He tried to shake off the hands pulling him away from the heat of the blaze. Thoel wouldn't let go. "What happened?"

Adam looked around, not answering, searching among all the chaos suddenly around him. Shontese soldiers used shovels, axes, and poles to beat the flaming tent to the ground and battle the fire. Adam looked past them, trying to find Tajor and Jerryck.

He glimpsed two people near the edge of the camp moving away. One of them staggered like a drunk. He stumbled and reached out for the other. His companion stiffened at the touch. Then both men collapsed to the ground.

Adam struggled to get to his feet. Thoel held him down. "Just take a moment. Let others deal with the fire."

"Not... the fire..." Adam still couldn't get enough air. He sounded like he was gasping. "...let go... have to..."

"Hey!" One of the soldiers went to check on the two men. "I could use some help! Someone!"

No one responded until the fire was brought under control. Then three other soldiers went to help. By that time, one of the Shontese doctors approached Adam. "Are you hurt? Are you burned? What happened?"

"I am fine." Adam finally started getting his breathing under control. "Not burned. They hit me. I lost my breath."

He pushed the doctors away, refusing to let them try and treat him for nothing. He went to check on the two prisoners. All hope of escape for them was now gone. Jerryck lay completely prone, unconscious again. Tajor lay on his side, curled into a fetal position and shuddering like he was the one who'd been punched in the gut.

Shontese soldiers picked them both up, carrying them back into the camp. They got as far as the German tent where the men were frantically trying to protect the radio equipment from all the chaos and people running around.

The sea of bodies parted. Andreno came striding up to them. "What is going on here?"

"Fire's out!" Mirvian shouted at all the men now standing around. "Clear off. Back to your posts and assignments. All of you."

People moved off. Too bad Andreno didn't leave too. He yelled at all the Germans, as if they could understand him. "I give you one simple assignment, and you mess it up so badly I have to come out here myself to straighten you up?"

Adam yelled right back. "You think we set fire to the tent?"

"Get them out of sight," Mirvian told the Shontese soldiers that carried the prisoners. They turned to the closest tent, the one the Germans used.

"Do not enter our tent," Adam ordered.

375

"You there." Mirvian strode over to the next closest tent, addressing the men there. "Clear out. Go to your commanding officer. Find different shelter. We need this space for other purposes."

The soldiers sheltering there didn't so much as protest. They snatched up their meager belongings and vacated. Mirvian said to Adam, "Have your men take the prisoners in there."

Adam relayed the order in German. His comrades quickly obeyed. Neither of the men gave any trouble. Mirvian helped carry them in and lay them against opposite walls. He lit a lamp as Andreno pushed his way in. A couple of his bodyguards tried to follow, as if there was room for that many in the little tent. Andreno yelled, "Back off. Give us some privacy."

He slapped the tent flap closed in their faces. Their footsteps retreated. Andreno said to Adam, "You tell these men I'm setting guards around this tent and yours. If you mess this up again, I'll have them kill you all."

"What are your plans with these men?" Adam asked, absentmindedly rubbing his stomach where he still hurt.

"Are you injured?" Mirvian asked.

"I am fine," Adam snarled.

"Let me see." Mirvian reached out. He snagged the front of Adam's long coat.

"No." Adam jerked away. The sudden movement pulled at the muscles in his stomach, making him wince.

Thoel paused from re-examining the magician. "You're hurting."

Adam snapped at him. "I'm fine."

"Don't you try that." The doctor stepped over to him. "Lieber warned me about you. Open your coat and lift your shirt. Do it! Or I'll have our men hold you down and do it for you."

Opting for the lesser of two evils Adam opened the front of his knee length, standard issue coat. Impatiently, Thoel yanked the shirt up. A large purple and black bruise was blossoming exactly in the spot where he'd rammed into Tajor's steel arm.

"Good god!" Thoel said. "What happened?"

"Nothing," Adam said. "I'm fine."

"You're bleeding."

Adam pointed out the obvious stupidity of that statement. "I don't see any blood."

"What do you think a bruise is, you idiot?" Thoel didn't sound convinced.

Mirvian pointed at the growing bruise. "Did the prisoner do that?"

"It does not matter," Adam told him.

"It does matter," Mirvian said. "You took injury trying to keep the prisoners from escaping. Then they tried to burn you alive. Just for obeying our prince."

"I'm sending the two of them up to the forward camp." Andreno stared at the bruise. Adam covered it. Andreno blinked. He raised his eyes to Adam's face. "Ziegfried has been looking for a magician he can work with and learn from."

"You plan for men to approach Gerhardt's camp while they're in a battle zone?" Adam narrowed his eyes. To his relief, Thoel left him alone to check on Tajor. "You cannot communicate with them. If they do not know you are coming, they will shoot first and ask questions later."

"You have communications with him," Andreno said. "You can tell him they're coming."

"We tried to get through to him all afternoon," Adam told him. "It does not always work. And do you plan for the magician to wake up during the days it will take for him to get there?"

"Your doctor can do whatever it is he does to make him sleep."

"That takes continued doses," Adam said. "If our doctor does not go, he cannot give them. I ask again. Do you want the magician to wake up?"

"I guess your doctor will have to go too," Andreno said.

"Then I will also have to go," Adam announced. He pointed to Thoel, trying to help Tajor sit up. "If something happens, he cannot communicate to anyone without me. And since you cannot communicate to any of my people without me, I will be taking with me everyone in this camp who is from my country."

"You can't strip me of all of your people!"

"Yes I can," Adam said. "I am responsible for them. You have no need for them without me. If I go, they go."

Andreno stepped close, getting in Adam's face. "I say you can't go!"

Adam leaned in. "Then you cannot send your prisoners."

"Don't you tell me what I can't do." Andreno shoved Adam. "Servant!"

Adam lurched, shoving his shoulder into Andreno, grabbing his pant leg and yanking his leg out from under him, knocking him to the ground. Before he regained his legs, Adam planted a knee in his chest, dagger in hand, the sharp blade up against his jugular.

"I am not your servant." Adam's voice was nearly gone, almost a whisper. Rage filled his belly, making it hurt all over again.

"Weiss?" Thoel inched close. "What are you doing?"

"You did this." Adam tilted his head at the two prisoners, ignoring Thoel, still speaking to Andreno, his voice getting hoarser. "If you wanted us to stay, you should not have done something this stupid."

Adrenaline made his hands shake. He withdrew the dagger to keep accidentally slicing Andreno's throat. Andreno lay stone still even without the dagger pricking his neck. His pupils were dilated, and the whites of his eyes showed all around.

"I should have you killed." He also spoke barely above a whisper.

"Then Gerhardt will break ties with you," Adam said.

"Over an interpreter?" Andreno snorted. "I don't think so. Ziegfried would never allow that."

"Ziegfried is trouble," Adam said. "Gerhardt will kill him if he must. And he will break ties. You will never get any gold from us ever again."

Andreno swallowed so hard it was audible. Adam slowly removed his knee from the man's chest and stood. He sheathed his dagger, keeping his other hand close to his walther.

"You want these men to go to the forward camp," Adam said. "I will get them there alive. We will leave at dawn. Go arrange it."

"You don't give me orders."

Mirvian held out a hand to assist Andreno to his feet. "I'll arrange it."

Andreno refused the assistance. He scrambled to his feet, backing away from Adam. He backed all the way out of the tent. Mirvian quickly followed.

Adam waited breathlessly, expecting Shontese soldiers to storm the tent and kill them all, like they had the Brendish visitors. When no one came, when it didn't sound like anyone outside was being assaulted, he let his shoulders drop and willed his hands to stop shaking.

Chapter 52

THOEL BROKE THE QUIET. "What did you just do?"

"I just tried to prevent us getting into another front in this godforsaken war," Adam said.

"The war is back home," Thoel said. "Not here."

"Look around you." Adam windmilled his arms. "The war is here. Why do you think all these soldiers have gathered? What do you think Gerhardt and Velig are doing with most of our men a few days east of here?"

Thoel broke eye contact. He clenched and unclenched his jaw. Then he changed the subject, nodding his head at Tajor. "I can't find any physical signs of injury on him, no reason for him to be acting this way. No broken bones. No swelling. No bruising. Not even a mark. Still, his body is giving all the signs of trauma. All I can do is treat for shock until I figure this out."

"Do that," Adam said. "Then prep them both for a journey."

"Are we keeping the magician asleep?"

"As asleep as he needs to be to keep him from talking and casting spells at us," Adam said. He stepped outside and told the rest of his comrades, "Dismantle. Pack up. We're leaving at dawn to join up with Gerhardt."

One of the radio guys asked, "You want us to make the call at dawn first?"

"No." Adam wasn't about to risk testing Andreno's patience any further than he already had. "Just keep handy whatever you need to set up quickly for sending and receiving while on the move."

"You don't know much about radio, do you," the operator said.

Adam shook his head. To prevent further discussion, or tutoring attempts, he turned his back. Shontese guards now ringed them, watching them as if they were Andreno himself. He made a point of ignoring them and went back inside.

None of his men questioned him. They packed everything up while Thoel kept an eye on the prisoners. By the time they finished they had less than half the night left. After a few hours of sleep, the sky grayed with dawn. A wagon pulled up in front of their tent with a couple dozen Shontese soldiers escorting it.

Mirvian brought the man who was supposed to teach Adam the mountain language. He said to Adam, "So much has happened. You remember Chouthan, don't you? He's going with you."

"We could be going into fighting," Adam warned him.

"It's war, isn't it?" Chouthan shrugged. "Of course there'll be fighting. I can handle myself. And I can help you with the Chemwanee tribes. Besides, I'm bored. And I hate being harassed by all these soldiers."

Mirvian and Chouthan helped them pack everything into the wagon, making sure to leave space for Tajor and Jerryck. The magician was strapped to a pallet and laid in the back. Tajor sat near the back end, his reshackled wrists tied to the side of the vehicle.

Adam didn't tell anyone that wouldn't stop Tajor from escaping. Not if he really wanted to leave. Not with the kind of strength he had demonstrated the previous evening.

Mirvian introduced Adam to one of the Shontese guards. "This is Chandler. He's in charge of the men who will keep you all safe on the journey. Be nice to him. Or he'll tell Nolrien to beat you harder when you get back to the palace."

"Great." Adam didn't mention that he probably would never set foot inside the palace again, not after how he'd treated Andreno. Which also meant he probably would never see the people who resided there again either.

Adam and Thoel rode in the wagon. Chandler jumped up to the seat beside the native driver. They pulled away from the camp. Everyone else walked on foot, in front, to the sides, or behind the vehicle.

The radio guys stuck close behind, constantly eyeing their equipment every time it jostled. They headed uphill, toward the peaks in the east. The radio operators complained about missing the dawn call time. Adam told them to use alternatives like the smaller, handheld two-way radios, or making contact in the evening when they stopped. He almost stuck his fingers in his ears when they gave him all the technical reasons why that wasn't feasible.

During the entire day Tajor said nothing. The doctor never did figure out what had caused the trauma the night before. He didn't act like he was in shock anymore. He just sat there saying nothing.

He watched everything. For all the good it would do him. The Shontese soldiers were as quiet as he was. The only people talking were the Germans. Tajor couldn't possibly understand what they were saying.

He watched silently as Thoel re-administered a dose of drugs to the magician. A catheter was used to keep his bladder empty, and an IV was inserted. Thoel didn't want to keep him completely under. He wanted to lighten the dosages for health reasons, just enough to keep the magician too sleepy and groggy to be aware of much, or do anything for himself. He claimed an IV would help with that. Tajor did nothing to inhibit.

That evening when they stopped, the radio operators set up. They didn't finish until after dark. They waited until dawn to make contact. The barely got through. On top of the spotty moments of clarity in the transmissions, the timing was bad. The Germans were doing a hit and Gerhardt wanted to keep the lines clear for coms from that. Adam relayed that they were incoming with a couple dozen Shontese soldiers and two prisoners. After that the spotty contact broke.

Adam told them to contact the palace. If Gerhardt knew they were trying to talk to him and couldn't, he might turn to them to see if Adam had left a message to convey.

"How much do you want us to say?" the operators asked. Good question. It had to be enough that Gerhardt would understand, not so much that it could leak out to any German on this world.

"Have them put Strom on," Adam said. He could talk to Strom in a different language. That would help.

They got through quickly enough. Then they had to wait for the radio operator there to find Strom and get him on. By that time Chandler was standing over them, itching to get everything rolling, complaining about the delay and how much travel time it would cost them.

Adam ended up just telling Strom that there had been an incident with the Brendish. He had taken them and all his comrades away from Andreno and was moving up to the forward base camp.

When they moved again, Tajor spent the morning staring at Adam. After a few hours, he had to ask, "Why do you keep staring at me?"

"I remember you," Tajor said.

"When?" Adam asked. "Where?"

Tajor smiled. Amusement filled his eyes. He looked away for the first time that day, gazing at the passing landscape. They passed a patch of snow that had drifted up during the winter and hadn't yet melted in the early spring weather.

"Hey." Adam tried to get Tajor's attention back. "Where did we meet before?"

Tajor quirked his head just enough to look at Adam. "You don't remember me?"

"From Andreno's tent?"

"From Andreno's palace."

Adam thought back over all the people he had met in the palace, everyone who had presented themselves to Andreno, both high and low noble. He ran all the faces he could recall through his head. None of them belonged to the Brendish priad.

Tajor laughed. "I suppose I should give you a bit more information. This was before that palace belonged to Andreno and before I was the priad to the king of Brend."

"I have not been around very long," Adam said.

"I haven't been the priad very long," Tajor said. "I rose through the ranks rather quickly. I think I may have even skipped a few."

"Did we just run across each other?" Adam asked. "Or did we speak? There was only one Brendish person I spoke to and that was... oh."

The smirk did it. The ash hair, the laughter in the eyes. The memory fell into place. This was that guard who had come to the balcony. "You threatened me. You told me to stop watching that pretty girl."

"Nita?" Tajor's smirk grew. "Yes, that was me. And from your reaction when you heard about her I'm guessing you're still sweet on her."

"Were you serious? Would her guards really have killed me?"

"Yes," Tajor said. "They would kill anyone who inappropriately approached her."

"They do that with all delegates they guard?"

"You don't know who she is?" Tajor laughed again. "Even though you have her name, you still don't know who she is?"

"So just for her they will kill," Adam surmised. He pouted, crossing his arms. "Thank you very much for laughing at me. I appreciate it."

"Not just for her." Tajor sobered. He looked down at the shackles on his wrists, then over at Jerryck. "For this, they will certainly kill."

"Nita's bodyguards?"

"They have more than one function. Being a bodyguard is only part of their job. And there are a lot more than just those who came with her. I'm sure someone told you about the Brendish palace elite?"

"They were mentioned," Adam said. "Were you one of them because you are so strong?"

"No." Tajor smirked again. "Though I'm sure that didn't hurt my chances."

Adam pointed to the shackles. "Could you break those as easily as you did at the camp?"

"Yes."

"So why don't you?" Adam asked. Tajor looked down at Jerryck, all the mirth was gone. Adam snorted and rolled his eyes. "Do not try and tell me it is because Jerryck cannot walk. You could kill all of us and wait for him to wake up. Or you could just carry him away. Tell me why you do not."

"That's not my choice to make." Tajor said it so quietly, Adam had to strain to hear.

The nonsense answer was infuriating. "Whose choice do you think it is then?"

"Yours." Tajor cocked his head at him. "At the moment. It would seem other people's lives are in your hands. Tell me, if you would, when faced with this kind of decision, knowing the consequences will be bad either way, how do you choose?"

Adam beat his fists on the bed of the wagon. "What kind of game are you playing?"

Tajor looked away again. "Sadly, this is no game."

The wagon lurched over a rock, jostling everything. The magician stirred some. Thoel immediately examined everything, including the tubes he had hooked up.

The two radio guys practically jumped in the wagon to check their equipment for the umpteenth time. The other Germans laughed at them, jeering until one of them tripped over the rock that had jostled the wagon. The laughter all turned in his direction. Even some of the natives joined in. The soldier jumped up, swinging at the nearest man laughing.

The two tussled, oblivious of the entire group moving forward without them. Adam stood and shouted to the driver, "Stop!"

Everything ground to a halt. Adam jumped out of the wagon and threw himself at the two fighting men, knocking them both to the ground. One stayed down, scuttling out of reach and spitting apologies, blaming the cold, the thin mountain air, the trek, everything but himself. The other took a swing at Adam. Stupid from his position on the ground. Adam kicked him in the stomach.

His breath left in a whoosh, a cloud of fog leaving his mouth in the chilly air. He dropped back to his knees, clutching his arms over his middle.

"Get back in formation." Adam growled at the two of them. "I don't care how thin the air gets up here. I don't care about the cold. I don't care how tired you are or how much your feet hurt. You fight, and I will beat you senseless. *Understood?*"

Every one of the Germans snapped a reply. "Yes, sir!"

It was an odd feeling, being addressed as if he really were an officer. They all formed up. The trek continued. Adam walked behind his comrades this time, keeping an eye on them. Chandler looked back at him from the wagon seat and gave him a nod of approval.

Chapter 53

THE FARTHER THEY WENT, the higher they got. The air thinned further. The temperature dropped. They passed more and more snow. Well before sunset Chandler called a halt. The natives set up camp with a defensive perimeter. Chandler posted guards on rotation. The men not on duty acted edgy, keeping their backs to the fires, eating while keeping an eye on the darkness closing in around them, curling up in their bedrolls with their weapons in hand.

"Is there something I should know?" Adam asked Chandler. "You all are acting nervous."

"Just keep your men in line," Chandler said.

Adam pointed away from camp. "Your men are watching out there. Not my men. Why?"

"Three Brendish elite escaped Andreno's camp," Chandler said. "They don't leave their own behind to gain freedom. They don't allow their own to be captured and transported elsewhere without returning and attempting to free them."

"You think they're out there somewhere?"

"If not now, they will be," Chandler said. "At some point or another. Maybe they're behind us and catching up. Maybe they went ahead to look for a good spot to set up an ambush. Maybe they're somewhere out there now, just waiting for us to drop our guard or split up. Keep your men in line. If any of them fall behind, consider them as good as dead."

"Between yours and mine, we have over twenty men. Three have no chance against that."

"You don't know the Brendish palace elite if you think that." Chandler shook his head. "The odds won't stop them from trying, and possibly succeeding."

Adam nodded and turned away. He said nothing to his comrades. If the prisoners escaped, or were rescued, Adam wasn't going to prevent it. He went to the wagon.

He stood on the ground and leaned over the side close to Tajor. "If you can hear whispers outside a tent, how much do you hear now?"

Tajor raised an eyebrow at him. "Are you asking me to volunteer information to you?"

"You must be staying for something," Adam said. "Why not that?"

"I stay because the decision is not within my authority to make."

"You have the ability to make this situation change," Adam said. "If you do not use it, that is a choice you have made. You cannot put this entirely on me."

Tajor closed his mouth. He looked away, hunched his shoulders, and shuddered. Adam ground his teeth and clenched his fists. "What is wrong with you?"

Tajor wouldn't look at him. "What are you doing?"

"I am trying to stop a war."

"By suggesting I kill you? Not just you, everyone around you?" Tajor looked up, still not at Adam. He looked past Adam, just over his right shoulder. He stared so intently, Adam turned to see if anyone was standing behind him. No one was there. Tajor asked, "Did your mother ever claim you have a guardian angel?"

Adam was so startled by the abrupt change in subject, it took him a moment to respond. "What?"

"If not your mother, then perhaps someone else?" Tajor stared directly in his face, just as intently as he had stared past Adam's shoulder. "Anyone who was nearby while you grew through childhood."

As a matter of fact, his mother had claimed Adam had a guardian angel. On several occasions. And his father had never argued it, had stopped anyone else from arguing with her about it. So had several of the neighbors.

"What does that have anything to do with right here, right now?" Adam asked. "It has nothing to do with the fact that you could kill us all and walk away."

Tajor looked away again. "I'm not going to kill you."

"No." Adam snorted with frustration. What was wrong with this man? Why wouldn't he use the ability he had? "You are going to choose to do nothing. You asked me how I choose the way I do. I want to know how you can choose to do nothing."

"I already answered that question."

"No, you gave an excuse to avoid responsibility for the choice you make."

Tajor frowned. He looked out into the darkness around them. With each passing moment, his frown deepened. When he spoke again, it was quieter than before. "If the only way I can choose to leave is by killing every one of you, why are you so determined to make me choose that? Do you want to die?"

"No. But if it stops a war here, I am willing to die."

"If you're really trying to stop a war, why not just order everyone to go on ahead and leave the two of us behind?" Tajor asked. "That would save all of your lives. And Jerryck and I could report to King Terrance how concerned you were for our safety."

"And if Chandler refuses?"

"Good question," Tajor said. "Which goes back to my earlier question you never answered. How do you make decisions like this? Either way, something bad will happen. How do you do this?"

"There is no need to make fun of my situation. Especially when you refuse to act."

"I'm being serious," Tajor said. "How do you do this?"

"Serious. Sure, you are being serious. I do not believe you. I am doing everything I can for you, without putting these men in more danger, and all you do is sit on your own strength and mock me. You have no idea how bad it could get, what things are like where I come from."

"Are you certain?"

"It is not possible," Adam said. "Unless you have traveled someplace that is more similar to my home, you cannot know."

"How do you know I haven't traveled that far?"

"I am certain of it," Adam said.

"Why?" Tajor tilted his head to one side. "Just because you're from a different world, you think no one else is?"

Adam leaned in closer, dropping his voice to nearly a whisper. "Who told you we are from a different world?"

"Besides your reaction?"

"Are you from a different world?" Adam asked.

"Technically—" Tajor paused a moment, then said— "not really."

"What is that supposed to mean?"

"It means exactly what I said."

"Are you from my world?" Adam asked.

"No."

Adam stood straight again. "Then you are from this world?"

"Recently," Tajor said.

"Recently? How recently?"

"Ever since lately," Tajor said.

Adam stomped his foot on the cold ground. "That is not an answer."

Tajor looked down at Adam's foot. "You try and fight with the ground, you'll lose every time."

"Why will you not answer?"

"I gave you an answer," Tajor said. "Why would you think I didn't?"

"You gave me no information I can understand or use."

"Then why is it my answer that's at fault?" Tajor asked. "How do you know it isn't your question that's the problem?"

Adam pushed off the side of the wagon and walked away without another word. This was getting nowhere fast, except annoying and frustrating. He couldn't even remember the original reason he'd gone to talk to Tajor in the first place.

The native soldiers sweated out the night. The three unaccounted-for Brendish elite failed to make an appearance.

The Germans failed to make radio contact in the morning too. The operators dismantled and stowed the equipment. When they moved Adam walked, avoiding Tajor.

The journey took a couple more days. Tajor didn't offer any more conversation, and Adam wasn't sure he would have taken it anyway. Instead, he got Chouthan to start teaching him the Chemwanee language.

Finally, they drew near the forward base and went through the protocols of approach. They passed through the sentries at the perimeter and were allowed to enter. Jorgan took in hand the few supplies they'd brought. Helmut stood right by his side counting it all. Velig took charge of the two prisoners and used Kiefer to interpret directions to the natives.

Adam quickly found himself standing at attention, alone before Gerhardt in the command tent, trying to explain his actions and everything that had happened. He started where Andreno had received the Brendish visitors.

He described Andreno's decision to commit acts of war against his northern neighbor. He made certain to include the possibility that there were three men out on the loose somewhere that the native soldiers feared. He explained how he had tried to facilitate the prisoners' escape so they could gain the possibility of using that to open communications. He tried to fuzz over the details that led up to him taking everyone up to the forward camp.

"You threatened Andreno?" Gerhardt wouldn't let it go with just that. "How exactly did you threaten him? With what?"

"I, uh," Adam still tried to gloss over it. "I told him that if he had no one who could speak the language approaching the camp, our men would shoot first and ask questions later."

"Andreno knows that Kiefer is here," Gerhardt said. "He can interpret for incoming. We're not going to automatically shoot men wearing Shontese uniforms. What else did you do?"

"I also said that in order to keep the magician under, the medic had to go. If the medic had to go, I had to go to interpret—"

"—and if Andreno didn't have you, he had no need for anyone he couldn't communicate with," Gerhardt finished the sentence. "You already told me that. I asked what else."

Adam clenched his jaw. He couldn't think fast enough to make up something believable. He was going to have to come clean. "Sir, please don't punish any of the men I brought with me. They were just following my directions. They didn't do anything wrong."

"What did you do?"

"I threatened Andreno with my dagger," Adam almost mumbled.

"Threatened? Or did you draw it?"

"I had it at his throat."

"And his guards just let you?"

"They were outside," Adam said. "He'd shut them out again. I was already mad that he'd committed acts of war, forcing us to assist when you had ordered me to try and open a line of communication. Then he pushed me, and I just, I sort of lost it."

"Sort of?"

"This is entirely my fault," Adam said. "Please don't send a bad report home about any of the other men. I don't want anything bad to happen to their families because they did what I told them."

"You should have thought of that earlier," Gerhardt said. "But I won't. I am surprised, though. You're more concerned about their families than your own."

Adam clenched his teeth together while he said, "That's kind of a moot point after how I messed up at the palace with Ziegfried's bodyguards."

"Moot how?"

"Didn't you already send home details of how I failed you?" Adam asked. "I figure my family is already dead."

Gerhardt blinked, leaning back in his seat. He opened his mouth. It took a few moments for any words to come out. "I did nothing of the sort. As far as I'm aware, command at home knows nothing of that fiasco and your parents and brother are fine."

Adam's breath caught. "They are?"

"Is that why you're acting so out of control? Because you think you have nothing left to lose?"

"I..." Adam's gut clenched. "I thought, maybe, if I couldn't help my own family anymore I could find others who needed help. Andreno didn't. And he was ruining any chances you had for that communication you wanted. The two prisoners needed help. I tried. I failed. And they won't help themselves. So I brought them to you."

"If you wanted to help them, why didn't you let them go after you left Andreno's camp?"

"Because he sent more than a dozen soldiers with us," Adam said. "As much as you want peace with Brend, I didn't think you wanted war with Shontarra instead."

"As for helping themselves," Gerhardt said. "That's rather difficult when one is drugged and the other bound."

"He's not bound," Adam said.

"He's wearing shackles."

"That's not holding him." Adam came clean about that part too. "He's stronger than anyone I've ever met. He could snap those in two any time he chose. He's just not choosing to for some reason I can't figure out."

"How about we go ask him." Gerhardt headed out.

"Good luck, sir," Adam muttered.

"What was that?" Gerhardt paused just outside the command tent.

"He doesn't give any information in his answers. Or he distracts and annoys you until you give up." Adam looked over at the man in question. He was watching them. "He has the best hearing I've ever come across too. If he spoke German, he'd be listening to every word we're saying right now."

"There's a lot of noise here," Gerhardt said. "And we're talking rather quiet."

"And he can hear us," Adam said.

"Sir?" Velig called from over by the two prisoners. Gerhardt crossed over to them, Adam right behind him. Velig said, "We need to get these two out of the open."

"Escort our guests to the back of my tent," Gerhardt said.

Lieber and Thoel wasted no time picking up the magician and carrying him. Tajor followed without being told, keeping his friend in sight.

Gerhardt's tent was pitched right next to the command tent in the center of the camp. Just as the two men were escorted inside Ziegfried ran up, trailed by a Shontese soldier who looked about fifteen or so. Ziegfried called to them, "Wait!"

Gerhardt stepped inside. He shooed Velig to take the two men into the second room in the back and dropped the entrance flap in place. That didn't stop Ziegfried. He burst inside with the Shontese soldier.

Gerhardt turned a cool eye to him. "What do you want?"

"I was told Andreno sent two men to meet with me," Ziegfried said.

Gerhardt glared at the soldier. He said, "Weiss, verify."

"What did you tell Ziegfried?" Adam demanded in the native language. "And who gave you permission? Where is Chandler?"

The kid stuck out his chin. "He's not doing what my prince wants."

"That is not for you to decide," Adam said.

"Leave him be," Ziegfried said. "He did the right thing."

Adam rounded on Ziegfried, repeating what he'd said in German. "That's not for you to decide."

"Whatever." Ziegfried snorted and rolled his eyes. Had he drawn from the kid or something? Why was he acting like an immature little teenage brat? "Doesn't matter how exactly I heard. I did. That's the important thing."

"You heard wrong," Gerhardt said.

"Tell me where they are!" Ziegfried demanded.

"Doesn't matter," Gerhardt said. "They're not here to see you."

"Adam," Ziegfried turned to him. "Did you or did you not bring two men that Andreno wanted me to see?"

"I brought two men for Gerhardt to meet with," Adam said.

Ziegfried stamped a foot. "And me."

"No," Adam said. "I brought them to Gerhardt."

"I know who those men are." Ziegfried put a hand on the kid's shoulder. "I got a good description of them. I'm the one Andreno would send them to."

"Really?" Gerhardt raised an eyebrow. "Even though he's very much aware that I've been attempting to contact the king of Brend for more than a year now? Two important men representing him wouldn't be sent to me? Is there something you're not telling me again?"

Ziegfried took his hand off the young man's shoulder. A flicker of fear shadowed his face. "No, I've told you everything."

"Have you?"

"That is the Brendish court magician that was brought here," Ziegfried said. "Andreno knows what I'm looking for. It has to be why he sent him. You don't perform magic. I do."

"And you have several new assistants to train up," Gerhardt said. "Five of whom are in this very camp. You haven't done much with them. I have no reason to believe you'll do anything with any other magic user you have access to. Leave. Now."

Ziegfried crossed his arms. "Not until I've seen those two men."

Gerhardt pulled back the partition that divided the main area from the tiny sleeping chamber, revealing everyone inside. Velig and the two doctors all squished in there. With so many bodies in such a tight space it was difficult to make heads or tails of which body part belonged to whom, let alone get a good look at the two guests.

Ziegfried frowned, taking a step toward the back of the room. Gerhardt dropped the partition back in place and stood in front of it. "There. You've seen them. Now, get out of my tent."

"Not good enough," Ziegfried whined.

"Velig!" Gerhardt shouted.

Velig stepped out from the back room, hand already on his luger. Ziegfried spun around. "I'm going. I'm going."

He stomped out, the young soldier following him. Gerhardt said to Adam, "Get some rest while you can."

"You're bunking with Kiefer, Jorgan, and Helmut," Velig told him. "Anyone can show you which tent. I already had your rucksack delivered there."

Chapter 54

ADAM DUCKED INSIDE the tent he'd been directed to. His sack already sat on a laid out bedroll to one side. Kiefer sat in there too. He looked up at Adam and grimaced. "Ah, man! They're sticking you in here with us?"

"Yeah." Adam grinned at him, playing along with the hazing. He plopped down by his sack. "Gerhardt said you're in trouble again. So he's punishing you."

"More like you're in trouble so he stuck you with me." Kiefer laughed. "Did you really strip Andreno of every one of our people in his camp?"

"Yes."

"Why?"

"Because he's an ass."

"I'm such a bad influence on you." Kiefer laughed even harder. "This is great! I can't believe you pulled off something this rebellious. How did you convince Andreno to cooperate? Did you threaten him?"

"Something like that."

"Give me details." Kiefer leaned forward. "I want to know everything. How exactly did you threaten him? And why did his bodyguards not threaten you right back?"

"He'd shut them out." Adam skipped giving details on the threat. "One of his commanders was in with us so they must have figured everything was okay."

"I bet he won't let you back into the palace now," Kiefer said. "That's why I'm never there. Last time Andreno saw me, I threatened to rip off his head and spit down his neck."

Adam snorted laughter. Jorgan entered with Helmut on his heels. "What are you going on about?"

"Adam!" Helmut barreled past Jorgan with outstretched arms. Adam scrambled backward. The tent was too small. The meaty arms wrapped around him and squeezed the air out of his lungs. "I missed you!"

"Put him down," Jorgan said. "Let go before you suffocate him."

Helmut let go of Adam. "You want to see all my new drawings?"

Adam gasped the thin air. "I'm supposed to get some rest."

"Me too!" Helmut said.

Oblivious to any privacy, Helmut stripped. He put on his sleepwear and climbed into his bedroll. Instead of lying down, he sat and dug out a stack of papers. Pencils rolled off them across the ground. He showed Adam the drawings he'd put on every piece of paper while Jorgan and Kiefer picked up the pencils.

When he finished, he went on about all the other drawings he was going to make as soon as he got more paper. Jorgan told him to lie down. The sun was setting. It was time to sleep. Helmut laid down and kept talking.

Eventually he fell asleep. One moment he was talking. The next he was silent. Kiefer and Jorgan also turned in, so Adam did the same.

They were all awakened before sun-up. Everyone emerged from their tents to go about their business before Adam could drag himself from his bedroll. Velig stuck his head in the entrance of their tent and said, "Weiss, get dressed. Get something to eat. Then report to Gerhardt in the command tent."

"Yes, sir," Adam said. Velig left.

"Too tired." Helmut yawned, rubbing his eyes. All around them the camp buzzed.

"Is there normally this much activity this early in the morning?" Adam pulled his uniform on.

"Half of the men are leaving today to do a hit." Jorgan was already dressed. He prodded Helmut into doing the same while he talked to Adam. "Only two mountain villages left in this vicinity. There's a group gathering at the farther one, so we're hitting the closer one first. Give time for the scouts to check out the other. Helmut, you've got your buttons crooked again. Here, let me help you fix them."

"A group gathering?" Adam asked.

"We think it's just some of the leaders from farther away," Kiefer said. "Deciding what to do about us, maybe. Gerhardt's hoping they'll threaten us. Then he'll have an excuse to leave the campaign."

They went and ate a hurried breakfast. Then Adam reported to Gerhardt as ordered. Gerhardt gave a few grumbled orders to the men already there. Then he said to Adam, "I have some last minute things to do. Go to my personal tent and wait for me there."

Without waiting for an acknowledgment, he left. Adam followed orders, going to Gerhardt's tent just next door. He passed the time by running vocabulary words through his head, making sure to include the new ones from the Chemwanee language.

There was so much activity outside, men running around, calling to each other, the clanking of equipment moving, then the marching of feet. At least half the camp had to be moving out. Adam tried to mentally block them out and focus. He didn't know nearly as many words as he should. At least Chouthan had relaxed some when he figured out that Adam was serious about learning. More of the language would come.

The activity outside died down after a couple of hours. Still Adam waited. Finally Gerhardt came. He went to the back and lifted the partition. The two men were still there. A German soldier stood guard over them.

"You're relieved," Gerhardt told the soldier.

Without a word the man saluted and left. Gerhardt dug a small metal key out of his pocket. He handed it to Adam. "This opens Tajor's shackles. I want these two out of my camp. I didn't allow another dosage of sedatives so Jerryck should be waking up about now, according to Lieber. He's going to be very groggy and he'll need assistance. Have Tajor help him. Those two traveling packs there by the door are for them. It should be enough to help them go find some way to get home. Hopefully they'll connect up with those three men that escaped Andreno's madness. If they happen to run across any

Chemwanee people, it would be ideal for us if they told them to get out of this area. I don't like killing them for something they didn't do."

"You want me to just stroll with them out of camp?" How was Adam supposed to pull that off? The camp was smaller than Andreno's, but there were in the center of it.

"Give me a few minutes, then go to the north edge," Gerhardt said. "I'll keep as many people away from that area as I can. But yes, I want you to just walk them out. Getting them to the perimeter is on you. After that they're on their own. And if they're feeling grateful at all, they'll have some Chemwanee people send me threats so I can leave."

"I'll convey the message," Adam said.

Gerhardt gave one curt nod. He strode out of the tent. The entrance flap dropped back into place. His footsteps receded outside.

Adam gave him a few minutes as ordered. He crept into the back room. Both the men appeared asleep, though Jerryck was beginning to stir the way he had in Andreno's camp. All the tubes had been removed. If Adam could manage the escape, Jerryck was free to leave as soon as he woke enough to do so. He just needed help through the waking process. Adam leaned over Tajor to jostle him awake.

"Get away from me," Tajor said before Adam touched him.

Adam blinked, startled. He cleared his throat, pulling himself together. He presented the key saying, "Give me your hands so I can unlock them. Or do you want to break them again."

Tajor smirked. Then opened his eyes. He held up his hands for Adam to unlock. "Should I break them? Or are you going to get in trouble for this?"

"Gerhardt wants you and the magician to leave." Adam tossed the shackles aside. "He says you should try to connect with the three men that escaped Andreno. He has two packs with supplies for you in the other room. It is not much. But it will have to do."

"Just like that?" Tajor sat up. "He's releasing us? He's demanding nothing in return? I'm supposed to believe it's this simple?"

"It is why he did not allow our doctors to dose the magician again," Adam said. "He does not want war with Brend. We will not be part of this. Help me with your friend."

Jerryck groaned. He flopped one hand over his face, not quite rubbing his eyes. Tajor scooted over and shook his shoulders. "Wake up. Open your eyes. We have to move."

"Moooo wwhhhhhaa? Jerryck moaned unintelligibly.

"Anywhere but here." Tajor talked like he had understood it. "Open your eyes."

Jerryck's eyes slitted open. He groaned again. They didn't have time to lallygag around like this. Adam had no idea how long Gerhardt would be able to keep the northern side of the camp clear for them. He hooked his arms under the magician's shoulders and heaved him up to sit.

"Wwhhaa LLleeeeaaaahn," Jerryck still tried to talk.

"We'll go find her." Tajor still spoke like the slurring made sense. He helped Adam lift Jerryck to his feet. "Open your eyes again."

Her? That second syllable was a name? Adam tried to mimic the sound without so much slurring, guessing at the name while Jerryck mumbled something else unintelligible. He said the name again, a bit clearer this time. Adam asked, "Who's Leanne?

"His wife." Tajor slipped Jerryck's left arm over his shoulders.

"He's *married*?"

"Why sound so shocked?" Tajor asked.

"I was told Magicians did not marry because—"

"Are we leaving or not?" Tajor interrupted him. Adam put his shoulders under the magician's other arm. Jerryck's knees buckled, not holding his weight. Tajor refused to move forward unless his friend put effort into it. "Jerryck, move your feet. Walk forward."

Jerryck's feet twitched and he put some weight on his legs. Tajor used his own foot to nudge one of Jerryck's forward. "Put one foot in front of the other."

Jerryck took one step, and stopped. Tajor said, "Good. Now do it again."

Jerryck lifted the same foot and set it back down. Tajor said, "No, with the other foot."

Adam and Tajor got Jerryck out into the front room one step at a time. Then Jerryck looked at Adam with unfocused eyes and jerked away from him, nearly stumbling down to the ground.

Tajor kept him upright. "It's all right."

"There are the packs." Adam pointed at them. Someone walked by outside the tent. Tajor's eyes followed the sound of the footsteps. Adam let go of Jerryck entirely. "I will go make sure no one is outside."

Adam ducked through the entrance. Two men headed away toward the south. He walked all the way around the tent. No one was directly to the north. The two men in the tent moved around, mumbled some. Adam went back in to get them moving while the coast was clear.

"We are clear for now. We should go while we can," Adam said. Jerryck leaned on the small portable table by the entrance, not supported by Tajor. Adam asked, "How is he?"

"He'll manage." Tajor slipped one of the packs onto his back.

Adam took the other one. They could probably move faster if Jerryck didn't have to worry about it for now. The magician leaned on Tajor again, stumbling outside.

They moved in spurts. They would cross an open space and duck behind a tent out of sight. Adam would make sure no one could see them, then they could cross the next open space and duck again. After a few of these spurts, Adam realized Helmut was following and ducking too. When Adam saw him, he ducked behind a crate giggling.

"Stay here a moment," Adam said to Tajor.

Keeping an eye out for any other possible followers, Adam went to the crate. Helmut was still giggling. He covered his eyes with his hands. Adam reminded himself to be patient and said, "Helmut, what are you doing?"

Helmut took his hands off his eyes. "Playing hide and seek with you and the new guys. I used to play this sometimes at home with my friend before the bad man killed him. It was fun."

Adam blinked. Hide and seek? He thought this was a game? No wonder he was giggling like a child.

What was it Jorgan or Kiefer would always ask him when they needed him to go away? Oh, yes. "Helmut, what are you supposed to be doing right now?"

"Nothing," Helmut said. "Velig told me to count the bullets left in camp, and I already did that. I went to find him to ask him what to count next. And I saw you playing hide and seek. And you're heading toward the edge of camp.

And I've been meaning to count how many steps around the outside of the camp is anyway. I'll go with you to the edge and then count."

Tajor hissed Adam's name. He looked over. A couple of soldiers were passing off to the right. Adam ducked down with Helmut until they were out of sight. He had to keep the two natives moving. The sooner they were gone, the better. Perhaps he could combine efforts.

"Helmut," Adam said. "There's a couple of guys over that way. Do you think you can distract them so that our new friends can go hide easier?"

"Sure!" Helmut's face split into a grin. He jumped up and bounded off in the direction of the two men.

Adam breathed a sigh of relief. He went back to the two natives. They got Jerryck back on his feet and hopped the next spurt forward. As they proceeded to get closer and closer to the edge of camp, Adam saw Helmut a couple more times. Always he was off to one side or the other, never so close as the first time. And it looked like he was chasing more people away, so Adam left him to it.

They approached the edge of camp when a breeze carried a naggingly familiar scent across Adam's face. What was that? Metal? And poop?

"Adam." Tajor tapped him on the shoulder. "How far can you get us?"

"To that line of trees over there past where the tents end." Adam pointed north. He continued looking around. Where was that smell coming from? It was like being in an infirmary with wounded after a battle. Tajor tapped him again. Adam said, "You will have to move quickly over were we cleared the brush, to where the trees start. The faster you are, the easier for me to make sure no one sees you. After that, you are on your own. Try to find those three men..."

There was the smell. Someone lay on the ground several paces to their left, halfway behind one of the tents. Adam dropped the pack he carried and headed over with a knot in his gut.

It was one of the men, lying face down in the dirt. Adam rolled him over. He was totally limp and non-responsive. Adam felt for a pulse before thinking it over. There was none. There wouldn't be. Not if the black blood seeping out of the hole in his chest was any indicator.

Adam caught movement out of the corner of his eye. He turned to his right, yanking out his walther. A man in a tattered crimson and gold uniform bored down on him, bloodied sword in hand. Adam raised the walther. Tajor came up behind him and snatched the gun out of his hand. Then he stepped between Adam and the bloody sword. The tattered guard checked his swing, barely missing.

Adam opened his mouth to scream out an alarm, something he should have done first. Another man grabbed him from behind, clapping a hand over his mouth so hard it was sure to leave bruises. The sword raised and began its downward arc right at Adam's face.

Helmut jumped out from between two tents. "You leave my friend alone!"

He tackled the man with the sword. The blade was knocked to the side. The man dropped it, grappling with Helmut's bulk. The two rolled on the ground.

Adam drew his dagger. Before he could stab it into the arm of the man holding him, he was thrown down and disarmed as deftly as Nolrien ever had. Since that released the hold on his face and head, he rolled. His own blade swept down in an arc right at his face.

In a blur of motion, Tajor swiped his hand out. The knife flew out of the man's hand. Tajor said, "You can't kill him."

The man who had taken Adam's dagger stood, raising his boot over Adam's face. "He'll raise the alarm."

Tajor stuck his palm under the man's boot just as it came crashing down. It stopped the momentum so short the man's leg recoiled as if he'd just hit steel. Adam used the opportunity to scuttle, striving to get at least a few inches of distance. He twisted. Tajor blocked his view of the other struggle. The grunting and scuffling noises had stopped, but the tent next to them was collapsing like one of its lines had been pulled up from the stake.

Tajor grabbed Adam by the collar with one hand and yanked him to the side quick enough he just about got whiplash. He held up his other hand to the man who'd taken the dagger and repeated, "You can't kill him."

The man held Adam's dagger with the same easy grip Nolrien used. "We can't leave him here to send everyone out after us."

A third man wearing crimson and gold brought over a length of what looked like tent cord. He said, "Problem solved."

He flipped Adam over to his stomach, away from where he could see if Helmut was all right. His hands were yanked behind him and tied at the small of his back. Tajor and one of the men went back over to Jerryck. The one who had Adam's dagger stabbed the ground right next to his face, leaned in close, and whispered in Adam's ear, "You scream, I slit your throat no matter what Tajor says."

"On your feet!" The other one yanked Adam up. Then pushed him forward, saying to the others, "Let's get out of here."

Tajor came back, hiking his thumb behind him toward Jerryck. He said to the one with Adam's dagger, "Help him."

The man squeezed the hilt of the dagger. He ran his thumb crosswise over the blade, as if testing the sharpness of the edge. Tajor stepped between him and Adam. Only then did he lower the dagger and head toward the magician. Only then did Adam take a breath.

As they dragged him out of camp he tried to look back, see if Helmut was all right. Tajor blocked his line of vision. "Face forward. Keep moving."

Chapter 55

TWO OF THE TATTERED and bedraggled looking men pulled the magician along, keeping him upright, keeping him moving. The third guard kept hold of the collar on Adam's coat, dragging him along out of sight from the camp, out of earshot, then up, up, up.

Adam tripped often, unbalanced without his arms. Every time, the guard growled and jerked him around. Every time, Tajor stopped it, picked Adam up and prodded him forward.

"I swear the next time he throws himself down—" the guard muttered after the umpteenth time a shale rock slid from under Adam's feet— "I'm going to just kill him and be done."

"You can't kill him," Tajor repeated yet again.

"Why not?" The guard pushed at Tajor, who remained immovable as a mountain.

"You really want me to answer?" Tajor asked. He nudged Adam forward again, still harassing the guard. "How much detail do you want? Think you'll understand it all? How about instead I just point out that he speaks our language? You don't think that could be useful?"

"Shut it." The guard snagged Adam's collar, nearly making him trip all over again.

Adam gasped at the thin air. Still they went up. Past conifers. Past clumps of sedge brush. Past groves of close growing aspens. It was a double jeopardy, really. As long as they moved, they got farther from anyone who might come to Adam's rescue. As long as they moved, they weren't beating information out of him.

He'd interpreted for enough interrogations. He knew what lay ahead. Though he'd never dreamed he would be on the receiving end.

The ground leveled with another grove of aspens. This one they entered. They came to small clearing in a tiny dell that butted up against a cliff face. One of the guards with Jerryck left him, disappearing back into the trees the way they'd come. Adam gulped. This was where they were stopping. No more delay.

"Sit." The guard on his collar pushed him down. He dropped to his knees, still wheezing from the climb.

The magician dropped too. He plopped down on his butt breathing as hard as Adam. He drew up his knees and ducked his head between them. The guard left with him tugged his arm, whispering something in his ear.

Tajor knelt in front of Adam. Out of all of them, he was the only one who's breath wasn't labored in the slightest. He may as well have just taken a light stroll through a flower garden. He didn't even show a bead of sweat.

He still had the walther. He held it clearly where Adam could see with the muzzle pointed at the ground. Keeping his finger straight and away from the trigger, he put the safety on. Then he flicked the catch at the bottom and released the clip. It slid out into his other palm and he pushed the bullets out one by one with his thumb, whispering a count as he went. He checked the chamber and extracted the bullet from there. He reloaded the clip and slipped that into his pocket with the extra bullet. He released Adam's belt and took the holster. He secured the walther in that and set it to the side, out of Adam's reach even if his hands had been loose.

Not once did he look curious. Not once did his fingers fumble. Not once did he turn the weapon in his hands the way someone unfamiliar with it would.

"Got your breath back?" Tajor asked. Adam said nothing, but breathed normal. Tajor smiled, "Good. I have a few questions for you."

Adam grit his teeth. Here it came. Tajor clucked his tongue. "Oh, come now, Adam. No need to look at me like that. It's not difficult. I ask a question. You answer the question. Simple. And the first question is, what year is it?"

Year? Not origin or intentions? Nothing about their weapons? The year? As if that would even hold any meaning for him.

The guard punched Adam's face. Without his hands he would have fallen prone if Tajor hadn't caught him. "Oh, I didn't tell you that part. If you don't answer fast enough, he'll hit you."

"You do not count years the same as my people." Adam's eyes watered from his smarting jaw. He tried to blink it away. It would only get worse from here. "Why do you need the year?"

The guard hit him again, this time clipping his nose. The salty taste of blood dripped past his lips and down the back of his throat. Tajor still held the front of his coat, keeping him upright. "That's another thing. I ask the questions. You don't get to, unless I give permission. Let's try this one more time. What year is it?"

Was he really serious? He still insisted on the year? The guard raised his fist. Adam flinched in anticipation and said, "1949."

The guard lowered his fist instead of using it. Tajor let go of Adam's coat and sat back, frowning. Adam had tried to warn him that he wouldn't understand.

"What year did the war start?" Tajor asked.

"1942." As if that would do Tajor any more good than the current year.

"It wasn't in the late 1930's?"

"No." As long as they were asking harmless questions, as long as he wasn't getting hit, Adam replied as quick as he could.

"When did the Great War end?"

Adam was more hesitant with this answer. How had Tajor known to ask that? Did these numbers have meaning for him after all? "1925."

"So late," Tajor murmured. Late? In relation to what? "Have the Americans entered the war?"

Adam had never used that word around Tajor. He'd never used it around anyone here as far as he knew. The guard flexed his hitting arm. Adam spit out the answer. "Yes."

"What provoked them? And when?"

"In 1945." Why hold back public knowledge that he shouldn't even know to ask about? "When the Japanese sank their fleet in San Francisco Bay."

"*San Francisco?*" Tajor straightened up, his eyes wide with surprise. "They didn't sink the American's Pacific Fleet in Pearl Harbor? Why did they skip Hawaii and go all the way to California?"

"They were in control of Hawaii at the time. They would not attack themselves." This was too weird. Tajor had said he wasn't from Adam's world. Had he lied? "How do you know these names and places?"

The question slipped out before Adam could stop himself. The guard's fist plowed into his left eye. Still kept from falling over he sat limp, hunched over, waiting for stars to stop floating in and out of his vision. Tajor straightened him up. He sniffed at the blood still dribbling from his nose.

Tajor put his face close, looking right in Adam's good eye. "You remember when we talked about you being from another world than this one?"

"Yes," Adam answered quickly. Another hit this soon wouldn't be good. The stars were still floating.

"If there are two worlds—" Tajor held up two fingers— "doesn't it stand to reason that there are bound to be more?"

There was a thought. One that hadn't occurred to Adam. The guard raised his fist. Tajor held up his hand. "That question was only to make him think."

It had worked. Tajor poked him in the chest. "Something you should know, and you can pass this on to your leader. Your people, in this war, you lose. Always."

No. That definitely was not something he could pass on to his leader. Any of his leaders. If they didn't use it as an excuse to kill his family they would only laugh, claiming it was enemy propaganda.

"One way or another," Tajor continued. "Something happens and you lose. Sometimes it's a major event that turns the tide, like the storming of the beaches of Normandy by the allies."

That had happened. It had put the war at a balancing point. At first it had looked unfavorable for the Germans. Then supplies had miraculously started appearing, fueling the war machine.

"Sometimes it's sabotage of the war machine from within," Tajor said. People kept trying. Again, the influx of supplies had allowed the government to pay more attention to insurgency, cracking down on it.

"Sometimes it's a slow process of attrition," Tajor said. "Everything winding down due to lack of resources. Sometimes with that one, your leaders go underground, feigning surrender and leaving the populace to the mercy of your enemies."

The more Tajor talked, the more Adam cringed. He was identifying things that were familiar. But why did he keep saying sometimes?

"Sometimes—" Tajor continued— "it's a sudden halt, such as a fire weapon dropped on Berlin that's so hot and destructive it razes buildings to the ground and melts people's flesh from their bones."

That sounded like the rumors of the new weapon the Americans kept propagandizing about. And again, there was that sometimes. Had it actually happened? Not where Adam came from. So why did Tajor refer to it in past tense? He caught himself this time just before the question escaped him, before the guard could hit him and increase the fuzziness growing in his head.

"You may ask a question," Tajor said.

The question popped out. "Why do you talk like my country is in many different worlds?"

"It is."

"How?"

"Some events are so large they splash across many worlds." Tajor spread his hands out, his fingers wriggling. "It's like echoes in a canyon, or ripples in a pond. They spread out from where they originate, bounce around, and touch everything around them."

Adam did his best to look like he was paying attention. His eye throbbed. He sniffled some more. The stars in his eyes had stopped floating, replaced by ringing in his ears.

"And just like echoes are sometimes distorted, or ripples are broken, as the event spreads out into neighboring worlds, variations occur." Tajor pulled his hands back to himself, rubbing his chin thoughtfully. "The biggest variation in your world seems to be the timeline. Your dates are all late. It's throwing off the major events. Let me guess. When you invaded Russia, it wasn't the worst winter they'd had in over a century?"

Adam's lips hurt from his swelling jaw. He shook his head instead of saying no. That was a mistake. The stars floated back into his vision.

Tajor nodded. "Usually by the time the Americans enter the war, your people are running out of resources and supplies. That was four years ago?"

"Three and a half," Adam said.

"Why haven't you run out of resources?"

Not a chance Adam was pursuing this subject. No matter what they did to him. Tajor already knew far more information than he should. And with the way he had toyed with Andreno, dancing around with words, evading all questions and controlling the conversation with ease, Adam didn't stand a chance of trying to string him along. Even if he tried to claim the resources were coming from this world, how many more questions would Tajor ask before he figured out that was a lie?

The guard socked him right in the mouth, probably loosening some teeth. Tajor took hold of Adam again. "Who's winning the war?"

"No one." Adam's words slurred and mashed together. If it didn't hurt to talk, that question would be an easy one to answer. The war had gone into stalemate after the influx of supplies from... somewhere.

"Is it because you're getting your resources from another world? Like this one?"

For the first time, Adam understood why some prisoners refused to answer questions no matter how much you beat them. He wasn't telling Tajor the supplies weren't coming from this world. He could just go on thinking that might be the case. The longer he thought that, the longer they stayed away from the real reason the Germans were here.

He saw the fist just before it smashed into his cheek. This time, no one caught him. The ground hit him on the other side of his face.

"Stop it!" Jerryck shouted, feet planted shoulder width apart, fists clenched. Was he talking to Adam? He wanted Adam to stop what? He wasn't hitting himself. Stop not answering? What would he do about it? Burn the entire forest down with them in it? Maybe. He probably had a way to save himself from his own fire.

"Now look what you've done." Tajor hauled Adam back upright. "The scary fire-throwing magician is upset. You should answer the question before he gets any angrier."

Burning to death wasn't going to be pleasant. But it would end their questions. It would end his need to refuse answers. Adam closed his eyes. One of them was almost swollen shut anyway. He clenched his aching jaw. And waited for the guard's fist. Or fire.

Neither came. Tajor said, "Your silence speaks volumes."

The guard who had disappeared into the trees ran up behind Adam. "Visitors coming! About ten of them. We have less than two minutes."

The hitter drew his sword. Adam cringed. But at least a blade might be quicker than fire. Would his family stay safe after his death?

Tajor jumped to his feet. "You can't kill him."

"We can't take him with us," the guard said.

Tajor focused on a spot just behind Adam. "Leave him."

The guard still held his blade up and ready. "So he can tell them what direction we went in?"

"How?" Tajor refocused on the guard, shrugging at him. "If he can't see or hear us go?"

They were going to blind and deafen him? Were they going to shove dirt in his ears and tie a strip of cloth over his eyes? Or would it be worse, like putting out his eyes and popping his eardrums? Either way, he was going to live after all?

The guard's arm flashed movement. Pain erupted with a sharp crack just below Adam's left ear...

Chapter 56

ADAM'S HEAD THROBBED. The mixed odor of dirt and blood surrounded him. One of his eyes wouldn't open. The other was mashed against the ground.

He tested the rope holding his hands behind him. It bit into his wrists. Oddly enough, that small pain distracted him from the raging inferno of agony that had exploded inside his head.

Someone shouted. "There!"

Feet slid down the side of the dell. Hands grasped at him, rolling him just enough to see from his good eye. Jorgan knelt over him, his face ravished by devastation and fear.

"Jorgan," Adam croaked, intending to ask about Helmut. His head hurt too much to get any more out.

Relief flooded into Jorgan's face. He rolled Adam back to his stomach, fingering the rope. Adam wriggled his numb fingers. The rope bit him again.

"Stop moving," Jorgan said. "I've got a knife and I don't want to cut you."

Two more men stood near, several more spread out at the lip of the dell. All toted mausers and looked about in every direction. One of the ones by Adam asked, "Did you see which way they went?"

"Yeah." Jorgan's voice dripped sarcasm. "He watched them go from behind his eyelids. You moron!"

"See if you can pick up their tracks," the man called to the ones on the lip. They all hesitated, looking to Jorgan.

"Belay that!" Jorgan called up. "We have who we came for."

The cord snapped. The pressure holding Adam's hands released. He dragged his leaden arms around to a more comfortable position. His hands tingled as he touched them to his aching skull.

"We should go after them," the man yelled. Adam winced at the sound.

"No, we shouldn't," Jorgan spoke quieter. "They left Weiss alive so we'd stop. Now they've had time to set up an ambush in case we weren't satisfied and moved on."

"So what?" The idiot brandished his mauser. "We have guns."

"Do you see a walther anywhere on Weiss?" Jorgan stood, nose to nose with the other man. "Because I watched him put it on this morning. They have a gun now too."

The man inched back. "They don't know how to use it."

Adam opened his mouth to refute that. His jaw and his tongue didn't want to work. It didn't matter anyway. Jorgan refuted it. "Point, pull trigger. It's not difficult to figure out. With a walther, they don't even have to cock it."

"It's right here." One of the men bent over and picked something off the ground. He held Adam's holstered walther aloft. "They must not have known what it was and left it."

"Then why did they take it in the first place?" Jorgan muttered.

"Made contact," one of the men at the lip of the dell called down to them, holding up a handheld radio. "Gerhardt said to bring him in immediately."

Jorgan knelt, putting a hand on Adam's back. "Can you stand?"

"I'm fine," Adam said.

To prove it, he put his hands down to push to his feet. Knives stabbed through his palms and up his arms. He clenched his teeth, involuntarily hissing at the new pain.

"Help him up," Jorgan said, taking hold of Adam's right arm.

The man who'd protested shouldered his mauser and took Adam's left arm. The two of them hoisted him to his feet. The sudden realignment made his vision swim and his stomach lurch. He almost doubled over to retch. He tipped his chin down and took a few slow, deep breaths until his vision cleared. He mentally ran a few vocabulary words, calming further until the worst of the nausea subsided.

By then they were coming down out of the aspens. He'd been putting one foot in front of the other toward wherever the two men at his sides guided him. He tried balancing his own weight better. It seemed to work okay. The man on his left let go. Jorgan kept hold on his right.

Adam made a half-hearted attempt to pull away. "I'm fine."

"Shut up." Jorgan retained his grip.

Back at camp, they passed the spot where Helmut had tried to defend Adam. Where Adam had found the body of that soldier he didn't know. The body was gone. And Helmut was nowhere around. If he was injured, he'd have been sent to Doc Lieber. The smell of blood lingered. Adam turned his face away, swallowing bile.

Jorgan gave orders to the other men. Adam tuned him out, focusing on not puking. The others ran off. Jorgan took Adam to a large tent near the command tent. This one was set up like an infirmary. He guided Adam to one of the cots lined up and said, "Sit."

Adam sat. "I'm fine, really."

Jorgan took a couple of blankets off a stack and told Adam, "Take off your coat."

Adam fumbled with the buttons. His hands ached, refusing to work right. Jorgan finished for him and helped him slide out of it. He shivered. Jorgan wrapped him in the blankets.

"I shouldn't be shivering." Adam clenched his teeth to prevent chattering.

Jorgan pulled the blanket tight. "It's not exactly warm in this tent."

"It's not exactly cold either," Adam said.

Someone entered carrying hot water bottles. Jorgan took them and stuffed them inside Adam's blanket under his arms. Someone else came in with a bucket of water. He was quickly followed by a third with a bucket of snow.

"I told you there was still some there," Jorgan said as he took the snow.

The man made a snarly face and left with the other two. Jorgan shoveled snow with his bare hands into another, empty hot water bottle. He capped it and brought it to Adam.

"Hold this on your face," he said.

"I really am fine," Adam tried again.

"God damn it!" Jorgan threw the bottle of snow down onto the cot with enough force that it bounced off onto the floor. "Stop saying that. You were just captured. They beat the crap out of you. You're covered in blood."

Adam stared at his friend. Jorgan never swore. He especially never took the Lord's name in vain. No matter what pressure he was under. That was one edge he never went over.

He turned away, wiping a hand over his face. "I have to help somebody, and it can't be Helmut." Jorgan's voice cracked. "There's nothing I can do for him. Please, just let me help you."

"Nothing you can do, because he's okay?" Adam asked, hoping against the dread building up inside.

"No." Jorgan's voice was a whispery rasp. His eyes filled with unspilled tears. "I guess in a way, if you believe in heaven, he's okay now. I can't believe someone like him wouldn't go to heaven when…"

Adam couldn't look at Jorgan anymore. He bent down to pick up the snowpack as an excuse to look away. The angle made his head want to pop off. His stomach rose up. He slipped off the cot and puked on the ground.

Gerhardt and Doc Lieber both entered the tent. Lieber's nostrils flared and he sniffed. He rushed over to Adam as Gerhardt ducked back out and called for someone to bring a shovel, a bucket, and dirt.

Lieber sat Adam back on the cot, wiping his mouth like he was a baby. "You're so dizzy you're puking? How hard were they hitting you?"

"He didn't know about Helmut," Jorgan said. "I just told him."

"Ah," Lieber said. He pointed, "Hand me that water and those rags. Let's get him cleaned up. Then I can examine better for serious injuries or head trauma."

"I'm sorry, Adam," Jorgan said. "I thought you knew. He was right there where it looked like you'd scuffled with them."

"He was trying to save me," Adam said. "One of them would have killed me right then if he hadn't attacked them."

"So he did save you," Lieber said.

"Not the way he wanted to," Adam said. "Not the way he was trying."

"Nothing in life ever turns out the way we want or expect," Lieber said. "And if our goal is valuable enough to us, there's always more of a price than anticipated. But he did save you."

When put that way, Adam had to agree. He was still alive. Helmut had accomplished what he was after on a very basic level.

Jorgan passed a hand over his eyes and turned away. Gerhardt put a hand on his shoulder and said, "Come with me. Everything's under control here and I need some help with things."

Jorgan nodded and followed the Oberst out of the tent just as a soldier arrived with the shovel and bucket of dirt. Lieber directed him in cleaning up the puke and moved Adam to another cot on the other side of the infirmary. It had to smell bad. The soldier almost gagged while he scooped it up and covered it and the new hole with the dirt. Lieber hadn't done any more than sniff when he first walked in. Adam couldn't smell a thing with the way his nose was swollen.

Lieber washed Adam's face, leaning in close and examining everything as he did so. Then he put the bottle of snow on Adam's left eye and said, "Hold that there. It'll help bring down the swelling."

Then Lieber went to work on the back of Adam's head. He couldn't help but flinch every time the doctor touched a sore spot. Lieber said, "Sorry. I'm trying to be gentle. Some of the blood has dried, so it's congealed and matted in your hair."

"I'm not going to need stitches anywhere, am I?" Adam asked. "I'm told stitches leave scars if you don't have constant treatment afterward."

"Constant treatment?" Lieber asked. "Is that what you did, why you don't have a scar where you were stabbed in your hand?"

"So I'm told," Adam said.

"Hmm," Lieber grunted. "I'd be interested to know what concoction that doctor used to erase the scar."

"Will I have scars from this?"

"Small ones, maybe," Lieber said. "I don't think anything on your face will need stitches. You'll need a couple here though."

He fingered the spot behind Adam's ear where they'd hit him last and knocked him out. Adam slouched. "Great."

"It'll be fine." Lieber threaded a needle where Adam could see. "It's right on your hairline, so probably no one will even notice if they don't know it's there."

"You're sure just a little one?" Adam asked. The little pricks and stabs from Lieber sewing his flesh did nothing for his mood. "There's a lot of blood down my shoulder from it."

"Head wounds bleed a lot," Lieber said. "It's small. They certainly knew right where to hit you to knock you out for a bit though."

"They hit me behind my ear. Not over my head."

"You're thinking of what you see in the cinemas." Lieber finished off and wiped down all his tools with rubbing alcohol. "Conking someone over the head doesn't work like in the movies. There's a nerve that runs down the side of the neck, just behind the ear. Hit that hard enough and it acts like a breaker switch for the human body. Ever stick too many plugs into an electrical outlet and blow a fuse?"

"I'm not an electrical box for a house," Adam said.

"It's just a comparison. When you replace the fuse and flip the switch to reset the box, that's similar to what hitting that nerve does to the human body. You reset. Hit it hard enough and you'll black out for a few moments."

"Did they just get lucky or something then?"

"They hit you exactly on that nerve. I doubt luck had anything to do with it. And what that tells me is that not only do they have incredible medicines in their magic potions, they're also more familiar with human anatomy than the average third world country. These people may seem backward to us, but in a lot of ways they're very well educated."

"Educated in human anatomy enough to kill people," Adam muttered. He looked around the infirmary. "I found another dead guy before Helmut attacked them. But they're not in here. How many people died?"

"We found nine bodies," Lieber said. "I won't allow them in here contaminating a place of healing. We set up a temporary shelter for a morgue at the edge of camp until we can record everything, bury them, and get everything cleaned up and sanitary. Now, let's check you out for other trauma."

They went through the rigamarole doctors loved torturing people with. Listening to lungs breathing, heart beating. Then, as if hearing the heart

beating wasn't enough, Lieber insisted on taking blood pressure and counting pulse rate. He made Adam focus on several objects at varying distances,
checked his pupils, made sure he wasn't cross eyed or something. He looked
in his ears. And all the while, Adam wanted to scream that he was fine so
Lieber would just leave him alone.

He was rescued when Gerhardt came back and asked, "Doc, how much
longer do you need?"

"I'm finished," Lieber said.

"I need a minute with him."

"Of course," Lieber said. He gave Adam a friendly slap on the back, and left.

"First thing's first." Gerhardt drew close, standing right in front of Adam.
"I apologize. I was preoccupied. That doesn't excuse the fact that I overlooked
what strategy those three men might have taken to try and rescue their charges.
I gave them the perfect opportunity by trying to empty the northern side of
camp, and if I'd been in their shoes I'd have done the same thing. That said,
I should also have taken into account the chance that they might have taken
you with them. They interrogated you?"

"Sort of."

"What did they ask?"

"Dates."

"Dates?" Gerhardt raised his eyebrows. "What dates? Who asked?"

"Priad Tajor asked." Adam answered the second question first. "He asked
what year this is, when the war started, when the Great War ended, when the
Americans entered the arena—"

"The Americans? Did he just allude to them?"

"He called them by name. And he knew that San Francisco is in California.
I didn't tell him that. He knew Berlin, and Normandy, and some place called
Pearl Harbor. I don't even know where Pearl Harbor is, but he seemed to
think it was in Hawaii."

"It is," Gerhardt said. "The Japanese thought it was too shallow for tor-
pedoes, so they kept their Pacific fleet there. Then the Americans got clever
enough to figure out how to sink it anyway. That was their foothold to taking
the islands away from Imperial Japan."

"Oh, that place. I didn't know that was what it was called."

"But he did."

"Sort of," Adam said. "He seemed to think it was the Americans who were in control of Hawaii and the Japanese attacked them, and that was what provoked them into entering the fight."

"That's backwards. Why would he think that? And how did he know these names? Did he mention anything about being from our world?"

"He said he's not."

Gerhardt's eyes unfocused. "Why would he want dates then?"

"He said our timeline is late."

"Late for what?"

"He said there are lots of worlds that go through our situation, this war. And there are variations. The variation in our world is a late timeline that's skewing some of our major events. Whatever that's supposed to mean. I didn't really understand it all, and my head was spinning by then. He did try to get me to tell him that we're getting resources from here to fuel the war machine."

"Did you?"

"I didn't say anything."

"That doesn't mean he didn't get what he wanted from you." Gerhardt rubbed the stubble on his chin. "Did he say anything else or give any other kind of indication that he was familiar with our world?"

"He knows how to handle a walther," Adam said.

"You're sure he knew how to handle it? He wasn't just exploring it and checking it out? Studying?"

"He handled it like any trained soldier," Adam said. "Took the ammunition out. He even knew to check the chamber for one extra. If he was exploring or studying, he wouldn't have known to point the barrel away from anything he didn't want to shoot, to keep his finger off the trigger, let alone how to put the safety on or anything else he did with it. He knew what he was doing."

Gerhardt's eyebrows drew together. "Odd. Jorgan said they left it. If they knew how to use it, why would they give up that advantage?"

"I have no idea," Adam said. "That's a riddle better suited for Jorgan, not me."

"Probably true," Gerhardt said. "Unfortunately, Jorgan is doing busy work at the moment to make him feel useful. Not solving riddles. He's not exactly working at full capacity right now."

"Helmut," Adam surmised.

Gerhardt nodded. "He's trying to make it look like he's not taking it as hard as he is. Don't let him fool you. I'll need you and Kiefer and others to keep an eye on him for a while. And between when you're doing that, I need you to write me up a report on today, starting with when our visitors overpowered you in my tent."

"No, no," Adam said. "It was near the edge of camp when those three—"

"In my tent," Gerhardt said. "Where Tajor and Jerryck overpowered you."

"They didn't—"

"They did," Gerhardt said. "I know they did, because that's how you're going to write it up. Understood?"

"I think so?"

"Good." Gerhardt turned and walked out.

Chapter 57

LIEBER STEPPED BACK IN IMMEDIATELY. He checked Adam's face again. "Swelling is going down. That's good. You can probably do without the cold on it if you want."

Adam tossed the snow bottle beside him on the cot. Lieber took his forearms. "Let me see your hands and wrists."

Adam held them up. "I'm fine."

"You won't be if you try and tell me that again." He scrutinized Adam's hands, flipping them over, pinching the fingers.

"Ow." Adam flinched. "That hurts."

"Good, you can feel it. Move your fingers for me." He grabbed some gauze and wrapped Adam's chafed wrists while he wiggled away. "Good. Looks better. Swelling is gone. They must have tied you pretty tight for that much chafing and circulation loss in that short a period of time. Have you ever falsified a report before?"

"What?" What did reports have to do with circulation loss?

"Have you ever falsified a report before?" Lieber repeated.

"No."

"It's an unfortunate necessity sometimes when you're dealing with lying thugs who will jump on any excuse to cause harm to people," Lieber said. "Make it good."

"You heard Gerhardt?"

"I'm the one who suggested it to him," Lieber said. "Though he probably would have told you anyway."

"I wouldn't have thought you would suggest someone lie. You get mad at me just for telling you when I'm fine."

"That's different," Lieber said. "That's lying to yourself. As for intentionally lying to others, I've been corrupted by being involved in politics in the past. One thing you need to keep in mind. A partial truth will bear more weight than a blatant lie."

"What's that supposed to mean?

"At some point you were definitely overpowered." Lieber held up one of Adam's hands and tapped the bandage around his wrist. "Use some of the facts involved in that when you write your report."

"I don't like lying," Adam said.

"Good." Lieber dropped Adam's hand and turned away. "You're free to go for now. You'll need to come back tomorrow so I can make certain you're healing properly. Go keep Jorgan company. He'll think he's keeping an eye on you rather than the other way around. It'll give him something to occupy his time and his mind. You'll find him at the north edge of camp in the temporary morgue."

"The north edge?"

"That's where we found all the bodies."

"Easier than moving them all here," Adam surmised.

"I keep this place ready for incoming wounded on the day of a battle," Lieber said. "Not that we've been unfortunate enough for that to happen yet. If someone is already dead there's no reason for them to be here. I don't believe in mixing the dead with the living."

"I'm the only one here." Adam looked around him at the empty infirmary. "There're no wounded from the battle."

"And every time that happens, it makes me more certain that the next battle is the one that will blow up in our faces," Lieber said. "Too many things going easy makes everything crash after a while. A single pebble can change the course of a river. Only one thing has to change for this campaign to stop working so well for us."

"Like men who attack us with swords and leave dead bodies in their wake?"

"Among other things," Lieber said. "Like making an enemy out of a magician or a politically powerful man. Or key people like Jorgan Gruber becoming nonfunctional due to mourning. That's a big one."

"Is that the only reason you want him occupied?" Adam's temper flared. "So he can get back to work?"

"Beyond that," Lieber said. "Jorgan heals through work. Gerhardt learned that when he felt so helpless over Kiefer shortly after they arrived here. They told me all about it. That's how they figured out how good he is with puzzles and logistics. Getting him back to work isn't just a matter of necessity for us. It's a form of compassion toward him."

Adam's temper deflated. "Got that."

He went in search of his friend. Since Lieber refused to give him back his coat with the claim that it was too bloody and, therefore, unhealthy, Adam kept the blanket Jorgan had wrapped around him. The morgue wasn't hard to find. He made his way through a crowd of oglers standing around outside. Armed guards blocked him at the entrance.

"Lieber sent me," he said. One of them ducked inside. After a moment he came back out with Velig.

"He's supposed to be here," Velig said, and gestured Adam to come in. The inside was quiet as a church. Nine covered bodies lined up in the small space. The oder of blood and other bodily fluids hung so thick Adam could smell it even through the swelling in his nose.

Jorgan sat cross legged at the feet of the largest body. His shoulders slumped. His head hung low hiding his face. His hands hung limp over his knees.

Adam sat beside him. "Hey there."

Jorgan didn't move. "Doc cut you loose?"

"Yeah. You okay?"

"Better than him." He moved just enough to flick a finger at the body. He raised his face to Adam. "Doc said it was clean. Fast. Sharp edge severed an artery."

"Better for him that way," Adam said.

"This was needless." Jorgan's eyes were red rimmed. No swelling or puffiness though. He still hadn't shed any tears. He needed to. "There was no reason to kill him."

"He attacked them," Adam said.

"He was unarmed."

"He didn't need to be. He killed a man with just his bare hands. Remember? He cried over it."

Jorgan drooped further. "It's my fault."

"What are you talking about? You're not the one who stuck a knife into him."

"I'm the one who convinced Gerhardt to bring him along instead of leaving him at base," Jorgan said. "He'd have been safe there. He'd still be alive."

"Don't do this to yourself."

"It's true." Jorgan looked up at him again. This time, there was anger in his eyes mixed with the unshed tears. "Why shouldn't I?"

Adam pointed to Helmut's covered body. "Because he wouldn't want you to."

"You don't know that for sure."

"What if your positions were reversed? What if you were the one lying under that shroud? Would you want him to blame himself for it?"

Jorgan cast his eyes down. The anger drained out leaving his face slack. "No."

"Come on, let's get out of here." Adam stood, tugging on Jorgan's arm. "Sitting here like this isn't doing you any good. And Helmut wouldn't like what you're telling yourself. Let's go for a walk."

Jorgan slowly got to his feet. It took a bit more prodding to get him to leave Helmut. Even then, he kept trying to turn back before Adam could get him all the way out of the tent. In the end it was Velig ordering him out that finally did the trick.

As soon as they stepped outside, one of the gawkers tried to latch onto them. "What's going on in there?"

"None of your business." Jorgan bared his teeth. "Get away from here."

"I'm not harming nothing," the man said. "I can be where everyone else is."

"No one else is poking their nose in my face," Jorgan said. "Get out of here."

"Speaking of noses and faces…" the man wouldn't leave off. "Your interpreter friend there looks mighty pretty. What'd he do? Run into a tent pole? You should boss him around, tell him to watch where he's going."

Jorgan pounced. Adam grabbed him, pulling him back, losing his blanket. One of Jorgan's fist swung wide and clipped Adam's nose.

"Oww!" Adam let go of Jorgan and clapped his hands over his smarting face. It stung so bad it brought tears to his eyes.

"I'm sorry!" Jorgan sounded appalled. "I'm so sorry! I didn't mean to!"

"Ha! Hahaha! Haha!" The man that wouldn't leave them alone laughed so hard he sat down on the ground. "Yeah! Hit him instead. He looks like he's used to it. Try and hit me again and I'll make you look just like him."

Velig strode out of the tent. The man on the ground scuttled backward away from him. That didn't save him from getting Velig's boot in his face. Adam kept his hands over his own face, hiding that his nose was bleeding again, keeping Jorgan from getting in trouble over it.

Velig jabbed a finger at Adam anyway. "Back to the infirmary."

Jorgan picked up the dropped blanket and steered Adam along. Lieber had left the infirmary. Thoel was there. He looked at the nose, despite Adam repeatedly insisting that he was fine. He decreed that no extra damage had been done. The only reason it bled was because the tissues were already damaged. He held a cloth to it, sopped up the blood, and waited for it to stop on its own. Then he checked it again. He proclaimed it passable then sent him and Jorgan to their tent.

Adam plopped down on his bedroll. It wasn't even lunch time, and he was as tired as if he'd spent the entire day in hard labor. Jorgan sat too, looking away from Helmut's possessions. His expression of deep grief returned.

"I really am sorry," he mumbled. "I don't know what came over me."

"I do," Adam said. "Don't worry about it."

"I know we're at war." Jorgan's voice was flat and empty. "I know people die. This is the first time someone I cared about this much has died. You were closer to the fighting back at home. How do you deal with it?"

"I didn't really get close to anyone and I wasn't at the front," Adam said. "I thought recently that my family was as good as dead, after that fiasco with Ziegfried and his bodyguards."

"Gerhardt didn't send anything home about that," Jorgan said. "Not that I'm aware of."

"He told me he didn't," Adam said. "I didn't know that until I got here to this camp. When I was at the palace I went and got a good drunk on over it. One of Nolrien's friends told me to just honor their memory by saving other people, doing as much good as I could for individuals whenever I got the chance."

"That sounds like something that would please Helmut." Jorgan spread his fingers wide in a helpless gesture. "I'm religious. I believe I know where he is now. He's better off. Why is this so upsetting?"

"Religious beliefs or not, it still hurts," Adam pointed out the obvious. "This certainly tops the death that bothered me most up to now. Maybe because Helmut meant more to me than the other guy."

"Who was that?"

"A stranger. An American POW named Brandon Cooper. I got him to talk some before everything went to hell in a handbasket. He was the last surviving son of a woman who probably would have a heart failure when she found out he had been killed. And his widow would be on her own raising their son that he'd never even gotten to see. They just found out she was pregnant when he shipped out."

"That's terrible."

"That's war," Adam said. "Things like that are why I hate war so much. And he knew he was going to die. He was provoking us into killing him faster, before we could extract any valuable information out of him. It worked."

"What did he do?"

"He somehow got out of his restraints, got hold of a guard's gun, shot the guard in the head, and then shot me in the leg."

Jorgan gaped. He shook his head. It was a full minute before he said, "That was the wound you had when you were transferred here through the portal."

"Yeah."

"He shot a guard in the head and not you?"

"He aimed at my head," Adam said. "Then he said I seemed like a good guy who was working for the wrong side and he aimed lower."

"I don't even know what to say to that."

"There aren't any words for that."

"No wonder it bothers you," Jorgan said. "And here I am. Helmut never once threatened me, let alone spared me for no reason."

"You were friends."

"More than that." Jorgan's eyes filled. This time the tears finally spilled over. He wiped at them. They kept coming now that they'd started. He sniffed. His voice cracked and rasped as he spoke. "I always thought that after the war was over, when we were all allowed to go home, I'd take him with me, take care of him like a sort of kid brother. I never had a brother."

The tent flap lifted from the outside. Keifer came in. He handed some lunch to Adam and said to Jorgan, "Gerhardt wants you."

Jorgan wiped at his eyes some more. Without a word he got up and left. Kiefer sat down, got out his mauser, and took it apart. His motions were slow, meticulous. He asked, "How's he doing? He okay?"

"He'll survive." Adam lay back on his bedroll. "He'll hurt for a while. He's looking for someone to blame. Then he'll survive and move on like everybody else. You were close to Helmut too. Are you okay?"

"I'll deal with it," Kiefer said. "Eat."

Adam went through the motions. He tasted none of the food he swallowed. It sat as a lead lump in his stomach.

Kiefer put the gun back together just as slowly and meticulously as he'd disassembled it. Since he seemed disinclined to chat, Adam got out his vocabulary pages and went through them. He tried to add notes about what little he'd learned of the Chemwanee language. Writing in phonetics reminded him of Helmut getting so excited over the sound pictures. For the first time, the exercise left him more agitated then calm. He took out one of his precious few remaining cigarettes and lit it.

From the first whiff of smoke, Keifer zoned in. His hands paused. His eyes narrowed and focused on the small glowing flame. Adam got his case back out and shook one out for him to take.

"You sure?" Kiefer asked. "You've only got a few left in there."

"I don't smoke often," Adam said. "I don't need more than a few."

Kiefer accepted the gift. Adam lit it with his own cigarette. The two of them filled the tent with a pungent haze.

"I should have offered one to Jorgan," Adam said.

"He doesn't smoke." Kiefer took another drag. "Not even to settle his nerves. He probably should on a day like today. He won't. He thinks smoking and drinking alcohol are sins."

"Alcohol?" Adam rolled his eyes. "Now that's just ridiculous. The Bible says Jesus drank wine. That's alcohol. There's nothing sinful about a good beer."

"Agreed. Not that it matters here. The only ale the natives make is crap. And Gerhardt has been refused every time he's tried to get us some from home with the rations."

"I made the mistake of tasting the native ale," Adam said. "It's worse than crap. The natives' sausages are crap too."

"And their roasts," Kiefer said. "And they have no kraut."

Adam chuckled. "We've got to stop. This is making me homesick."

"You look more tired than homesick."

"I'm exhausted." Adam crushed out the stubby remains of his cigarette.

"Take a nap." Kiefer still slowly drew off of his.

"I shouldn't be this tired this early."

"Screw that," Kiefer said. "It's been a rough day. Take a nap."

Chapter 58

ADAM WOKE TO VOICES outside the tent. Several hours must have passed. It was dark out. A lantern had been lit inside. Someone had been going through Helmut's corner. But he was alone in the tent.

One of the voices outside was unfamiliar. The other was Kiefer. The stranger said, "Ziegfried wants him. That's all you need to know. You don't have the right to argue with him. You just obey."

"No I don't," Kiefer said. "And I don't like repeating myself. He's asleep. He's staying that way."

"I don't know how some of you people can be so disrespectful. Ziegfried is a very important man. Do you have any idea how easy it would be for him to leave you here when everyone else gets to go home?"

"So what?" Kiefer said. "There's nothing left for me there."

"Not even your family?" The other guy sounded skeptical. "No girl? No friends? No promise of a career in the new world regime? Ziegfried can either make all that happen, or he can take it all away."

"Take what away?" Kiefer sounded unimpressed, and even less intimidated. "What's he going to do? Encourage everyone to throw rocks at me and then laugh in my face because people give me a blanket party every other week? How about he takes away my ability to communicate with everyone around me for a few months. Or he could go after my family. How about he fires my dad from his job, throws the family out of every church in town, then blacklists them from every grocery store."

"He could, you know."

"Why stop there?" Kiefer continued. "Why not gang rape my little sister and hang her from the nearest light post. Then he can convince the chief of police to shoot my father in the head when he tries to insist her death is a murder, not a suicide. Then all the neighbors can lock my mother in a room so she can't get out when they light up the house and burn it to the ground around her."

"You're demented!" The stranger said with a gasp. Adam caught his breath too. He doubted Kiefer was making up a pretend scenario that hadn't already happened.

"Am I?" Kiefer challenged. "You can tell Ziegfried that I said he can do the world a favor and eat a bullet. There's nothing he can do to me that I fear. If there's anyone or anything he wants, I will do all in my power to stand in his way. Especially including one of my friends. Adam Weiss is not available. He is sleeping. Now get out of here before I push your face out the back side of your head."

"You'll regret this." The stranger moved away.

"Doubtful!" Kiefer called out. He came inside, pausing in the doorway when he saw Adam awake. "How much did you hear?"

"I didn't hear a damn thing." Adam certainly wished that were true.

"Good." Kiefer let the flap of the tent door fall closed behind him. He went over to Helmut's corner, organizing some of the things that had been gone through. He gave Adam a guilty look. "Someone has to do it, go through it all. And I'm not going to make Jorgan be that someone."

"That would be hard on him."

"He's a good guy." Kiefer dropped his shoulders a couple inches. "So was Helmut. Too bad those Brendish men didn't rid us of Ziegfried instead."

"You hate him so much, why haven't you killed him?" Adam asked. "Just curious."

"Gerhardt told me not to. He hasn't figured out how to do it without risking the lives and families of the men who've been assigned to him."

"They hate you for no good reason. You care about them and their families?"

"I respect Gerhardt," Kiefer said. "He protects me like no one ever has. I owe him. I'll do what he asks."

The tent flap opened. Velig came in followed by one of the civilians that had come to learn magic from Ziegfried. He saw Adam awake and got a smug look.

"Fritz, give me your hand," Velig said. Kiefer obediently held up his left hand. Velig reached out and lightly slapped the back of it. "Naughty Fritz. No antagonizing little Ziegfried's new pets."

The civilian clicked his tongue. "So disrespectful."

"What was disrespectful?" Velig asked. "Do you take offense to your job?"

"My job title is not 'pet.' And a slap on the wrist is not an appropriately harsh punishment. And you called Ziegfried little."

"That's his name," Velig said. "Ziegfried Klein. Isn't that what Klein means?"

"You used it in a derogatory fashion. Not respectfully as his name."

"Sounded more respectful than he deserves," Kiefer said.

"There, you see?" Velig said. "It sounded respectful."

The civilian shook his head and clicked his tongue again. He looked at Adam. "Are you Adam Weiss? Ziegfried wants you. Come with me."

"He's Adam Weiss," Velig said. "He can't come with you right now. He's sleeping."

"He looks awake to me," the civilian said.

"Close your eyes," Velig told Adam. He obeyed. Velig said, "He looks asleep to me."

"Unbelievable," the man said. Adam couldn't resist opening his eyes and watching everything.

"What's so unbelievable?" Velig asked. "He deserves some sleep. He's tired. He had a hard day."

"He had a hard day," the civilian repeated. "That's why Ziegfried wants him, wants to see for himself that one of his favorite friends is okay."

"He's fine," Velig said.

"*Fine?* How can you say that? His face is purple with bruises."

"I'm fine," Adam said. "Ask the doctor who looked at my nose. I told him that too."

"Stop talking in your sleep." Velig scowled at him. Then he said to the civilian, "He's fine. He said so to the doctor who looked at his nose. You can ask him."

"You said that just because he said it."

"Did he?" Velig asked. "I don't listen to what people say in their sleep. I was referring to the complaint I got from the doctor. This man annoys doctors. Instead of cooperating with them, he says he's fine when others would be whimpering like little babies. Let's go back outside and let him keep sleeping."

Velig grabbed the civilian's arm and forcibly steered him out. Kiefer waved. "Bye-bye."

"But…" the man squawked. Even when he was outside, he continued protesting until he was out of hearing. "He's not sleeping. I saw. He's awake. Ziegfried wants…"

Kiefer laughed. He tipped his chin to Adam. "Gerhardt isn't the only man I respect and obey. I owe both Velig and Grippe too."

He resumed organizing Helmut's corner. Adam watched for a bit. Then asked, "You want some help?"

"No," Kiefer said. "This helps. I didn't get to do it for any of my family. You should probably try and get some more sleep."

Adam lay back and tried to relax. He threw an arm over his eyes to block the light of the lamp. That hurt. He rolled over to his left, putting his back to the light. That pulled at the stitches behind his ear. He rolled to his right side.

Kiefer snickered at him. "You want me to blow out the lamp?"

"I'm fine." Adam grumped.

He closed his eyes, doing the best impression of sleep he could muster. Kiefer quietly went back to sorting. Adam pulled the blanket up over his head. Eventually, sleep found him.

In the morning he didn't want to get out of the tent. Or even his bedroll. It was cold out and he still didn't have his coat back. Jorgan was gone. Kiefer teased Adam. "You're just making excuses so you don't have to go out where everyone can see your pretty face."

"Whatever." Adam rolled away, not caring how many stitches he pulled by laying on them.

With a sigh, Kiefer got up and left. Adam rolled back to his right, off the side of his head that hurt the most. Then he was bored. He sat up in the chill, digging into his pack. He took out all his notes to continue studying what little he had learned of the mountain language. Goose pimples prickled up his arms from the cold so he snuggled back down into his bedroll, spreading his notes on his pillow.

Someone scratched at the entrance flap of the tent. Chandler called, "Adam? Are you in there?"

"I am here," he called out. "You can come in. I am not coming out."

The flap lifted enough for Chandler to look in. "I've got Chouthan with me. Is that all right?"

"Sure," Adam said.

"Hey!" Kiefer called from outside in the native language. "What do you think you're doing?"

"I told them it is okay," Adam called to him.

Kiefer came in, allowing the two natives to do the same. He had a plate of food and a coat. He handed both to Adam, reverting to German, "I think the coat may be a little too small. It's the only one I could find for you. I'd give you Helmut's if I didn't think Jorgan would have a conniption fit. Besides, it's so big it would just fall off you anyway."

"Why can't I just have my own back?" Adam asked

"Because you got blood all over it," Kiefer said. "Not only does it stink, Lieber says that's unhealthy. We don't exactly have optimal laundry facilities here to wash it."

"Fine." Adam puffed out his breath. He took the plate of food.

Chouthan squatted right in front of him, inspecting his face. "So something bad did happen. We wondered."

"Wondered what." Adam turned away. "I am fine."

"We know there are dead men," Chandler said. "Chouthan was concerned and—"

"I was not!" Chouthan sat back on his heels.

"—and I need to know how this is going to affect my men," Chandler finished.

Kiefer got up, beckoning Chandler to follow him outside. "I'll take you to Gerhardt. We can ask him."

Chouthan lingered. "You can be a difficult man to find. Why does everyone here call you Weiss? I thought your name was Adam."

"Identification," Adam said. "Weiss is my family's name."

"A cultural thing then. Understood," Chouthan said. Adam set aside his now empty plate. Chouthan's eyes followed the bandages around his wrists, then flitted back up to his face. "Have you used any medicine or anything? You can pick up some nasty things in a place like this, a group of clustered men, no good place to wash up, no decent food."

"I am fine," Adam said.

"You're lucky, is what you are," Chouthan said. "Chandler suspects those three men we were watching out for caught up. If he's right, and you had a personal run in with them, you're lucky you're not dead."

Adam shuffled his papers, rustling them loudly, hopefully distracting Chouthan from that particular topic. He must have gotten the hint. He eyed the papers Adam had spread out and changed the subject. "You want another language lesson?"

That was an offer Adam dove into with relish. He soaked in as much as he could for as long as he could. Around lunchtime Kiefer came back with more food. He tried to join in the lesson. Chouthan wasn't nearly as patient with him and seemed far more interested in learning about them. What did they like? What sort of things did they have in their culture? What might they be interested in trading for? Adam asked Kiefer to leave and reclaimed his teacher's attention.

Several more hours passed before Adam was summoned to the command tent. He grumbled as he squeezed into the coat Kiefer had brought. It stretched tight across his shoulders, dug in under his arms, pulled away at the buttons, and fell short of covering his wrists.

Looking ridiculous in the small coat, he grit his teeth all the way to the command tent. Velig and Gerhardt were bent over maps spread out on the table that took up the main space. They both straightened up. Velig sent everyone else out, then went to a corner to pick up some equipment.

"You didn't go to the doctor today," Gerhardt scolded Adam.

"I'm fine," Adam said.

"That's for the doctor to decide. Velig will escort you to them as soon as I'm through with you in here."

Adam tried to sound respectful, but suspected he sounded petulant when he said, "Yes, sir."

"I'm sending the next battle group out tomorrow morning." Gerhardt leaned on the map with both hands. "You're going with them."

Adam's stomach clenched. "Sir?"

"Velig and I are going too," Gerhardt said. "So is Ziegfried with a couple of his new cronies. So far the enemy hasn't really fought back. This time there's a new element."

"The Brendish men that escaped," Adam said.

"Correct." Gerhardt nodded once. "I'll be holding you in reserve during the fighting. I expect we'll still win. But I believe there will be more of a cost. And when we figure out the precise location of those Brendish men, I'm sending you and Velig in to talk to them if possible."

"What will we say?" Adam asked.

"Don't worry about that for now," Gerhardt said. Velig brought over a mauser, some extra ammo, webbing, and other traveling gear. Gerhardt said, "I don't think you'll have time to sight in the weapon, unfortunately. It'll have to do for now. Take it. Secure it. Then report back here after supper for a briefing along with everyone else that's going."

"Yes, sir." Adam reached to pick up the equipment.

"I'll carry it for now." Velig grinned maliciously. "You didn't really think I'd forget to escort you to the infirmary, did you?"

Adam held back a sigh. It wouldn't go over well with the Brass. He left the command tent and went with Velig to the infirmary. There he had to subject himself to the doctor's administrations with all the poking, prodding, and stupid questions. By the time he returned to his tent, Chouthan was gone.

Chapter 59

AFTER SUPPER ADAM WENT TO THE COMMAND TENT. About half the men in camp gathered in the space outside it. Jorgan came out and set up a frame with a map tacked to it. When Gerhardt emerged, everyone got quiet.

"Pay attention," Gerhardt addressed everyone. He gave a standard go-and-fight pep talk before getting down to specifics. He tapped a spot on the map. "This is our forward base camp. We'll go from here, climb up this slope, and follow this ridge-line."

All eyes followed his finger as it moved, tracing the route he described along the drawn contours. "At this point right here, we'll descend into this valley. We'll skirt around the edge over to the northern side. Here we'll stop until we get the all clear from the scouts. Then we climb up the backside of this face and position ourselves."

Jorgan tacked up a new map over the old one. Gerhardt hardly paused. "This is our target area. This spot here in the center is a sort of guest lodge, from our best estimate. This is where they're housing all the visiting spiritual leaders, what the Shontese call... Ziegfried, was it shaman?"

"That's how my interpretation spell translates it from what Andreno calls them," Ziegfried answered.

"This is their magic user," Gerhardt continued. "Not sure what the difference is between a shaman and a magician, don't care except for the fact that they have to be eliminated. This is the building where we'll be initiating. Feldstetter, you have the longest arm and the greatest accuracy tossing grenades. When I give the go, you hit this building. It's essential that your aim is accurate. I can't stress enough that this building go first, in this battle more than any other so far."

"I'll hit it," Feldstetter said with a confident tilt of his head.

"There's one more added element to take into consideration," Gerhardt went on. "The perpetrators of the incident here were spotted earlier today heading in the direction of this village. If they're present when we make our hit, it could be problematic. Keep alert for new difficulties. Aside from that you all know the routine. Those of you with a *Maschinenpistole* will be given your specific locations where you'll position yourselves and act as a replacement for a *machinengewehr*. And if I hear one more complaint about not bringing those up here with us, some heads are going to roll."

"It's taken care of," Velig interjected.

"Very good," Gerhardt said. "Due to the likelihood of the Brendish and their magician adding unexpected elements, Ziegfried will accompany. Velig and I both will be coming along as well. So will Weiss, in case we need an interpreter, though I prefer to keep him out of the fighting. Questions."

Someone asked, "How long will it take us to reach the target location?"

Velig answered, "Barring unforeseen difficulties, two days. I'll go over specific gun placements as we close in."

One of the doctors asked. "Who's going to be in charge of the camp with both you and Velig gone?"

Gerhardt pointed at Jorgan. "Gruber."

"If you believe there'll be unexpected elements," the same doctor said, "what's the chance you'll bring back casualties this time, aside from the usual ankle sprained in the dark?"

"Unknown," Gerhardt said. "Which is why you're here, even though you're not going. We have no information on how a magician fights. While we're gone, prep for the worst. Gruber will put together teams standing by to come pick us up if we're too wounded to move far enough, fast enough."

The briefing wrapped up. They were given their time and placement to muster for head count and launching. People filed away, mumbling to each other.

One man groused that they could do their job. They didn't need the Oberst breathing down their necks while they did it. Another told him that it was just a sign of how important it was that those Brendish men pay with their lives for the damage done to the camp. Adam shook his head. Those Brendish were important all right. Just not the way others were thinking.

He hung back when Ziegfried sidled up to Gerhardt and said, "I can take care of them. You really don't need to trouble yourself to go along."

"Rest up, Ziegfried," Gerhardt said. "You're going to carry as much as everyone else."

Ziegfried tried again. "Listen—"

"Good night, Ziegfried." Gerhardt turned away and walked into the command tent. Ziegfried took a step to follow. Velig stepped in front of him.

"Fine. Be that way." Ziegfried turned to Adam. "That's okay. I've been trying to get some time with you anyway."

"Good night, Ziegfried." Adam walked away.

Kiefer met him not far away. They passed a couple of men that had been at the meeting. One of them grumbled about the lack of machine gewehrs. Kiefer muttered, "Idiot."

"Do we even have any MGs here on this world?" Adam asked. He hadn't seen any since coming through the portal.

"Of course we do," Kiefer said. "We have a whopping total of three of them. They're permanently placed on the walls of Far Base for defensive purposes. We've got some mortars too. Those are locked up in the armory. These idiots think that since the castle isn't going to be attacked, there's no reason to keep the defensive placements, and we should have brought them with us here to use for convenience. As if MPs aren't already mowing people down efficiently enough."

Adam frowned. "Who says the castle isn't going to be attacked?"

"Exactly!" Kiefer exaggerated a nod. "Although I have no idea who would be suicidal enough to even think of attempting it, it's best to be prepared."

They passed a small knot of men who hadn't attended the briefing. They talked about Gerhardt leaving the camp for the first time since they'd set up and speculated on why he'd do so now.

"Word's spreading fast," Adam said. "I'm wondering how many people will guess that he's most likely going so he can keep an eye on Ziegfried."

"Probably no one." Kiefer wrinkled his nose with distaste. "Most people aren't around him enough to know what an ass he is."

"Oh, I don't know." Adam needled. "His bodyguards are around him constantly and they dote on him like he was a movie star or something."

"That's because they're stupid," Kiefer said. "A lot of people are stupid. In fact, most people are stupid. There's only a few people I've met that aren't."

"Who?"

"Helmut, for one," Kiefer said. "He wasn't stupid. Simple, yes. Stupid, no."

"What definition of stupid are you using?"

"If you have brains, and intelligence, and you refuse to use them, that's just plain stupid," Kiefer said. "I would say that Strom is stupid if I was convinced he ever had any brains or intelligence to begin with. Otherwise, he's disqualified from the stupid category."

"Someone under-qualified to be considered stupid." Adam laughed. "They're pretty bad off."

Kiefer grinned. "Yeah!"

They reached their tent and went inside. Kiefer paused long enough to look over at Helmut's corner. He sighed and dropped onto his bedroll. Not much later, Jorgan came. He looked at just about everything but Helmut's corner. Both of them insisted on helping Adam pack and get ready to go.

They mustered before sunup. Their gear and arms were inspected. They all hefted their packs and secured various gear and food on their webbing. Then they launched.

The trek cross-country was neither difficult, nor a walk in the park. It wasn't so wintry that they trudged through deep snow. The patches of snow they did come across they went around or cleared out of the way. It wasn't raining. It wasn't blistering hot. They climbed up and down slopes with their webbing straps fully loaded across their shoulders and hips. The first time they dug into their bread bags, Adam had to resist the temptation to eat more than needed just to get rid of some of the weight. It was amazing how something as light as a single bullet could accumulate to the pounds he now hauled.

The only person complaining about it was Ziegfried. Everything was too heavy. The water in his canteen sloshed around too much. The food rations tasted disgusting. It was undignified to act like a common pack mule. He was too out of breath to reach the top of the climb. His legs were too tired to keep up the pace.

Two of his new underlings had come along. One of them lifted some of the weight off of Ziegfried, loading it onto himself. Gerhardt unclipped everything the underling put on his belt and hooked them back onto Ziegfried's.

"That's not fair." Ziegfried yelled a little bit. Gerhardt hooked more things onto him. Ziegfried whimpered. "That's more than I was carrying before."

"And if you carry enough that you can't breathe anymore—" Gerhardt clipped a second canteen at the small of Ziegfried's back— "then I won't have to listen to your whining."

"You can't do this to me." Ziegfried puffed out his chest. "I'm an important person."

"So is Velig." Gerhardt took some of the ammo off of Velig and put it on Ziegfried. He unclipped something Adam couldn't see from his back, relieving him of a bit of weight. "So is Weiss. And Lieber, he's important too."

He went through the men. He called each of them by name, claiming they were important. He took a little something off of every one of them, clipping it onto Ziegfried.

"Stop! Stop!" Ziegfried begged. His knees sagged under all the extra added weight.

"You stop whining like a snot nosed little brat first," Gerhardt said. "March. Move those feet. Pick up the pace. Keep up with everyone else. I'm going to pick up a stick. And for every step you lag I'm going to switch you if you don't move it fast enough."

"Please," Ziegfried whimpered. "Put everything back. I'll stop complaining. Just please, take some of it back off."

"The longer you spend whining, the longer you're going to carry it," Gerhardt said. "Shut your mouth. Do your part. I'll take off the extras one by one as we move, as long as you keep up."

Ziegfried stopped complaining. By the time they stopped for the night all the extra weight had come off and been redistributed to the original carriers.

Their stop was shorter than the night. They cleared out of their campsite before the gray light of dawn seeped in from the east. A second day of moving made them all weary and snippy. No one dared complain. Not after what happened to Ziegfried.

They descended from the ridge line. They skirted the valley below. At the northern side they stopped and hunkered down in the brush while the scouts were sent out to clear the way.

This close to the intended enemy everyone felt the pressure to remain undetected. No one spoke save in hushed whispers. They only moved if they had to. When they did, they used extreme care to prevent as much rustling in the bushes as possible. Although most of them glugged water from their canteens and snacked from their bread bags, no one lit up a smoke. No one took off any of their gear. Weapons were kept in hand. Everyone was ready to jump at a moment's notice.

Some of the scouts returned. The immediate perimeter was clear. Gerhardt spread the command to stand down. He broke them up into shifts, making them take turns sleeping and standing guard.

About halfway through the night they moved again. They climbed up a steep slope. The scouts guided them, one by one, through the dark to their individual locations.

Adam was guided to a shelf of rock with Gerhardt, Velig, and Lieber. A few feet to the right, Ziegfried and his two assistants were positioned. The other two doctors with them were elsewhere among the men, to the left and to the right.

Once everyone was positioned, they waited. Adam stared into the darkness below. Down there, people slept oblivious to the death sneaking up on them. He swallowed down the sick rising from his gut.

Gray light seeped into the east, easing back the darkness. A couple of early risers emerged and wandered about below. Gerhardt and Velig pressed binoculars to their eyes, watching for a few minutes. A couple more people joined the first few. Gerhardt lowered the binoculars, raised the handheld radio, and gave Feldstetter the go.

On the rocks just below, still well above the roofs of the village huts, Feldstetter armed a grenade. He stood, and lobbed. It flew end over end, spinning through the gray light. It hit the near side of the target building. The ensuing explosion shattered the quiet of the early morning.

Chapter 60

THE MEN OPENED FIRE, hitting other buildings. People screamed and cried. Pain and terror. Feldstetter continued lobbing grenades. Smoke and fire rose, carrying with it the stench of blood and charred flesh.

People scurried through the madness toward the far side of the valley. People dropped as they neared it. Older ones shielded the younger with their own bodies.

Adam turned away from the sight, his stomach recoiling. He didn't bother covering his ears. It would do no good. He looked up. If ever he had been tempted to believe in god, he wished the deity would save those people down there.

A face popped out above the rock, peeking down at the Germans. Then it was gone. Adam blinked, and shook his head, trying to make sense of what his eyes told him. It had been the size of a child, but looked somehow full grown. It had pointy ears and a red tint to its almost translucent skin. And its leer put Nolrien's scary smile to shame with a mouth full of sharp teeth that were pointier than its ears.

The face appeared again with that same smile. This time, whatever it was, it held a rock above its head. It took aim and let fly. The rock thunked somewhere. One of the Germans manning an MP stopped shooting and started cussing in pain. The face giggled and disappeared again.

Adam tried to get Gerhardt's attention. "Sir?"

"Not now," Gerhardt snapped at him.

"Sir?" Adam insisted. The face appeared again, popping up from behind a rock somewhere farther down and to the right. "Sir, this is important!"

"What is it?" Velig scowled at Adam. He pointed at the creature that eerily reminded him of some sort of imp or demon out of folklore. Did they have kobolds on this world? Maybe that's what it was. Velig spotted it. "What the hell?"

"It sure looks like that's where it's from," Adam said.

A small explosion went off near one of the MPs. Its operator screamed and jumped up with his clothes aflame. Rocks gave way beneath him, showering down on the men directly below him. Two of his comrades grabbed him, keeping him from going over the edge. They pushed him to the ground and beat at the flames.

"HA! HA! HA! HA!" The kobold didn't giggle this time. It let out a creepy laugh that rang loud and clear, easily heard even over the din of the battle.

"I think we're seeing the work of the magician," Gerhardt said.

"Definitely," Velig agreed, watching the kobold vanish again. He shouted orders into his radio. They had an enemy at their backs. He dispatched men to locate and eliminate.

"We have an enemy behind us?" Gerhardt lowered his binoculars. He waved his hand toward the valley. "I was referring to all that."

Velig and Adam both turned to look out across the valley. A deep fog blanketed everything. The entire floor was obscured to the point of invisibility.

"When did that roll in?" Velig asked.

"It didn't," Gerhardt said. "It was just suddenly there."

"Wow!" Ziegfried slowly stood, wide eyed and slack jawed. The guns had quieted, having no immediate targets now. "I've never seen anything like this. How incredible! I'd never thought of using magic to manipulate the elements of nature like this. I'd never thought of how something so passive could be so effective."

"You're certain this is magic?" Gerhardt called over to him. "I need confirmation."

"This is definitely magic," Ziegfried looked as awed as he sounded. "I can feel it. There's a lot of strength behind the spell causing this."

"Where is the spell caster?" Gerhardt asked.

Ziegfried pointed vaguely at the valley floor. "Down there somewhere."

"Where exactly?" Gerhardt growled at him. "I want the location pinpointed."

"Oh!" Ziegfried blinked like he was coming out of a little bit of a trance. "Of course. I knew that. I'll get right on a search."

He sat down and took a couple of charms out of his pockets. His lips moved. One of the assistants asked if they could help. He shook his head and continued silently mouthing.

The MPs continued intermittent spraying. The mausers had gone silent with no visible targets. The men were calling to each other, pointing down, talking about the sudden appearance of the fog.

Velig shouted through the radio, bringing their attention back around. He said to Gerhardt, "We can't hold like this. The men won't keep focus, especially not with an unknown at our backs. If there's no change, we're going to have to start going down on foot to search and eliminate."

"Ziegfried!" Gerhardt shouted over. "Can you focus on more than one thing at a time? We need that fog cleared if possible. I don't want to send men down into that if I don't have to."

Ziegfried gave him a distracted glance and a short nod. He said something to his two assistants. They sat down and took on looks of concentration as intense as his.

"Weiss," Velig said. "Keep your eyes peeled behind us."

Adam turned and scanned the area where the kobold had last made an appearance. He glanced from rock to rock, watching for it to pop up again. He held his mauser ready to shoot it.

Off to the left, far from the area Adam was watching, someone screamed. Adam looked over in time to see the kobold tossing someone over its head and down the slope. The man desperately clutched for any kind of a handhold he could as he went tumbling. A couple of shots were fired at it from other locations. It was already gone. The shots ricocheted off bare rock.

"*Mein Gott!*" Velig gasped. "That can't possibly be real!"

"*Barmherziger Gott!*" Gerhardt had a similar reaction, his binoculars back at his eyes.

Adam turned to see what they were blaspheming over. In the steadily increasing light, the fog swirled over where some of the buildings had stopped. It rose up in height, about three or four times taller than a man. The swirling picked up speed, making a funnel like a tornado. Two protrusions stuck out from either side as crude arms. Two dark spots appeared on the side that faced the Germans. They blinked. The arms stretched up, tendrils of fingers popping out at the tips. At the same time, a gaping hole opened directly below the eyes in the shape of an irregular mouth. It let out a low rumble that reverberated through Adam's bones.

"Ziegfried!" Gerhardt shouted. Ziegfried gaped. His mouth hung slack. He stared wide eyed at the behemoth across the valley. Gerhardt grunted with disgust. He ordered Velig, "See if that thing is bullet proof!"

Velig relayed the order to half the mausers, keeping the MPs laying down cover fire over the invisible valley floor. The mausers opened up on the monstrosity.

"Interesting," Gerhardt grunted, his binoculars glued to his face. "Velig, take a close look. Tell me what you see."

Velig raised his own binoculars. After a few moments, he said, "I see slight reactions to the bullets."

"Every hole fills back in fairly quickly," Gerhardt said. "Still, it's a reaction. Concentrate fire. Ziegfried, tell me what that thing is!"

"It's what we've been looking for." Ziegfried giggled, even as the foggy, wind monster started moving. Slowly, inch by inch, it crept toward them.

"Weiss!" Velig snapped at Adam. "Behind us!"

Adam dutifully wrenched his eyes from the horrifying scene and turned around. He readied his mauser, scanning the rocks. Search as he might, there was no sign of the kobold.

He tried to keep his eyes everywhere at once, desperately pushing distraction to the back of his mind. Bullets flew. Explosions went off. Lieber kept up ongoing transmissions on the medical channel of the radio. Gerhardt and Velig kept making comments to each other that were like information teasers, rousing curiosity.

The constant fire on the wind behemoth was having some sort of effect, causing it to look a bit ragged at the edges. Some of the fog pulled back, revealing the buildings at the edge of the valley closest to their slope. Then it stopped ebbing and remained steadfast.

"How long do you estimate before that thing gets in range of a grenade?" Gerhardt asked. "If bullets are harming it, I want to know what an explosive will do."

Another explosion went off. This one was too close, within the vicinity of some of their men. Down where Feldstetter had continually lobbed stick grenades, body parts and pebbles of blasted rock went flying. It looked like every one of the remaining explosives had gone off all at once. The hideous kobold laughter followed.

Velig swore violently. Gerhardt said, "So much for it staying behind us. How'd it get down there?"

"I don't see it move," Velig said. "It just pops up here and there. By the time we know where it is, it's already wreaking havoc. Weiss, I told you to keep your eyes behind us!"

Adam refocused. He panned from rock to rock. He could see more and more in the growing light. There was no sign of the little creature.

"Ziegfried!" Gerhardt called. "You pinpoint that magician yet?"

"No," Ziegfried called back. "I think he's moving around."

Gerhardt cursed under his breath. Velig said, "You know we have a finite amount of time before we're fighting off predatory fauna. We're not going to be able to keep at this for much longer."

"I'm aware." Gerhardt worked a muscle in his jaw. "Send the men in. Sweep it clean."

Chapter 61

VELIG DIVIDED THE MEN into two main groups. Those closest to the valley floor, he sent in to begin a sweep on the side farthest from the wind monster, on which the rest concentrated their fire.

Adam heard giggling. He looked in that direction. The kobold popped its face up from behind a rock with a look of anticipatory glee. Adam aimed his mauser just in time for the creature to pick up another MP operator. That blocked Adam's shot.

With a flick of the kobold's wrist, the man went flying over the edge with a scream of terror. Adam's finger twitched on the trigger. The creature vanished. Only its maniacal laughter remained.

Velig reminded everyone going into the fog to stay in vocal contact with each other. Gerhardt estimated the wind monster close enough and demanded to know if anyone had any grenades left.

Adam heard the giggles again. This time he raised his mauser and aimed before he got a visual. The moment the kobold popped its face into view, he fired. The shot pulled to the left. He cursed over not having had a chance to sight in the weapon. He drew back the bolt to reload the chamber. The kobold turned and looked him straight in the eye. It bared its pointy teeth and disappeared again.

Several minutes passed without the kobold reappearing. Then Adam heard a low growling, right above his location. He raised his rifle.

The kobold didn't pop its face out. It took a leap right at Adam. Its teeth were still bared. Its fingers extended like talons. The growling morphed into a raging battle cry. Adam squeezed the trigger.

The bullet hit it square in the chest, right where its heart should be. It was knocked out of its arc of trajectory. It slammed up against the rock wall behind it with a look of startled surprise. It gurgled. Then it vanished.

This time when it disappeared there was a loud whump. Air sucked into the space it had occupied. Then all that air exploded outward. Adam turned, shielding his face with his arm from the shower of rocks and pebbles knocked loose to rain down on him, the doctor, and the brass.

All three of them paused. They looked at him as he peeked out from behind his arm. Velig clapped him on the shoulder. "Good shot!"

One of the men below them stood and flung a stick grenade. It landed just beneath the wind behemoth. What was left of it shredded in the resulting blossom of fire and smoke.

Ziegfried giggled, eerily reminiscent of the imp. Gerhardt shouted at him, "What is your problem?"

"Look!" He jumped up and down, pointing at the valley.

Gerhardt looked, without his binoculars. "Interesting."

Adam looked too. Heading to the far side of the valley, they could see a man in the fog. Everywhere he went, the fog avoided him, like he was inside some sort of bubble or something. While the fog continually thinned and lowered, he kept pausing and looking behind himself.

Gerhardt pressed the binoculars back to his eyes. "Looks like he's talking to someone."

Velig used his binoculars too. "Is that who I think it is?"

"It certainly is," Gerhardt said. "That is the Brendish Priad. And it's a good bet that if he doesn't know exactly where the magician is, he'll know where to find him."

"Either way…" Velig left the sentence hanging.

"It's time," Gerhardt told him. "Take Weiss. Get down to him."

Velig tapped Adam on the arm. "Let's go."

"Watch yourselves down there," Gerhardt said as the two of them got up. "The men don't know you're going to be down there and they'll be jumpy inside that fog."

"With limited vision and itchy trigger fingers," Velig said what Gerhardt didn't.

Adam followed Velig back up to the top, then around and down to the bottom of the slope. Several of the buildings were completely exposed at the edge where the fog ebbed back. Velig plunged in.

The stench hung thick. Blood and excrement mixed with charred hair and flesh. Adam choked in the reek. Velig glance back at him.

"Hold it down," he said. "Breathe through your mouth until your nose adjusts."

Adam gagged. "I can taste it."

"I know." Velig didn't pause his forward march. Several paces farther he lifted up a hand. "Hold up. I think this is about where we saw him. Listen for movement."

Adam held his breath, a relief from the putrid air. He opened his ears. Everything was quiet, a testament to the still forms they had passed on the ground, in a pile here, in bits and pieces there. Somewhere behind them and to the right, one of the men called out his position. Farther away, someone else responded.

Velig crept forward. His hand hovered over his luger. Adam followed. He took another breath, unable to hold it any longer.

A mauser shot rang out directly ahead of them. At the same time, the fog lit up red in that direction with a small explosion. It didn't have the same sound as one of theirs. It was smaller, sharper, more like a sudden ignition of fire than the percussion of a grenade cap.

A burst of violent wind knocked Adam and Velig backward to the ground. When Adam was able to look up again the fog was gone. Not one wisp of it remained.

"Something's happened!" Velig cursed and surged forward, drawing his luger.

Adam followed, mauser in hands. They came around yet another shattered building to see three dead bodies. Jerryck lay bleeding on the ground by the one wearing crimson and gold. The other two wore German uniforms. Tajor stood by them, firing a mauser in the direction of their men on the rocks. He held it properly against his shoulder, as well as any trained soldier. And he was looking down the barrel. Aiming. Not firing randomly.

"Put it down!" Velig shouted, aiming his luger at Tajor.

Too late. The shot was already fired. Even though Tajor couldn't possibly understand the words, Velig kept shouting anyway. "I said put it down. On the ground. Let go of it. Get your hands up in the air where I can see them."

"Put it down," Adam interpreted. "And keep your hands where we can see them."

Tajor knew how to handle guns. He had to know he couldn't pull back the bolt to reload the chamber and swing it around to aim at them without getting himself shot. He let go of the stock. Holding the barrel, he lowered the butt down to the ground. Keeping his empty had where they could see it, he lowered the rest of the mauser until it was only a few inches from the ground. Only then did he let go of it, letting it drop the rest of the way.

"Tell him to move away from the weapon." Velig motioned to Tajor at the same time he said it. Tajor must have understood well enough. He backed away from the mauser before Adam said anything. Still keeping Tajor covered, Velig tilted his head in Jerryck's direction. "Get status."

Jerryck was staring at the rock face where the Germans had attacked. Adam lay down his mauser just out of the magician's reach and knelt by his side. He leaned in close to get a good look at the shoulder leaking blood. He said to Velig, "Looks like he took a bullet."

"Did it hit his lungs?" Velig asked.

"How am I supposed to know that?"

"Is he wheezing? Or gurgling? That'd be one sign." Velig still kept the luger trained on Tajor as he pulled the two-way radio from his belt.

Adam listened to Jerryck's breathing for a moment. Then he said, "No, not that I can hear."

Velig raised the radio to his face and depressed the button to talk. "Gerhardt, this is Velig. Contact made. In need of medical assistance. Requesting Lieber sent in."

"That's a negative," Gerhardt's voice came through the radio, drawing Jerryck's attention away from the rocks. "All medical are occupied. Ziegfried took a bullet in the chest."

Adam whipped his head around to Tajor. "You shot Ziegfried in the chest!"

"The *chest?*" Tajor sneered, looking anything but repentant. "That's too bad. I missed. I was aiming for his head."

"How badly injured are the targets?" Gerhardt's voice scratched through the radio. "Are you able to move them? Bring them closer to us?"

"Unknown," Velig said.

Jerryck turned his head to look at the rocks again. Adam spoke in German to Velig. "Tell him that if Ziegfried is injured, no one should touch him. He's liable to drain them out of reflex."

"We're aware of that!" Velig snapped at him. "And if you think we're going to relay that over the air waves—"

Gerhardt's voice came through the radio. "I'm working on getting someone to you to ascertain their condition. Stand by."

Jerryck pushed himself to roll onto his side, hissing and gritting his teeth while he did so. Adam put a hand on his chest to hold him down. "Lie still."

Jerryck pushed against him anyway. He even sounded like he was in pain when he spoke. "That man has to be stopped."

The only men in the direction he was rolling were Tajor and Velig. Was he going to do something to Velig? Adam quickly tried to reassure him. "You are safe. I will let none of our men hurt you more."

"No, not me." Jerryck pointed with a shaky hand past Velig and Tajor, toward the rock face where the Germans had attacked. "That man."

Which man? There were still a lot of men over there. Adam shook his head. Those men weren't shooting anymore. What was it Jerryck wanted them to stop?

Jerryck lay still. He closed his eyes and whispered something Adam couldn't quite catch. Whatever he said to himself, it must have helped calm him. He completely relaxed for a moment.

Only for a moment. Then he gasped, tensing up. He jerked toward Adam. Tajor arched his back and took on an expression of absolute agony, then dropped to the ground on his hands and knees. And Ziegfried lay by Jerryck's side.

"Ziegfried!" Adam scuttled back in shock.

"What the… What's going on? What happened? How'd he get here?" Velig spluttered, looking just as shocked as Adam. Gerhardt screamed much the same over the radio.

Ziegfried looked at Jerryck. He reached out and grabbed the magician's arm. Adam gasped, knowing what Ziegfried was doing, not knowing how to stop it. Velig still kept Tajor covered, but shouted, "No! Ziegfried, no! Weiss, kick him, break the contact."

Adam scrabbled to his feet. He lurched over and pulled one foot back to kick Ziegfried's arm away. Then he and the magician both rolled away from him. A few times. The contact broke. Tajor gasped again and curled up in a fetal position. Then all three of them were still.

Adam and Velig stared at the three of them for a moment. Then looked at each other. Velig looked just as confused and lost as Adam was, while Gerhardt still demanded explanations through the radio.

"Sir?" Someone called out. The two of them turned. A couple of their men were approaching, covering both of the prone Brendish men with their mausers.

Velig waved his arms wildly at them. "Hold your fire!"

The man cocked his head. "What orders then, sir?"

Others converged from different directions. Someone stopped at the two bodies wearing German uniforms with smoking, charred remains where their heads should be. Another crept to Ziegfried, while yet another used a toe to nudge the dead man wearing crimson and gold. He bent down and dug out a sheathed dagger hidden on the man's body.

Adam reached for it. "That's mine."

The man held it away. "Finders keepers."

"That's his," Velig growled. "Give it. Now."

The man reluctantly surrendered the dagger to Adam. Velig looked around at all the men gathering. He called, "Who has basic medical?"

The man by Ziegfried raise his hand, so did a few others. Velig pointed at Jerryck, Tajor, and Ziegfried, "Tend them."

Chapter 62

MORE OF THE MEN converged on their location. Velig had them all report in, then run off to do whatever task he had a mind to set them to. Some gathered the papers of their own dead. Others gathered materials to put together makeshift litters to move the wounded. Lieber came running with Thoel. Gerhardt came close behind them. Adam turned away so he wouldn't have to watch whatever medical procedures they decided to torture people with.

Before long Gerhardt and Velig rounded everyone up, prepping to get on the move. Thoel complained about risking Ziegfried's life by it. One of the men aiding him pointed up at a large bird circling overhead. "More of those are going to come, along with other predators. We'd be risking everyone's life not to move."

"Weiss, can you help me out here?" Thoel called him over to Tajor. "He's not completely out like in Andreno's camp. If he can help us figure this out, or tell us what's wrong, we might be able to help him this time."

Adam leaned in close. "Tajor? Do you know if there's anything we can do to help you?"

Tajor drew in air and let it back out with a few quiet, strained words. "Nothing you can do."

When Adam told Thoel he frowned and said, "If he's sure of that then maybe he knows exactly what the problem is."

Adam said to Tajor, "Tell us what is wrong."

"Magic." Tajor only got out the one word this time. Then he shuddered and curled up tighter.

A couple of men came over with a litter and set it down next to Tajor. One of them pointed up to where a few more of the strange birds had gathered and said, "Gerhardt's ordered everyone to move before more of those get here and start feeding."

"We have to move," Adam told Tajor. "And we cannot leave you or you will get eaten."

He slitted his eyes open again. The muscles in his neck flexed, but he didn't quite lift his head. "Jerryck?"

The magician had already been loaded onto a litter and picked up. Adam said, "Do not worry. We are not leaving him behind either."

Tajor didn't help move himself onto the litter. But he didn't resist either. The two men assigned to carry him fell in line right behind Ziegfried and Jerryck. Adam loaded up what he was given to carry and put himself right behind them. That way he could keep both the Brendish men in sight and hear anything if they spoke.

The trip was short and quiet. They only went a few miles when the scouts led them to a sort of cave under an overhanging cliff face. Ziegfried was taken to the back where the ceiling was low enough that the men had to duck to keep from hitting their heads on the rock above. Jerryck and Tajor were put closer to the outside. That was as much separation from Ziegfried as they could manage while still keeping them properly guarded.

Adam sat down at their feet. He sloughed off his pack and drew up his knees. He lifted his arms to rest his elbows on his knees. His coat pulled uncomfortably, reminding him that it was too small. He shifted to sit cross-legged instead so he had a place to rest his elbows more comfortably.

Lieber and Thoel hovered over the two Brendish men. Gerhardt left Velig giving out orders to the soldiers and came over to them. He demanded, "What have you done for them so far?"

"We extracted the bullet from the magician's shoulder," Lieber said. "It was touching bone, so we couldn't just sew him up and leave it in."

"Mauser?" Gerhardt asked.

"Affirmative." Lieber leaned in over Jerryck, peeling back some of the makeshift bandage that had been applied. "The clotting looks good, bleeding has slowed, but he'll need stitches. Haven't had a chance to do that yet."

Velig came to Gerhardt. "All heads are accounted for. I need the go to send the men out to prep for the night."

"Get it done," Gerhardt said. Velig moved off, calling some of the men by name and doling out assignments.

"What about the Priad?" Gerhardt asked.

"I haven't been able to find anything causing the distress he's exhibiting," Lieber said.

"He did this in Andreno's camp too," Thoel told them.

"Weiss, ask if he knows what's wrong," Gerhardt ordered.

"I did," Adam said. "In the village. He said it was magic and there's nothing we can do to help him."

"What did you do last time?" Lieber asked.

"Treated for shock," Thoel said. He shrugged. "I didn't know what else to do."

"Did it work?" Gerhardt asked.

"I don't know," he said. "It didn't seem to make him any worse as far as I could tell. And he did come around to normal by the next morning."

"Treat for shock then," Lieber said, digging in his supplies. He pulled out a wickedly curved needle. Adam turned away.

Some of the men were gathering rocks, piling them in a line just outside the cave. Others were heading in pairs into the trees. A few patrolled back and forth on the other side of the line of rocks, their weapons in hand. The rest stayed inside the cave sorting supplies or tending injuries.

Since two of the doctors were with the Brendish, Adam looked for the third among those tending injuries. Instead, he was lying on another pallet with the wounded.

"What happened to the third doctor?" Adam asked, pointing.

"Doctor?" Lieber leaned over Jerryck while he worked. "I'm the only doctor."

"You mean Koen?" Thoel glanced over that way, then took a tool Lieber handed him and gave him another. "He and I are just field medics, not doctors."

"What happened to him?" Adam asked. "He's not wearing any more bandages than Tajor."

"Ziegfried happened to him," Gerhardt said. "He'd already completely drained his two assistants we brought to help him. Koen was going to be the third man he killed after he was shot."

Adam shuddered. "He's still alive?"

"Ziegfried let go for some reason," Gerhardt said. "I don't know why. I suspect the Brendish magician may have interfered somehow, because it was just after that when he was all of a sudden gone from the ledge and down in the village next to you."

"He did say something about some man that needed stopped." Adam kept his eyes off of Jerryck and off whatever the doctors were doing to his shoulder. "Then he jerked and Ziegfried was laying beside him."

"It was definitely the magician then." Gerhardt nodded, looking to the back of the cave where Ziegfried lay. One of the men tending the injured leaned over him. Gerhardt called out, "Get away from him!"

"Sir, he needs help," the man called back. "He's still bleeding. And this injury looks pretty serious."

"Are you a doctor?" Gerhardt asked him.

"I'm trained for triage and first aid," the man answered.

"So not a doctor," Gerhardt said. "Get away from him."

The man didn't back off. "He needs help."

"Weiss," Gerhardt said. "Go let off some steam and take care of that."

Adam jumped to his feet, snatching the opportunity to get away from the doctors, however temporary, even though it meant getting closer to Ziegfried. The man stood to face Adam bearing down on him, fists up, teeth bared. He said, "If he dies, we're all stuck here."

Adam stepped to the right, grabbed the man's pants by the knee, and pushed on his shoulder at the same time. He went down easy, whapping his head on the ground in the process. Adam leaned his weight in on the man's torso, pinning him, just the way Nolrien had to him so many, many times.

"Ziegfried kills people when he's weak," Adam said in the man's ear. "That's why neither of his two assistants are with us anymore. That's why Koen is comatose. If we lose too many to him that way, Command will abandon us. We'll be stuck here anyway."

He didn't know if that was exactly true or not, but it sounded good. The man must have bought it. He went limp. Adam added more stuff that sounded good. "Those men that the doctors are treating, they're important officials in a country that can help us if we get stuck here. You want them to leave off? Maybe let them die? So the doctors can maybe come over and let Ziegfried kill them?"

"What about Andreno?" The man spoke quietly, timidly. "Wouldn't he help us?"

"After the way he forced us to come here and do his dirty work?" Adam let up the weight and stood. He sneered down at the man. "He's trustworthy only as long as we're useful to him."

Some of the others had paused their work, watching him. He clenched his fists. "Anyone else have anything to say in the matter?"

Some of them looked over at Velig. When he did nothing to contradict Adam, they turned and went back to work. Velig gave Adam a slight nod of approval.

Adam went back to sit by Jerryck and Tajor. Lieber had finished whatever he was doing to the magician and had him re-bandaged and covered. The blanket looked like one of theirs. Either someone gave up the blanket from their bedroll or the owner didn't need it anymore.

The men out in the forest brought in armfuls of wood, chopped them, and built fires at the long opening of the cave. The men piling rocks in a line finished that off to waist height with extra branches and wood. The low wall reflected the heat from the fires back into the cave, warming the air as the sun set and the temperature plummeted.

Tajor showed no signs of improvement. Neither did Jerryck. Gerhardt eventually gave Liber and Thoel permission to work on Ziegfried. He didn't suck the life out of them. He didn't do anything except lay there, as comatose as Jerryck.

Adam pulled out his breadbag, then stared at the food in his hands. His stomach growled. But visions of dead body parts put a lump in his throat that no food would be able to pass. He stowed the bread bag and laid out his bedroll and dozed.

Halfway through the night he was awakened by shouts. On the other side of the fires one of the men on guard duty called out, raising his mauser to his shoulder. Others turned on their pocket lamps to shine where he was pointing. A little girl stood at the edge of the trees. Her golden hair shined in the light where she stood blinking and holding up a rolled parchment, or skin, or something.

"Hold your fire!" Velig shouted, striding over to the inside of the wall.

"Weiss!" Gerhardt called. Adam scrambled over to him. "How much of the mountain language did you learn?"

"Enough for a greeting," Adam said.

"Go see if you can get her to come closer so you can greet her," Gerhardt said.

"Closer, sir?"

"I don't want you near those trees," Gerhardt said. "Or the brush in front of them."

The little girl, still blinking in the pocket lamps aimed at her face, called out. "Adam?"

Gerhardt and Adam both froze, staring at her. Velig glanced back at them. The little girl called his name again.

"How does she know my name?" Adam asked.

"My bets are on our Brendish guests," Gerhardt said. "Get her closer to the wall, figure out what she's holding, and what she wants."

Adam went out as far as the fires. There, Velig stopped him momentarily. "Don't go past the wall, in case this is a trap and you need to duck behind it for cover."

Adam nodded. He stepped past the fires. Velig called out to the others, "More light. Watch the trees and brush for movement."

Half a dozen more men turned on their pocket lamps and panned them across the landscape behind the girl. She looked at Adam at the wall, and questioned his name. He nodded and did his best to ask her name. She laid one shaking hand on her chest and said, "Khata."

"Here?" he pointed to the ground on the far side of the low reflector wall. "Khata here?"

He didn't know how else to ask her to come closer. It worked. She stepped right to where he pointed. She looked at the guns pointing at her. She shivered, then looked at Adam and held out the roll in her hand. The roll shook, along with her entire little body.

Her clothing looked thin, not enough for the chill of the night. Her golden hair was tangled and matted. Her face was dirty. And her eyes were so wide they were white all around her blue irises.

One of the men holding a mauser on her lowered the muzzle a bit. "She looks like Goldilocks."

"Stand your ground," Velig said. The man re-aimed properly.

Adam reached out to her outstretched hand. Her fingers were cold when they brushed against his, transferring the roll to him. It felt like soft leather. He held one end and let it drop open, revealing words written in Brendish with some sort of black, dusty lettering. Charcoal? Some of it had smeared. He held it up to the light of the fires behind him.

"Light!" Velig called. One of the men came over and shined a pocket lamp right on the letters. After a moment, Velig asked, "What does it say?"

"Uh..." Adam wasn't sure he should be saying it out in the open where everyone could hear.

"Jerryck?" Khata asked, rising to her tiptoes and craning her head to look at him. She said something more, but Adam couldn't understand the words. She still shivered. And her lips were getting a purplish tint to them.

"She's cold," Adam said. "She's not going to hurt us. And if we treat her right maybe she'll take a message back for us."

Velig looked skeptical. "You going to write a message in their language?"

Adam held up the leather and waved it a bit. "Someone out there can read and write in the same language used in Shontarra."

"All right, bring her in, if she'll come," Velig said. "Don't force it."

Adam gave the leather to Velig. Moving slowly to keep from startling anyone, he slipped over the low reflector wall. She stepped back, eyeing the walther at his right hip. Keeping his right hand out where she could see it, he used his left to release his belt and set it on top of the wall with the gun in its holster.

This time, she didn't back up when he approached. But she did shiver again. Then he got close enough to hear her teeth chattering. He opened his coat, took it off, and wrapped it around her shoulders. Her jaw dropped. She stared at him, looking more shocked than a troublemaker with a good grade on their report card.

The cold bit through Adam's shirt. He opened his arm back toward the fires. "Khata come? See Jerryck?"

He hoped he had the words right. She closed her mouth, confusion leaking into her eyes. Then she craned her head toward Jerryck again. Holding the coat closed, she stepped past Adam to the wall. She startled when he touched her, then let him lift her over to the inside. He climbed over himself, into the immediate warmth the wall reflected back from the fires. He put a hand on her back and pointed to Jerryck. She ran to him and sat down, still holding the coat closed.

Adam grabbed his belt with his gun. Velig gave the order to stand down, to kill the lights, then followed Adam over to Khata. Gerhardt met them there.

Velig handed the leather back to Adam. "What does it say?"

"Uh…" Adam angled it to the light of the fires and went over the words again. "It says Jerryck's sister demands the release of him and Tajor, or she'll gather all the shamans in the mountains and kill us all. Didn't we just kill all their shamans?"

"Doubtful," Gerhardt said.

Chapter 63

LIEBER WOKE ADAM with a tap on his shoulder. "Weiss, I need you again."

"Hmmph?" Adam grunted. It was still dark except for the warming fires. "You said I could sleep 'til morning."

"I said hopefully." Lieber scooted to sit closer to Tajor. "You're the one that said last time he was better by the next morning. It's almost morning and he's not showing any improvement at all. Talk to him again."

"He'll just say the same thing, that there's nothing we can do," Adam complained. "Besides, it's cold."

"We found you another coat," Lieber said.

Adam pulled his bedroll tighter around himself, trying not to think of where that coat had come from, or the owner who didn't need it anymore. "It's too big."

Lieber kicked him lightly, more of a nudge than anything else. "Stop making excuses and get over here."

Khata sat up. Their talking must have woken her again. And he didn't know how to tell her everything was fine, to go back to sleep. Maybe if he gave her another little something. That had worked so far. He was running out of little things to use as gifts. Lieber had helped him some with that, providing a piece of candy and a cookie. She hadn't eaten them, but she seemed pleased with them anyway.

One of the men patrolling near the wall took a moment to light a cigarette. Khata gasped at the striking of the match. That would work. Adam dug out a few of the matches he carried.

He held them out to her. "Khata like?"

She stared at them blankly. Adam took one of them and struck it. When it flared, she flashed the first smile he'd seen on her. It was brief, only a couple of seconds long, but it was there. She gingerly accepted the remaining matches and added them to her stash, then laid back down.

"I'm not sure that's the smartest thing to give her," Lieber said.

Adam sat up and put his coat on. "It's only a few. They won't last long."

"Like the cookie didn't last long? Or the maple candy?" Lieber pointed to them. Adam shrugged. He was too tired to care.

Jerryck jerked, like something had startled him, the first movement he'd made since they'd taken him from the village. Khata sat up again, holding her coat closed. Gerhardt must have noticed too. He came over just as Jerryck turned his head to the side and groaned.

Lieber frowned. "Tell him to lie still."

"Jerryck?" Adam put a hand on the magician's good shoulder. "Lay still. Try to relax."

Jerryck opened unfocused eyes and looked around blearily. Lieber said, "Help him focus. Keep him grounded."

Adam held up his free hand helplessly. How was he supposed to do that? Lieber said, "Ask him easy questions. Who he is, who you are, where we are, if he remembers what happened, stuff like that."

Adam leaned closer to Jerryck. "Do you remember me?"

"I'm sorry we hit you so much." Jerryck's words slurred so much Adam had to concentrate to make sense of them.

"Do not worry about that," Adam said. The more they stayed away from that subject, the better.

"What did you ask?" Gerhardt demanded. "What did he say?"

"He remembers me," Adam told him.

"I didn't hear your name," Gerhardt said.

Adam turned back to the magician. "Do you remember my name?"

Jerryck shook his head. Then his face turned green. He looked about how Adam had felt after the Brendish guards had finished with him. He squeezed Jerryck's good shoulder with sympathy. "It's Adam. Do you know where you are? What happened?"

"Village," Jerryck said. "Fighting."

Some reassurance was in order. Without asking permission, Adam went into the pattern he used whenever he'd needed to set a POW at ease. If you gave them a little information, it always calmed them, and made them more willing to reciprocate. Even though Jerryck wasn't going to be considered a POW, it probably felt that way to him at the moment.

"The fighting is over," Adam said. "And we are not in the village. We moved under an overhang of rock to shelter. A day has passed. We have stayed the night here. It is almost morning. You were injured. And we cannot figure out what is wrong with Tajor."

Jerryck slowly blinked. He turned his head the other way, just enough to see Tajor curled up beside him. He lay there for a moment, doing nothing, saying nothing. He didn't even look all that upset over Tajor's condition. Perhaps he was still in some shock himself? Or he was hurting? Or had Lieber given him something for the pain and it was making his head fuzzy? Adam didn't know.

Jerryck shifted his head enough to look at Khata. He lay there staring, just as emotionless as he had looked at Tajor. Adam pointed at the girl. "Do you know her? She asked for you by name."

"Why is she here?" Jerryck asked. Khata flashed him the same smile she'd given Adam.

Adam switched to German and spoke to Gerhardt. "He's asking about the girl. How much do you want me to tell him?"

"Tell him whatever he asks about her," Gerhardt said.

"Even the letter?"

"He won't know to ask," Gerhardt said. "You'll have to tell him. He might be able to confirm if the threat is valid or not."

Jerryck was still staring at the girl. Adam told him, "She came to us in the night."

"You didn't kill her?" Despite the slurring still in Jerryck's words, Adam caught the bitterness in the tone now.

"Such a pretty little Goldilocks?" Adam smiled at her. She flashed her smile a third time. Adam continued the reassurance. "And so brave, to come to us after what we did."

"There were a lot of little kids in that village," Jerryck said.

This wasn't going to be something Adam could ease over. He was going to have to give some sort of answer to move past it. He met Jerryck's eyes and tried an explanation. "There is nothing that can make good what we did in that village. Or any of the other villages. But understand, we were ordered to come to these mountains by people who will kill the families of these men if we do not obey."

He used his hand to indicate all the Germans around them in the cave. Jerryck curled his upper lip a bit. "Does that include the raided villages in Brend and Shontarra this winter?"

"Ziegfried did that," Adam blurted out, before he even thought about whether or not Gerhardt might want them to have that information. Gerhardt cocked his head at the name. Adam continued to try and smooth things over. "Without permission. We have stopped him. And if we could talk to your king, we could give him an apology. We should have figured out what he was doing long before we did."

"Would you also apologize for the poison in our river last year?"

Adam paused to absorb that. "Poison?"

"The poison he made with magic," Jerryck said. "That was put in our river."

Magic poison. Like what had been in the food that had made Adam so sick? He turned to Gerhardt. "Has Ziegfried ever used magic to make poison?"

"Not that I'm aware of," Gerhardt said. "I wouldn't put it past him if he thought he had something to gain by it. Why?"

"Jerryck says their river was poisoned last spring, and Ziegfried is the one who did it."

"I know nothing about this." Gerhardt exchanged glances with Lieber, who gave him droll look as if to silently say, 'I told you so.' Gerhardt glowered at the back of the cave where Ziegfried still lay motionless. "It would certainly motivate him to keep me from making contact with the King of Brend. This sounds like something we need to have a long conversation about when he wakes up."

"You think he will?" Adam asked. Ziegfried hadn't even twitched the entire time they'd been there.

"If he doesn't, it'll save me the trouble of killing him," Gerhardt muttered. "Get whatever confirmation the magician can give us. And let him know we're going to the forward camp."

Adam switched back to the Brendish language. "We do not know of any poison in a Brendish river."

"I know his signature," Jerryck said. "He did it."

"We believe you," Adam said. "It sounds like something he would do. You can tell us more later, when you are more healed. Maybe after we get back to our camp."

"I'm not going to your camp," Jerryck said.

Where else did he have in mind? The Germans had just slaughtered the last village in the area. Adam said, "There are dangerous animals around. You are injured, and it is our fault. We will keep you safe and make sure you heal enough that you can return to your home safely."

"Why would you care for our safety?" There was that bitter tone again.

"I cannot give you a short answer for that." At least not one Adam expected the magician to accept. He sighed and rubbed his eyes. He was too tired to deal with all this right now. Tired enough that he pressed too hard on the healing bruise around his eye where Jerryck's friend had hit him. He dropped his hands and looked at Tajor and the little girl. They deserved an answer too.

Perhaps tired was an answer they could accept for now. He said, "Some of us, we are tired of all the fighting, all the killing. Too many people have died."

"So you're going to risk King Terrance attacking you by making us go back to your camp?"

"We will not make you. We are hoping." Adam hoped Jerryck and Tajor wouldn't put that statement to the test.

This was a lot trickier than relaxing the tongue of a POW. They didn't just need information out of this person. They needed peace with his people. And he was obviously still upset about the attack. Perhaps some confirmation that someone out there was still alive?

Adam turned to Gerhardt. "You said you wanted me to ask about the letter the girl delivered to us?"

Gerhardt nodded once. Adam pulled out the leather with the charcoal writing and held it up for Jerryck to see. "Khata brought us this."

Jerryck rubbed his eyes. "I can't read that."

"It is in your language." Adam used his head to point at Khata. "Not hers."

"My eyes won't focus right," Jerryck said. "The letters are blurry."

Easily solved. Adam handed the letter to Gerhardt and told Jerryck, "It says that your sister demands we release you and Tajor, or she will gather shamans from everywhere and kill us all. We are waiting for morning when it is light before we send Khata back with our answer."

"That you're making us go to your camp?" He just wasn't letting that go.

Adam corrected him. "That you are injured and we want to heal you."

"They'll kill you."

"With what?" Adam asked. Then he snagged the opportunity to ask about Gerhardt's suspicions. "Their shamans? We just killed them all."

"No you didn't."

Even if it wasn't true, perhaps Gerhardt could use that. Adam told the Oberst, "He says not all the shamans were killed in that village."

"Good," Gerhardt said. "That means we're all in danger here. As soon as we have evidence of just how much danger, that's the perfect excuse to quit this campaign and leave. Keep the talk going in this direction. This is good."

Khata was using the lull in the conversation with Jerryck to show him everything she'd been given during the night. He asked, "Where did she get all this?"

"I gave them to her," Adam said.

Jerryck picked up the spinner Adam had put together. It was the first thing he'd given her after the coat. One of the buttons had come loose from trying to keep the coat closed around him, even though it was too small. He'd hunted up some string, threaded it through the holes, tied it into a loop, and showed her how to use it.

"I made it a toy for her," Adam said. "You wind up the string and see how long you can keep it spinning."

"And the coat?"

"I gave her that too," Adam said. "She was shivering when she first came, like she was cold. So I took off my coat and gave it to her."

"You're wearing a coat."

Adam worked to keep a grimace off his face. "After this last battle, we had a few extras."

Jerryck picked up one of the matches. Adam gave him the name of it, and said, "We use those to make fire."

Jerryck dropped the match and said, "Among her people, a gift is an apology."

"It *is*?" If Adam had known that he'd have given her everything he carried, and not just to get her to lie down and go back to sleep.

"They have some sort of system to measure how sorry you are." Jerryck paused for a moment, closing his eyes. Lieber dug into his bag and came out with a small vial of morphine. Gerhardt shook his head. Then Jerryck opened his eyes and continued as if he hadn't stopped at all. "I don't really understand it. I do know that a Chemwanee never threatens anything they won't actually do. So maybe my sister hasn't killed you because you gave Khata gifts? Maybe? I don't know."

He stopped again. Gerhardt waved his hand, motioning Adam to keep it going. Adam said, "You really do have a sister here in these mountains?"

Jerryck nodded. Then he closed his eyes and sighed a little. Adam prodded, "And you really do think she could get shamans together to try and kill us?"

He mumbled something about shamans getting together. Adam puzzled over that for a moment, hoping he had the words correct. He mumbled right back, "Would that not put them in danger of us killing them?"

No response. Lieber still held the vial of morphine. Gerhardt crossed his arms. Velig came over to them. Still, Jerryck didn't respond.

Adam prodded. "Perhaps we should ask her not to gather them so we do not have to."

"You might not even know they're in the area," Jerryck said.

Adam wasn't so sure about that. "We knew about the shamans in that village."

"They were talking. Not acting. You killed them. The next group will act, not talk."

Now they might be getting somewhere. "What will they do?"

"I don't know, not for sure," Jerryck slurred.

He twitched. Then he grit his teeth, putting his right hand on his wounded left shoulder. Lieber leaned forward with the vial. He had a needle on it. Adam didn't want to know when he'd put that on there. And he didn't want to watch Jerryck getting dosed again. He put out a hand to stop it and kept talking. "You do not know, but you are sure they will kill us?"

"Somehow, someway, they'll kill you all, if you can't convince them to let you leave," Jerryck said. "They work with earth magic. They could uproot trees on your head... Break a natural dam and flood a creek you're trying to cross... Make the side of a mountain slip and bury you... I don't know exactly what they'll do. When they fought with the gathering of seats, they made that (unknown word) explode."

Adam repeated the word he didn't know, and said, "I do not know that word."

"A mountain that blows up," Jerryck said. "Spits out fire and rock that flows like water, burns everything in its way. And that's what doesn't get buried by all the ash raining out of the sky from the explosion."

"Oh! A volcano!" Adam said it in German. Then told Jerryck, "I know what that is."

Adam repeated the new word several times before Gerhardt interrupted him. "What do volcanoes have to do with anything?"

"The shamans in these mountains made one erupt during some fight with magicians," Adam said. "He was talking about all kinds of different ways the shamans here can kill us, if we can't convince them to let us withdraw."

"Perhaps if we begin a withdrawal before more of them can gather in the area that will help," Gerhardt said. Gerhardt went over to Velig and they moved farther back into the cave.

"I think that will work," Adam said to Jerryck.

"What will?" Jerryck's eyes followed Gerhard as he moved off.

"That is enough of a threat, I think we can stop killing and leave these mountains." And it was possibly a good step to keeping the war from spreading to this world. "We will make this work."

To Be Continued

About the author

REBEKAH OLSON IS a Story Grid Certified Editor who lives in Salem, Oregon. Her earliest memories are her love for stories. When she couldn't get 'big people' to tell her enough stories, she would fill entire sheets of notebook paper with squiggles writing stories of her own. Unfortunately, she couldn't read yet and so had no idea what the story was. Since none of the 'big people' would tell her what the squiggles said, those stories are lost. So now she makes up new stories. When she's not writing, she's reading, watching movies, playing piano, knitting or crocheting.

Please help the author by leaving a review where you purchased this book. You can visit here for a list of retailers where this book is available https://www.authorrebekaholson.com/books.

If you liked this story, visit her website at https://www.authorrebekaholson.com/ or you can visit her blog https://www.authorrebekaholson.com/blog and read chapters for free. While Adam struggled in Shontarra, find out what was going on in Brend from Court Magician Jerryck's point of view.

www.ingramcontent.com/pod-product-compliance
Lightning Source LLC
Chambersburg PA
CBHW071731110726
47908CB00006B/1560